Douglas Schofield is a Canadian-trained lawyer. He currently holds the position of Assistant Solicitor General with the Cayman Islands Government. He makes his home on Grand Cayman with his wife Melody, and Juno, their highly intelligent talking cat.

Praise for Flight Risks

"Flight Risks is a fast-paced, snappy thriller that hurtles through the worlds of law, finance, politics and family. ... How Schofield winds everything together is marvellous. He keeps readers enthralled in the chase by developing Grace as an enormously resourceful and courageous figure, whose primary goal is to get her daughter back."
– Victoria Times-Colonist

"I spend most of my time reading screenplays, and I very seldom take the time to read novels. But this novel is an exception. The way Mr Schofield writes is refreshing. His choice of words... the way he uses words... just astonishes me. I kept re-reading sentences just to enjoy them. And what a fabulous story! When I had to put the book down, I couldn't wait to get back to it. It kept me awake at night. I don't like using the word "fantastic" - it's so overused - but this really is a fantastic novel!"
- Graham Greene, film and TV actor

"Sadly, but completely satisfied, I finished reading Flight Risks. *I arrived on the set of Diary of a Wimpy Kid two hours before my call time. I wanted to be alone without any interruptions and I spent it down with all the characters in* **********ng story! I just could not wai********* where I*
- Alf Hump

FLIGHT RISKS

DOUGLAS SCHOFIELD

HIRST
publishing

First Published in the UK in August 2010 by Hirst Publishing
Second Edition published in June 2011

Hirst Publishing, Suite 285 Andover House, George Yard, Andover, Hants, SP10 1PB

ISBN 978-0-9566417-0-0

Cover by Robert Hammond
Printed and bound by Good News Digital Books

Paper stock used is natural, recyclable and made from wood grown in sustainable forests. The manufacturing processes conform to environmental regulations.

www.hirstpublishing.com

For My Sweet Melody

AUTHOR'S FOREWORD

It will come as no surprise to the reader that *Flight Risks* is a work of fiction. But beyond the usual disclaimer about any similarity between the novel's characters and real persons being purely coincidental, another point should be clearly understood. Many novelists writing about international financial skulduggery seem unable to resist resorting to the facile device of 'secret bank accounts' in the Cayman Islands. This is pure mythology. In fact, the Cayman Islands' anti-money-laundering regulations are far more rigorous – and far more vigilantly enforced – than those of many 'onshore' jurisdictions. Anyone who doubts this statement should try opening a bank account in the Cayman Islands.

PROLOGUE

Dawn.

A late model Grand Am sped along the Interstate. On either side of the dual ribbons of asphalt, a sere, bone-dry landscape sifted past. Flat. Unchanging. Mind-numbing.

In the car, five dark-eyed young men sat erect, staring ahead at a dramatic city skyline, starkly silhouetted against an opalescent sky.

Each man was silent. Each man was eerily still. Each man's face was freshly shaven, the skin of his cheeks shiny and taut.

Flickering taillights signalled congestion ahead. The inside lane – the lane reserved for high-occupancy vehicles – appeared clear. The front passenger checked his watch. He muttered to the driver in a foreign language.

The car slipped left and accelerated, speeding past slower traffic.

The car closed on a freightliner in the neighbouring lane. Its long trailer was laden with a lopsided load of heavy steel pipe. The transport drifted left, straddling the two lanes. The car's driver muttered a curse. He swerved to the right, changing lanes to pass.

On the trailer, a wide strap restraining the rear of the load suddenly parted with a report as loud as a cannon. The load abruptly shifted, pipe ends splaying.

A horrifying chain reaction of failure followed, as a second strap let go and, with a shriek of grinding metal, tons of pipe rolled off the trailer.

The truck driver stood on his brakes. The huge rig jack-knifed, taking out a line of cars in a roar of demolition, and came to rest lying on its side on the highway median.

The Grand Am lay under the load of pipe. Crushed.

A single length of pipe flexed rhythmically, one end tapping on the pavement.

Tapping . . . tapping . . .

PART I
BRITISH COLUMBIA
SEPTEMBER 28 – OCTOBER 12

ONE

By the time Grace Palliser pulled her car into her ex-husband's driveway, she'd worked herself into a state of nerve-wracked nausea. It was only the prospect of a few days alone with Shy that got her out of her car and onto the front walkway.

Brent's pickup wasn't parked in its usual spot under the old Garry oak, which was something of a relief. The New Brent was self-righteous and judgmental, constantly spouting memorised psychobabble he'd picked up from his live-in girlfriend. The New Brent had forgotten the Old Brent.

Grace hadn't.

Grace climbed the steps and tapped on the door, hoping it would be Shy who answered.

Immediately, the door swung open.

Bad luck. The bitch was waiting.

Hilary Holt's blonde-streaked hair was pulled straight back and secured with an alligator clip. The tight hairline gave her thin face a permanent look of sanctimonious severity.

Maybe she thinks she looks elegant.

Grace noticed with satisfaction a few grey roots lining the woman's brow.

Hilary hadn't looked like this at the hearing. When her name was paged, she'd made an entrance through the courtroom doors like a daytime television personality, hair curled and bouncing, cocooned in an earth-tone mohair sweater and pleated skirt. The sweater had been carefully chosen – loose enough not to look sluttish, tight enough to highlight her well-formed breasts. The overall effect was that of a warm and loving woman, comforting to every weeping child who had ever skinned a knee.

By the time Hilary Holt left the witness box, the presiding judge's face had been alight with admiration.

"Oh, it's you." Hilary pretended surprise, as if she hadn't expected Grace to come. "She's almost ready. She's running a

10

bit late because she didn't tidy her room. Brent is very insistent about that."

Really? That's new.

Hilary's tone made it clear that she was enjoying her new position. "Just give us a moment, please."

Grace suppressed the urge to punch her in the face.

Hilary turned and walked off toward the back of the house, leaving Grace seething on the porch.

Her ass jiggles.

Grace savoured a moment of immature pleasure.

She felt better when she heard the familiar thumping of small feet in the hallway. Shy materialised around the corner and launched herself at her mother.

"Mommy! You're here!"

Grace opened her arms. She enveloped her little girl, inhaling the scent of her hair and sweet cream skin. She forced back sudden tears. Hilary reappeared and stood a few feet inside the door. Her face wore a faint smirk.

Grace stood up. Shy's fingers clutched possessively at the sleeve of her jacket.

Hilary held out a bulging Winnie-the-Pooh backpack. "Everything she'll need. Clean clothes. Rain slicker. Some Merry Berry drinks boxes. And Blackie. She can't sleep without Blackie."

Shy's stuffed poodle. She'd had it since she was ten months old.

Grace saw red. She clenched her fists. "How many children have you had, Hilary?" she hissed.

"None," the woman replied warily.

"And how long have you lived with Brent?"

"Eighteen months – you know that."

"And Brent has had primary custody of Shy for, what, five weeks?"

"Yes."

"Right!" Grace raised her voice. "So don't try to tell me how to take care of my daughter! You sound ridiculous!"

11

"Mommy!" Shy cried, tugging on her sleeve. "Don't argue, Mommy!"

"You're right, honey. Let's get going."

Grace grabbed the backpack from the woman, who flinched as if she expected to be slapped. She took Shy's hand and started down the steps.

"The court order says Sunday at eight!" Hilary called after her angrily. "Have her back on time! And if we hear about any medication problems, we'll go back to the judge!"

She slammed the door.

That went well.

Grace strapped Shy into the middle of the back seat. Her daughter wouldn't look at her.

"Come on, baby," Grace said softly. "Let's get some supper. How about the Macaroni Grill?"

Shy's face lit up.

"Cool," she said.

Grace started her car.

Let the weekend begin.

When the phone rang at eight o'clock on Sunday morning, Grace was kick-starting her day with a strong French roast. She wondered darkly if it was Brent, calling to harass her. Shy was upstairs on Grace's bed watching cartoons with Fraidy curled up beside her. Grace's Burmese cat was high-strung and he hated kids, but he'd made an exception for Shy.

It had been a delightful weekend so far. Mother and daughter had scrambled around Thetis Lake Park, watched videos and munched junk food. Shy had refused to sleep in her own bedroom. She'd insisted on sleeping with Grace, and so she had, a restless little package of bony elbows and sharp toenails and Blackie the stuffed dog. This situation had both gratified Grace and concerned her. She was thankful that Shy had not displayed the agitation or remoteness of earlier visits, but this new display of neediness was worrying.

She'd feel a lot better if once in a while Shy would put her hands on her hips and behave like the Little Miss Bossy Boots she'd once been.

Grace was also alarmed by Shy's statement, matter-of-factly delivered while she was industriously crayoning on the paper tablecloth at the Macaroni Grill, that Hilary and Dad were 'being mean' to her. She hadn't been able to get her to specify in what particular way the two adults were mean. Insisting that she tidy her room wouldn't qualify; other things might.

Grace had read somewhere that the birthing of a child released a substance called oxytosin in the female brain, causing immediate strong and protective bonding with the newborn. Oxytosin must last a lifetime, she thought. Her need to protect Shy was desperate and unremitting.

Grace gulped down a mouthful of coffee and answered the phone.

Grace and Shy stepped into the elevator.

"We won't be long, sweetheart. Mommy just wants to photocopy something to show Mr. Vallee when he comes to see us."

"We won't be late for the movie, will we?" The child's voice carried a note of panic.

"No, no, sweetie. It doesn't start for another hour. Push the button for Mommy."

Shy pushed the button for the sixth floor. She kept pressing it until the door closed and the elevator started up with a bump.

When the door slid open to reveal the reception lobby, Grace was startled at the sudden appearance of an older man waiting on the threshold. He was dressed in a linen suit and a Tilley hat. He looked like he'd just stepped out of a Bogart movie. Shy jumped with fright. Her hand shot out and grabbed her mother's.

Armand Dimitri seemed equally nonplussed. He stood aside and removed his hat. "Miss Palliser! What a surprise! A very good day to you, my dear."

"And you, Mr. Dimitri," Grace responded, recovering quickly. She and Shy stepped out of the lift. "What brings you here on a Sunday?"

"Grave and weighty matters, my dear," he intoned with mock solemnity. His accented English was delivered in a courtly tone. "It seems that Sunday is the only day when Attorney Nader can find time to attend to my various affairs." He turned his attention to Shy, who was peering up at him, her eyes as big as saucers. "This beautiful child must be your daughter."

"Yes, she is. Shy, say hello to Mr. Dimitri. He's the man who owns the coffee shop where you had that nice muffin this morning."

"Shy, is it!" Armand Dimitri exclaimed, bending down. "What a pretty name!" He held out a huge hand. "Would you shake an old man's hand, or are you indeed a shy young lady?"

"My real name is Sherry," Shy replied flatly, quickly reaching out and shaking two of his fingers. "Shy is only a nickname my Mommy and Daddy gave me when I was little."

"Ah, I see. And would you prefer to be called Sherry?"

"No, Mister. I like to be Shy."

The old man chuckled. "In name only it would seem, my child." He straightened, addressing Grace. "My nephew joined us for brunch this morning. He told us about the trial. The crime is most distasteful, but Michael counts it a great honour to be assisting Mr. Devereaux. He also speaks with great admiration about you, Miss Palliser."

Michael Dimitri was a newly qualified lawyer who had recently joined the firm. It was said that Eric Nader, one of the senior associates, had insisted on offering a helping hand to his client's nephew. Two weeks ago, the managing partners had assigned the young man to help Andre Devereaux and his assistant, Grace, as junior counsel on a murder case. "He needs some courtroom experience," they'd said.

Up to this point, Dimitri hadn't contributed much to the defence effort.

14

Grace was certain that Michael Dimitri's admiration of her was mainly focused on one thing. She gave a cautious *pro forma* response.

"Really? I know Andre is very grateful for the extra help. It is, as you say, a difficult trial."

"Yes, of course." Imperceptibly, he leaned closer. "Perhaps you would care to join us for brunch some Sunday morning. My friends and I have a regular table at Romanoff's. You would be most welcome, my dear. And I'm sure Michael would be delighted if you came."

Grace kept her expression neutral. The man who had delivered this unexpected invitation with such evident sincerity was a millionaire many times over. Armand Dimitri had emigrated from Lebanon to Canada as a young man and set up shop as an importer of coffees and teas. In three decades, his business had grown from one small shop on Yates Street to become 'Dimitri's', a chain of designer-coffee outlets and emporia that, in British Columbia at least, rivalled the success of Starbucks.

Armand himself was known to live a quiet life, eschewing extravagance and attending only select gatherings of the glitterati. Grace knew that the invitation she had just received would excite the envy of many a social climber. But she also instantly understood that the offer probably came with a price.

"That's very kind of you, Mr. Dimitri. Unfortunately, I have a number of uncomfortable distractions in my life these days. Perhaps at some time in the future."

"Grace, of course! I understand! I may use your first name?" He waited for her nod before continuing. "I do understand, my dear. It is the way of life, *n'est-ce pas?* Everything seems to flow smoothly, then suddenly we are swept up by currents that tumble us about."

"Sometimes currents of our own making."

Dimitri smiled. "In my country, there was a saying: 'Bad decisions make good stories'." He continued without giving her a chance to reply. "Well now, I must be off! Your Shy is

15

showing signs of impatience. No doubt she is eager to get on with your day."

"We're going to a movie!" Shy piped in, her tone a bit friendlier now that this dull adult conversation seemed to be ending.

"Good for you! Don't eat too much popcorn. You wouldn't want to spoil your dinner."

Shy stuck out her chin. "You sound like my Mommy."

Armand Dimitri chuckled like an indulgent grandfather. He boarded the empty elevator and gave Shy a little finger wave as the door closed.

Grace led Shy to Andre Devereaux's office.

Andre Devereaux, Queen's Counsel, was the firm's senior trial lawyer. His career in the courts had spanned nearly five decades in three Canadian provinces. His exploits were legendary. Grace always jumped at the chance to work with him. She was usually assigned to one of the civil litigation partners, or to Associate Counsel Leddi Dixon, but whenever Andre had a lengthy case he would lobby the senior partner, Cameron Pomeroy, emphasising that Grace was more valuable to him than a junior lawyer. "She's sharper than most of the lawyers around here!" he'd insist. "She notices things I miss."

Grace's recent difficulties with prescription drugs had not changed his opinion.

Currently, Andre and Grace were defending Horace Assu, a seventeen-year-old Native Indian youth from the small logging and fishing community of Port Hardy, on the northeast coast of Vancouver Island. The boy's first-degree murder trial had been transferred three hundred miles south, to Victoria, the provincial capital.

Grace went to Andre's desk and retrieved one of the coil-bound booklets she'd prepared for Monday's proceedings. She herded Shy toward the photocopy room.

They walked past Eric Nader's office. The door was shut, but Grace heard a female voice. It sounded like Joan Van Zant, Nader's secretary. Joan was forty, divorced and childless. She was also something of a workaholic, which made her

16

perfectly suited to work for Eric Nader, who was notorious within the firm for his unconventional hours and frequent trips abroad.

When Joan wasn't working, she spent many of her evenings sipping gin and tonic in Pardee's, a waterfront nightclub owned by Armand Dimitri. The office gossip-mongers theorised that Joan Van Zant was a cougar, constantly on the prowl for younger men.

"Who's here, Mommy?"

"Mr. Nader must be working today, sweetie. It sounds like Joan came in to help him."

"Joan has Halloween chocolates in her drawer."

"Does she?" Grace glanced at Joan's workstation. The computer was turned on, its beach scene screensaver shimmering with colour. "And how would you know that, young lady?"

"'Cause she gave me some that time when Daddy brang me here after we came back from Nana's. You and Uncle Andre were doing court stuff and Dolly was getting lots of phone calls so I couldn't play with her telephone earmuff thing. Joan gave me some paper and pens and a whole bunch of little chocolate bars that people give out on Halloween."

"Hmmh. You were a spoiled girl, weren't you?"

When Grace finished the copying, they walked back toward Andre's office. Nader's door was still closed, but there was no sound coming from behind it. Joan's computer screen was black.

She hadn't heard anyone leave.

They returned to Andre's desk and Grace replaced the booklet. She noticed a stack of file folders with attached correspondence sitting next to the phone. Out of habit, she began to straighten them.

The corner of a lined writing pad poked out from the bottom of the pile. Andre tended to leave half-used notepads in odd places; often they contained interview notes that belonged in a specific file. Grace pulled the notepad out from under the folders. It was filled with writing.

Hell. What file is this from?

Grace scanned the first page.

"Are we going now?" Shy sighed from the doorway.

"In a second, sweetie," Grace replied, distracted. She sat down on Andre's chair. She turned over a page, then another. She counted eight full pages. Each was written in French, in Andre's distinctive hand. The text appeared to list dates and times, with cryptic explanatory notations. Grace's high school French wasn't up to the task of making sense of every word, but the dates were recent, spanning the past month or so. The letters "P" and "G" appeared singly, and sometimes together, at the beginning of each entry.

"OUT!"

A male voice, raised in anger.

Grace looked up, alarmed.

Shy was nowhere in sight.

"Shy?" Grace jumped to her feet and made for the door. As she swung into the corridor, she almost collided with Joan Van Zant, who was holding Shy by the hand. Over the woman's shoulder, Grace saw Eric Nader standing in the doorway of his office with his arms crossed. He levelled a hostile look at her, then turned on his heel and disappeared.

Shy's eyes were wide and her lower lip was quivering. She let go of Joan's hand and grabbed for her mother's. Grace quickly inspected her daughter's other hand, hoping it wasn't clutching stolen chocolates.

Nothing there.

She looked at Joan.

"You should try to keep track of Shy when you bring her here, Grace," Joan said. "She walked into Eric's office without knocking. You know how irritable he can get when he's busy."

Joan's tone didn't seem to match her words. Oddly, her expression conveyed a touch of embarrassment.

"That man yelled at me," Shy whimpered to Grace. "I just wanted to ask Joan if she's still got those Halloween chocolates."

Joan kneeled down. The front of her blouse gaped open, revealing a diamond-studded pendant floating between ample breasts. "Oh, Shy, I'm sure Mister Nader is sorry now that he raised his voice at you," she said, placating the child. She glanced up at Grace, who didn't try to hide her scepticism. "Anyway... you know what? I think Auntie Joan does have some of those chocolate bars left. Shall we get them?"

"That's not necessary, Joan," Grace interjected before Shy could reply. The 'Auntie Joan' performance seemed to be aimed more at dissuading Grace from confronting Nader than at salving the hurt feelings of a five-year-old. "We're on our way to a matinee at the Capitol Six. Shy can get something there." Grace rubbed the top of Shy's head as Joan stood up. "And I'll try to explain to her about poking her nose where it doesn't belong."

Joan shot her an apologetic look and returned to Nader's office. Grace went back to Andre's desk and replaced his notepad under the files. She and Shy left the building.

They set out on foot toward the movie theatre.

"What happened up there, honey? Why did Mr. Nader get so upset?"

"I don't know, Mommy. I opened the door 'cause I heard Joan talking. Then the man yelled at me."

How do you explain "asshole" to a five-year-old child?

"Well, Hon, they were probably working very hard, like Mommy does with Andre."

"They weren't working, Mommy. They were kissing."

Shy knew that Raymond Vallee was coming to visit. Grace told her to expect him around suppertime.

At twenty minutes past six, the old fashioned bell on the front door rang twice. Grace was rinsing dishes, so Shy ran to let the man in. But once the door was open, her courage failed her. The man wasn't very tall, but he was very big. Part of his huge belly was exposed between the bottom of his sweatshirt and his beltline. He had a broad face and a flat nose and sagging flesh under his chin.

He smiled at Shy, but before he could say a word, she backed away from the door and fled to the kitchen.

"Mommy, he's here!" she called. "He's here, Mommy!" She slid to a halt in front of Grace, who was drying her hands, and dropped her voice to a stage whisper, her eyes big and alarmed. "Mommy, he's a giant! Is he going to come in our house?"

"Of course, silly girl! You didn't leave him standing on the porch, did you?" Grace quickstepped out to the front entrance. Raymond Vallee was standing uncertainly on the mat.

"Hello, Grace." He pronounced her name "Gresh", in the endearing accent of his people.

"Raymond, please come in! I'm so sorry. Shy is sometimes a bit funny about strangers. Shy, please close the door." Grace led Raymond into the sitting room next to the foyer. She had furnished it carefully, over several months, with second hand pieces. It had a cosy, overstuffed look.

Raymond pulled a wad of paper towel out of his pocket and wiped the back of his neck. His face wore a greasy sheen left by several hours spent craning over the steering wheel of his pickup, and his clothes smelled faintly of stove oil. His thick hands were well scrubbed, but still bore the indelible signs of his occupation as a heavy-duty mechanic at a logging camp.

Raymond Vallee was Horace Assu's uncle. Grace had met him several months ago, on an investigative trip with Andre to the Port Hardy Reserve. And this past July, Raymond had been her guide, and occasionally her interpreter, when, at Andre's request, she had returned to the Reserve to interview potential witnesses.

Grace had come to know Raymond as a kind and intelligent man, with the gentle wisdom of someone who has seen too much.

Her guest looked around the room. Grace noticed the appreciative expression as his gaze alighted on a Kwakiutl Indian mask mounted over the small fireplace.

"You must be exhausted!" Grace ventured. "That's a long drive. Are you really going back tonight?"

Raymond turned to her. "Yeah. I wanted to stay over to see Verna and Horace, but there's no one to replace me at work. Winter shutdown's coming up pretty quick." Verna was Horace Assu's mother. She was staying at a motel in West Victoria and attending the trial every day.

"Can I get you something? A drink? Something to eat?"

The big man sank onto the end of the couch.

"Got any iced tea?"

"Sure do."

"That'd be nice. Thanks."

Grace went to the kitchen. When she returned with glasses of tea, Shy had taken up a position in a chair on the opposite side of the room. Her little girl was eyeing Raymond with undisguised curiosity.

"I hope I'm not too late to help Horace."

Grace set down her glass. "Tomorrow is critical, Raymond. The case hasn't been going well. But the tide could be turning. Andre and I discovered something very disturbing about Horace's first day in custody."

Raymond looked at her gravely. "So have I."

Grace met his eyes. "Your phone call this morning was a bit mysterious."

"My mother used to live with Verna. She was very old. Agnes Vallee. I think you met her."

"I remember. She seemed quite frail. The children were very good about bringing her things and making her comfortable."

"She was their favourite granny. She died in August."

"Verna told me. I'm so sorry, Raymond. Your family certainly didn't need the extra grief."

"It's okay. She had a long life."

"She didn't say anything when I was there. She just sat in that old chair with her hands in her lap."

"She never learned English. She understood some of it, but she only spoke our language. And she wasn't too comfortable around white people. Said they only brought trouble. A few

21

years ago her mind started to go over to the other side. Alzheimer's."

"Oh. I didn't realise."

Raymond fished into a pocket and retrieved a small cassette. He handed it to Grace.

"That's a tape from Verna's answering machine. It disappeared last year."

"What do you mean?"

"Verna noticed she wasn't getting any messages. When she checked the machine, the tape was missing."

"Last year?"

"Yeah. In November."

Grace opened her mouth to ask another question, then closed it. Raymond would tell the story in his own way.

"My mother had this really old housecoat. It had holes. Millie and I bought her a new one." Millie was Raymond's wife, a small woman with a kind face who had tried to fatten up Grace - 'that skinny white girl', as she'd called her – with huge helpings of smoked salmon and freshly-baked bread. "Millie saves all our credit card statements. We bought the new housecoat on November twenty-third. I checked."

"Five days after Horace was arrested."

"Yeah. I was cleaning out Mom's room last night. Verna couldn't face doing it, so I agreed to do it while she was down here at the trial. Mom's old housecoat was hanging in the closet. I found that in the pocket."

"Have you played it?"

He nodded. "Yeah. It's those two cops, talking to Horace. If Mister Andre plays it for the judge, I think it will help. Listen for yourself. Do you have an answering machine?"

"Maybe something better." Grace examined the cassette. "These things come in two sizes – micro and mini. Let's see if this fits my pocket recorder." She left the room and retrieved the hand-held device from a drawer in the kitchen.

The tape fit.

22

Because Grace wasn't sure what they were about to hear, she sent Shy upstairs to watch TV. Then she sat beside Raymond and played the tape.

She couldn't believe her ears.

When the voices stopped, Grace clutched Raymond's arm.

"How the hell...?"

"I figure the phone didn't go back on the hook after Horace left that message for Verna."

"But how would this cassette end up in your mother's housecoat?"

"My mother never answered the phone. But I guess she heard her grandson's voice on the machine, and then she heard those two white men's voices. She wouldn't have understood much of what was said, but she knew her grandson well enough to hear how scared he was. She must've taken the tape out to give it to Verna. Maybe she thought the next phone call to the house would make the machine erase the conversation."

"Was she showing signs of Alzheimer's last fall?"

"Yes and no. Right up to the end, she'd have her clear days and her lost days. I figure she put the tape in her pocket and then her mind drifted off and she forgot about it."

Grace stood up. "I have something to show you." She retrieved the photocopies she'd made at the office earlier in the day. "After you called and told me you were coming, I went to the office and made these copies to show you." She explained their significance to Raymond.

He studied the documents while he listened. After a moment of silence, he looked up at her with anger and hurt in his eyes. "Our people have always known that some of them cops lie! They're gonna ruin Horace's life!"

"Not if we can help it, Raymond. I'm phoning Andre right away!"

"Good. I know you and Mr. Andre will do your best for the boy." He lumbered up from the couch. "And now I have to get back to Hardy."

"Will you stop to see Verna?"

23

"Can't. I'm booked to take the floatplane back to Seymour Inlet at six in the morning. I'll only be out there for a couple of days. Company's shutting down the camp. Anyway, I don't want to tell Verna about this. It would just get her hopes up." Verna Assu had been devastated by the events of the past ten months. She'd lost so much weight she looked like a chemo patient.

Raymond ambled toward the door, still talking. "I'll stay in touch with Millie by radiophone. She'll tell me if anything comes of this."

"Something will come of it," Grace said firmly. "Count on it!"

TWO

"I've always thought that the worst thing about this trial is our grinning little client. But now it looks like his condition is an asset."

Andre Devereaux spoke in the faint French Canadian accent that had always sounded so intimate to Grace. He was sitting behind his desk, perched like a raptor on the leading edge of his oversized executive chair, staring out the office window. He swivelled and clutched the edge of the desk, pulling himself forward on the castors. Intelligent blue eyes locked on to Grace's. Their whites were still as clear as a teenager's after sixty-eight years.

They were wonderful eyes. Many times, Grace had watched them cut like a laser through courtroom liars.

She had also seen them filled with affection and concern.

Today they looked tired. She worried that Andre wasn't getting enough sleep.

"Foetal Alcohol Syndrome. Very fashionable defence ploy these days. Wonderful material for impassioned sentencing arguments. But damned unhelpful when you're trying to mount a substantive defence!" He smiled and tapped the answering machine tape on the desk in front of him. "This could cut the legs off Oatway's case. All he'll have left is the evidence of that evil little cretin, Chernoff."

Bert Oatway was the prosecuting attorney assigned to the case. His irritating personality was just one of the tribulations they had faced in *Her Majesty The Queen* v. *Horace Alvin Assu*. Another was their client's sometime friend and schoolmate, Frank Chernoff, who claimed that Horace had shown him the murder victim's severed penis just before he'd thrown it into a skunk-cabbage swamp behind the community centre on the Native Reserve.

Grace had secretly obtained a psychological evaluation on Chernoff, done when he was a child. It recounted how he had once hung a puppy in a tree and beat it to death with a piece of pipe. When Grace read that passage to him, Andre had looked nauseated. *"Mon dieu,* Grace!" he'd said. "That's exactly how psychopaths get their start in life!"

But because Chernoff had been seven years old at the time, the report was sealed and technically unusable. Andre couldn't even refer to it in cross-examination.

Oatway had opened his case on Frank Chernoff's evidence and on the strength of a signed confession, obtained from Horace by two wily police officers. Since Day One of the trial, Oatway had been swaggering around the courtroom as if he'd already won a conviction.

On their side, Andre and Grace had a client who seemed mentally incapable of assisting in his own defence. Horace was sweet-tempered and eager to please, but he'd been unwilling or unable to offer them a coherent account of his activities on the date of the murder, or – just as critical – of the events at the police detachment after his arrest. Instinctively, they both knew his confession, such as it was, had been improperly obtained, but Horace's meandering narrative hadn't helped much in developing that line of argument. He'd only told them one thing that now seemed significant.

"I guess we now know what Horace meant when he kept saying, 'Them cops got a dog'," Grace said.

Andre sat back in his chair. "It starts to make sense."

Horace had always denied to Andre and Grace that he had killed Melvin Hanuse, the notorious alcoholic and general nuisance on the Port Hardy First Nations Reserve who had been bludgeoned to death on the gravel shores of Johnstone Strait. In fact, despite his confession to the police, at his meetings with Andre and Grace the boy had repeatedly denied any part in the crime. He had also denied all suggestions that Melvin Hanuse had sexually abused him in the past, or on the day of the murder – a suggestion that Andre had made in the hope that there might be grounds for a lesser charge of manslaughter.

Each time they sat down with the boy in the interview room at the Pembroke Street Detention Centre, Horace just smiled at them with doggie-like trust and asked when the judge was going to let him go home.

There was a brief knock and the office door opened. Michael Dimitri stepped in. He nodded and smiled at Grace – she didn't miss the fact that his glance lingered for a few extra milliseconds on her partly exposed thighs – and then he stood just inside the doorway, shifting from foot to foot, waiting for some acknowledgement from Andre.

Preppy Boy, Grace thought, taking in Michael's fifty-dollar haircut, button-down shirt and private school tie.

The older man's eyes slowly migrated to the doorway.

"Yes, Michael?"

"Just checking to see if you need me this morning, sir." His tone was neutral, even respectful, but his eyes said he wasn't really looking for work. He was just going through the motions.

Grace couldn't recall Michael Dimitri offering a single creative contribution to the defence strategy. On the few occasions when he'd been present while Andre and Grace consulted with Horace, his face had worn a look of unconcealed distaste. Distaste because Horace was a Native Indian? Distaste at having to dirty his hands with such a case? Grace didn't know, but she guessed that Michael Dimitri's professional ambitions were focused on something more lucrative than defending common criminals.

She wondered, as well, if he was conflicted: attracted to her physically, but harbouring a certain amount of resentment as well. After all, twenty-eight year old Grace Palliser – holder of no diplomas, heir to no fortunes, five-foot-eight and far too attractive to actually possess an IQ – enjoyed a higher status on the defence team than he did.

Maybe that was why he appeared to show so little interest in the case.

Andre's voice interrupted her ruminations.

"No, that's fine, Michael. Meet us at court at nine forty-five."

"Okay. See you there."

He sidled out slowly, like a shoplifter trying to avoid attracting attention as he edged toward a store exit. Grace was relieved when he was gone. She had long ago admitted to herself that she was quite selfish about working with Andre.

The old lawyer opened a binder that was lying on the desk in front of him. "Give me a moment, my dear."

She waited while he ran a finger down the index in the trial ready-book she had assembled for him. She had made two copies, one for each of them, and later a third one for Dimitri. She wondered if the young man had even bothered to read through his.

As Andre thumbed through the tabs, Grace's eyes roamed around the familiar office, taking in for the thousandth time its curious mix of modern and antique furniture, the mahogany wainscoting, the silk wallpaper, the overflowing bookshelves, and the dark etchings of nineteenth century European alleyways brooding from behind mildewed matting. The thick carpet still gave off a faint scent of cigar smoke, even though it had been over a year since Andre had been literally ordered by the partners of Pomeroy & Associates to stop smoking his beloved Bolivars on the premises.

Andre's cigars hadn't offended Grace. In fact, they had comforted her.

Many things about this old man comforted her. Some of those things, by agreement between them, were never mentioned in the office.

Andre brought her back to the present. "Okay, Grace. What I need to do is-"

"-think out loud, with my assistance?" she asked, smiling at their old private joke.

"No." He looked at his watch. "We've only got two hours. I need to plan my cross-examination of Perry. Meanwhile, there's something I want you to do."

*

28

At ten minutes before ten, Horace Assu was led from the prisoner holding area into the courtroom. Even though he had spent many days in this room, absently listening to testimony designed to imprison him for a very long time, his eyes glanced apprehensively around the room. He spied Grace, sitting in the front row of the gallery, behind Andre and Michael Dimitri, and he grinned in recognition.

Grace had become quite fond of the gentle young soul they were defending. Every time she'd seen Horace's happy, otherworldly look, even in the darkest days of the case against him, she had become more convinced that he couldn't have committed this crime. Now she was almost certain of it. She gave him a kindly smile, and tried to convey some encouragement by nodding her head a few times.

Horace waved to his mother and other family members, sitting two rows behind Grace, and took his seat in the dock.

At five minutes before ten, Corporal Perry strode into the courtroom. He spoke briefly with Bert Oatway, and then took a seat in the front row of the gallery, behind the prosecutor. Grace watched him. He was a short, sinewy man in his mid-thirties, with dark hair, ruddy cheeks and a Roman nose. Today he was decked out in his full dress red serge uniform, which made him look slightly larger than life. RCMP policy on courtroom attire was not as strict as it once had been, but smart prosecutors still insisted that officers wear their red tunics whenever they were called to testify in front of a jury. The uniform might be a nineteenth century throwback, now largely ceremonial, but it still retained a certain historical mystique for older citizens. Many Crown prosecutors believed it lent credibility to an officer's testimony.

But the jury had been excused, and Perry's attire wouldn't impress the judge. Justice Jack Roney was a round, balding man whose personality bore no resemblance to the jovial stereotype often associated with his physical appearance. He had a caustic tongue, which he reserved mostly for easy targets like ill-prepared advocates and dishonest witnesses. Some of the more lazy and accident-prone members of the local legal fraternity lived in mortal fear of Justice Roney. After his appointment to the Supreme Court of British Columbia, a shocked and frazzled lawyer had nicknamed him 'Pepper Roney'. The name had stuck.

Despite this, Jack Roney was a first class criminal trial judge and, more important for Horace Assu's defence, he had great respect for Andre Devereaux, Q.C.

His Lordship entered the courtroom at exactly ten o'clock, wearing the ceremonial garb of his high office. He nodded curtly, and settled into his chair. He surveyed the courtroom and then looked at the prosecutor.

Oatway rose. "I ask for a declaration of *voir dire*, My Lord."

"So declared. Call your first witness."

"Yes, My Lord. Corporal John Perry."

Perry stepped through the gate and crossed to the witness box.

The *voir dire* commenced.

Voir dire, meaning "see speak", was a French phrase that had crept into the legal lexicon of Great Britain at some ancient time and eventually crossed the Atlantic to the English-speaking colonies in the New World. In the United States, it had come to refer to proceedings relating to the selection of a jury. In Canada, it referred to a sub-trial within the main trial, held to determine the admissibility of certain types of evidence. Most frequently, the evidence under scrutiny was a confession to the police. In Horace's case, the *voir dire* was being held to determine whether the record of his interview with Corporal Perry and his partner, Constable Biddlecomb, could be admitted into evidence, marked as an exhibit on the main trial, and read to the jury. Since Justice Roney had sole power to rule on admissibility, the jury was excluded.

Bert Oatway wouldn't have had to bother with a jury at all if he hadn't forced through an application to have Horace tried as an adult.

Corporal Perry swore to tell the truth and stated his name for the record.

30

The prosecutor, robed and tabbed, his black vest tugging at its buttons over an abundant paunch, edged to the lectern. Oatway's shock of red hair and booming courtroom delivery had earned him the moniker 'Foghorn Leghorn'. Today, his notable voice was full and confident. It reached out to every ear in the courtroom as he led Corporal Perry through the preliminaries: occupation, rank, present posting, posting during the latter half of the year 2000, investigation of the Hanuse murder, and arrest of the suspect Horace Assu. The arrest had been made shortly after Perry interviewed a sixteen-year-old Port Hardy resident named Frank Chernoff.

After ten minutes, with this preamble out of the way, Oatway moved to the real meat of the hearing.

The burden on the prosecution was to satisfy the presiding judge that Horace Assu's confession was given freely and voluntarily, that it was not obtained by threats or actual violence, and that it was not the product of improper inducements or promises made by the police interviewers.

There were two additional issues to be canvassed. First, as with any person in police detention, the prosecution had to satisfy the judge that the accused had been advised of his right to contact a lawyer, and that he had been given a reasonable opportunity to do so. Second, because Horace had been a youth, Oatway would want to show that the boy had been given an opportunity to contact an adult relative or friend.

Corporal Perry testified that all of the proper criteria had been met and that, in the end, Horace had freely agreed to be interviewed without speaking to his mother or to a lawyer.

"Constable Biddlecomb and I carefully explained his rights to him," Perry stated, using the clinical tone of a professional witness. "First, I read him his rights when I arrested him at his mother's home, early in the afternoon of November 18th. Then we both explained his rights again, in the interview room, after he had tried unsuccessfully to place a telephone call to his mother."

"What did you say to him about the matter of legal counsel?" Oatway asked.

"I explained that he had the right to contact a lawyer and also that, if he couldn't afford one or if he didn't think his family could afford one, there was a toll free number he could use to speak to a Legal Aid duty counsel in Vancouver. He declined the opportunity."

"What happened next?"

"Well, we went over the whole thing again. Constable Biddlecomb sat with Horace and went through the waiver form with him, reading each section aloud and making sure he understood. He then signed in the space provided. Constable Biddlecomb and I signed as witnesses, and Biddlecomb filled in the date." He opened the file in front of him and produced a sheet of paper. "I have the original of that document here."

Oatway looked at the judge. "Exhibit 'A' on the *voir dire*, please, My Lord?"

Roney looked at Andre. "Mr. Devereaux?"

"No objection, My Lord."

THREE

Andre Devereaux rose from his seat and moved to the centre of the courtroom. Grace watched him with fascination, her heart beating a little faster. Her friend was never just *in* a courtroom - he *inhabited* it. He seemed taller within these walls. Larger than life.

Andre never did anything deliberately dramatic in court. He never raised his voice. With most witnesses, when he was cross-examining, he merely invited them to confirm any parts of their evidence that supported his client's case. He politely helped them to correct their errors.

There were exceptions, of course. He was merciless with liars. Slowly and methodically, he would close off every avenue of escape. Then he would move in for the kill.

It was never pretty.

Andre stood in the well of the court for long seconds, his hands clasped behind his back. He didn't need any notes.

Corporal Perry eyed him, then looked away, fixing his gaze on the opposite wall. He exuded professional detachment.

"Corporal," Andre began, "you testified about your years of service, but that part of your evidence has slipped my mind. For how many years have you been a member of the Royal Canadian Mounted Police?"

"Eleven years, sir."

Perry's tone was carefully flat and disinterested.

"And how long does it usually take to be promoted from Constable to Corporal?"

"Fifteen to eighteen years."

"So you received an early promotion?"

"Yes, I did."

"Before or after November, 2000?"

The witness hesitated.

"After."

"Are you now attached to a special federal enforcement unit – something to do with narcotics investigations?"

"No. I mean, I was, for several months, but because of the World Trade Center attacks, I've been transferred to an anti-terrorism unit."

"Are these desirable postings for a member of the RCMP? I mean, from a career point of view?"

"Yes. Depending on your performance, of course."

"Of course. By the way, did you apply for the narcotics position, or was it just offered to you."

"I put in for it."

"When?"

"A couple of years ago. '99, I think."

"And Constable Biddlecomb – was he promoted as well?"

"No."

"But he has been transferred out of the Port Hardy Detachment?"

"Yes."

"Where does he work now?"

"With me, on the Anti-terrorism Task Force."

"Do you know if he applied for a transfer to a federal unit?"

"I believe he did, but I can't tell you when."

Andre paused for a moment, watching the witness. He deliberately allowed the silence to last too long. Perry shifted uncomfortably.

"Tell us, sir, are you married?"

"Divorced."

"Children?"

"No."

"And Constable Biddlecomb?"

"Single."

"Where is your new office located?"

"In Vancouver. At E-Division Headquarters."

E-Division covered the entire province of British Columbia, an area larger than the state of Texas.

"What is the population of Vancouver?"

"I don't know – couple of million, I think."

"And what is the population of Port Hardy?"

"Fifty-five hundred."

"Corporal, are you happier now, living in Vancouver?"

Oatway, who had been squirming impatiently, suddenly exploded out of his chair.

"Objection, My Lord!" he boomed. "An inquiry into the Corporal's satisfaction level is hardly relevant to these proceedings!"

Justice Roney stared very hard at Andre, who looked up at him innocently, awaiting an invitation to respond. Pepper Roney seemed to think for a moment. Then he shook his head. He obviously wanted to see where this was going.

"I'll allow it. There's no jury here, Mr. Oatway. Mr. Devereaux is an experienced counsel. I'm sure he'll demonstrate relevance. I'm going to give him some latitude."

Foghorn Leghorn flopped back into his chair, no doubt wondering if he would be allowed any 'latitude' when he tried to re-examine.

"Should I repeat the question, Corporal?"

"No. Yes, I am happier living in Vancouver."

"And Constable Biddlecomb?"

Oatway sighed loudly. Perry took the prosecutor's hint. He smirked. "You'd have to ask him."

"Yes. Perhaps we shall. Tell us, Corporal Perry, did you think that a successful investigation of the Hanuse murder case might help your transfer application?"

"Not necessarily. I mean... I knew it wouldn't hurt. But decisions by the Staffing Branch are a constant mystery to most of us." He smiled wryly, trying to propel his wisecrack along.

No one chuckled.

"Corporal, please tell us the exact time of young Mr. Assu's arrest."

"I would have to refer to my notebook."

"Of course."

Perry unbuttoned a breast pocket in his tunic and removed a small notebook. There were elastic bands wrapped around sections of the book, leaving free only those pages pertinent to this case. It was an old trick, often employed by police officers to prevent nosy defence lawyers from flipping through unrelated entries while they were examining an officer's notes during cross-examination.

Perry opened the book to a marked page.

"I arrested him at 1:18 p.m. on November 18, 2000."

"And would it be correct to say that he was booked into the cells at the Port Hardy detachment at 1:35 p.m."

Perry looked at his notebook.

"That would be about right."

"Horace Assu was then left in his cell until around 3:30 p.m., when either you or Mr. Biddlecomb removed him and took him to an interview room, is that correct?"

"Yes. Constable Biddlecomb brought him to the interview room at 3:35. Then we both left the room so he could try to call his mother. Then we re-entered the room, went through his rights again, and started to take his statement."

"Which interview room was this?"

"Interview Room Number Two."

"I see. By the way, did this young man have any money on his person when he was booked in?"

"I believe he did. I think the guard found twenty or thirty dollars in his pocket when he searched him."

"Thank you. Now, what were you and Constable Biddlecomb doing from 1:35 p.m., when Horace was placed in his cell, until 3:35 p.m., when he was taken to Interview Room Number Two?"

Grace stopped taking notes so she could watch the witness.

"We were doing paperwork and discussing possible strategies for our interview of Mr. Assu." Perry sounded defensive.

"Were you and Constable Biddlecomb together for that entire two-hour period prior to the interview?"

"Yes, except perhaps when one of us went to the washroom or something like that."

"You were both continuing to work together on this case, and preparing to interview the suspect?"

"That is correct. And we spent some time briefing the detachment commander."

"Staff Sergeant Chadwick?"

"Yes."

"Do you have anything *specifically* recorded in your notes about what you and Mr. Biddlecomb were doing during that two hour period?" Perry didn't react right away. He kept looking at Andre while he opened his notebook. His face had already answered the question. He briefly shifted his gaze to the small book in his hand. Grace noticed that his fingers fumbled a bit with the pages.

"No," he eventually replied in a low voice. "All I have for the period 1:35 to 3:35 is 'P.W.O.' That's my abbreviation for 'paper work office'."

"Oh well," Andre said brightly. "Let's try this... Think back to 3:35 p.m., when Constable Biddlecomb brought the boy to the interview room. Have you got that in your mind?"

"Yes sir." Corporal Perry tried to look bored, but it didn't work. His eyes were wary.

"Now we'll work backwards. Where were you and what were you doing just before 3:35, during, say, the previous *twenty-five minutes?*" Andre emphasised the last few words.

The courtroom was quiet, broken only by the background sounds of people in the public gallery whispering and shifting in their seats. Bert Oatway, awakening to trouble, sat up in his chair. Justice Roney looked up from his note taking and watched the officer in the stand.

Grace put down her pen. Perry had only two choices.

The policeman didn't know he was dead either way.

He chose the coward's route.

"I... I don't recall, sir. Without having a note to refer to, I wouldn't have any reason to recall."

From forty feet away, Grace could see a slight sheen of sweat on the policeman's forehead.

Up to this point in the cross-examination, Andre hadn't moved from his position. Now he turned his back on the witness and strolled over to the barrier behind the counsel table. He stood directly in front of Grace. Michael Dimitri looked momentarily perplexed, but he shifted his chair sideways so that all observers might think that he was part of some carefully planned defence move.

"What's the first rule of cross-examination?" Andre asked Grace gravely.

"Same as carpentry. Measure twice. Cut once."

"Are we finished measuring?"

"Yes, I believe we are."

He held out his hand.

Grace handed him the four coil-bound booklets of documents that she had put together on Friday. He turned and walked toward the witness, holding up one of the books, open at the first tab.

"Corporal Perry, we're in luck, sir. We have some notes you can refer to."

Perry's eyes were fixed on the open page. Even from twenty feet away, he would have recognised a prisoner booking sheet. Grace saw him go pale.

Oatway saw an opportunity.

"My Lord!" he cried, getting up. When he had Justice Roney's attention, he changed his intonation, trying to sound like the sweet voice of reason. "My Lord, unless counsel is producing notes written by this very witness, cross-examination on them would be improper! He can't ask a witness to review someone else's notes!"

Pepper Roney was glaring down from his perch, but not at Andre. He hadn't missed Perry's reaction and he smelled a rat.

"Mr. Devereaux, do you have an extra copy of that document for me to look at?"

"Yes, My Lord," Andre replied cheerfully, "and one for Mr. Oatway as well!"

Oatway started to fulminate.

"But, My Lord-!"

38

Roney cut him off.

"Hold your horses, Mr. Oatway." He gestured to Andre. "Let me see that, please."

Andre passed a booklet to the clerk, who passed it up to the Judge.

"My Lord, under the first tab you will find two documents," Andre explained. "We have highlighted the relevant entries."

The booklet contained photocopies of two different versions of Horace Assu's RCMP prisoner booking sheet. The forms were known as 'C-13s'. There were spaces on the lower half of the sheet for jail guards to record a prisoner's movements.

Grace watched Perry. The policeman looked like he was coming down with malaria. She shifted her eyes back to her note pad, then felt suddenly uncomfortable. She looked up quickly.

Michael Dimitri wasn't following the proceedings. He was staring at Grace.

It only took a few seconds for Pepper Roney to comprehend the significance of the documents before him. Meanwhile, Oatway had taken his copy of the booklet from Andre and was examining the two C-13's. Grace watched him run his finger across the highlighted entries once, then again. Suddenly, his head came up. He stared at the witness for a few seconds, and then rose to his feet again. His face sagged as he faced the bench.

"I withdraw my objection, My Lord."

"Quite right. Thank you, Mr. Oatway." The judge turned to Andre. "Proceed, Mr. Devereaux."

"Corporal, I have extra copies for you, sir." The clerk passed them to the stricken witness.

"Look at the first page. That is the C-13 we received with the Crown's disclosure material. It's the same one Mr. Oatway received from your office. Do you see that?"

"Yes."

"There is a space on that document for the jail guard to record the movements of prisoners. Correct?"

"Yes."

"Look at it. What time was Mr. Assu removed from his cell?"

"3:35 p.m."

"Do you recognise those initials in the column to the right?"

"Ranjit Gill." Perry coughed nervously. "He's a civilian jail guard."

"Quite so. Now, sir, look at the second page. My assistant obtained this document from Horace Assu's mother." Andre held up his copy of the page and pointed to a hand-written notation. "Can you explain what this entry refers to?"

Perry coughed again. "It appears that a twenty dollar bill and a ten dollar bill were removed from the prisoner's effects and signed over to Mrs. Assu."

"Thank you." Andre paused. "Now, sir, at what time was Horace Assu removed from his cell, according to this version of the document?"

Perry didn't answer.

"Corporal?"

"3:10 p.m.," Perry croaked.

"Thank you. Now then, does this second C-13 refresh your memory regarding your activities just prior to 3:35 on the afternoon of November 18, 2000?"

Perry was down, but not out. He straightened up and fired a defiant salvo back at Andre.

"Biddlecomb and I had a brief interview with Mr. Assu. But he didn't tell us anything of value. Just small talk. So later we let him try calling his mother, and then we went on with the actual interview. We didn't threaten him or promise him anything during that first meeting, and, anyway, he didn't give a statement. So we figured it wasn't really relevant, like, at this hearing." He looked over at Oatway, as if he was expecting him to applaud.

Oatway's jaw was tight as he studied his fingernails.

Andre turned back to the page under the first tab. He held it up. "If that is true, sir," he asked mildly, "why would you think it necessary to alter the record of the prisoner's movements before providing this first document to Mr. Oatway's office?"

Perry didn't look at his copy. He didn't need to. He knew what was on it. His head swung back and forth between Andre and the Judge. "I didn't. I... I don't know what... I can't think what could have happened." He stammered on briefly through a constricted throat, then subsided into silence.

Justice Roney fixed Perry with a baneful eye. "The word 'forgery' comes to mind," he intoned. He sat back in his chair and looked at Andre. His instincts told him there was more to come.

"The court now knows," Andre stated, "that Mr. Assu was removed from his cell at 3:10 p.m., not 3:35 p.m. as you led us to believe. The commencement time written on the first page of Horace Assu's written statement is 3:42 p.m. He was not returned to his cell until 4:30. Where was he between 3:10 and 3:35?"

"He was in Interview Room Number Two."

"With you and Constable Biddlecomb?"

"Yes.

"These twenty-five lost minutes are what you are now referring to as a 'brief interview'?"

"Yes, well, not very much was said," Perry responded lamely. His counter-attack was faltering.

"I believe you referred to it as 'small talk'?"

"Yes, that's right."

"If that is true, sir, why have you tried to hide this interlude of 'small talk' from this court?"

Perry gnawed on his lower lip. He looked at Oatway, then at the judge, then back to Andre.

"I wasn't... we weren't... we just didn't think it was relevant."

"I see. You didn't think your deliberate manipulation of an unsophisticated young man into confessing to a murder he didn't commit was relevant to any issue at this hearing?"

"We didn't do any such thing!" Perry raised his voice. "Your boy's guilty, sir! He's admitted it! And no amount of–!"

Oatway struggled to his feet, apparently intending to intervene before the officer dug himself in any deeper. He wore the look of a man who thought he should be working harder, but just couldn't find the energy.

Pepper Roney reacted faster. He swung on the witness. "Corporal! You're a witness in this courtroom, not a judge! Keep your opinions to yourself!" He turned to the prosecutor. "Yes, Mr. Oatway?"

"My Lord, with respect, Mr. Devereaux is overstating. Despite this morning's revelations, there is no evidence before this court that any such manipulation occurred in this case. The last question was unfair to this witness. I repeat, My Lord, where is the evidence that Mr. Devereaux's client was deliberately manipulated in any way?"

Justice Roney rolled back his chair. He looked inquiringly at Andre. "Indeed, Mr. Devereaux. In front of a jury, perhaps, a question can do as much damage as an answer. But in this proceeding, I am the fact finder. You have raised grave suspicions, I grant you that. Suspicions that may well lead to severe consequences for certain individuals-" he glared at Corporal Perry "-but nothing more than that. Do you have other evidence to offer on this issue?"

"Indeed I do, My Lord. My assistant, Miss Palliser, has been keeping it safe for us."

Andre signalled to Grace. She hoisted a portable compact disk player from the floor next to her feet. The CD was already loaded in it. Andre had persuaded one of his former clients, who managed a sound studio, to open the facility at seven thirty this morning and provide a technician. The technician had electronically enhanced the conversation on Raymond's cassette, and then burned the results onto a compact disk. Both men were sitting in the back of the courtroom, waiting to see the results of their handiwork.

Grace carried the CD player to the clerk's desk. All eyes in the courtroom were on her. All eyes except Corporal Perry's. His were fixed on the piece of equipment in her hands. He looked like a man in dire need of medical attention.

As Grace returned to her seat, she noticed a uniformed RCMP officer sitting in the back row of the gallery. The man's eyes were fixed on the witness.

Bert Oatway seemed thoroughly dispirited. He sat stiffly upright in his chair, trying to look detached, waiting for the next gale to blow through his case.

"My Lord," Andre began, "yesterday, my assistant, Ms. Palliser, came into possession of a most extraordinary piece of evidence – a recording on a small cassette tape, the type used in answering machines. I have the original tape with me and I can produce it, but on this disk player I have an enhanced version of its contents. Strictly speaking, I should first prove such matters as provenance and chain of custody before playing this recording for you. But if you will permit me to play it immediately, it is my sincere belief that the good Corporal here-" Andre gestured at the sweating witness "-will be able to attest to its authenticity."

Pepper Roney's curiosity was now fully aroused. He didn't invite Oatway to respond. He nodded to the court clerk.

"Play it."

The clerk pressed a button. There was a momentary pause and then Horace's thin voice, with its distinctive Native accent, filled the courtroom.

Uh, Hi! Mom? Mom? Hey, Mom? I'm at the police. Them cops say I killed Mr. Melvin, but I didn't! Come 'n talk to these guys, Mom, okay? Come 'n get me, okay? Please come soon, Mom, okay? Uh, okay, talk to you later.

There was a sharp sound as the receiver was replaced on its cradle, but the connection seemed to remain open. There were a few quiet bumps and scuffling sounds, a click, as if a door had opened, followed by the thump of footsteps and the scrape of chairs. Then, a male voice…

Corporal Perry's voice.

Okay, kid, no luck reaching your Mom?

In the witness box, Corporal Perry blanched.

No, sir. Guess she's out – maybe bingo – she likes to go to bingo.

Too bad. Well, let's get started-

43

At the prosecution table, Oatway let out a strangled sound. He fixed Perry with a malevolent glare.

I wanna talk to my Mom. She's... not home.

And you said you don't want a lawyer, so-!

Don't need no lawyer. I dint do nuthin...

Perry's voice on the recording got suddenly louder.

Quit fuckin' us around, kid! We know you killed him! Maybe you'd like to spend some time with Tyson, eh? Would you like that?

Who's Tyson?

Our office pit bull, kid! And he hates Indians!

Don't like them dogs! Why you got one here?

To help us with snotnoses like you who jerk us around!

On the recording, Horace started to cry. In the courtroom, a chorus of gasps erupted from Verna Assu and her son's supporters. Tears ran down Horace's face as he listened to himself being terrorised.

I never kilt that guy! He never tried touchin' me, just some other guys!

Perry shouted at him.

You knew about his dick being hacked off! Only the killer would know that!

In the recording, Horace was blubbering.

Lotsa people knowed 'bout that! I heard guys talkin' about it!

You're lying, kid! We kept that back!

Another male voice interceded.

Easy, John. He's just a-

A loud slam exploded from the speakers, followed instantly by the boy's squeal of fright. His cry was cut off by the distinct click of a telephone receiver dropping into place.

Silence settled over the courtroom like dense fog. The witness looked as if he'd been harpooned. At the prosecution table, Oatway sat stunned, his face pale, his breath shallow.

Justice Roney's eyes lasered into the witness. For ten seconds, he didn't utter a word. Everyone waited for his reaction. His expression transformed through visible stages, from shock to cold rage and finally, to pity.

"I trust you have plans for a new career, Corporal," he rumbled. "Get out of my courtroom!" He turned to the

44

lawyers, all business. "Gentlemen, I'd like to speak to you in my chambers." He leaned forward, addressing the official court reporter. "Madam Reporter, please attend with us and bring your equipment. And when we're finished there, we'll take an early luncheon adjournment so you can replay that CD and put every word of it on the trial record." He turned to his assistant. "Madam Clerk, please bring young Mr. Assu's so-called waiver form and voluntary statement into my chambers."

Roney slammed his bench book shut and stood up. The Sheriff's officer turned and faced the body of the court.

"All rise! This court stands adjourned until 2:00 p.m.!"

Constable Biddlecomb was standing in the lobby, waiting his turn on the stand. He was tugging at the collar of his tunic, which looked a little tight on him. Grace watched as Perry emerged from the courtroom, stepping carefully as if he was negotiating rough terrain. He was gripping his case file tightly in his right hand; she noticed his left hand was trembling. He walked about ten paces into the lobby area, and then stopped. He seemed confused about where to go next. Biddlecomb spotted him and walked over. Perry stared at him, opened his mouth to speak, closed it, and stood in dumb shock.

"What?" Biddlecomb asked. He received no answer. "What?" he repeated, louder.

Verna Assu and two friends were standing in a far corner of the waiting area, watching the two policemen as if they were large insects. Just at that moment, a tall RCMP officer emerged from the courtroom and walked directly over to the two men. He was the officer Grace had noticed earlier, sitting in the back of the courtroom. His collar dogs told her that he was an Inspector. He looked about forty. His face bore the timeless good looks of a prairie farm boy, but one glance at his eyes told Grace he was no country rube.

At this moment, those eyes were filled with distaste and regret.

Grace overheard the conversation. The Inspector spoke in a quiet voice, but there was no doubting his authority.

"Perry, you will not discuss this with Biddlecomb. Leave the building and return to your hotel room. Don't leave there until I call you. If you want lunch, order room service." He turned to Biddlecomb and pointed at a nearby lobby seat. "Constable, I want you to sit over there until one o'clock. At that time, you may leave to get some lunch. Be back here by two o'clock. Eat alone and don't speak to anyone about this case!"

Corporal Perry trudged toward the stairs. Biddlecomb sat down, trying to look calm but not succeeding. For the first time, he seemed to notice that several bystanders were staring at him.

The Inspector turned to leave. He spied Grace standing nearby. He walked over.

"You're Mr. Devereaux's assistant aren't you, ma'am?"

"Yes, I am."

He held out his hand.

"Tom Naaykens. I'm an Inspector at Courtenay Subdivision. Port Hardy is one of the detachments under our jurisdiction."

Grace took his hand and felt a gentleman's grip.

"Grace Palliser. I was impressed by the way you handled that just now."

"Yes, well, as you can imagine there's going to be plenty of fallout after that little show in there." He smiled apologetically. "I'm not referring to your boss's performance. It was a set piece. I'm referring to the three-card-monte with the booking sheets... and that recording."

"I knew that's what you meant."

"I foresee what the Force calls 'a disciplinary review'. I'm also guessing that the Crown's case against Horace Assu is about to be flushed. In fact, I imagine Mr. Oatway will be withdrawing the charge even before the judge makes his ruling. Whatever happens, I'd like to meet with you and Mr. Devereaux and ask some questions. Nothing touching on lawyer-client privilege. Just-" he glanced over at Biddlecomb "-about this mess."

"I'm sure Andre would be agreeable. I'll give you one of his cards."

"Let me give you one of mine as well," he said.

Grace dug in her purse, retrieved one of Andre's business cards, and they made the exchange.

"I'm giving you two," he said. "One for each of you."

Grace studied his face. No, he wasn't trying to pick her up.

Too bad, she thought mischievously.

FOUR

Tom Naaykens was right. After an hour with Justice Roney and Bert Oatway, Andre emerged from the judge's chambers to tell Grace that the case was over. They would reconvene court at two o'clock and Oatway would formally withdraw the indictment. He'd conceded during their meeting with the judge that he'd always been uneasy about Frank Chernoff's anticipated evidence. Hearing this said, Andre had taken a chance. In exchange for Oatway's undertaking not to report the social worker who had leaked it, Andre had given him a copy of the psychological report on Frank Chernoff.

After skimming through the document, Bert Oatway had vowed to re-open the investigation.

Andre and Grace brought the good news to Verna, who hugged them both and then collapsed sobbing into the arms of her friends. Next, they went down to the cellblock interview room. Horace was hunched over a Styrofoam tray, picking at some unidentifiable glop that passed as a prisoner's lunch. His eyes flickered back and forth between the two of them as Andre explained that the charges would be dismissed and he would be released from custody later that day.

"I'm going home with my Mom?" he asked in confusion.

"Yes, Horace," Grace said gently, "you can go back to Port Hardy."

Tears rolled down his small face.

"That Mr. Perry was right."

Andre sat back, dumbfounded.

"What do you mean, Horace?" Grace asked quietly.

"He tole me the judge'd take care of me."

"Take care of you?"

"Yeah. 'Once 'n for all', he said."

The courthouse rumour mill operated with its usual efficiency. As two o'clock approached, a half dozen media jackals and about twice as many rubbernecking lawyers joined the swelling crowd outside the courtroom's double doors. When the Sheriff slipped the latches, middle-aged professionals in three-piece suits competed with pungent old ladies in rug coats for seats in the front pews. Grace had entered the courtroom earlier through the side door, along with Andre, Bert Oatway and Michael Dimitri. She soon found herself surrounded by warm bodies on all sides.

Andre was standing near the prosecution table, talking quietly with Bert Oatway. Michael Dimitri sat alone at the defence table, trying to look important. Grace watched as he gazed out over the filling gallery, apparently searching for a familiar face. Finding one, he nodded gravely, as if to convey that today's victory had been his weighty responsibility.

This guy's unreal, Grace thought.

Perry and Biddlecomb were nowhere to be seen.

If the courthouse insiders were expecting one of Pepper Roney's famous performances, full of sound and fury and quotable quotes, they were disappointed. The proceedings were short and anticlimactic.

Justice Roney marched in and took his seat. He opened his bench book, as if he actually intended to take notes, than nodded to Bert Oatway, who was already poised at his lectern.

"Mr. Prosecutor?"

"Thank you, My Lord." Oatway took a deep breath. He began speaking. Grace detected a slight quaver in his foghorn voice. "My Lord, in light of the evidence heard in this courtroom earlier today, and in light of certain matters brought to my attention for the first time during the luncheon recess-"

That's covering your ass.

"-I now apply to this court to withdraw the indictment against Mr. Assu."

"Thank you, Mr. Oatway." Justice Roney leaned forward. "Your decision to take this course is a credit to you, sir, and to the office you hold. Your application is granted." He turned and directed his next remark to Horace, who was sitting quietly

49

in the prisoner's dock, looking up at him like a frightened squirrel. "Horace Assu. The charge against you has been withdrawn. You are free to go, young man."

Sounds of relieved weeping erupted from behind Grace. Pepper Roney actually smiled indulgently and added, "Why don't you leave that box and go sit with your mother."

The Sheriff opened the gate and Horace, oblivious to courtroom decorum, ran to where his mother was sitting. There were hugs and fresh paroxysms of noisy thankfulness.

While most eyes in the courtroom were distracted by the emotional scene behind her, Grace noticed Roney whispering to his clerk. Finishing, he looked up.

"Mr. Oatway, does that complete your business with the court today?"

"Yes, My Lord."

"Thank you. Mr. Devereaux?"

"I am content, My Lord."

"So you should be, Mr. Devereaux. Sheriff, please adjourn the court."

Roney disappeared into his chambers, and the chattering crowd began filing out. Grace watched the court clerk leave her seat and work her way through shuffling bodies to the back of the gallery. A moment later she reappeared, followed by Tom Naaykens. She and the tall Inspector disappeared into Roney's chambers.

Apparently the fallout had begun.

They were silent as they walked back to the office. They were each burdened with overstuffed briefcases, the remains of Oatway's misconceived case against Horace Assu. After court, Michael Dimitri had thoughtlessly disappeared in the direction of the Registry offices, his mind no doubt preoccupied with some fresh young secretary, leaving his briefcase under the counsel table. To make room for the CD player she was carrying, Grace had been forced to empty her own briefcase of its accumulated debris — collapsible umbrella, makeup,

magazines, and unopened mail – and pile it in the bottom of Andre's courthouse locker.

Andre had shrugged into his wrinkled Colombo raincoat and now he trudged beside Grace. Unruly strands of his immaculately white hair fluttered and danced on a rising wind, but he was oblivious. He was hunched in thought, his eyes fixed on the pavement a few yards ahead.

Grace knew Andre too well. He was taking no great pleasure in their victory. He was re-spooling the morning in court, replaying the evidence and, she guessed, sorrowfully reflecting on the sad fact that, once again, police officers had forgotten that they were supposed to be investigators, not judges.

The cold wind carried the scent of kelp and ocean swells. A southeaster was brewing – unusual for this early in the fall. A few fat raindrops spattered against the wall of the building next to them. Leaden clouds, their lower margins as black as clinical depression, rolled in from the Strait of Juan de Fuca. Soon sheets of rain would be slashing down the avenues of the city.

Grace moved closer to Andre, shortening and quickening her pace to match his. They proceeded north on Blanshard Street, over sidewalks and crosswalks crowded with ambling American tourists. When they reached Fort Street, they turned east. Their firm's building was halfway up the block. They entered the lobby and rode the elevator to the sixth floor.

When the doors slid open, the firm's receptionist was on her feet, signing for a FedEx delivery. Her telephone headset was askew, giving her the look of a frazzled air traffic controller. She peered past the deliveryman's uniformed shoulder.

"Grace! Mrs. Dixon has been asking for you! I think she just left Mr. McCormick's office. You might catch her at her desk."

"Thanks, Dolly," Grace replied. "If she calls again, tell her I'm on my way."

They headed down the carpeted hallway to Andre's office. Grace plunked her briefcase on one of his client chairs and turned for the door.

"I won't be long."

"Take your time." He gestured at a row of phone message slips arranged on the seat of his chair.

Grace located Leddi Dixon in her office, staring at her computer monitor and clicking away on the mouse. The woman looked up and smiled worriedly.

"Grace! Come in." Her eyes slid back to the computer. "This terrorism thing is turning American foreign policy upside down," she said absently. "For years, they've been criticizing the Russians for their tactics in Chechnya. Now they're agreeing that the Chechen rebels are terrorists. Looks like they want to be sure of Putin's backing when they start dropping bombs on Afghanistan."

"I've stopped watching the news," Grace replied. The terrorist attacks on the World Trade Center had thrown the world into turmoil. The horrific scenes at Ground Zero in New York, the endless memorial services, and the increasing international pressure on the Islamic fundamentalist government in Afghanistan to surrender Osama bin Laden had dominated the news for the past two weeks. On September eleventh and the days following, Grace and millions of others had spent every spare moment glued to CNN. Finally, drained by it all, she'd resolved to preserve her mental health by ignoring the swirl of events in the world outside and concentrating on the vicissitudes of her own life.

She watched as Leddi scrolled quickly through a Web news report. The woman was ten years older than Grace, but her striking features were still smooth and unlined. Considering the stress she must have endured as the only female lawyer in the firm, this seemed to Grace rather remarkable. Leddi's married surname belied her Mediterranean features, inherited, Grace guessed, from her Macedonian parents. Leddi had once told her that her father, an immigrant barber in the ethnic polyglot of East Vancouver, had raised his daughter single-handedly from the age of ten after his wife had succumbed to a brain tumour. A photograph of her mother, in an antique frame draped with a strand of yellowing pearls, occupied one corner of Leddi's broad desk. The portrait was originally done in black-and-white, but it had been retouched with colour so that the woman looked mysterious and faintly exotic, like an obscure princess in Czarist Russia.

Leddi's seemingly unique genes had awarded her with raven black hair, shiny and thick, and dark, enigmatic eyes. She was slightly overweight, but she dressed carefully – and expensively, Grace noticed with envy – covering her few extra pounds with stylish flair. At social functions, with her luxurious hair spilling over her shoulders and a touch of makeup, Leddi Dixon never failed to turn men's heads.

Grace eased herself into a plush client chair. "You were looking for me?"

"I was." Leddi pulled her eyes from the screen and turned her chair toward Grace. "I hear you and Andre got that boy off."

"News travels fast. Yeah, the charge is withdrawn. The policemen were lying and... well, you know Andre. He demolished the case in less than an hour."

"How did Michael work out?"

"The truth?"

Leddi raised an eyebrow. She nodded.

"Frankly, he was useless," Grace said sourly. "He didn't even wait after court to help us pack everything up. He wandered off to smooth-talk some registry clerk." Grace had been with the firm since high school graduation and she'd earned the right to speak plainly. And she had heard that the young lawyer had not received Leddi's vote when the hiring decision was made.

"I understand he has great regard for you, my dear," Leddi said, with a crooked smile.

Grace made a face and changed the subject. "Why did you want to see me?"

"How's it been going with Shy?"

The reference to Grace's daughter dropped like a rock into the conversation.

When Grace walked out on her husband four years ago, she had taken Shy with her. For a few weeks, Brent had cried and threatened and carried on about his baby girl, but those displays ended abruptly when he discovered the benefits of being an unattached male in a city overpopulated with single women. Victoria was the provincial capital and its hundreds of government offices teemed with nine-to-five secretaries. After a few dates, Brent had been content to leave the single-parent juggling act to Grace. He'd considered his duty done if he dropped around from time to time to take the youngster for an ice cream or an afternoon at Beacon Hill Park. He'd show his friends what a cool Dad he was, striding around for a few hours a week with his toddler hoisted on his shoulders. He had even been loutish enough to brag to Grace that Shy was a "chick magnet".

No, the day-to-day drudgery of rearing a daughter hadn't been for Brent Taylor – especially on Friday and Saturday nights.

But lately that had changed. Shy had learned to talk, Brent had met Hilary – using Shy as bait, no doubt – and Hilary had turned out to be one of those nurturer wannabe's that plagues the second marriage market.

And, at about that same time, Grace had been falling down a hole. Angry and adrift and frustrated by the loneliness of single parenthood, she had inevitably telegraphed her vulnerability to the wrong man. A world-class smooth talker, he had stepped into her life just long enough to obliterate her bank account and demolish her mental health.

To Grace's everlasting shame, she'd been forced to ask for Brent's help to throw the guy out.

In the course of all this turmoil, Grace had discovered tranquillisers. Then she'd taken up with an American attorney who lived in Florida. Then she'd derailed that relationship in a senseless, drug-addled scene witnessed by the man's teen-aged daughter.

Then Brent had struck.

He hadn't succeeded at first. But with Hilary pushing from behind, and with a relentless lawyer, he had kept up the pressure with an avalanche of court motions, psychologist's reports, custody and access reports, drug screening orders and histrionic complaints about Grace's long working hours, late pickups at day care, and lack of extended family support. The court proceedings turned into a state-sanctioned Inquisition, as every aspect of Grace's life was sedulously examined for fault.

Finally, in August, Brent had emerged smirking from the Burdett Street courthouse – the same building where Andre and Grace had been sweating through Horace's case – with an interim custody order. Grace's pain, humiliation, and devotion to her daughter had been reduced to a few curt phrases on a court document: *Specified access to the Respondent, as set out hereunder...*

That had been the worst day. That had been the day when even Grace's fear of losing all access to Shy might have been overcome by the ache, by the craving, by the overpowering need to float away on valium-induced cloud.

She would surely have fallen if someone hadn't caught her.

Andre.

All these memories tumbled through Grace's mind as she formulated her reply to Leddi's question.

"This was my weekend. We had a wonderful time together, but sometimes it can be pretty awful. One weekend, she'll seem miserable, the next one she'll be offhand, like she doesn't care at all. It just hurts. Everyday."

"I'm sure it does." Her eyes strayed to the photograph on her desk. "The mother-daughter bond is very special. Just remember: as much as she tries, Ms. Holt will never replace you. All I can say is that you'll just have to be strong and struggle through it. When we get the Notice of Trial, we'll have a possible end date to your troubles."

"'Possible' being the operative word."

Leddi nodded sadly. A tone sounded, announcing an incoming e-mail. Leddi's eyes strayed back to her computer screen. She seemed slightly preoccupied. Assuming their chat was over, Grace started to stand up. Leddi waved her back to her chair. She seemed to be wrestling with a decision.

"I'm sorry," she said regretfully, "but there's something else we need to discuss. It might as well be now." She opened a drawer and brought out a pill vial. It was half full with small blue pills.

Grace recognised their shape.

Instantly, a familiar craving gnawed at her.

She pushed it back.

"I opened the top drawer of your desk," Leddi continued. "I was looking for one of those big bulldog clips. I found these." She read the label. "Diazepam." She looked up, her eyes suddenly hard. "I thought you'd put this behind you."

Grace sighed wearily. "Look at the date on the label. Those pills have been in my drawer for months. I haven't touched them. I promised you. I promised Cameron. I've kept my promise."

"Then why haven't you thrown them away?"

"They're a warning."

"A warning?"

"They were in plain view, weren't they?"

"Yes."

Grace leaned forward. "Every time I open that drawer, I'm testing myself. Just the sight of them reminds me of how easy they are to get and what a bitch they are to stop. Resisting them makes me feel stronger. It's a little mental trick I learned from my grandfather. It might upset a rehab counsellor, but it works for me."

Leddi looked bewildered. "Your grandfather?"

"He was an alcoholic. He wasn't very likeable, drunk or sober. We didn't get along. But when he finally quit drinking, he kept a can of beer on the top shelf of the refrigerator, where he'd see it every time he opened the door. It was there for years."

Leddi Dixon shrugged. "Okay, Grace. I don't pretend to understand these things." She handed the pill bottle across the desk. "Just remember what Cameron said: one more incident and you're out of a job. I'd hate to lose you, and I know Andre would be devastated, but Cameron has the last word on things like this." She waved a finger. "Losing your job wouldn't be the worst of it. Brent could get permanent custody of your daughter." She paused to let that sink in. "Okay, interview over." She turned back to her computer screen. "I'd better check my e-mails and then get home. Graydon and I are entertaining some VIP from his head office." She grimaced. "Not my favourite way to spend an evening." Leddi's husband, Graydon Dixon, was the regional manager for a large international bank.

Grace headed for the door.

Leddi called after her.

"Cassie's off this week. Any chance you can help with some of my tapes?"

"If you want me to work on your boring files, the least you could do is get me a raise," Grace responded, grinning, as she exited the office.

"Not until you treat me with the respect I deserve, you insolent child!" Leddi called after her.

Late Tuesday morning, as Grace backed out of a conference room carrying a banker's box full of documents, she collided with a large male.

It wasn't really an accident. The man had been standing perfectly still, waiting. Even before she heard his voice, Grace knew that he had staged the encounter. She nearly dropped the heavy box.

A big hand and frayed shirt cuff, followed by a thick arm, reached around, rubbing across her shoulder. Her nostrils were assaulted by a familiar odour.

"Gracie, my girl! Let me help you with that!"

Harvey Pendergast.

The bulky torso of a tall middle-aged man followed the arm around, taking the weight of the box and removing it from her grip.

"Harvey, I've said this before, but let me repeat it. I'm not your girl! Not today! Not any day!"

His grinning face appeared in front of hers. The man's eyes were small and set close together. Dyed hair puffed over his forehead, like a Fifties greaser.

"Where are we headed?" Pendergast asked.

Grace sighed, resigned to putting up with him, and pointed down the corridor.

"Andre's office." She turned back into the conference room doorway. "There's another box. I might as well get it."

"Don't strain your back, my girl. You might need it tonight." He smirked at her.

"Oh fuck off, Harvey!" Grace stomped into the boardroom. She heard Harvey laughing as he went off down the hallway. She snatched the other box off the table. In her anger, she almost did wrench her back.

Smart move, she thought, pausing to make sure her vertebrae were properly arranged. *Like I really need Harvey saying 'I told you so'.*

Harvey Pendergast was a private investigator and process server, a sometime Vancouver City cop, and apparently a long-time acquaintance of Eric Nader. He spent a lot of time hanging around the office, picking up documents to be served and conducting investigations for the litigation lawyers. He also spent a lot of time in Nader's office, usually with the door closed. Office gossip held that the two men were involved in some sort of business deal, but if Nader's secretary Joan knew anything about it, she was keeping her mouth shut.

Eric Nader himself took some getting used to. The man who had yelled at Shy was an inch or so shorter than Pendergast and rail thin. His straight hair, dark and sleek as an otter's, swept back from a narrow face. His eyes were pale and watchful. It was said that French was his first language, but his manner of speech was clipped and precise, delivered in an accent quite unlike Andre's.

Whatever the connection between the lawyer and the ex-cop, it was of little interest to Grace. Her attempts at friendly conversation with Nader, though infrequent – and, since Sunday, unlikely to be repeated – had always left her with a vague feeling of disconnection.

Pendergast, on the other hand, was simply a boor.

Andre had always made it plain that he too had little use for Pendergast. He avoided using the man's services for anything other than service of court documents. When he required an investigator, he engaged an outside agency. Pendergast probably knew this, but he'd never attempted to discuss it with Andre.

When she arrived at Andre's office, Pendergast was leaning against the doorframe. The old lawyer was sitting at his desk, his expression deliberative and distant. The box of documents was sitting on a chair. Grace squeezed past Pendergast. Her nostrils caught an unwelcome whiff of unmetabolised liquor, as acrid as smelter tailings. She set her box on top of the first one.

"-listening to the news," Pendergast was saying. "Sounds like you pulled a rabbit out of your hat for that teen killer."

"Yes, well I seldom pay attention to press reports about my own cases," Andre replied thinly. "That 'rabbit', as you call it, was clear proof that a police investigator was lying." He attempted to end the conversation by pointedly turning his attention to the papers in front of him.

Grace bent over her box, straightening up document binders. Pendergast's eyes slid away from Andre and fixed on Grace.

"You and Girl Friday here dig up that evidence yourself?" Pendergast asked, his eyes on Grace's backside. Andre, looking up to answer the question, saw Pendergast drinking in the sights.

"I didn't. Girl Friday did." Andre stood up, his usual signal that a discussion was over. "But, as you know, it wouldn't do for us to discuss our sources." He addressed Grace. "How about an early lunch? On me."

Andre's eyes told her to agree without quibbling. She tucked a loose strand of hair behind her ear, glancing at Pendergast.

"Sure. Sounds good."

FIVE

When they emerged onto the sidewalk, a brilliant day reached out to tantalise their senses. The weather system had fled eastward overnight. Apart from a few impossibly white cumulus clouds floating over the Navy yards at Esquimalt, the sky was a freshly laundered blue.

Andre breathed deeply. "Grace, some days are like fine wine!"

They made their way west on Fort, past the Easton's Centre, across Government Street and through the tourist traps in Bastion Square.

It was October, but the midday air behind the weather front was still and warm. Many of the tourists were in shorts, with precautionary windbreakers tied around their waists. Andre began to perspire in his worsted suit, and his arthritic knees were complaining. He half regretted that he and Grace had not taken his car.

Then he caught himself and chuckled. *No*, he thought, *the walk is better.*

Grace touched his arm as they negotiated their way through an oncoming gaggle of teenagers in a crosswalk. He glanced sideways at her as they moved from sun into shade. Grace's arresting eyes seemed to shift from green to blue in the changing light.

Walking with Grace Palliser, working with her, being near her, were among the most treasured delights of the seventh decade of Andre Devereaux's life. She moved smoothly along beside him on her long legs – legs that seldom wore nylons or needed them. On high heels, which she also seldom wore, she towered over him. He didn't mind. His wife had been a few inches taller than he was; his surviving daughter, Annette, was taller as well. Andre's long life as an alpha male, in the courts and in the wider society, had taught him to his own satisfaction that size didn't matter.

He kept track of Grace in his peripheral vision as they crossed Johnson Street. She always adjusted her longer stride when she walked with him. He knew that and appreciated it. Even so, even off her natural pace, she moved fluidly, erect and straight-backed, her remarkable face framed by bouncing waves of soft auburn hair. On her worst day, Grace Palliser was gorgeous.

It contented Andre to know this beautiful woman. Behind her florescent beauty was a mind like a razor, intelligence he enjoyed and admired. This rare combination may have been occasionally evident to others in the office, but Grace would only accept praise from Andre. He believed on good grounds that he was Grace's only close friend, a notion that both gladdened him and saddened him. Most young women, he knew, had a close girlfriend or two to confide in. Someone to giggle with as a teenager, to laugh or cry with as an adult. To share secrets with. To run to in a crisis. But Grace's female peers didn't take to her very well. The magnetism that attracted all that male attention — usually uninvited by Grace, it was clear — tended to repel her female contemporaries.

Years ago, Andre had come to the conclusion that many beautiful women moved through life in daily pain. Only their less well-favoured counterparts imagined that they must be enjoying lives of endless dream fulfilment. In truth, many women like Grace were trapped in demon-haunted psychic landscapes, fraught by self-doubt and mistrust of others. No matter what their outer conduct, inner serenity often eluded them.

Grace didn't have parents. Her brother was dead. She had her grandmother, an apparently remote and intolerant woman whom Andre had never met. She had her daughter Sherry, nicknamed Shy, aged five years, with her brown curls and eyes like dark forest pools. She had her righteously reborn ex-husband Brent, aged thirty, pretending to be fifty, who had made it his recent business to mount a determined assault on Grace's mental health.

And, from time to time, she'd had her pills.

Because of them, she no longer had a relationship with Myles Rothwell, a Florida attorney she had loved so very much.

But she did have Andre.

The Italian restaurant, "Il Terrazzo", was located near the north end of Waddington Alley, off Johnson Street. The alley had been recently paved with cobblestones, designed to quaintly charm visitors. They didn't charm Andre or Grace, but the restaurant itself was a favourite with locals. They arrived ahead of the lunch crowd and took a quiet table under ivy in the courtyard. The hostess showed them to their seats and left a basket of bread. Andre sat silently for a moment, rubbing his knees.

"They're bothering you again."

He smiled. "A little, yes. Nothing that a glass of wine won't cure."

"Maybe we should have driven today."

Andre shook his head. "It's better to keep the joints active. Hurts a bit, but the walking keeps them from stiffening up."

Andre carefully spread his linen napkin across his lap. "Pendergast is divorced, you know. His wife's grounds were mental and physical cruelty."

Grace looked up from her menu, momentarily startled.

"Okay…" she replied, a bit uncertainly.

"Is he becoming a problem for you, my dear?"

"Harvey? Not really. I have to give him the stiff arm once in a while, but he's not difficult to handle. He just has no class."

"He is a dangerous man, Grace."

"That sounds a bit ominous. Dangerous as in pinch-my-ass, or dangerous as in dangerous?"

"Dangerous as in vicious."

"Why are you saying this?"

"I can't tell you now, but I will tell you."

"Then why are you saying anything?"

"So you'll be careful. So you'll stay clear of him."

"I do."

"Good."

Grace eyed him curiously. Andre smiled. "And watch out for young Dimitri as well."

"Why?"

"Because he spends too much time looking at your legs when he thinks I'm not watching."

"Oh, for God's sake, Andre!"

He chuckled. He plucked at his napkin. "Have you spoken to your friend Myles lately?"

Grace pressed her lips together. Andre immediately regretted the question. After a second, she answered.

"Every time I pick up the phone to call him, I lose my nerve. After that disaster..." She trailed off and looked at Andre with sad liquid eyes. "We had a good thing, but I guess I broke it."

"How are you doing with the...?" He stopped, searching for the right words. Gentle words.

"I'm clean, Andre."

"Your purse rattled when you put it down. Pills in a container have a distinctive sound."

"Tylenol. Want to see?" Grace reached down beside her chair.

"No. Just checking. Because I love you. You know that, don't you?"

"Yes, I know that. I love you, too. If I was twenty years older, I'd ask you to marry me."

"If I was twenty years younger, I'd accept."

"You would, wouldn't you?"

He favoured her with a look of deep affection. "Young wine in an old bottle, my dear. It's a cursed existence." He put down his menu. "Ready to order?"

"Sure."

They passed the time discussing the case. Grace told Andre about her encounter with Tom Naaykens.

"A policeman with integrity," Andre remarked. "That's encouraging."

Lunch arrived. They ate their pasta in comfortable silence, enjoying the food and the day and the quiet.

They both decided to resist dessert and settle for strong coffee.

"Have you ever thought of working for another firm?" Andre asked her, stirring thick cream into the dark brew.

"Have I-? Now that's an odd question, coming from you!" She studied his face, then, apparently deciding that he wasn't making idle conversation, she went on. "I've been there since high school. Leddi isn't charging me for her work on my custody case. And I get to try cases with you! Why would I want to work anywhere else?" Grace leaned forward, her eyes fixed on him. "What's this about?"

Andre backtracked, dissembling. "There's word that Leddi might be appointed to the Supreme Court. It could happen at any time."

"I've heard that. But that's not the reason for your question, is it?"

He took the plunge.

"What if I felt I had to leave Pomeroy's? Would you come with me? Wherever I went, another firm, my own office, whatever I might decide?"

Astonishment spread across Grace's face. "Andre, what's going on?"

"Would you, my dear?"

He watched his question work its way across her face. For about one second.

"You know I would! But only if I'd be working for you alone." Her tone said: that's my final answer. She crossed her arms. "Now what's this all about?"

"As with our friend Mr. Pendergast, I can't tell you now, but I will tell you. I will tell you first. But not now."

"But…?"

"For your own sake, Gracie. Trust me."

Her eyes searched his face. She retreated, satisfied.

"I do trust you, Andre. I'd trust you with my life."

They walked back to the office.

"Come over for supper on Thursday evening," Andre said as they stepped into the elevator. "I'll make Filets Provencal."

"I'd love to! But I have Shy for a sleep-over on Thursday."

"Bring her! I can always heat up a tin of Alphaghetti or some other abomination suitable to the sophisticated palate of a child."

"Deal! I get her at five. We'll come straight over."

By four that afternoon, Grace had finished the accumulated work on her desk. Andre had left early. He'd told Grace to take the rest of the day off, but of course she'd ignored the invitation.

She cleared her desk, and then went to check with Leddi. She found her looking at some photographs.

"Andre's gone for the day. He told me I could knock off early. Okay with you?"

"Sure, go ahead" Leddi replied vaguely.

"What are those?"

"Hmmh?" Leddi looked up. "Oh, just a few photos from our trip to Arizona."

Leddi and Graydon had taken a holiday in Arizona at the beginning of September. Their return had been delayed several days by all the flight disruptions after the 9-11 catastrophe.

"Can I see?"

"Sure."

Grace leaned over the desk. The air around Leddi smelled faintly of wildflowers. It was remarkable to Grace that even after a long day the woman showed no signs of wear. Leddi laid out a handful of prints. They were taken at a desert resort. One of them showed a stunning swimming pool surrounded by trimmed lawns and date palms. In the distance, dramatic red sandstone spires rose from rolling foothills that were covered with pinon and chaparral. Grace picked up the picture.

"My God, Leddi!" she breathed.

"What's is it? What's wrong?"

"Nothing's wrong. It's just so beautiful! What is this place?"

"It's called Maroon Mountain Inn. It's near Sedona."

Maybe Myles would meet me there. Grace's stomach tightened at the thought. She pushed the fantasy away.

Leddi's husband appeared at the office door. Graydon Dixon was about the same age as his wife, with hardier good looks than those usually associated with denizens of the banking profession. His full head of wavy brown hair was just starting to grey at the temples. On the several occasions when they'd met, Grace had noticed that he was always impeccably dressed, his shirts crisp, his ties precisely knotted, his shoes like mirrors.

Graydon stood by as Leddi explained a few of the more dramatic scenery pictures.

"I don't see any pictures of you, Gray," Grace said lightly. "I thought it was only women who were camera shy!"

Graydon looked faintly discomfited. "Leddi's in charge of the camera. She's usually too intent on scenery to think about the family album."

"There's nothing to stop you from taking the camera with you on your trip," Leddi interjected. She turned to Grace. "Graydon leaves Sunday for two weeks in London and Basel. Poor man, a banker's life is hell."

Graydon's smile seemed a bit strained.

At that moment, Cameron Pomeroy appeared from the hallway and, with a friendly nod to Graydon, he eased into the office. Pomeroy was the reverse of Graydon Dixon. Grace had always thought that he looked more like a stereotypical bank clerk than a lawyer. He was short, with a small bespectacled head perching on a neck that seemed to be slightly too long. Grace seldom worked on the senior partner's files, but she liked the man. He often stopped by her desk to chat. He was engaging and well read and, despite his appearance, no pushover. Grace had learned this the hard way when he'd called her into his office to discuss her use of tranquillisers.

"All right, people," Pomeroy said in a tone of mock authority, "what's going on here?"

Leddi explained. Cameron glanced at a few of the photographs. Knowing the man's inquiring ways, Grace was surprised that he seemed only mildly interested. He had something else on his mind. He wasted no time in revealing it.

"Nice spot," he said, replacing the photos on the desk. "Now, Leddi, what do you hear about your appointment?"

"Oh, Cameron!" Leddi sounded slightly exasperated. "Let it go. If it happens it happens."

"It will happen. I have it on good authority that you have the inside track." Pomeroy was referring to the open secret that Leddi Dixon was short-listed for an appointment to the Supreme Court bench.

But the legal profession's rumour mill was renowned for grinding out confusion and false hope. Leddi wasn't about to take the bait. "You know as well as I do that there is no such thing as 'good authority' in these things. If I am on the short list, too much idle talk could ruin it."

More than one lawyer's elevation to the bench had been cancelled on the eve of its official announcement after word got back to the appointment committee that the candidate had been bragging to colleagues. Apparently, Leddi knew that.

The following morning, while Grace was working on some of Leddi's dictation tapes, Dolly buzzed through to tell her that Horace and his mother were in the waiting area. Grace found Verna standing at the reception counter. Horace was sitting nearby, reading a comic book, as if this day was no different from the hundreds he had just spent in the Pembroke Street Youth Detention Centre. He beamed when he saw Grace, and then went back to his pictures.

"I wanted to bring Horace here so we could thank you and Mr. Devereaux," Verna said, her round face glowing.

"That's very thoughtful, Verna. I'll call Andre."

They trooped into a conference room and Grace buzzed Andre on the intercom. He said he'd be right in. While they were waiting, Verna told Grace about their immediate plans.

"I've learned about a special school here in Victoria that can help Horace. You know about his condition?" she asked in a low voice. Grace nodded. Foetal alcohol syndrome was disturbingly common on some of the coastal Native reserves. The history of the collision of European and Native cultures was not a pretty one.

"It's my fault," Verna continued. "I was drinking in those days. Because of that, Horace has always had a tough time in school. Now, after all those months he spent locked up, he's really behind. But our Band Manager has found some federal grant money to put Horace in special classes."

Horace didn't appear to be interested in the conversation. He sat at the table reading his comic book.

"Sounds like a good plan," Grace said, watching the boy. "But he's missed the start of the school year. Can you get him in now?"

"Yes. But they want him to have a medical exam first, so we're staying over at the motel until all the paperwork's done."

"When will you go back to Port Hardy?"

"In a few weeks. It's a boarding school, but I'll stay around for a while to be sure he settles in."

Andre arrived a moment later. After general discussion, and thank you's all around, Verna gave them both a hug, Horace shyly shook hands, and Grace walked them to the elevator.

At two, Grace's extension rang.

"Your ex is on the line," Dolly reported. "Want me to say you're in a conference?"

Grace was tempted to let Dolly give Brent the brush off, but she thought better of it. She was going to have to deal with this man until Shy was eighteen. She might as well get used to it.

"No, that's okay. Put him through."

There was a click on the line, and then she heard Brent in mid-sentence, his mouth away from the phone as if he was speaking to someone in the room.

"I'll do it in a minute! I'm on the phone here!"

He sounded snappish. Grace's antennae went up. She knew his moods.

"Hello, Brent."

"Grace!"

There it was, that inflection when he spoke her name. It always brought back the bad old memories. Never any good ones. Maybe there weren't any good ones. Odd how that was – only the bad memories seemed to linger. Even the pills hadn't been able to make them go away.

"Yes. What do you want?"

Don't let him get to you.

"I left a message! Why haven't you returned my call?" he demanded. He had always been able to count on bullying Grace. He'd rant; she'd be mild. He'd blame, she'd be submissive and apologetic, even if she hadn't done anything wrong.

Not today. Not this year.

"I've been busy," she replied coldly. "Why are you calling?"

"Shy tells me that you had some Native guy in your house." She could hear him striving to regain the old control. "A man with dirty hands, she says. What the hell is this about? You getting your pills from street dealers now?"

"I haven't touched a pill in months and you know it."

"I don't know it. Your drug screens only go to the social worker."

"Well, don't you think you'd hear from her if they were positive? Shy was talking about Raymond Vallee. His nephew is Horace Assu, the boy Andre was defending. The case ended on Monday."

"You mean that perverted butcher job up in Port Hardy?"

"Yes. Horace was acquitted. As a matter of fact, the prosecution dropped the charge in the middle of the trial. Read the papers. God, Brent, it must be exhausting!"

"What?"

"Living two lives – yours and mine!"

"I have to protect Shy!" he erupted.

Shit. Here it comes...

"And I *did* read the papers! That kid walked on some bullshit technicality!" The man was fulminating. "He confessed to the cops, but the judge threw out the confession. All that means is he's guilty and that sleezoid old lawyer pal of yours outsmarted the prosecutor and put the cops on trial!"

"Brent, you couldn't be more wrong! About everything! But I'm not going to waste my time explaining. If you're unhappy with the justice system, write a letter to the editor! What's the point of this call?"

"The point-" Brent's voice got louder "-is I don't want my daughter around these people! If you want to work on these lowlife cases, that's your business! If you want to have these creeps in your house, that's your business!" He was shouting now. Grace held the receiver away from her ear. "But if you're going to expose my daughter to them, that's my business!"

Grace forced herself to reply calmly.

"That man was Horace's uncle. He spent six hours on the road from Port Hardy to bring us a piece of evidence. That evidence helped exonerate his nephew. He was sober and he was polite! You've got yourself wound up over nothing!" Grace paused, thinking. "Or is it just that you don't like Native people? Is that it, Brent? You don't want Shy to be around any of 'those drunken Indians'? I remember how you used to talk!" Now Grace was raising her voice. A few of the secretaries sitting nearby looked up from their work to stare at her. She didn't care.

"Don't be stupid! There are Natives working at my job. Good workers, too."

"How many of them have you invited for a beer? How many of them have you asked over to one of your barbecue parties?"

"I'm not going to have this argument with you, Grace! Hilary and I believe your lifestyle is a danger to Shy! For Chrissake, she's even got a story about some lawyer in your office groping his secretary right in front of her! We're not going to stand by and let you expose Shy to this kind of thing.

71

Hilary and I have decided to stop the visits until we can talk to our lawyer and get this case back into court."

"*Hilary and I* believe? *Hilary and I* have decided? Really? So those were *your* pants she was wearing the other day! Never once in our years together did I hear you say 'Grace and I believe...' or 'Grace and I have decided...!' You really are a pathetic little worm, Brent! I suppose if I'd cared more about myself when I was with you I'd have noticed how small you really are! Listen to me! You and that woman can scheme all you want, but the court order is enforceable both ways. I have specified access! You can't get the order varied without a hearing, and you can't get a hearing this week. And when you do get one scheduled, I'm really looking forward to hearing you explain to the judge how dangerous it is for your daughter to be around Native people." She shouted into the phone. "Thursday at five for her overnight! Have her ready!"

Grace slammed down the receiver. Heads turned. A few of her crisis-loving neighbours stood up from their desks, obviously waiting to see if she was going to break down. She sat hunched in her chair, head bowed, teeth and fists clenched.

Then she went looking for Andre.

He wasn't in his office. She went in anyway and closed the door. She sat in his chair and put her head on her arms.

She started to cry.

SIX

Grace decided that it wouldn't be fair to burden Andre with her latest child custody woes. She told Leddi they might be served with another application from Brent's lawyer. Leddi asked a few questions, shook her head and went back to work. Graydon was away on his business trip, and Leddi had been staying late to wrestle with some of her problem files.

She's clearing the decks, Grace thought. She must know she's going to be appointed.

Now that the murder case was over, Grace was feeling a vague sense of loss. A criminal trial might be draining – it might even be a cursed, damnable experience when it was happening – but the office days that followed often seemed too long, too quiet, and too depleted of urgency to replace the adrenaline rushes of courtroom work. Grace wasn't a lawyer, but she'd ridden that roller coaster often enough and her reactions were the same.

At six o'clock, craving relief from her creeping sense of ennui, she went in search of Andre. Maybe they could go for a drink. But his office was still empty.

I wonder if it's a medical problem...

She pushed the thought away. Andre had always exuded good health. He'd seemed a bit tired lately, but that was understandable. The Assu trial had been stressful and, after all, the poor man was nearly seventy years old.

Grace tried calling Andre at home, just to check on him, but there was no answer. Finally, restless and not yet ready for supper, she walked alone to Swan's Brew Pub. On the way, she bought a newspaper – a handy prop to discourage the inevitable pickup artists.

Grace took a table in a corner, ordered a pint of Rickard's Red, and opened the newspaper. She was pretending to any would-be womanisers that she was there to read her paper and enjoy a quiet drink. She was also pretending to herself.

Mostly, she sat scanning the same paragraphs over and over, her eyes out of focus, her mind divided between the latest War on Terror debates – sky marshals, bullet-proof cockpit doors, emergency police powers – and the disorganised tumble of her own uncomfortable existence.

She wondered idly if she'd ever receive a sign that there was some point to her life, and if she'd even recognise the sign if it came. She tortured herself over her cowardice during her years with Brent and her months on prescriptions. She wondered – now that she was standing up for herself and 'setting the boundaries', as the self-help books said – why it didn't seem to make any difference to most of the people who knew her. It didn't matter to Brent. He continued as before, obsessively determined to prove that he was somehow better than she was, somehow a more virtuous and upright member of society.

It didn't matter to Pendergast. He continued with his habitual stream of the low-grade remarks.

It didn't seem to matter much to Shy. She had stopped parroting her father's snide remarks about 'pillheads', but mostly she just kept on being a child, sometimes loving her Mom, sometimes needing her, and sometimes acting as if Grace was just some incidental adult in her life, like a spinster aunt who visited occasionally.

And then there was Myles. He hadn't noticed her rehabilitation because he was three thousand miles away, and because Grace hadn't yet overcome a certain morbid fondness for emotional self-mutilation.

There was a phone call to be made, but she was the one who had to make it.

She was staring distractedly at a page six op-ed piece when an unwelcome voice intruded on her gloomy reveries.

"Is this seat taken?"

Grace looked up.

Preppy Boy Dimitri was standing in front of her with a beer in his hand.

Grace made a point of leaning sideways to peer past him.

"Do you need an extra chair for your table?" she asked.

"No."

"Then it's taken."

Preppy Boy set his glass on a spare beer mat and sat down.

"Look-!" Grace began.

"Not 'Look'. Michael. Call me Michael."

"I didn't call you at all. Why are you sitting here?"

"Because it's after hours, and we're not in the office. We *do* work in the same office, right? We should get to know one another. Who knows, we might work on other cases together. How old are you, Grace?"

Grace raised an eyebrow. She took a sip from her beer, looking him over. He'd obviously driven home after work for a quick shower and a change of clothes. He was dress-down cool in slacks and a polo shirt. The jacket he was carrying looked like lambskin. His hair glistened with sculpting product. She detected a whiff of cologne.

"Are you trying to win a bet?"

"Maybe. How old?" He favoured her with his best smile. Grace's long pause and cool regard had apparently raised his hopes.

"Younger than you. And also, too old for you."

"Clever. Come on, Grace, it's after hours! I admire you, lady. I do. You're not only damned good looking, you're smart. Great combination – could take you a long way."

Grace's eyes narrowed. He couldn't have missed her change of expression, but he pushed on without taking a breath.

"Old Andre didn't really need me on that trial – you had it covered. Fact is, I doubt he even wanted me there. Never told me about the little goody bag of surprises you had for that cop. My opinion – you won the case for him. You ever think of going to law school?" He affected a tone of understanding and tolerance. "I mean… the law used to be a man's domain, but not any more. Sixty percent of my graduating class was female."

Interesting technique, Grace thought. When he needs to take a breath, he does it in the middle of a sentence so the other person won't feel comfortable interrupting.

She turned and surveyed the growing crowd of young people gathered at the bar. Then she leaned forward and answered in a low voice. Dimitri bent closer to hear her over the background chatter.

"Mr. Dimitri. Michael. I'm sorry, really I am. But you see, compared to you, I've had a pretty crummy life so far. I had a miserable marriage and a ferocious divorce. I've just lost custody of my five-year-old, who hates strange men anyway. I live in an old rental house, and I don't do office affairs or one night stands. Even if your intentions tonight are entirely honourable, and even if something developed between us, you'd lose interest in a month or two. Add it all up and it doesn't look too promising." She paused to let that sink in. "On the other hand, there are a few tight little units standing over there by the bar. Maybe you should try your luck with one of them and let me read my paper."

Dimitri leaned an elbow on the table, tilted his head to one side, and made a theatrical show of scratching behind his ear. Grace waited for a smart aleck response, but all that came out was, "Can I finish my drink?"

"Sure. Do you follow sports?"

"Uh, yeah…" he replied, suspiciously.

Grace removed the sports section from the newspaper and pushed it over to him.

"Live it up," she said, and went back to her editorial.

After a few seconds of staring at the top of Grace's head, Dimitri picked up his beer and stood up. "Upon further consideration," he said, with elaborate politeness, "I've decided to take your advice."

He wandered away and was soon engaged in earnest conversation with an anaemic-looking young girl who was wearing too much eye shadow.

Thirty minutes later, Grace walked back to the office to get her car.

Dimitri had done her an unwitting favour. He'd convinced her to phone Myles Rothwell.

It was around eight when she reached the firm's building. She needed to use a bathroom, so she walked through the car park to the elevator and used her security card to activate it. She rode up to the sixth floor. The reception area and the lawyers' offices were dark, but the lights over the secretarial stations had been left on.

Grace was just finishing in the ladies' room when she was startled to hear male voices. Her heart sank when she realised that one of them sounded like Harvey Pendergast. Then she heard the outer door to the ladies' room thump open.

"Hello?"

It *was* Pendergast!

Grace heard the inner door start to open.

"Anybody in here?"

What the hell?

Grace didn't want to deal with this jerk. She raised her feet off the floor and held her breath. The self-closing mechanism on the washroom's inner door hissed open, there was brief silence, and then it closed again.

"Not in there," she heard Pendergast say.

Another voice replied from the hallway outside. "She must have stayed in town tonight." The conversation faded as the outer door swung shut, but not before Grace recognised the other man's voice.

Eric Nader.

Grace put it together. They'd seen her car in the underground garage and were making sure she wasn't in the office.

They wanted privacy.

Andre's warning about Pendergast replayed in her head.

She stood and eased open the door of the stall. She stepped out. She removed her shoes and crept to the inner door. No sound. She opened the inner door wide enough to slip through into the space beyond. Pendergast's distinctive body odour lingered faintly in the dead air. She listened at the outer door for a second, then opened it a crack. Voices came from the direction of Nader's office.

Grace was about to exit in the opposite direction and leave by the stairs when Pendergast's gravelly voice drifted up the corridor.

"- that damned Devereaux again!"

Grace stopped. She made a snap decision. She reversed course and strode quickly down the carpeted hallway. Leddi's office was next to Nader's. The voices got louder; Nader's office door was wide open. Leddi's was closed, but not completely. Grace ducked in and pushed the heavy door almost shut, then stood close to the gap, listening. She could hear Pendergast's voice clearly.

"You don't think him prowling around Fisgard Street is important? He might have seen me with Getz."

"A coincidence," Nader replied. His tone conveyed disinterest.

"I don't know... Once is a coincidence, twice is a problem! I mean, what's a shiny-shoes lawyer doing in that part of town?"

"Perhaps something to do with one of his cases. Keep your eyes open, of course. But don't do something we will regret!"

"Okay, while we're on that subject, when do I close this file?"

"It will have to be after you-"

The door to Nader's office clicked shut. Grace opened Leddi's door wider, but all she could hear was an indistinct rumble of conversation.

She was afraid to take the risk of slipping away now. She lowered herself to the floor behind Leddi's door and waited. Minutes passed. Then Nader's door opened. Grace peeked out. She saw the lawyer remove a folder from the bottom drawer of Joan's desk and return to his office. He left his door open.

"Here they are," he said. "I need signatures on the bottom left of these three. And on the back of this one. I'll seal them later." Pendergast mumbled a response while Nader continued speaking. He seemed to be returning to a previous discussion.

His tone was icy. "Koop will cut us off if he suspects a problem. Koop is the key. We must not lose him."

"There won't be any trouble. You have my-"

Nader's door clicked shut again.

Grace was still debating her next move when the two men left Nader's office. A few minutes later, she heard the elevator bell. She sat frozen by Leddi's door, trying to understand what she'd heard. She'd recognised the name Getz. He was one of Nader's clients. He'd supposedly filed a claim against a fund created by some Swiss banks to compensate Holocaust survivors, or their descendants, for forfeited dormant deposit accounts. Grace had never seen the client, but it was rumoured around the office that he was the sole surviving heir of a man who had died in Dachau during World War Two. The deceased had deposited a substantial amount of money in a Swiss bank account during the 1930s. Getz's claim was supposedly worth millions of dollars in today's money.

Grace also remembered a Swiss bank official named Koop. He had visited Victoria for a couple of days earlier in the year and spent a lot of time with Nader. The firm had even allowed him to use one of the conference rooms as an office.

Grace waited another fifteen minutes. When she was satisfied that the two men weren't returning, she stepped into the hallway and went directly to Joan's desk. She opened the bottom drawer.

No file.

She hesitated over what to do next, then, gathering courage, she went to Nader's office door. It was closed. She could probably count on her fingers the number of times she had been in this office since the man joined the firm. She felt like she was about to trespass in the private apartments of royalty.

She opened the door, took a deep breath, and strode quickly to Nader's desk. The desktop was as clear as a bowling alley. She looked around. There was nothing on top of his credenza; she tried its sliding doors. They were locked.

She was about to try the desk drawers when she spotted a brown banker's box sitting in the back of the foot well. She slid it out. A typed label on the lid read: "Getz, David Samuel".

Grace removed the lid and looked inside. There were two large binders, a few bulging file folders, a thin photo album, and a boxed videotape. She kneeled there for a second, her hands shaking.

Now or never, she thought.

She emptied the contents of the box on the floor, being sure to keep the components in the right order, replaced the lid on the box and shoved it back under the desk. Then she carried the file material to Andre's office. She kicked the door shut and set her armload on his desk. She switched on his reading lamp.

She sat in his chair and started to read.

There was a daunting amount of material, but it was actually quite straightforward. The smaller of the two binders contained reproductions on glossy, sepia-toned paper of hundreds of transactions on a Zurich bank account. The entries started in June 1926 and ran continuously until April 1962. There was a notation in German on the final page, with a sticky note next to it bearing a handwritten notation in English: "Closed to suspense account".

There were only six withdrawals, all in the late 1930s. Every other major entry represented a deposit. After December 1940, only interest credits and bank charges appeared. The account was held in Swiss francs. It was a numbered account, but there were copies of account opening documents in the back of the binder, dated in March, 1926. They identified the account holder as Herr Israel Leopold Getz, of Warsaw, Poland.

The second, larger binder appeared to document the identity of the claimant, David Samuel Getz, allegedly the grandnephew and sole heir of Israel Getz. Along with official claim forms and exchanges of correspondence, there were copies of what appeared to be rail transport records. They were written in German, but some bore over-stamps in Cyrillic characters – Russian, Grace thought – and bore dates from the autumn of

80

1941. The names of various Getz family members, including one Getz, Israel L., had been marked with a yellow highlighter.

Grace grimaced at the sight of these meticulous records of mass murder, so neatly typed and initialled.

She looked through the thin booklet. It contained a dozen or so photographs, mounted in plastic sleeves, each bearing a number. Judging from the clothing and the surroundings, several of the black and white pictures must have been taken somewhere in Europe during the 1920s or 30s. A typewritten legend taped to the inside front cover of the booklet confirmed this. Other photos were in colour and had been taken recently. They were obviously pictures of Nader's client. Grace studied them.

David Getz had wispy, salt-and-pepper hair, a narrow, almost cadaverous face and dark watery eyes. His left eyelid drooped a millimetre or two lower than the right one. His prominent nose was slightly offset, as if it had once been broken. He had a scrawny chicken neck, and in two of the pictures he was wearing a dress shirt and a tie that was cinched too tight, spilling loose skin over the collar.

This man looks like an alcoholic.

She flipped through the second binder until she found his address. It was an apartment in one of the downtown towers, a few streets over, north of Yates. She copied it down on a scrap of paper.

She returned to the old black and white photographs. The client did bear some family resemblance to the elder, deceased Mr. Getz, and also to one of the middle-aged males who appeared in two of the pictures. But it was difficult to tell, because none of the older photographs had been taken from close up.

There was one other file folder. It bore the logo and inscription of the Swiss Bankers Association. She flipped through the material, glancing at titles.

Report on Dormant Accounts of Victims of Nazi Persecution in Swiss Banks.

Decree of the Federal Assembly of the Swiss Confederation Concerning...

Guidelines for the ICEP Audit Firms for Completion of...

Report on the Pre-War Wealth Position of the Jewish Population in Nazi-occupied...

Valuation of Accounts with a Probable Relationship to Victims of...

Rules of Procedure for the Claims Resolution Process.

The file contained too much information to absorb at one sitting. Grace picked up the videotape. It bore a hand-written label: *Getz – Koop interview – June 24, 2001.* She was tempted to take it home and watch it, but that seemed a bit risky.

She bundled up the file material and carried it back to Nader's office, replacing it in the box exactly as she had found it. Then she left, being sure to close the office door.

She rode the elevator down to the parking level.

I need to talk to Andre...

The parking garage was empty. Grace walked over to her six year old Escort. It was sitting in a stall near the rear wall. She cranked the starter. The engine coughed and then caught. She let it warm up for a few seconds, and then released the brake. She pulled over to the exit gate.

As she slid her card into the gate control, a sudden movement caught her eye.

Harvey Pendergast's Jeep screeched to a stop in the middle of the exit lane, nose to nose with Grace's car.

The steel grid between them started to rise.

Pendergast's door swung open. He got out of his vehicle. Grace was suddenly afraid. She struggled to compose herself as he strode toward her car.

The big man leaned down at her open window. He was chewing a wad of gum.

"Night on the town, doll?"

Grace let the 'doll' thing go by. "Just some shopping and a couple of beers. What are you doing? Why are you blocking me?"

He peered into the back seat.

"What did you buy? Something slinky?" He wasn't smiling.

"Harvey, I'm tired! Get out of my way!"

"Don't see any bags back there."

"In the trunk!" she retorted. Her tone dared him to push the issue. He stared at her, chewing his gum.

"Heading home a bit early, aren't you? Bars are just waking up."

"It's late enough for me. Move your car!"

Pendergast leaned closer. His breath was a pungent combination of beer and fruit-flavoured gum.

"I've been parked across the street. Didn't see you come in."

Grace had half expected the question. She jerked a thumb over her shoulder.

"I used the door from the lane!" Pendergast's stare said he didn't believe her. "Are we finished here?"

"Sure." He straightened. "Have a good night." He turned and headed for his car.

Grace gripped her steering wheel, watching as Pendergast climbed into his Cherokee, gave her a little wave, backed out and drove away.

She had a queasy feeling that she'd just stepped over some invisible line.

SEVEN

Andre usually arrived at the office before seven. When he walked in on Thursday morning, Grace was waiting in one of his guest chairs.

If he was surprised, he didn't show it. He put down his briefcase and hung up his coat. Then he closed the door and took the chair next to her. He put his hand on top of hers.

"What is it?"

"We need to talk. Something happened last night."

"More trouble with Brent?"

"No. Well, yes, there's always trouble with Brent. But this involves the firm."

"The firm?"

"You remember our conversation at lunch? About Pendergast?"

Andre's eyes narrowed.

"Yes."

Grace glanced at the door. "Feel like going out for a cup of coffee?"

For a moment, Andre sat very still, his eyes on Grace's face. Then he got up and put his coat back on.

Grace waited until the waitress had left.

"You told me Pendergast is dangerous."

"And I meant it. What happened?"

"Last night after work, I thought I'd go for a drink. You know what it's like after a trial – hard to settle down. I came looking for you, but you were gone."

"I left early. I had a dinner engagement up in Sidney."

Sidney was a small town at the north end of the Saanich Peninsula, a few miles north of Andre's home at Cordova Bay.

"That's okay. I went down to Swan's for a beer. It turned into a very strange evening. First, Dimitri junior tried to pick me up." She waved off Andre's reaction with a quick laugh. "I dealt with it. After that, I walked back to the office to get my car. But by then I needed to pee, so I went upstairs."

As carefully as she could, Grace recounted the details of what she had heard and seen in the office. Then she described her encounter with Pendergast at the parking lot exit. When she finished, she sat back and sipped her coffee. Andre was about to respond, but she leaned forward and cut him off.

"You know what I think? I think there's something fishy about Mr. Getz's claim. And I think you know it! And I think those two men suspect that you know it! And I think you told me Harvey is dangerous because you think he might be dangerous to you. Maybe to Mr. Getz as well." She grabbed his hand. "I'm worried about you. What have you been up to? If there's real danger, Andre, why aren't the police involved?"

Andre chewed his lower lip. He seemed to be considering how to reply.

"We'll come back to Pendergast in a minute," he said. "Tell me first – when you read the file, did you come across any incorporation records for an offshore company? Maybe a Cayman Islands company?"

"No." Her eyes narrowed. "What have we got here, Andre? Another Jensen case?"

Lance and Terry Jensen had been prosecuted for an extensive mortgage fraud. Andre had been retained by a number of bilked investors to trace and recover assets. He and Grace had been able to arrange for court orders in the Cayman Islands, freezing the Jensen brothers' bank accounts there. Ultimately, the funds had been recovered and disbursed.

But it had been no simple thing. The opposition had thrown up one obstacle after another. During a year-long legal wrangle, Andre and Grace had learned quite a bit about the confidentiality laws of offshore banking centres. There were severe criminal sanctions against anyone who breached confidentiality without local court authority.

Andre let out a long breath. He spoke to her softly and earnestly.

"David Getz is a waterfront derelict. They're exploiting him. I want you to stay out of this. I'll handle it. Trust me. For your sake, you don't want to get on the wrong side of this. You have a daughter. You have to think of her."

"You have a daughter too! Why haven't you gone to the police?"

"Suspicions, Grace. All I have are suspicions. I might *suspect* that Pendergast has been pressuring Getz. I might *suspect* that Nader's Swiss Fund file is some kind of scam. And I might report these suspicions to the police. But what if the Getz claim is legitimate? As a member of this firm, I would have breached lawyer-client privilege by discussing the file with the police. I'd be in trouble with Getz, with the firm... and let's not forget the Law Society. And what about Leddi? A scandal right now might ruin her chances for an appointment to the Supreme Court." He sighed. "No, Grace. There may be something to this, but it's too soon for the police. I need clear evidence. If it exists, I will find it. Patience is what is needed. Just patience.

"Notice, please," he continued, "that I said 'I' need evidence, not 'we'. Stop playing Nancy Drew! Just keep your eyes down, work on Leddi's cases, and don't start showing sudden interest in the Getz file, or in the comings and goings of Harvey and Eric." He squeezed her arm. "And don't go into the office after hours unless you're there with me or Leddi."

She tested him. "What about Cameron, or McCormick, or, you know, the associates?"

He smiled. "Don't be cute. Best to just stay away after hours."

They walked back to the office.

As they were waiting for the elevator, Grace couldn't resist a mischievous dig.

"I thought you liked me playing Nancy Drew."

"I do... on our cases." He looked at her. "They're safer."

The elevator arrived. They stepped in.

"By the way, my dear," Andre said. "I'll have to postpone our dinner date tonight. There's something I have to do. I hope Shy won't be too disappointed."

"What? Disappointed at not having a gruff old man to torment? Or disappointed at missing out on his *haut cuisine* version of Kraft dinner?" Grace's response was joking, but something about Andre's manner gave her the uneasy feeling that she had just been lied to. "Just promise me you'll take your own advice…"

"What do you mean?"

"Stay away from the office."

"I will." He paused. "Bring Shy over on Sunday instead. I promise I'll dazzle her." His expression gave the impression that he positively relished the prospect.

"It's not my weekend."

Andre's face fell. "Of course. Well, you come along anyway. We'll have that drink we missed last night, and relive some of our greatest courtroom triumphs."

"This is the radio telephone operator. I have a call for Grace Palliser."

"Speaking."

"Go ahead, please."

A voice emerged from background clutter.

"Hello, Grace? This is Raymond."

"Raymond! Are you calling from the logging camp?"

"Yeah. Listen, I heard all about it, Grace. The tape did it, eh?"

There were electronic beeps between their transmissions. It was like talking to a space shuttle.

"It sure did. You found it just in time!"

"Great! I want to thank you and Mr. Devereaux – Verna told Millie about that last day in court. Wish I'd been there!" Raymond motored on. "Listen, I can't talk on this phone too long. The bosses don't like it. I'm flying out of here this morning. Camp's pretty well shut down and they don't need us. Me and Millie and some of the family, we're driving down there tonight. Millie's reserved the cabin next to Verna's. I'm bringing a big barbecue and some fresh salmon and we're going to have a little celebration, you know, to give thanks for having young Horace sent back to us. Tomorrow night. There'll be lots of grilled salmon and potato salad and good stuff! We want you to come. Mr. Devereaux too."

"Well, thank you, Raymond. That sounds nice. I don't know about Andre, though, but I'll mention it to him."

"Okay, Grace. Hope to see you tomorrow."

This was just the kind of thing Andre would enjoy, Grace thought, but even as she headed down the corridor to his office, she had a feeling that he would find some reason to beg off. And she was right. When she told him of Raymond's invitation, he seemed momentarily intrigued, but then said there was something else that might need his attention so he wasn't sure if he could make it.

"I'll try. I'll have to meet you there."

As Grace walked back to her desk, she couldn't shake the feeling that Andre was hiding something from her.

At lunchtime, just before she left the building, Grace dug in her purse for some lipstick. She spotted the scrap of paper with Getz's apartment address written on it. She studied it. The address was only a few blocks away.

What's the harm if I take a look?

The building was a high rise. It had a seventies look. On the wall of the covered outer alcove there was an intercom panel with a small typewritten nametag next to each button. Grace looked for number 803. The tag next to the button read 'Getz, D.'

She looked around. She wanted to get a look at this 'Getz, D.' without him seeing her. The apartment complex across the street had a thick hedge running across the front of the property. She decided she would tell him she's from the Post Office with registered mail and that she's double-parked, so he'd have to come down to sign for it. Then she'd wait across the street.

She held her breath and pushed the intercom button. She didn't get a chance to try her little ruse.

"Hello?"

Pendergast!

Grace quickly walked away. She had to get out of sight before Pendergast got the idea of going out on his balcony to see who had buzzed him.

"Hello, who is it?" his voice repeated impatiently through the speaker. Grace was already halfway back to the street. She pulled up the hood of her coat and headed for the corner.

Should I tell Andre?

He'd be upset with her.

She rounded the corner.

I'd better tell him.

Joan Van Zant had worked for Eric Nader for several years. She was as secretive as her boss. Grace knew better than to question the woman about any of his files. Especially after that Sunday encounter at the office.

But there was another way.

When Grace returned from lunch, Dolly's relief was working at the reception desk. Dolly invariably spent her midday break in the office lunchroom, nibbling like a bird on Melba toast or chewing on cut up pieces of fruit in a seemingly endless – and apparently vain – effort to shave pounds off her spreading bottom.

Grace went to the lunchroom. Dolly was there, alone, reading a fitness magazine. Grace put the kettle on. She waited quietly until it boiled, then stood at the sink, dipping a tea bag.

"Dolly?"

"Mmm?" She looked up.

"That man who was in the waiting room when I left for lunch, is he that Getz fellow who's getting all the money from Switzerland?"

There had been an older man near the elevator when Grace had left the office earlier. She knew he wasn't David Getz.

"No, that's Mr. Wheeler. He's Mr. McCormick's client. Actually, I've never seen Mr. Getz. He only meets with Mister Nader in the evenings. Even Joan says she's never seen him."

"You're kidding."

"That's what she says. I asked her one day why no one ever sees Mr. Getz." Dolly's top lip curled in remembered disgust. "She got real snotty about me asking, like Getz was *her* client. Sometimes I don't know about that woman. She acts so high and mighty, like she was a partner or something. She's just a secretary!" She snorted. "It's not like the bitch is *that* good-looking!" Dolly was echoing a widespread sentiment among office staff. Many of them resented Joan's often grating attitude. Some speculated that she was sleeping with her boss. Nader lived in a large secluded house on the waterfront north of the city and, as far as anyone knew, he had never been married. The latest theories held that Joan was high on herself because she was bedding her boss and was privy to all the firm's secrets.

Dolly prattled on. "As for Mr. Getz, maybe it's like being one of those lottery winners. You know. Word gets out that they've come into all that money and then people start beating down their doors trying to sell them something. He's probably just trying to keep a low profile."

"Yeah," Grace agreed, happy to have an easy way out of the conversation. "I suppose that must be it." She looked at her watch. "Guess I'd better get back to Leddi's tapes." She carried her tea to her desk and sat down to think.

Grace knew something was wrong the moment she drove into Brent's driveway.

Hilary's car was usually parked in front of the garage door.

When Brent was home, he always parked his truck on the gravel apron under the oak tree.

Both vehicles were gone.

She found a note pinned to the front door. It was unsigned, but she recognised Brent's uneven hand.

Grace

We've decided there will be no visits until the court decides on our lawyer's application. We've talked it over with Shy and she is fine with it.

The two cold sentences embedded themselves like shrapnel in Grace's heart. Her fingers clutched the porch railing so she wouldn't collapse into a weeping wreck right then and there. Brent's arrogance made her want to scream. She pounded on the door, then kicked it, and kicked it again. All but overcome, she stormed back to her car.

She noticed a middle-aged woman standing on the sidewalk, staring at her. Grace shouted, "What are you looking at?" The woman hurried off. Grace got into her car. She took a moment to compose herself. Then she backed into the street and drove off in a squeal of tires.

After parking in the garage behind her house, Grace plodded up the back stairs and let herself in. When she dropped into a chair at the kitchen table, she realised that she had no memory of the drive home.

She didn't eat supper. She had no appetite. She phoned Brent's number, but all she got was the man's annoying answering machine greeting:

Hi there! Brent...(female voice cuts in)...and Hilary! (child cuts in, giggling)...and Shy! (Brent's voice takes over)...are not available to come to the phone. You know what to do! Wait till you hear that beep!

Grace tried again every hour until midnight. It was all she could do not to smash her phone. Finally, her heart aching, she curled up on the bed. Fraidy jumped up next to her and pushed a wet nose against her face. She stroked him for a moment. The cat made a nest in the curve of Grace's body and instantly fell asleep. But it was hours before sleep came to Grace.

The lights of the Swan Hotel spilled out over the south end of Store Street, highlighting the bobbing heads of a youthful drinking crowd that was fully engaged in getting a jump on the

91

weekend. The rest of the long street, a mixture of warehouse businesses and derelict buildings, was black and still. The Swan was on the northern boundary of the waterfront hospitality industry and, at night, few pedestrians ventured further.

Andre Devereaux eased his SUV along the darkened street and turned into a large parking lot next to the Radcliffe building. There were a handful of cars parked on the upper end of the lot, near the street. He drove slowly down the slope toward Selkirk Water, a narrow saltwater inlet off Victoria's inner harbour, and parked under a tree near the shoreline. He switched off the engine and sat very still, allowing his eyes time to adjust to the dark. To his left, higher up the slope, the Radcliffe was a boarded-up hulk, brooding between the street and the water. In front of his vehicle, thirty feet away, a chain link fence marked the edge of the parking lot. Beyond that, a half-acre of scrub lay between the rear of the Radcliffe and the water's edge.

Andre waited a good three minutes. As he was about to get out of his vehicle, movement caught his eye. Beyond the link fence, he could just make out the shape of a man standing on the shoreline. His back was to Andre. He was wearing a light-coloured jacket or shirt that stood out from the surrounding darkness. Just as Andre focused on him, he bent over. A growth of gorse near the fence line obscured what he was doing.

Some drunk vomiting.

He opened the centre console next to his seat and retrieved a small penlight. He exited his vehicle. He swung the door back quickly to extinguish the interior light, stopping it before it slammed. He gently clicked it shut.

No point in attracting the drunk's attention.

Andre buttoned his coat and made his way back up the slope until he was abreast of the rear wall of the Radcliffe. His arthritis was acting up, but he forced himself to ignore it. The parking lot fence terminated at the untended remains of an ornamental hedge. There was a beaten pathway leading from the edge of the paved surface to the back of the abandoned building. Andre knew there was a stairwell there, leading down to a basement entrance. He moved cautiously forward along the path until he reached the top of the steps. The stairwell was deep and black. He descended four or five steps and then shone his light into the darkness below. Apart from an empty wine bottle and a few used syringes, the landing was empty. He trained the light on the door.

It was secured with a shiny new padlock.

The barman had told him the man often spent his nights here. He must have been mistaken.

Andre climbed back to ground level, knees aching. Urgency nagged at him. He had to find Getz. Tonight.

It suddenly occurred to him that the figure he'd seen on the shoreline might be the man he was seeking. He shone his light across the patch of beaten grass adjacent to the top landing of the stairwell. There was a narrow path leading through the scrub toward the water.

He started down the slope, his penlight pointed near his feet so he wouldn't trip on the uneven terrain. In a few moments, he could hear the soft lapping of water. Then he heard a violent splashing sound. He stopped and switched off his penlight.

He moved cautiously forward and peered over a growth of broom.

The man was in approximately the same location he'd been in earlier. He was still bending over.

What is he doing?

Light from the Johnson Street Bridge glinted off the ink black surface of the water. Andre could see a form lying in the shallows. As he watched, the man shoved it out from the shore, then straightened up, waded out a few feet, and pushed it under the surface with his foot.

Before it sank from sight, Andre realised it was a body. Andre stood there, frozen in horror, momentarily unable to move. He realised he had better move, and quickly. He was standing on the man's most likely path away from the beach.

93

The man turned, waded back to shore, and squatted down. He seemed to be checking the ground.

It was Harvey Pendergast.

Andre felt suddenly dizzy. He drew an involuntary breath. The sound must have carried on the still night air, because Pendergast's head came up and he stood up quickly. Andre whirled and fled up the path. He fumbled for his light, but it slipped through his fingers and he lost it. He heard scrambling footsteps behind him. He kept going, panic rising. He lost the path on a bend and plunged chest high into shrubbery. He reversed, regained the path, and staggered up the slope toward the back of the building. His knees screamed with protest at each step, and his breath was coming in ragged gasps. The terrain rose suddenly and he stumbled. His right knee almost gave out. In his desperation, he clutched at his pant leg, trying to pull the leg along. The heavy footsteps on the path were gaining.

Suddenly, they stopped. *He's out of breath!* Andre exulted. *I may be old and lame, but-*

There was a sound like a horse's cough and Andre felt a sharp blow in his lower back. Dark earth rose up to meet his face. He wondered vaguely why his knees had stopped hurting.

Before he could thrust out an arm to break his fall, his face smashed painfully into the ground. He was momentarily stunned. He struggled to get up, but he couldn't feel his legs. As he tried again, a rough hand seized the back of his coat and yanked his head off the ground. Foul breath assailed his nostrils and a harsh voiced hissed in his ear.

"Meddling old fuck!" His face was dropped back in the dirt.

"Pendergast, are you crazy?" Andre croaked.

A blow landed behind his ear; his brain exploded and he sank into darkness.

Andre Devereaux's final moments of conscious life were spent in unendurable pain. He awoke screaming, but the scream was cut short when his lungs filled with superheated gases. He couldn't feel his legs, but the upper half of his body was immersed in a fiery, blistering hell. Only a cold surface next to his cheek seemed to offer relief. He tried to press himself into it, to submerge into its depths. But it was concrete, hard and unyielding.

At some central datum point inside the remnants of his brain, anguished final thoughts registered and then evaporated into the simmering surrounding stew.

I'm going to die...

In his last second of life, a paroxysm of realisation blocked out the agony of incineration.

Gracie!

Dear God, you trusted me!

EIGHT

The afternoon shower was violent, but brief. She stood under a big cedar tree until it stopped, then she resumed her walk. The August sun burst from behind the fat cloud overhead and the air around her filled with the warm metallic smell of rain-quenched dust. After a few minutes, she angled off the steaming asphalt and walked on the shoulder of the road. She kept looking down, watching her feet, watching every step. The fine dust, damp on the surface but dry underneath, stuck to the treads of her sandals, then fell away, leaving perfect castings of her footprints. The process fascinated her. She was still absorbed in its investigation when she reached the little green footbridge in front of her house.

A playmate was calling to her. It sounded like Bobby Martin, but she couldn't be sure. His piping voice seemed to be everywhere at once, down the street, no, down the lane towards the bushes, no, there, behind his house. Bobby's house was directly across the street from her own, the only unfinished dwelling in the subdivision, its rough plywood a constant reminder of Bobby's father's drinking and no-account ways.

"Stay outside! Don't go in yet! Play some more!"

She squinted into the glare of the bright afternoon. She couldn't locate Bobby. A voice with no body. She shook him off and crossed the little bridge over the drainage ditch.

Daddy's police car was in the driveway. She stared at it for a long time, puzzled but oddly not puzzled. Something nagged at her memory, but it wouldn't come. The car ticked at her, hot metal cooling.

Then the car was gone and she was in the kitchen, next to the old four-burner gas stove with the big chip in the enamel where Daddy had hit it with the iron skillet the time he got drunk and yelled all day. The linoleum was greasy under her feet. She looked down. Her sandals were missing. She thought she must have taken them off at the front door, but she couldn't remember coming up the front steps or opening the front door or taking off her sandals or calling for her mother. She couldn't remember doing any of that.

The air in the kitchen was as dead as a vacuum. She saw that the door at the top of the cellar stairs was open wide, a black maw leading down, down, down. Cold fingers closed around her spine.

Wake up! You can! You can wake up!

Clawing up through darkness, up from yesterday's kitchen, she glimpsed the forest of dresses and skirts and blouses on hangers in her closet, her bedside lamp with the stained shade, the cover curling back on her latest paperback.

Thank God, I'm out of the dream.

The gunshots pulled her back. They echoed up the stairway from the basement and they pulled her back to her place by the stove. She felt herself running toward the black maw and running down wooden stairs that her feet didn't touch and didn't feel.

No, Daddy! We're children! We're just children!

Her heart pounded in her chest and in her throat and in her eardrums. She heard her gasps for breath inside her head and they sounded like someone else's struggle for air. She strained to listen, but all she could hear were her pulsing heart and her desperate gasps and the echoes of the gunshots.

The gloom of the cellar sucked the warmth out of her skinny body. She froze, shaking, at the base of the stairs. Pale light from the kitchen seeped past her and she peered after it as it moved out into the darkness. It came to rest on something on the floor, right in front of the cupboard where Daddy kept his cans of paint.

Something long and white and red.

Mommy.

As she took a few steps forward, a door slammed somewhere upstairs and the house shook and she squealed with fright. After a minute, she got up more nerve and crept forward again. Mommy was lying on her back on the hard

97

cement. Bright red blood ran everywhere. It spread in a great stain across her breasts and it ran out of the corners of her mouth and dripped into the dust on the cold grey floor. It smelled like metal. It smelled like the damp August dust by the roadside. It ran and it dripped and it stuck to the dust and the dust stuck to it and it spread like a creature.

Mommy's eyes watched her but they didn't move.

She reached for Mommy's hand but it didn't reach up to meet hers and when she touched it, it felt cool and limp. And then her feet were in Mommy's blood and in the dust and it was sticking and oozing and not falling off and not making little castings.

It was sticking and sticking and sticking...

She heard moaning from somewhere nearby. Then she realised it was coming from her...

At 6:35 a.m. on Friday, October 5, 2001, Grace Palliser woke up screaming.

When Detective Sergeant Hank Farrell's extension rang at ten in the morning, he was working his way through a cup of cappuccino and a copy of yesterday's sports section. His file work was pretty much up to date, and it had been a quiet week.

His partner, Paul DaSilva, was on the line.

"Sarge, I'm in the radio room. We've just had a call from the uniforms at that fire on Store Street. Looks like an arson."

"Yeah?"

"Yeah, and something else."

"What?"

"They found a crispy critter."

Farrell set down his coffee. "A body?"

"Yeah. In the basement."

"Meet me at the car."

The Victoria Police Headquarters was on Caledonia Street, only a few blocks from the scene. The detectives were there within minutes.

They were greeted by the usual commotion after a fire call. Two marked cars were parked across the end of the block at

Pandora Street, in front of the Swan Hotel. Uniformed officers were directing traffic and keeping the gawkers back. Three fire trucks were parked at odd angles. A tangle of hoses criss-crossed the street and led into a parking lot on the north side of the building. Fifteen or twenty firemen were busy with cleanup. TV crews were scrambling about, capturing footage for the noon news.

Farrell knew the building. It had been abandoned for as long as he could remember. It was three stories high, constructed of red brick, with a deep basement. Today, gutted by fire, it looked like a scene from the Balkan wars. Faded 'For Lease' signs, scorched from the heat of the fire, hung from the upper stories. At the top of the front fascia, now weathered and darkened by a century of soot, a foot-high inscription was still legible.

THE RADCLIFFE 1899.

Farrell had never understood why this building hadn't been renovated with the rest of Victoria's waterfront revival. It was less than a hundred paces from the Swan, a structure of similar vintage. The Swan had been completely redone and it now attracted flocks of tourists and locals alike.

Paul DaSilva parked their unmarked car against the curb in front of a neighbouring building, well out of the way. They walked through the parking lot to join a group of uniformed officers and fire fighters gathered near the rear corner of the building. Frank Donovan, a uniformed sergeant, left the group to meet them.

"Hank. Paul. We've got a body."

"So we heard," Hank said.

"The report came just after midnight. Fire guys didn't get control of it until early this morning. Looked like it started in the basement, so they went in to see if they could figure out the cause. There are these incredible heavy timbers supporting the first floor – man, they really knew how to build them solid in the old days! The FD captain spotted a place where the fire had burned right through a couple of them. A few scrapes with a shovel and they find tattooing on the cement floor, like from a liquid accelerant. They're thinking arson. Bit more poking around and one of them comes running out to me. Got a charred body. It's in the first room to the right, down the back stairwell. Patrol officers say some of the local rubbies used to set up housekeeping in that room. Dry place to flop... good place to drink in the winter. Owner kept putting bigger locks on the door, but the piss-tanks would just pry them off.

"Anyway, I got everyone out of there and called Ident and you guys. Mitch is in there now."

Mitch was Corporal Greg Mitchell, a crime scenes officer from the Identification Section. Farrell was relieved. He was the best man on the Section.

"Mitch got a portable down there?" Farrell asked.

"Yeah."

"Call him. Tell him we're coming down."

The back of the Radcliffe faced onto a half acre of scrub that sloped down to the shoreline. The waste ground behind the building was a tangle of weeds and shrubs, its southern edge forming an embankment that abutted the city-side approach to the Johnson Street Bridge. There was a beaten down area of grass near the top of the stairwell. It was littered with empty wine bottles, beer cans, and food wrappers. A portable generator was running at full throttle. Electrical cables ran down into the darkness.

An acrid smell of urine in the stairwell had somehow survived the deluge of water from the firemen's hoses. When the detectives reached the bottom steps, Farrell saw that the door had been chopped through. It hung at a crazy angle.

The other side of the doorway was an evil-smelling hellhole of burned out walls and timbers. There were extensive gaps in the ceiling above, and water was dripping from the upper floors. A powerful fan had been set up to help expel smoke from the area.

They found Mitch in the rubble of what had once been a large room. Floodlights were set up in three corners. The crime scenes officer was wearing a borrowed fire fighter's hat and coat, and he had a camera with a flash attachment slung around his neck. He was standing there, eating an apple.

Just in front of him, an area of ash and quenched cinders had been partially cleared. A blackened form, barely recognisable as human, was lying in the middle of the cleared area.

Mitch looked over as DaSilva tried to shake some black filth off a shoe.

"You guys shoulda borrowed some hard hats. Shit's still falling in here."

"Yeah," Farrell replied. "Just wanted a quick look. Anything you can tell us so far?"

"He's male. Got a shoe. If he's one of the local winos, he must've been shopping the sales. Fancy Italian make, and the heel's hardly worn. The back half was under his top leg and it survived the heat. Otherwise, judging by the cooking he got, it'll take dental records or DNA to figure out who he is. 'Course, if he's one of the doorway derelicts, it'll be tougher to make an ID. Those guys aren't big on dental hygiene."

"What's the time line?" Farrell asked.

"Godfrey'll be here in a minute to help me." Curtis Godfrey was one of the Fire Department's arson investigators. Mitchell waved an arm at the black muck around him. "We'll have to do the archaeology first."

"Wouldn't want to be you, Mitch," DaSilva piped in, grimacing.

"Yeah, thanks. Anyway, I should be finished in here by early afternoon. Then he can go to the morgue. Pathologist is booked for two. If there's any blood left in the heart muscle or the aorta, we might have an alcohol level for you by the end of your shift."

"I'm predicting double shifts on this one." Farrell said. "Who's the exhibit man?"

"Bowers. He's out back somewhere."

"Okay, thanks. We'll get out of here and leave you to it. If you find anything in this mess that we should know about, call us. We're in Delta Six."

The two detectives returned to the daylight. Fifty feet down the slope, an officer wearing dog handler's fatigues was working his way along a path through the scrub, scanning the ground.

Farrell turned to DaSilva. "See if he's found anything. I'll have a word with Donovan."

Farrell located the uniformed Sergeant in front of the building, talking to a fireman. Farrell repeated what Mitch had told them. DaSilva joined them a few minutes later.

"Bowers hasn't found much. A few scuffmarks on the path, but no decent footprints – ground's too hard. Wouldn't mean much anyway – winos are probably up and down that path all the time. He did find a flashlight, one of those little flat ones people keep in their cars. Looks new. He photographed and bagged it, just in case."

As they were discussing a canvass of all known local derelicts, to see if any of them knew who had been using the basement room, a young uniformed officer walked up from the parking lot and interrupted. He nodded to the detectives. Out of habit, he reported directly to Donovan.

"Something weird here, sir. I was taking down the licence numbers of all the cars in the parking lot, like you said. One of them is Ford Explorer – looks like a '99. Its driver's window is smashed out. And the licence plates are missing."

"Did you check for registration?" Farrell asked.

"No sir. Figured Ident should go over it first, in case it's tied into the fire somehow."

"Let's take a look."

They followed the young officer down toward the water. A large asphalt parking area, with marked stalls, bordered the north side of the Radcliffe property and the waste ground behind it. There were four rows of parking, with room for a hundred or so cars.

"How many vehicles were in this lot when you guys arrived?" DaSilva asked Donovan.

"Well, I wasn't first on the scene – got here about ten minutes after the fire department. There were maybe ten or

102

fifteen cars here then. A few owners showed up this morning and we took their details and let them take their cars. I asked Burns here to take down the plate numbers on the rest and have dispatch run them on the system."

"Might be nothing," Farrell said. "Could've been some shitrat with no insurance looking for plates with a current sticker."

A midnight blue Explorer was parked near the bottom of the lot, thirty feet from the water's edge, under a yellowing alder tree. It faced a chain link fence that marked the parking lot's boundary with the undeveloped land behind the Radcliffe Building. Farrell noticed that several leaves had dropped from the tree and were lying across the hood and roof. The window in the driver's door had been completely smashed out. Cubes of auto glass lay across the front seats.

Farrell pulled latex gloves out of his coat pocket. He tugged them on. He opened the driver's door and checked behind the visor. Then he leaned in, opened the centre console, and peered inside. It contained a few CDs. He checked the titles. He walked around and opened the passenger side. He checked the glove compartment and behind the visor.

Nothing.

He pushed the door closed and pulled off his gloves.

"Clean. No insurance. No registration. CD player's still in the dash, CDs in the console. Just classical stuff, no top forty, no country and western, so I'm thinking the owner's middle-aged or older. If this was a typical boost, that CD player would be history." Farrell glanced at the young uniformed officer's nametag, then turned to Donovan. "Frank, would you mind letting young Burns here give us a hand?"

"Not a problem."

Farrell turned to the rookie.

"When do you go off shift?"

"Three and a half hours ago, sir."

Farrell looked at his watch.

"Any problem with overtime?"

"No sir. Glad to help."

103

"You know who I am?"

"Yes sir."

"This is Paul DaSilva, my partner."

They shook hands.

"I'd like you to continue with what you and Sergeant Donovan started here – run all these vehicles through CPIC and save the printouts for us. On this one here-" he gestured at the Explorer "-run the VIN through MVD and get the name and address of the owner. Call us as soon as you have it. Also, get hold of Ident and ask them to send another crime scene guy to climb through this car. If they give you a hard time, tell them to call me. Keep everyone away from this vehicle until Ident is finished with it, then have it towed to the secure compound. Report whatever you learn and whatever Ident turns up to me or Corporal DaSilva, but make sure you keep Sergeant Donovan here in the loop."

"Yes, sir. It's done."

As the three NCO's walked up the incline of the parking lot toward the street, Farrell noticed a TV crew had been taping them.

After crawling out of her dream, Grace stumbled to the bathroom and gulped water directly from the tap. She examined herself in the mirror. A pale and sweaty face stared back at her. She hadn't seen that face in months.

It was a workday – she had to pull herself together. She took a long shower. She made some coffee and sat on her bed, watching CNN. She pawed through the clothes in her closet, searching for something to wear. But she felt empty and disorganised. Stupidly helpless. She couldn't seem to get herself moving at daytime speed.

Finally, she gave up. For the first time in months, she called in sick. In her present state, she just couldn't face another day of Leddi's mind-numbing dictation. After she finished talking to Dolly, she started dialling Brent's number, to ask him where the fuck he got off defying the court order, but she slammed the receiver down before the first ring. If she couldn't face

Leddi's files, she sure as hell couldn't face a screaming match with her pious prick of an ex-husband.

She headed for the bathroom. Alarms were going off in her head, but Grace ignored them. She walked down the hallway, into the bathroom, and leaned her forehead against the mirror. Her hands gripped the edges of the counter, as if they had been blessed with independent will and were trying to convince her brain to turn her body around and get the hell out of that dangerous little room.

Grace knew that the pathways to wise decisions and stupid ones were roughly similar. The difference lay in the complex rationalisations required to validate a bad choice.

She stood there, trembling, locked in indecision.   She opened the cabinet.

The prescription container Leddi had found in her desk was sitting on the lowest shelf, where she would see it every day.

Today, the little blue pills weren't a reminder. More and more, with each passing second, they represented a sanctuary.

As a small child, she had lost both parents. A few terrible minutes had snuffed out beauty and laughter and safe loving hands.   Better than most, Grace knew one of life's coldest realities:

Things fall apart.

That knowledge had never made it any easier to carry her burdens.

With a sigh, she grabbed the container and opened it. She shook two pills into the palm of her hand, then two more. She went downstairs, holding onto the banister and taking each step carefully and deliberately, as if she were part of some carefully synchronised ritual.

As if the ritual somehow relieved her of responsibility for what she was doing.

She made her way to the back of the house, to the kitchen, taking slow deliberate paces of exactly even length. She took a glass from the cupboard and a container of orange juice from the refrigerator.

She filled the glass.

Fraidy appeared.   He wound back and forth between
Grace's legs, purring and meowing in his breed's weirdly un-
feline accent.

She hesitated.

"Bad decisions make good stories," Armand had said.

So, I'll write a book...

She swallowed the pills.

Then she fed Fraidy, unplugged her phone and went back to
bed.

Just after three, Dolly looked up to see two big men step out of
the elevator.   They were wearing sports jackets.   For some
reason, she knew instantly that they were policemen.   The
younger one was quite handsome.   His quick smile made
Dolly's stomach flutter.   The older one looked dishevelled and
slightly world-weary.   He reminded Dolly of an unmade bed.

"Hello, Miss.   Does Andre Devereaux work here?"

"Yes, sir."

The man had a billfold in his hand.   He opened it and
showed her his badge.

"I'm Detective Sergeant Farrell.   Victoria P. D.   We'd like to
speak with Mr. Devereaux."

"I'm sorry, sir.   He's not in."

"When do you expect him?"

"Actually, I'm not sure.   He didn't come in this morning and
he hasn't called.   One of the lawyers may know where he is."

"Could you find out for us, please?"

"Yes sir."

Dolly rang through to Leddi Dixon.   "Ma'am, two police
detectives are here to see Mr. Devereaux."   She listened, and
then continued.   "No.   I haven't heard from him."   She
listened again, then disengaged.

"Mrs. Dixon will be right out."

Leddi appeared seconds later.   After introductions, she
escorted the two officers to a conference room and offered
them seats.

"I understand you're looking for Mr. Devereaux?"

"Yes, ma'am," Hank Farrell replied. "Your receptionist says she hasn't seen him or spoken with him today. Do you know where he is?"

"Actually, I don't. I haven't spoken with him today. He's usually very good about keeping the front desk advised about his schedule. But, he's between cases right now, so…" She paused and asked, "May I know what this is about?"

"We'd rather not say just now. We need to confirm certain information first. Mr. Devereaux is the only person who could help us."

"He's is not in any kind of trouble, I hope?"

Farrell drew in a breath and held it for an extra millisecond.

"Not to our knowledge, ma'am. Would anyone here be able to help us locate him?"

"Well, normally, I would suggest that you speak with Grace Palliser. She's one of our secretaries. She and Andre are close friends. But she's off sick today." Leddi got up. "If you gentlemen wouldn't mind waiting, I'll ask around the office and see if anyone has heard from him."

"Thank you. That would be helpful."

After five minutes, Leddi returned.

"I'm sorry. I've checked with everyone in the office who might know Andre's whereabouts. No one has spoken to him today. On the chance that he might be ill and hadn't thought to phone Dolly – our receptionist – I called his home. No answer. I also tried Grace Palliser's number, but no answer there either. Dolly told me this morning that Grace sounded pretty rough when she called in, so she may have unplugged her phone." Leddi stopped talking. She bit her lower lip. "I must admit you have me worried. Is there something I should know?"

"Well, ma'am. Let's just say that Mr. Devereaux's vehicle has come to our attention in circumstances that need explaining. Beyond that, there isn't much we're at liberty to say right at this moment. What we'd like from you, if possible, is to confirm that we have the correct residential address for Mr.

Devereaux. We'd also like any information you have on family members, so we can try to contact them."

"Andre's wife passed away about ten years ago. He has a daughter. Her name is Annette, but I don't know her surname, unless it's still Devereaux. She lives over on the mainland. Her name and address might be on Andre's group life form. Our accounting department could give you that."

"Well, that's a start. Thank you. And one more thing. We'll need to contact this Miss Palliser you mentioned. If she and Mr. Devereaux are close friends, she may know what his plans were for today."

"I'll get you her address and phone number while you talk to accounting."

Ten minutes later, as the elevator door closed behind them, the two detectives exchanged a long look.

"Sounds like he might be our dead guy," DaSilva ventured. "Question is… what was he doing in that building?"

Farrell shook his head. They rode the elevator in silence. As they stepped out in the lobby, Farrell said, "Let's ask Saanich PD to go to his house. If there's no answer, they should break in. Based on what we know right now, they won't need a warrant."

They returned to their car.

"This Devereaux… Ever run across him in court?" DaSilva asked.

"Couple of times." Farrell grunted to himself. "Once he really fried my ass."

NINE

Grace woke at three. She lay among her pillows, staring at the ceiling, trying to overcome the feeling of hopeless lethargy that had been lurking in wait for her return to consciousness. Finally she sat up, spilling Fraidy off the bed, and swung her feet to the floor.

She managed to make some toast and coffee, and then sat dumbly on her bed, nibbling and sipping and watching a mindless daytime talk show. She contemplated plugging in her phones, but she couldn't muster enough energy to rouse herself.

Endless insincere chatter on the TV finally drove her to take a shower. When she was finished, still wet and wrapped in a towel, she retrieved the pill container from the cabinet and went downstairs to the kitchen.

This time there was no hesitation. She took four pills, and then counted what was left.

Enough to get me to Sunday, she thought.

Then what?

She dressed, threw on a jacket and, with her hair still wet, went out to her car and drove five blocks to a liquor store. She bought a bottle of The Balvenie, a single malt scotch that Andre had taught her to appreciate. "An acquired taste, as they say," he'd told her. "But once conscientiously acquired, it is an experience of subtle grace and intimate pleasure."

Sure, Andre, she thought sardonically. *Everyone says that about scotch.*

The cashier took in Grace's damp hair and too-wide eyes and gave her an appraising look. She shook her head as she rang up the sale.

Grace was beyond noticing.

At four fifteen, Farrell and DaSilva emerged through a metal clad door into the corridor outside the morgue. Greg Mitchell followed a moment later, his ever-present camera slung around his neck like a permanent appendage.

"Okay, here's the quick summary." Mitch held up a clear plastic exhibit bag, stickered and marked. "The pathologist spotted these keys when we were transferring the body onto the X-ray table – man's got sharp eyes, missed them myself. Keys and key ring were burned right into the flesh of the right thigh, so they must have been in the right front pocket of his pants." He held up the other exhibit bag. "These here are the slug fragments." Farrell took the bag from him and examined the contents through the plastic. "They showed up right away on the film," Mitch continued. "As the Doc was saying, the guy was shot from behind, right through the spine at vertebra L3. One shot, three-two calibre."

"Can ballistics do anything with pieces this small?" DaSilva asked.

"An educated guess? There might be sufficient markings on the largest fragment for a match. But don't quote me. You'll have to wait for the final word from them."

"That's for down the road anyway, since we've got no weapon," Farrell said. "But the keys could tell us something right now."

"Yeah. I'll clean them up and try them in that Explorer." Mitch fingered the small plastic bag containing four heat-discoloured keys. They had bits of charred material adhering to them. "They don't look too deformed." He pointed to one of them. "The plastic grip has melted off, but this sure looks like a Ford key to me. These other ones look like they're for a residence or office." He dropped the two smaller exhibit bags into a larger one. "When I'm done, I'll sign them over to you if you want to try them at that house in Saanich."

"Good idea." Farrell turned to DaSilva. "Heard back from Saanich P.D. about Devereaux's house?"

"Not yet."

"We'd better call them." He turned back to the Ident officer. "Mitch, call us if that key fits the Explorer. We'll pick up the exhibit from you later. Paul and I need to see a woman named Palliser. She's supposed to be a good friend of Devereaux's. She might have some information we can use."

At five thirty, Grace made some scrambled eggs. She sat at the kitchen table and picked at them with her fork. After a few mouthfuls, she scraped the rest into the garbage and poured herself a scotch. She added a blue pill chaser to her first swallow. Soon she felt a warm glow spread out from her stomach, heading for her limbs and her head. The glow helped mask the damned guilt.

It was an evil guilt that rippled through her insides and wouldn't let go and wouldn't stop reminding her that she'd made another bad deal with her conscience.

She thought again about plugging in the phones and turning on her cell. She pushed the thought away because she knew she would immediately want to call up Brent and scream at him, giving him more evidence to use against her. Or, if she managed to stop herself from phoning Brent, she'd be phoning Andre and begging him to come over and rescue her.

She couldn't do that to her friend again. She'd just finish the pills and then put a stop to this on her own.

Anyway, she wasn't ready to be rescued. Maybe she'd call him later. Or maybe tomorrow, after she'd slept this off.

She dropped some ice into her glass, grabbed the scotch bottle and drifted into the living room. She sank onto the couch and stared at the chair where Shy had been sitting last Sunday, eyeballing Raymond. She wanted her little girl to be sitting there right now. She'd pour the whiskey down the drain and they'd go to the movies.

But Shy wasn't sitting there and she had the scotch bottle in her hand. She poured a few ounces over the ice. Then she got up and put on the CD soundtrack from *Pretty Woman*, which somehow felt like a perfectly droll choice. She set the player selection on 'random', and then sipped her scotch and sat there and hated herself for wallowing in self-pity, but went ahead and did it anyway.

*

Farrell and DaSilva returned to the office just as one of the squad members, Constable Lori Graham, put down her phone.

"Two things for you. That was Mitchell. Radio room told him you were on your way up. He said to tell you the key fits the Explorer. Next thing... ten minutes ago, I had a call from Andy Shaw, one of the Saanich guys. They went to the house and found the back door wide open. No sign of Devereaux. They're wondering if the place's been B-and-E'd. Lots of valuable stuff in there. Hard to tell if anything's been taken."

Hank Farrell leaned on the end of his desk for a moment, tapping a pencil.

"I'm thinking we should take a drive out there and try those keys in the door. Have a look around the house. Then go see this Grace Palliser."

"Her place is only a couple of miles from here."

"Yeah, I know. But remember what that lawyer lady told us? She said Devereaux and Palliser are good friends and that Palliser booked off sick this morning. She said the receptionist told her Palliser sounded really rough and that she wasn't answering her phone."

"Too much of a coincidence?"

"Hard to say. Maybe." Farrell's extension rang. "I'd like to go out to Cordova Bay and look around." His extension rang again. "I want to see what we can learn about Devereaux before we talk to Palliser." He picked up his phone.

It was Farrell's wife. The expression on his face told the others that the discussion was going to be serious, so they moved back to their desks to give him some privacy. After several seconds, DaSilva heard Farrell bark, "Okay, Janey! Calm down! I'll be there in fifteen minutes!" He hung up the phone. He was up and halfway across the room before DaSilva could swivel his chair to face him.

"It's my kid. He took a header off his skateboard. They're up at Vic General. Janey's pretty upset. I'd better go."

DaSilva stood up. "Want me to come?"

112

"No, that's okay. Thanks anyway. Why don't you pick up those keys from Mitch and go out to the Devereaux place? See what you can see."

"Sure. What about Lori?"

"I've got her working with Burns. Just keep your cell on and I'll check with you later. If my boy's okay, we can arrange a meet. I'd like to get to Palliser before we go off shift tonight. Oh, and Paul..." he added, stopping by the door, "before you go, get Palliser's DOB from Motor Vehicles and get someone to run her through CPIC – see if she's got a history."

Grace lived in a rented house in Vic West, a district of older, mainly pre-Second World War homes that hadn't quite kept up with the rest of the city. One of the surviving charms of Grace's neighbourhood was the line of mature oaks that ran down both sides of the street. Their limbs and foliage met above the centre of the roadway, forming a shaded bower that ran for several blocks. Grace's house – two stories plus a daylight basement – sat on a narrow lot in the middle of a block.

DaSilva arrived early. He drove slowly up the block peering at house numbers until he identified Grace Palliser's. Lights were on inside, so she was probably home. He drove past, wheeled around in the next intersection, and parked on Palliser's side of the street, four houses up. He didn't want to spook her. Farrell was coming straight from the hospital in his own car. He'd asked DaSilva to wait until he got there so they could go in together.

DaSilva's visit to Andre Devereaux's house had been instructive. Two of the keys recovered from the body fit the front and back doors of the house. A third, smaller key, fit the padlock on a detached garage. The Saanich PD officers had cut off the padlock, but the key worked in the mechanism. Inside was an MGTD, a sweet little car with low mileage. It had obviously been lovingly maintained. There was a tweed cap sitting on the passenger seat.

DaSilva had wandered through the house. It was small and tidy and expensively furnished. The largest room was a book-lined study. It was warm and inviting, with richly grained hardwood flooring and thick oriental carpets. It smelled faintly of expensive tobacco. There was a large antique desk that looked like something out of *The Three Musketeers*. DaSilva had spent a few extra minutes rummaging through drawers. He hadn't seen anything that would explain why a sixty-eight-year-old lawyer had been shot and incinerated. He and Farrell would have to arrange for Mitch and his crew to do a thorough search. He'd locked up the house and left.

It was seven thirty when DaSilva parked the unmarked car and turned off his lights. Farrell had promised to be there by eight o'clock.

The street was dark and quiet. The detective sipped lukewarm coffee and used the time to relax. It had been a long day, and Farrell was making it longer. Hank Farrell lived for his work. He seemed to think that, because Paul DaSilva was single, he had nothing better to do with his evenings than clock unpaid overtime. "I know the budget is tight, but the bad guys don't work banking hours," Farrell liked to say.

It wasn't Paul DaSilva's fault that Hank Farrell couldn't stand his wife.

DaSilva didn't usually mind the extra hours, but it was Friday night and that delicious blonde would be working behind the bar at the Fourways Pub. Just a few days ago, she'd made it pretty clear that she hoped he'd be around some night when she got off her shift.

Right now Paul DaSilva had the distinct feeling he was about to miss out on a night of sensational sex.

An SUV approached from the far end of the block. It pulled over on the opposite side of the street, two hundred feet beyond the Palliser residence. DaSilva didn't pay much attention until the vehicle's lights went off and it abruptly executed a reverse turn and came to a stop against the opposite curb. The SUV was now on DaSilva's side of the street, facing away from him.

A police turn, he thought.

Not many civvies do those.

A big man in dark clothes got out of the vehicle and started walking along the sidewalk in DaSilva's direction. There was something familiar about his gait.

Walks on the balls of his feet. Like a cop.

The man was peering at each house as he passed it. When he reached the front of the Palliser residence, he crossed the front lawn and stopped in front of the lighted windows. He appeared to be listening. DaSilva could see that he was holding something in his right hand. Light from the windows glinted off a rectangular piece of metal. It looked like a licence plate.

The man disappeared down the side of the house.

DaSilva waited for him to reappear.

He didn't.

DaSilva grabbed for his radio mike.

"Victoria, Delta Six."

"Delta Six, Victoria." He recognised Carly Reynolds' voice, thin and professional over the air. He'd slept with her one night, after a Christmas party. Carly hadn't sounded quite so professional during that memorable event.

"Carly, DaSilva. I'm parked in the seven hundred block Sonora. I'll be out of the car for a minute."

"DaSilva, Victoria. Ten four, Paul. Is Sergeant Farrell with you?"

"Negative. He's on his way."

DaSilva got out of his police car and crossed to the sidewalk. He walked toward the Palliser residence. When he reached the home next to Palliser's, he worked his way along the neighbour's side yard toward the rear of the property. A low fence separated the two back gardens. He scanned the small lawn area behind Palliser's house. There was no one there.

DaSilva retraced his steps and surveyed the front of the Palliser house. There was no one in sight. The SUV was still parked on the street. He crossed to the far corner of the property and peered down the other side of the house.

Nothing.

He continued cautiously along the side of the building and checked the back garden again. He was beginning to think the man had just cut through the property to the rear lane.

Why do that?

DaSilva crossed the back garden. Just past the porch, there was a sliding glass door, apparently leading into a daylight basement. It was open about eighteen inches.

DaSilva listened at the opening.

Music drifted down from upstairs.

Either the guy went through the property to the lane, or he's in the house.

Something the hell wasn't right.

DaSilva wasn't carrying a portable radio. He backed away from the open door and pulled his cell phone out of his pocket. He dialled 911.

"Wakey, wakey, girlfriend!"

At first, the unwelcome voice and the unwanted greeting was a very small sound, far away.

Grace wondered if it was part of a dream. Sluggishly, she roused herself and opened her eyes. Her field of vision was filled by twill cloth. She blinked a few times. The cloth resolved into pant legs. She was confused. It wasn't a dream – the carpet was hers, and she could hear Lauren Wood's preternatural voice singing *Fallen*. This was her house, her living room. She tried to push herself upright.

A strong hand helped her up to a sitting position. Fetid body odour assailed her. In that same instant, an unshaven face appeared in front of hers, hair puffed over a sweaty brow, piggy eyes leering.

Pendergast? What the...!

"Hey, Grace!" the face said. "Bottle of fine whiskey? Romantic music? Like I always say – the best things in life are old scotch and young women."

116

Grace struggled to find her voice. "H-Harvey...? What are you doing in my house?" She tried to sound indignant, but her thick tongue slurred the effort.

Pendergast sat on her coffee table and put his face close to hers. His breath smelled of beer and onions; his little eyes were full of danger. "You and I are gonna have a little talk."

Grace shook her head, trying to clear away the cobwebs of substance abuse.

"A talk? You break into my house to have a talk? Get the hell out of-!"

"Yer eyelids are at half mast, girlfriend. And that tongue of yours don't seem to be working too well." His voice was heavy with mock disappointment. "Don't you know it's unhealthy to drink alone? You should have waited for me, so we could get drunk together." He ran his hands up her leg. "I've always wanted to fuck that Grade A frame of yours..."

Grace noticed he was wearing gloves, but she was so offended by his words that the observation didn't register. She heard herself shouting.

"Get out of my house, you revolting creep! Get out now!"

Pendergast didn't react to the insult. He continued in the same calm tone. "Your swipe card gave you away, Ice Lady. Program tells me you went upstairs at 8:06 and didn't come down till 10:23. The office is a funny place to be shopping for clothes. What were you and that little weasel Devereaux up to? Doing a little surveillance of your own?"

Grace tried to stand. "I don't know what-!"

In one quick movement, Pendergast put her in a wristlock. She yelped in pain. "Sit down!" he hissed.

Grace fell back onto the couch. She looked up at him in fear. The pig eyes were as cold and hard as ball bearings.

He released her wrist. "I knew Billie Palliser, you know," he said, with eerie lightness. Grace flinched at the unexpected mention of her father. "Yeah. Vancouver PD, back in the day. He was a good cop when he was younger. We even worked together for six months or so. Good times we had, Grace – 'kicking doors and smacking whores', as your Dad

117

liked to say. Cops weren't as politically correct in those days. But at the end there, Billie was mostly a fuck-up. We were hard drinkers, but he just didn't know when to stop. Some of the guys said he was drinking the best part of a bottle a day." He gestured at the scotch bottle. "Guess they're right when they say it runs in families." He patted her knee. "Sorry about your mother."

Grace felt icy fingers close around her spine. She could smell her mother's blood. She had to stop him.

"What do you want, Pendergast?" She addressed him by his surname so he wouldn't know he was pressing on a nerve.

He didn't seem impressed by her lame attempt at bravado. He reached casually under the back of his jacket and drew out a revolver. A black metal tube appeared in his other hand. He threaded it onto the barrel. Grace watched in disbelief. For the first time, it registered with her that he was wearing thin black gloves.

The fog of her intoxication began to lift under a sudden onslaught of adrenaline. She felt her heart rate double.

"What the fuck do you think you're doing?"

Her protest was cut off by the black muzzle of the silencer being pressed against the soft skin of her upper lip. Pendergast leaned forward and used the gun to push her head back until it was pressed against the back of the couch. Tears of fear blurred her vision.

Her tormentor put a finger to his lips. "Shhh." Grace was immobile, waiting to die. "That old bastard Andre lifted something from one of Nader's files. Don't even try pretending you don't know what I'm talking about – you two have been joined at the hip for too long. I want it back now! I know you know where it is."

Pendergast eased the pressure on her lip so she could reply. He watched her mouth like a predator, waiting to pounce on a lie.

Grace concentrated on responding slowly and reasonably, but her voice shook, and the combined effect of valium and alcohol made it difficult to get her tongue to co-operate.

118

"Harvey, I honestly don't know what you're talking about. Andre hasn't given me anything." Pendergast sighed, smiled at her, and took the gun away. She relaxed slightly.

He gave her a backhand that made her ears ring. "The film! Where's the film?"

Grace let out a cry, as much from shock as from pain. She spoke quickly, hoping to avoid another blow. "I don't know what the hell you're talking about! You have to believe me!"

Pendergast's left arm snaked out and his fingers clamped like a vice around her throat. He shoved the muzzle of the gun against her cheekbone.

"You have a daughter," he whispered. The words penetrated her brain and erupted like seizures. "Would you like me to pay her a visit?"

While he was waiting for his cell phone to connect, DaSilva heard a woman's voice from inside the house. She was shouting. He made out the words clearly.

Get out of my house, you revolting creep! Get out now!

DaSilva shoved his phone back in his pocket and drew his service automatic. He slipped through the opening in the sliding door and tried to locate some stairs leading up to the main floor. Ahead of him, a shaft of light fell at an angle from above, shedding dim light into the basement. He appeared to be in some sort of recreation room. He moved forward quickly, threading his way through the shadows of furniture and children's toys, found the stairs, and mounted them two at a time as quietly as he could, keeping his weight on the outer ends of each step. The door at the top was partly ajar. DaSilva softly nudged it open. He found himself at one end of a kitchen.

Music was coming from a room toward the front of the house. Over it, DaSilva heard the smack of a hand on flesh, followed by a sharp cry.

"I don't know what the hell you're talking about! You have to believe me!"

DaSilva could hear the terror in the woman's voice. He strode across the kitchen and into a short hallway, counting on the music to cover the sound of his progress. Fifteen feet ahead, light spilled out from his left onto a front foyer area. The music and the disturbance were coming from a front room. He inched along the dividing wall, his weapon raised and ready.

He was three feet from the corner when a cat darted around the corner and ran between his legs. At that instant, his cell phone rang.

There was a sudden rustling of cloth, the crash of overturned furniture, and a sharp cry.

He had to act.

DaSilva stepped into the open archway and pointed his weapon toward the source of the sound. There was no one there.

Fraidy had been nervously watching the proceedings from under a chair on the far side of the room. When Pendergast smacked Grace, the cat began creeping along the wall. When he was halfway to the hallway entrance, he made a dash for it. Through a blur of tears, Grace saw her cat disappear around the corner. Then a telephone rang in the hallway, as if the skittery feline had somehow set it off.

My phone doesn't sound like that, Grace thought.

Pendergast exploded into action. He grabbed Grace's arm and pulled her to her feet, knocking the coffee table on its side. He swung her body in front of him. Then he quickly backed the two of them away from the couch toward the wall that divided the living room from the hallway, keeping Grace's body between him and the entrance to the room. He held his silenced revolver in front of her, pointed toward the doorway. The whole process took less than two seconds. They were eight to ten feet away from their original position when a man with a black automatic pistol appeared in the archway. He spun around the corner and pointed his gun at the couch.

What followed was a terrifying sequence. The man shouted "POLICE!", the alien phone rang for a second time, the man's eyes and the muzzle of his gun tracked left, he looked at Grace and then above and behind her, his eyebrows narrowed, and then Pendergast's gun spit once and the man's right eye disappeared.

The intruder's automatic dropped from nerveless fingers and fell to the floor. His knees buckled and he collapsed like a dynamited building, straight down into an awkward heap. The front windows rattled. The phone rang again. The sound came from under the man's body. The horror of what she had just seen stopped Grace's breath. Pendergast released her and she slumped to the floor, on her hands and knees, struggling for oxygen. Pendergast walked forward three paces and picked up the man's gun, pocketed it, then stepped over the body and strode to one side of the front window. The drapes were closed. He drew the end section of the cloth aside a few inches and surveyed the street outside. He repeated the operation at the other end of the window.

The man's phone rang again.

Grace found her breath and her mind started to work. Panic seized her as she realised the obvious.

I'm next!

Pendergast might torture her for a while, trying to get her to give up those documents or whatever they were, but in the end, he would kill her.

It was the realisation that she might only have minutes to live that got Grace off her knees. She stood up slowly, using the wall for support, and then leaned against it with her arms wrapped around her. She tried to look frightened and vulnerable while she forced her brain to start working.

Having a dead man – apparently a policeman – lying in her living room, with blood trickling from his face, and the madman who shot him pacing around the room, made it easy for Grace to look frightened.

But her mind was in a fever.

I need a weapon.

121

Pendergast left the window, glanced in her direction, and then waved his gun hand at her. "Don't move!" he said. He went to the foyer, turned off the hallway light, and peered out the small window next to the front door.

Grace moved quickly and silently to the fireplace. Her bare feet made no noise on the carpet. She seized a small hearth shovel and then walked swiftly over to the body. She stood looking down at the dead man, holding the shovel in her right hand, behind her leg.

Pendergast reappeared.

"I told you to stay put," he hissed.

"He said 'Police'," Grace whimpered. "You killed a policeman."

"If he's a cop, he's got a partner out there somewhere. I need to check the back." Pendergast pointed his gun at her. "Where can I see the whole back yard?"

"Laundry room, or upstairs," she said weakly. He gestured with his gun. "Laundry room. Let's go." He took his eyes off her for an instant. She'd been waiting. She swung the shovel with all her strength, aiming for his head. He caught the movement and put up his gun hand to stop the blow. In her intoxicated and nerve-jangled state, Grace's swing wasn't very powerful, but the sharp metal edge of the shovel was like the back of a machete blade. It caught Pendergast squarely on his right wrist. He swore loudly. His revolver flew across the room. So did the shovel.

Grace bolted.

Pendergast was taken by surprise, but he recovered quickly. With his good hand, he made a grab for the back of Grace's shirt, but she managed to slip his grasp. Her muddled brain was working well enough to realise that he'd be able to corner her at the front door before she could open it, so she ran toward the rear of the house. Pendergast sprang after her, but tripped over the dead man's legs and landed heavily on the floor. She heard him fall and sobbed with relief as she dashed through the kitchen. She couldn't hear him behind her yet.

She flung open the back door and fled down the steps and across the lawn toward the garage.

She heard heavy steps arrive on the porch behind her.

She waited for a bullet.

It didn't come.

Pendergast stood on the porch and watched Grace Palliser's fleeing figure as it disappeared into the garage. He cursed to himself as he lowered the cop's automatic. It was too risky without a silencer. Anyway, it was the wrong gun.

And a bullet in her back wouldn't work.

He'd come here to arrange a suicide.

He looked around quickly. There was no one about, nothing moving.

One cop? Alone? Fucking crazy.

Maybe. But soon someone would be looking for him. That call on the guy's cell phone...

He went back into the house. He lifted the corpse's jacket and replaced the automatic in its holster, snapping the leather clip tight over the hammer.

He looked around the room. He picked up his pistol and the fireplace shovel. He replaced the shovel on the hearth, and set the coffee table back onto its legs. The half-empty scotch bottle was still in its place on the floor at the corner of the couch. He left the overturned whiskey glass where it had landed, on the carpet.

Then he exited the house by the front door. He left the hallway lights on and the door wide open. The dead policeman's body could be clearly seen from the porch.

He walked unhurriedly to his car, and drove away.

TEN

After twenty minutes, Carly Reynolds started to worry. She tried a few times to raise DaSilva on the radio. No response. She called her supervisor, who dispatched a car to do a drive-by on Sonora Street. Meanwhile, Carly tried to locate Hank Farrell. He was in his private car, and he should have been carrying a portable radio, but detectives were notorious for leaving the things turned off. She couldn't reach him. She called the hospital. He'd just left. She called his cell phone, and got voicemail. It was either turned off, or he was on a call. She left a message.

At eight twenty, Farrell arrived in front of Grace Palliser's house to find two marked cars with red and blue lights flashing, and four patrol officers with ashen, stricken faces.

Farrell had been delayed at the hospital. It would be months before he learned that his call to DaSilva's cell phone had cost the young detective his life.

O'Grady's Motel and Cabins, off Route 1A on Craigflower Road, was no more Irish than any other establishment owned and operated by Native Indian people. The only blarney was in the name, which was handy for attracting tourists who didn't know they were actually standing on the Songhees Indian Reserve, and were too embarrassed to leave when a jolly lady in sweats appeared from the living quarters behind the counter.

The Elders on the Band Counsel quite enjoyed operating their little tourist trap. They thought it was great to have a joke on those white folks, who had played some pretty grim jokes on them in decades past. Jokes like taking them away from their parents and forcing them into residential schools. Jokes like punishing them when they were caught speaking their own language. Jokes like taking away their sacred spiritual symbols – their ceremonial blankets, their coppers, their masks, their elaborate potlatch regalia – and carting them off to museums in the east. Jokes like that.

The evening air was still and crisp. Raymond Vallee was stationed in front of a huge, smoking barbecue. He'd positioned it strategically on the clumpy grass between Verna's cabin and his own. He'd made the barbecue himself by cutting a forty-five gallon drum in half, lengthways, and then hinging the two halves to form a fire bed with a lid. It was a simple design, with a handle welded to the lid and a detachable leg assembly for the bottom half. With a full bag of charcoal, he could maintain even cooking temperatures for hours.

Tonight, most of the grill was covered with full-length strips of sockeye salmon, skin down to the heat. Around the edges of the fire, Raymond had positioned a dozen fish heads. Native adults still appreciated barbecued salmon cheeks, even though most of the youngsters turned up their noses. Woven over and between all this marine nutrition were the soft tips of green cedar boughs. They infused the grilling fish with a unique flavour.

The clan had gathered to give thanks for Horace's deliverance from custody. And for the fresh chance his new school would bring him. Seven family members had followed Raymond's pickup, in two separate carloads, from Port Hardy to Victoria. They'd arranged to rent cabins near Verna's. With three old friends from the Songhees Band who had joined them, the number of bodies requiring constant feeding had swelled to fourteen. But there was plenty of food. There was a huge cooler, brimming with salmon and three different salad dishes, perched on the tailgate of Raymond's truck. This was his second full grill since seven o'clock.

Everyone had piled into Verna's cabin to talk and eat and drink beer. To Raymond's relief, no one had become drunk and started acting stupid. So far.

They'd better not, he thought sternly.

Only two white people had been invited to the gathering. They hadn't appeared. Raymond was disappointed. Disappointed, and surprised. He didn't know the old lawyer very well, so he wasn't sure what to think about his absence. But he knew, with the certainty of a man who has faced prejudice and insincerity all his life, that Grace Palliser had been honoured to receive his invitation and had planned to attend. He could only think that something very important must have intervened to stop her from coming.

Raymond was processing those very thoughts when he heard a keening cry behind him. He turned.

Thirty feet away, Grace Palliser fell to her knees on the gravel pathway.

"Gresh!" Raymond dropped his spatula and lumbered over to her. When he kneeled down, she collapsed sideways into his arms. "What happened?"

She shook her head and pressed her face into his shirt. She managed to choke out a few words. "Andre! Call Andre!"

He smelled liquor on her. And something else. Fear. Raymond scooped Grace Palliser off the ground as if she weighed nothing and carried her toward his cabin. He noticed she was barefoot, and her feet were torn and bleeding. He wondered if she'd been raped.

He laid her on a bed and went to fetch Millie and Verna.

When Grace had fled through the garage and out into the lane, she'd been responding to the only message her shocked and confused brain had been capable of sending. *Get away!* It didn't give her any other message. It didn't tell her to run to the neighbours and beg them to call the police. It didn't tell her to run to the shopping centre, five blocks away, and dial 911 on a pay phone. It didn't direct her to do anything that even the most compassionate prosecutor might one day concede was the 'reasonable and prudent' thing to do at that very minute, in that very hour. It didn't tell her to do anything like that.

Get away to where? was all it asked.

She couldn't muster an answer until her feet had carried her several blocks. Her cerebral cortex was freshly stupefied by the extra valium she'd washed down with some more scotch an

126

hour or so before – although now she had no memory of doing this. Finally, the answer came.

Find Raymond.

That was her last clear thought before her conscious mind imploded. For the rest of her life, Grace would never be able to recall her three-mile barefoot journey in the black of night from the lane behind her house to O'Grady's Motel and Cabins on Craigflower Road.

Millie took one look at Grace, shuddering on the bed with her shirt pulled out and her feet bleeding, and turned to Raymond. "Don't tell the others she's here. Even if she hasn't been raped, something terrible has happened to her! And she's been drinking and God knows what else! She doesn't need gawkers, Raymond! Leave this to Verna and me!"

Verna agreed. And so did Raymond. He fetched his first aid kit from his pickup and then went back to his cooking. Verna returned to the party and tried to act like nothing had happened. Millie stayed to comfort Grace and bandage the raw flesh on the soles of her feet.

Millie Vallee had seen a lot of human wreckage in her forty years on the Port Hardy Reserve. Historically, the Reserve system had been a breeding ground for explosive violence, sexual abuse, juvenile crime, and every other degradation that could scourge a forgotten people neglected for a century by a smug and self-involved white majority. But the central curse, the one affliction that stood as the point of departure for every other social ill, was substance abuse. Liquor or drugs had killed uncounted members of Millie's extended family. Her experience and instincts told her that this disturbed young woman had consumed more than just the whiskey that was so strong on her breath.

Millie finally managed to extract Andre Devereaux's unlisted phone number from her distraught charge. There were no phones in the rental cabins, so she sent Raymond to make the call from the pay phone at the motel office. He returned to report no answer after a dozen rings – not even an answering machine. Millie tried to get another number from Grace – any number, any friend who could help. The young woman didn't seem to be able to focus on the question. She just kept repeating Andre's name.

Between trips from the barbecue to Verna's cabin, Raymond suggested that they take Grace to the hospital.

Millie wheeled on him. "Raymond, this is a good woman! She has an important job and a little daughter! She's had too much to drink and she's on some kind of drug. Maybe an illegal drug. Do you want to ruin her reputation? Maybe get her fired? After everything she's done for our family? We can care for her. Her pulse is strong and her breathing is fine. God help us, you and I have cared for worse in our own family!"

Raymond grunted his assent and went back to his cooking. He hadn't thought of it that way. Millie was right. He didn't know about these doctors here in the city, but he'd had lots of experience with the small hospitals on the north end of the Island. The medical staff constantly gossiped about patients.

After an hour or so, Verna arrived to relieve Millie. The Songhees folks were leaving; she thought Millie should say goodbye. A few of the Port Hardy cousins had drifted off to their cabins, and Horace, unpretentious celebrity that he was, had fallen asleep in a chair.

Millie went next door to put in an appearance. She explained her long absence from the party by saying that she was suffering from an upset stomach.

Verna made tea and tried to get Grace to drink it. The young woman took a few sips and then vomited it on her shirt. Verna cleaned her up as best she could, then just sat and held her hand.

After a while, Grace fell asleep. Or passed out. Verna couldn't tell which.

It was getting darker in the cellar. The light from the top of the stairs faded as day fell toward night. It was hard for her to see the little tag end of the thread she had to pull to get the paper off the Band-Aid. Other Band-Aid papers and threads littered the floor near her feet.

Pressing carefully with little fingers, she stuck another Band-Aid over one of those red holes in Mommy's chest.

"There, Mommy. Please get up now Mommy. It's getting dark now and we have to start dinner. Mommy. Mommy, please get up."

Mommy's hand was getting colder and colder. And she wouldn't move her eyes.

She was sleeping with her eyes open. Daddy said people have to close their eyes when they sleep so their eyeballs don't dry out.

"Your eyes will dry out, Mommy. If you have to sleep now, go up to bed and shut your eyes. Don't sleep on this floor… the cement is cold. And you have to shut your eyes."

There was sniffling and whimpering coming from somewhere. Not from her. From behind the furnace. Jeffery. Jeffery is behind the furnace.

She stood up and went toward the sound. Her feet left footprints on the cement. She stopped and looked down. Mommy's blood was on her feet. But it didn't fall off like the dust. She reached behind the furnace and tugged at her little brother until he came out. He looked at Mommy and started to wail.

And then some strange men crashed through the basement door and she and Jeffery started to scream.

It wasn't Jeffery Palliser screaming at seven o'clock on the morning of Saturday, October 6, 2001. It was Grace, clutched in Millie Vallee's arms, while Raymond, in his underwear, looked on in bewilderment from the doorway behind.

Inspector Gus Fisher loosened his tie and shifted his position. The straight-backed chair was too small to hold his considerable bulk with any degree of comfort. Hank Farrell, looking somehow smaller in yesterday's limp clothes, was sitting across the table. They were in Grace Palliser's kitchen. Mitch and a few designated assistants had secured the rest of the house and property. Farrell was holding an exhibit bag and copying something into his notebook.

"The bosses are going to order me to take you off this case, Hank," Fisher said quietly. "You've lost your partner. You have to go through the counselling thing. You know the rules."

Hank Farrell set down the plastic bag. It contained a pill bottle. He stared at Fisher through haunted eyes. "Fix it, Gus. I'll go to the counselling. Don't take me off the case. I owe this to Paul, Gus."

"Hank-!"

"I'll resign today and work the case on my own! I won't be sidelined – not on this! Just go back downtown for me and fix it. I need to be here while the guys work this scene, and Gus-" he paused and lowered his voice, but the words came out clear and cold "-I need to be there when we pull this woman in."

"Hank, I can't."

"Who do the guys always ask for when they need a confession? Who do *you* always ask for, Gus?"

"Yes, I know, pal, but the brass have their rules and you know-"

"Fix it, Gus! You can. I know you can! Just-fix-it!"

The Inspector sighed and climbed to his feet. He leaned forward, his knuckles on the table. "I'll try. No promises. But I want a promise from you."

"What promise?"

"When you get the call to see the counsellor, no arguments. You fuck around with that, I pull the rug. Understood?"

Farrell nodded, and Fisher headed for the front door. Farrell called after him.

"Who's going to handle the press? We need to get something on the noon show."

"Leave that to me. You got a picture of this woman?"

"Lots of them. Ask Mitch."

The patrol officers who had discovered DaSilva's prone body hadn't detected any life signs, but they'd called for an

130

ambulance anyway. The EMTs, arriving minutes after Farrell, confirmed that Paul was dead. Even though they weren't MD's and had no legal right to declare death, Farrell had gritted his teeth and told them to leave Paul where he was.

Then he'd gone behind his car, where he hoped he couldn't be seen, and retched violently into the gutter. The smartest thing he'd done after that was to ask the Watch Commander for permission to call Greg Mitchell. The Ident officers on duty that night were good, but they weren't Mitch. He'd phoned and woken him up, and told him Paul had been killed.

Within fifteen minutes of receiving Farrell's call, Mitch had taken control of the scene and rousted a pathologist.

When pale-faced top brass started descending on the scene, Mitch had the balls, if not the rank, to keep them on the street. He'd arm-twisted the pathologist into doing a three a.m. post-mortem and he'd had the bullet – extracted almost intact from Paul DaSilva's ruined brain – under the microscope of a firearms expert by quarter after six.

Farrell wasn't taken completely by surprise when Mitch told him that the bullet that killed Paul DaSilva was fired from the same gun that killed Andre Devereaux.

But Mitch said there was something else. Something unexpected.

"Steinhorst says the slug shows signs of scrubbing."

Farrell's jaw dropped. "A silencer?"

"Yeah. That's what he thinks."

"That's why the neighbours didn't hear anything! But shit, Greg, you ever heard of a woman using a silencer?" Farrell chewed on his lip. "What the hell have we got here?"

Greg Mitchell shook his head.

Grace Palliser had vanished. Farrell examined photo albums found in the house. She was a beautiful woman, with remarkable eyes and a seductively memorable face. She'd have a tough time blending into a crowd.

She was also a woman with problems. Booze and tranquillisers were a deadly combination. Mitch had found evidence of both. Either she'd been abducted – which Farrell didn't rule out, but thought unlikely – or she was the shooter.

But why?

By nine in the morning, Farrell had his case against Grace. Greg Mitchell's boots clomped into the kitchen. He sat down in the chair Gus Fisher had vacated not long before and carefully placed a clear plastic exhibit bag on the table in front of Hank Farrell. It contained a set of licence plates. Farrell looked up, startled,

"Don't tell me…"

Mitch nodded. "Devereaux's plates."

"Where did you find them?"

"In her car, under the front passenger seat."

"Was the car locked?"

"Yeah. Keys were in her purse."

"I don't get it. She leaves her car. She leaves her purse…" Fraidy brushed against his leg. "She leaves her cat."

"She panicked. Or somebody grabbed her."

"I thought of that." He picked up the licence plates. "But this changes things a bit. Maybe she left her purse because she'd just shot a cop. Panicked and ran. Fuck!" He slammed the palm of his free hand on the table. Fraidy bolted. "Why the hell didn't Paul wait for me?"

Mitch waited while Farrell worked through the spasm of guilt. Then he asked quietly, "Any ideas on motive?"

"No. You?"

"Well, the scotch bottle was more than half gone. The prescription bottle was here in the kitchen, on the counter by the sink. The date on it is from last spring. There's no telling how many pills were in it yesterday. There were only two dirty glasses in the entire house – one in the sink, with orange juice in it, and the one on the carpet in the living room. That one had definitely been used for the scotch. Looks to me like she was drinking alone and popping pills when Paul came calling. The combination of alcohol and valium can really fuck a person up."

Farrell looked at his notebook. "I thought the pills were called 'diazepam'."

"Diazepam, valium – same thing. My sister was on that shit for years." Mitch stood up. "There's something else… I'll be right back!"

Mitch slipped into the front hallway. A uniformed constable – the designated exhibit control officer - was standing guard over several boxes of seized items. Mitch rooted through one of the boxes and returned to the kitchen with a file folder.

"Found this in her bedroom. Take a look." Farrell opened the folder. It contained newspaper clippings. They were dated in October of 1978. The one on top was an entire page, folded to quarter size. Two obituaries were circled. He started to read, then looked up at Mitch.

"Her father was a cop?"

"Yeah. Mental case. Skip the obits and look at the stuff under it." Farrell put the sheet aside and read the headline on the next clipping.

SHOCKING MURDER-SUICIDE IN NORTH VANCOUVER
Two children orphaned.

Farrell skimmed through the article. On October 5th, 1978, Grace Palliser's father, William Palliser, had come home in the middle of his shift and shot his wife with his service revolver. Then he'd retreated into a nearby forested area with a bottle of rye. Propping himself against the trunk of an old Douglas fir, he'd finished off the bottle and then put the gun in his mouth and pulled the trigger. His body had been found by children later that day. When the local police eventually entered the house, they'd stumbled upon a grisly and unnerving scene. Four-year-old Grace and her two-year-old brother, Jeffery, had been found huddled and crying in the basement, next to the body of their dead mother.

Barbara Palliser had been shot three times in the chest. The front of her blouse had been unbuttoned. Each entry wound was covered with Band-Aids.

There were trails of tiny red footprints all over the concrete floor. Farrell glanced through a few other clippings. They seemed to be a repetition of what he'd just read. He looked up, his expression questioning.

"Notice the date," Mitch said. "October fifth. Devereaux was killed twenty-three years to the day after Palliser's father capped her mother and then himself."

Farrell nodded, thinking. "Where's the brother now? Maybe she's heading his way." Mitch reached over and took the bundle of clippings. He flipped through them, extracted one, and handed it to Farrell.

"Jeffery Palliser died in a car accident when he was fifteen. Our girl would have been seventeen then." Farrell read through the yellowed clipping. It was a familiar story – young driver showing off, loses control, a carload of teenagers end up in a lake. Everyone in the car was drunk. Everyone drowned.

"Who raised this woman? Where did she grow up?"

"Looks like North Vancouver. Lori Graham found some school records in a box. She read through the stuff, says Palliser was an honour roll student, but there's no evidence of a college education. She says it looks like grandparents raised the children. Must be on the mother's side, because the surname is different. She asked me if she should follow up and locate these people." He lowered his voice. "She didn't want to bother you, with you having to deal with Paul's death and… well, you know, Hank, she also didn't know if they'd let you stay on the case."

"Gus is fixing that," Farrell replied, with more confidence than he actually felt. "Tell Lori and everybody else that I'm running this investigation and that the bosses will have to fire me to get me off it!" He paused and tapped the folder. "Now, what about this? Sounds to me like you have a theory. You think she snapped? Went crazy? Killed the old man because

134

he was a father figure? Maybe killed Paul because he pushed the wrong button?"

"Not my field. Just thinking. Huge emotional trauma when she's just a little kid, raised by grandparents, good marks but never goes to university, trouble with booze and pills – she could've been a time bomb for years. Something set her off. The date, maybe. October fifth." He grimaced and looked apologetic. "Just an idea, since you asked."

Farrell's neck was stiffening under all the tension. He massaged it with his fingertips. "Guess we better find her and see if you're right."

ELEVEN

Grace's turbulent awakening on Saturday morning had almost exhausted her already depleted reserves of energy. After she'd recovered from the nightmare – its ghastly, repetitive details once more filed away in her memory vault – she lay on the lumpy mattress and watched a patch of eastern sky through the dusty panes of the window near her head. Dawn was a resplendent display of deep violets, slowly transforming through every intermediate hue of pink and rose, to a final, limpid amber. At another time, in another frame of mind, she would have been exhilarated by the pastel wonders of this new autumn morning.

Not today. She tried to concentrate on yesterday. On last night.

Was it yesterday? What day is this?

She attempted to align her memory and then use it to retrace her steps, hour by hour. It was frustrating. Wherever she focused, images parted like gossamer. There were gaps, black spaces, where nothing had been retained.

Nothing. Not even sensations.

How did she get here? How did she end up in Raymond and Millie's cabin?

Did I see Harvey Pendergast kill a man in my own house? I must have. That part seems real: Pendergast smacking me, that gun, the dead man. I ran away. What day is this? What the hell have I done?

Grace knew she had to move, to act, to take some initiative. If she could just clear away this haze of helpless lethargy. It wasn't the scotch. She could handle a hangover. It was those damned pills. She had to find Andre, and then they had to go together to the police.

Sometime after nine, Millie brought her a cup of strong black coffee. She pushed herself upright and sipped at it gratefully while Millie sat on a chair by the bed, her round face full of concern. Raymond stayed out of the way. He sat in the cabin's tiny front room, watching television with the volume turned low. Grace noticed the bandages on her feet.

"I barely remember coming here. What day is it, Millie?"

"Saturday. You've been here since nine thirty last night."

"Thank you for taking care of me."

"It wasn't just whiskey last night, was it?"

Shame washed through Grace like a storm surge. She took a long sip from her cup before answering. She couldn't lie to this gentle soul.

"Pills, Millie," she answered resignedly. "Diazepam. A lot of diazepam."

Millie regarded her for a moment. There was no judgment in the look and, when she spoke, there was none in her tone.

"You have a daughter, Grace." Millie had made the one observation that Grace couldn't answer. She nodded, her eyes full of tears.

Millie put a hand on Grace's knee. "Something else happened last night. The way you acted, Raymond and I thought you might have been-" she took a breath "-um, assaulted."

"Yes, but not like that." She knitted her brows. "There are parts missing in my memory and I'll need time to separate the reality from the delusions, but Millie-" she grabbed her friend's hand and leaned forward, whispering "-I... I'm sure I witnessed a murder." She let that sink in. Millie sat back, her breath still. "I have to call Andre. And the police." Grace closed her eyes and sighed. "But I just can't get my body to move."

As she finished the sentence, Raymond appeared in the doorway.

"Maybe you better move as far as the couch, Grace, because I just saw your house on TV. There's some kind of news report."

"We'll return to our shocking headline story later on in this special report. We'll be going live to Debbie Paulson, who is on location at the scene. But first, we have some background

137

for you that we've put together from police sources and our own investigation.

"You may have seen our coverage of Thursday night's fire at the old Radcliffe building on Store Street…"

The image on the screen cut away from the news anchor, while he continued his narrative as a voiceover. There was dramatic night footage of the warehouse blaze, and of dozens of fire fighters struggling to bring it under control.

What's this got to do with my house?

"Yesterday morning, as we reported, arson investigators working in the lower levels of the burned building not only confirmed that the fire had been deliberately set, but also discovered the charred remains of an adult male."

The footage now being shown was taken during daylight. It showed clusters of fire officials and police officers gathered at different locations near the burned out building. In one scene, a group of officers were gathered around a dark-coloured Ford Explorer, parked on pavement near the shoreline. One plainclothes officer was searching the vehicle, while two uniformed policemen and another man in plainclothes looked on.

Grace started and leaned forward, peering at the screen. The observer in street clothes looked familiar. And something else about the picture nagged at her brain.

The Explorer was the same colour as Andre's.

The scene changed. Two men were emerging from a stairwell at the back of the building, carrying a black body bag on a stretcher. The two ends of the bag were virtually flat. The raised section in the middle was about the size of a large dog.

The image dissolved back to the main news desk as the anchor smoothly continued his narrative.

"It was first thought that the deceased person might be one of the street derelicts who frequent the Store Street area, but, with last night's slaying of one of the investigators assigned to that case-"

Grace stiffened.

"-we understand that that theory has changed. Victoria Police verify that they have now identified the man who died in the fire, but they're not releasing his name pending notification of next of kin.

"As we told you at the top of this report, the city awoke today to the shocking news that Victoria Police Corporal Paul DaSilva, a twelve year veteran of the Department, was gunned down last night in a private residence on Sonora Street."

Grace felt the blood drain from her face.

"Corporal DaSilva was one of the detectives investigating Thursday night's arson fire, and the suspected homicide, at the Radcliffe building. We understand he was attempting to interview a potential witness when he was killed.

Did he say... 'witness'?

"We're going live now to the seven hundred block Sonora, where our correspondent Debbie Paulson is standing by with more details. Debbie?"

The next scene shook Grace to the depths of her soul. Over the shoulder of a breathless young reporter, she could see her own house. Her front yard was staked off with yellow police tape, and several officers, both in uniform and in plainclothes, were standing inside and outside the barrier. Twenty or thirty members of the public, a few of whom Grace recognised as neighbours, were gathered in small groups on the street and sidewalk. As she watched, a policeman carrying a cardboard box under each arm emerged from the front door and made his way down the steps. He locked the boxes in the back of a Suburban.

"Thank you, John" the reporter replied. "Residents of this normally quiet neighbourhood were badly shaken last night after police were called to the residence you see behind me. There they discovered the body of Corporal Paul DaSilva, a detective who has been a member of the Victoria Police for the past twelve years. We're told that he died from a gunshot wound. Police are now asking for the public's assistance in locating the occupant of this home, twenty-eight year old Grace Arlene Palliser, who is missing at this hour. Here with

139

me is Inspector Gus Fisher of the Victoria Police, who has agreed to provide us with more information. Good morning, Inspector."

"Good morning, Debbie."

The camera panned wider to include an overweight man in a tweed sports jacket and a thin tie. He had wispy brown hair, grey at the sides, and the podgy face of a fast food gastronome. He wore a look of deep sadness.

"What can you tell us about this tragic affair, and how can our viewers assist the police in their investigation?"

"I'm afraid I can't give you too many details at this time. As you can appreciate, the investigation is in its early stages. Shortly after eight o'clock last night, patrol officers were dispatched to this location to check on their colleague, Corporal DaSilva, who had not reported in for some twenty minutes after leaving his police car. He was due to meet another officer here for what was thought to be a routine inquiry, but that officer was delayed. We do not yet know why Corporal DaSilva left his vehicle. The patrol officers found the front door of this house wide open, with Corporal DaSilva's body lying in plain view several feet inside.

"Corporal DaSilva was one of the officers investigating the Thursday night arson fire in the Radcliffe Building on Store Street. As you know, a body was found in the basement of that building. I have already told you, Debbie, and now I can inform your viewers, that that death was a homicide and we now have strong evidence to suggest that these two killings are linked. Corporal DaSilva was conducting inquiries on the Radcliffe case when he died.

"We're seeking the public's assistance in locating the tenant of this house, this woman, Grace Arlene Palliser..."

Fisher held up an eight-by-ten colour photograph. Grace gasped involuntarily. The cameraman zoomed in on the photo and Grace's smiling image was frozen on the screen for several seconds while the Inspector continued his narrative.

"Miss Palliser is twenty-eight years old. She's employed by a local law firm. A car registered in her name has been impounded, but we don't know if she has access to another vehicle. We believe Miss Palliser will be able to help us with our investigation. Out of an abundance of caution, we ask that anyone spotting Miss Palliser not approach her, but immediately contact the Victoria Police or the nearest RCMP detachment."

The faces of the eager news correspondent and the solemn Inspector replaced Grace's photo.

"Inspector, when will you be able to release the name of the person who died in the Radcliffe fire?"

"Very soon. We haven't yet been able to reach the deceased's next of kin, but we're optimistic that we will be able to do that within the next twenty-four hours."

"Thank you, Inspector. Is there anything else you would like to say to our viewers?"

"I just want to emphasise how vital it is that we find Grace Palliser. We will be very grateful for any help the public can offer. And we'd like to thank Channel Six News for your assistance."

"Thank you, Inspector." The reporter turned back to the camera. "So, there you have it, John. An unidentified man killed on Thursday night, a police detective murdered on Friday night and, today, a young Victoria woman is being sought for questioning. We'll be standing by here for any new developments. This is Debbie Paulson, in the seven hundred block Sonora, for Channel Six News."

"Thank you, Debbie. We'll be getting a copy of the photograph the Inspector was holding and showing it to our viewers again later in the broadcast.

"In other news, there was another sudden death in Victoria yesterday. After receiving a report from an Air BC seaplane pilot, Coast Guard personnel recovered the body of a man floating in the water off Laurel Point Park. He has been tentatively identified as-"

Raymond clicked off the TV. "Grace, maybe you'd better tell us what happened last night."

Grace nodded. Her face was ashen.

Millie interjected. "Verna knows you're here, Grace. If she sees the news…"

"Yes," Grace said slowly. "She should hear this. What about Horace?"

"Don't worry about him for now. He'll be watching the cartoon shows."

Millie fetched Verna. Grace told them everything she could remember. It was after eleven before she finished. Her three friends, usually reserved about showing their emotions – especially around white people – were visibly stunned.

But they didn't hesitate to offer their help. Millie made some toast and another pot of coffee, and as time passed Grace's body and mind began to recover from yesterday's chemical onslaught. They sat at the small kitchen table and discussed what to do next.

Grace needed to make phone calls – to Andre, for sure, and to Leddi. She would have to turn herself in – they all agreed on that – but she had to do it on her terms. She had to have command of the facts and she had to be in actual possession of the evidence that would help clear her.

In other words… the Getz file.

There was one final and important requirement. They all knew that while Grace didn't suffer from Horace's mental handicaps, her consumption of whiskey and diazepam had created one of her own. The lessons of the boy's experience with the police were not lost on them.

Grace would need legal representation from the moment she arrived at police headquarters.

They agreed that Grace shouldn't risk going to the pay phone herself. So, while Millie went to buy her some socks and sneakers, Raymond plodded back and forth to the pay phone every half hour, trying without luck to get an answer at either Andre's or Leddi's number.

Grace washed the vomit off her shirt and changed into one of Millie's sweatshirts while she waited for it to dry. She kept thinking about the TV footage of the Ford Explorer. They switched the TV on at twelve to see if there were any new developments. There weren't, but when the footage of the vehicle search was repeated, Grace had an uneasy feeling in the pit of her stomach. She sat on the floor close to the screen and studied the vehicle.

It looked just like Andre's.

By late afternoon, with no luck contacting Andre or Leddi, Grace knew she couldn't delay any longer. She decided to call Cameron Pomeroy. Over concerned resistance from her companions, she insisted on making the call herself. Andre or Leddi might have accepted Raymond at his word, come and picked Grace up, taken her to the office to secure the Getz file, and then stayed with her through the police interviews. But Pomeroy, she argued, whose legal practice consisted of wills and conveyances and other dry and mostly non-contentious work, might not respond well to an anonymous call from a strange Native man. He was intelligent and usually open-minded, but he would probably feel he was out of his depth. He might pretend to cooperate and then hang up and call the police.

Grace knew that Pomeroy would have to hear her voice if there was to be any real hope of enlisting his help. She borrowed Raymond's ball cap, shoved her hair into it, and pulled the brim low over her eyes. Her feet hurt when she walked, but that couldn't be helped. At least Millie had found sneakers that fit.

Raymond led her to the pay phone and waited nearby, keeping watch.

She dialled.

"Hello?"

"Cameron! This is Grace."

There was a long silence on the line.

"Cameron? Are you there? I'm sorry, but Andre and Leddi aren't answering and-"

"Jesus Christ, Grace! I've been watching the news. What in heaven's name have you done?"

143

"I haven't done anything! Harvey Pendergast killed that policeman! For God's sake, Cameron, he was going to kill me next! I managed to get away from him."

"Pender-!"

Pomeroy's glottal stop gave Grace a sudden feeling that this man knew something. Was he involved in the Getz file?

"Grace, why was that policeman in your house?"

"I don't know. Pendergast broke in while I was asleep on the couch. He stuck a gun in my face. The policeman just appeared from nowhere and Pendergast shot him. I ran out the back door before he could kill me too!"

There was another long silence. Grace waited warily. She wondered why he hadn't asked her why she was calling. Or, where she was calling from. Or, why she hadn't gone to the police.

When he did speak, his voice was quiet and – so unlike the Cameron Pomeroy she had known – full of foreboding.

"Grace, were you working with Andre on a certain matter involving Pendergast and Eric Nader?"

There it was. Out in the open.

What do I say?

She felt her anger rising. She plunged.

"Yes! I've been helping him. I know about the Getz scam, and I swear to you, Cameron, I'm going to make damn sure the police know about it. So if you're-!"

"Grace! I'm not part of it! Believe me! Andre only told me about it on Wednesday, the night before-" He stopped. He seemed to be holding his breath.

"Before? Before what?"

When Pomeroy continued, he sounded deeply distressed. "Grace, earlier, when I picked up the phone, did you say 'Andre and Leddi aren't answering'?"

"I've been trying both their numbers all day, Cameron! They don't even have their answering machines on. That's why I'm calling you."

144

"Grace!" More gently. "Grace." A heavy breath. "How do I say this? Andre…" Grace had a premonition. Suddenly she knew what was coming. Her knees went weak.

"Andre is dead, Grace. He died in that warehouse fire on Thursday night."

Somehow…

Somehow, Grace had known it.

The Explorer in the parking lot, the police wanting to interview her, Andre's unanswered phone. She had known, but her convalescing conscious mind hadn't been ready to make the connection. Or, accept the connection.

A connection too dreadful to contemplate.

Her dear, wonderful, extraordinary friend.

Murdered.

By Pendergast. It had to be Pendergast!

Pain welled up from deep inside, choking off her air.

Raymond had been watching the street. He glanced around in time to see Grace sliding down the front wall of the motel office, the handset of the phone slipping from her fingers. The expression on her face tore his heart from his chest.

For the second time in less than twenty-four hours, Raymond Vallee carried Grace Palliser into his cabin and laid her, weeping, on a bed.

145

TWELVE

Grace parked Raymond's truck on Fort Street. Fort was one-way, eastbound, so she was facing in the right direction in case she needed to get away quickly. She wasn't completely sure she could trust Pomeroy.

Raymond had wanted to drive her, but she wouldn't hear of it. She didn't want to risk repaying his kindness with criminal charges for being an accessory. It was better this way. If she was picked up driving his vehicle, she'd just say she stole it. The police might be suspicious, but there would be no evidence to contradict her.

"Pomeroy will drive me from the office to the police station," she said. "I'll leave your truck on Fort, two blocks east of the office, and you can pick it up in the morning."

Raymond had finally agreed and then, to add some realism, he'd shown her how to hot-wire his truck.

"You know how to do that?" she'd asked.

"Injun spare key," he'd deadpanned.

She was early, so she shut off the engine and waited in the darkened truck cab. Pomeroy had agreed to meet her in the parking garage at nine o'clock. They would go upstairs and find the file. They would also dismantle Joan's computer and take it with them. Nader didn't have a computer in his office. He used a laptop and took it home every night. Pomeroy had said he'd always wondered about that.

When they'd collected every shred of evidence they could find, they'd go to the police.

Grace wanted desperately to end the news coverage. Not just for her sake. Shy would be traumatised. Brent and his pinched-face girlfriend would make sure of that. In her head, Grace could hear them smugly crowing to each other. She could hear them trying to poison Shy against her mother.

For most of the day, the city had been bathed in luminous sunshine. But change was in the air. Strong gusts from the southeast moaned through the struts of the truck's side view mirrors. Grace knew the signs. It would be raining by morning.

She was still numb from the shock of Andre's death. For an hour, she had lain in utter despair on the bed in Raymond's cabin. Desolate. Inconsolable.

Verna had taken Horace to a movie and then for a dinner out. The plan had been to keep Horace occupied so he didn't discover that Grace was staying in the neighbouring cabin with his aunt and uncle. Because she'd already left with Horace when Grace phoned Pomeroy, Verna still didn't know about the death of the man who had saved her son from prison.

It was Millie who had finally brought Grace back to life. She'd sat the whole time next to the bed, her gentle hand on Grace's shoulder, while Raymond periodically hovered in the doorway. Finally, Millie made a suggestion.

"Raymond, I want you to phone that Mr. Pomeroy back. Get him down here. This girl needs to go to the police, and every minute she delays makes her look more guilty."

That had roused Grace, as Millie had hoped it would. Grace had made the call herself, and Pomeroy had answered on the first ring.

She checked her watch. It was time. She got out of the truck. She was wearing Millie's old ski jacket. It was too big, which was good. She pulled Raymond's ball cap down low on her forehead and began walking west. The bottoms of her feet were bedded in fresh dressings, new socks, and the cushioned insoles of her sneakers, but they still hurt like hell. The left foot hurt more than the right, but she forced herself to walk without a limp. She didn't want to be noticed.

She kept her head down, careful not to make eye contact with oncoming pedestrians. She reached the building. In a flash of fear, she wondered if the police had it under surveillance. She gritted her teeth and forced herself to relax. Why would they? She'd left her keys and security card in her purse at the house. The police wouldn't expect her to come here.

147

Unless Pomeroy had tipped them off.

She passed the lobby entrance. When she was fifty feet short of the parking ramp, the automatic gate started to go up. A car was coming out. Grace stopped close to the wall and squatted down. She pretended to tie a shoelace.

With a squeal of tires, a black sedan shot out of the garage, swung right and sped past her. Darkly tinted windows hid the vehicle's interior. The car didn't belong to anyone from the firm. But it looked familiar. Grace couldn't think why.

She stood up, quickly covered the remaining distance to the ramp, and slid past the barrier. Pomeroy's sleek Lexus wasn't there. The garage was empty.

He must be late, she thought. She decided to wait near the elevator, out of sight from the street. She walked diagonally across the parking area to the door that led to the elevator and the bottom landing of the fire stairs. As she approached, she noticed that it was slightly ajar. It was held open by a man's shoe. Grace froze. The position of the shoe was odd. The man was lying down.

She crept forward, heart pounding. The foot didn't move. She slowly pushed the door open.

Cameron Pomeroy was lying face down. His head was on the bottom step and his neck was bent at an unnatural angle. The right side of his skull was crushed. Blood and brain matter dripped onto the floor.

Grace gasped and reeled back from the sight, releasing the door. It slammed closed on Pomeroy's foot. She leaned against the wall of the garage, her stomach heaving. Utter horror swept over her. Horror and exhaustion. She was exhausted by panic, exhausted by fear, exhausted by events spinning out of control.

Exhausted by death.

A voice in her head nagged.

Do something!

Grace took a deep breath and pushed the door open. She stepped into the small landing area. She used her foot to move Pomeroy's leg so the door would shut tight, and then squatted

148

down in a corner under the pale stairway lighting, her knees shaking. She scanned the scene. There was no sign of a weapon. A cluster of keys lay on the concrete next to Pomeroy's upturned right palm. She stared at them.

Where's his car?

Her mind started to work.

His security card! I need his card!

Grace knelt beside Cameron Pomeroy's leaking corpse and ran trembling hands along each side of his rib cage until she located his wallet in an inside jacket pocket. She flipped through it quickly, looking for the card.

Credit cards. A few hundred in cash. Driver's licence. No security card. She held her breath and forced herself to methodically check each of his pockets. She finally found it in the breast pocket of his shirt.

The inert air in the stairwell was cold on her face, but Grace was bathed in nervous sweat. She stood up and stepped over the body. On an impulse, she scooped up the keys – she might need them upstairs. She swiped the security card through the slot next to the elevator door and heard the distant whine of a lift motor engaging. She shoved Pomeroy's keys and wallet into her jacket pocket and waited tensely for the elevator to arrive.

I need that file!

As the elevator door began to open, she heard the sudden sound of a car engine going into fast idle. It came from the direction of the garage. Grace rushed back to the door and cracked it open a few inches.

A car was nosed against the in-ramp barrier. She heard the whirr of the gate mechanism as it engaged. She felt her insides loosen. Someone was coming in. Ten feet behind her, the elevator door slid closed. Grace stumbled backwards, praying that the elevator car wouldn't leave. She swiped Pomeroy's card through the slot again and pounded on the button with her knuckle.

She didn't have much time. She held her breath.

The stairs!

149

She was about to bolt for the stairs when the elevator door slid open. Grace threw herself inside and alternately stabbed the 'Close Door' button and the one marked 'Lobby'.

Close! Close!

The door slid shut. The elevator car started upwards. When the door opened again, Grace tore through the lobby to the rear exit, slammed into the door's crash bar, burst out into the service lane and ran for two long blocks. She could feel her bandages tearing from their moorings. The pain was pure torment. But she didn't slow down.

THIRTEEN

When Grace parked the truck next to the cabin, Raymond's bulky form appeared on the darkened porch. By the time she stepped out of the cab, he was standing a few feet away, brandishing a length of firewood.

He dropped the piece of wood. "Just making sure your friend Pendergast wasn't coming to call, using my truck as a cover. Guess I'm getting a bit paranoid." He looked puzzled. "I thought you and Mr. Pomeroy were going to the police?"

"Pomeroy's been murdered." Grace's voice was small and afraid. She leaned on Raymond as he helped her inside.

At 3:00 a.m., Hank Farrell and his detectives met with Greg Mitchell in a conference room at the Caledonia Street headquarters. They discussed the evidence from the latest scene. Farrell was so tired his legs were vibrating. He'd been driving himself and the rest of the team too hard. Even he was ready to admit that they all needed a night's rest. Mitch finished his briefing.

"So here's the bottom line: we've got two of her fingerprints on the inside handle of the stairwell door, one on the inside surface of that same door, and one on the lobby button in the elevator. There are just enough points in the lobby button print to make an ident. And we have that strand of hair. It was sitting right there on the back of his jacket."

"She's never been arrested or printed, so you're comparing these prints to ones from the house?" Farrell knew the answer, but he wanted everyone at the table to understand.

"Correct. 'Knowns' aren't a problem. We must've lifted half a dozen full sets from her house and her workstation at the law firm. Only two people showed up in her house – her and a child. I'm guessing her daughter."

"That's it?" one of the cops asked. "No other adults?"
Mitch shook his head.

"A few strays that don't match anything in the database. And they weren't found anywhere relevant. Not much of a social life, this girl."

"The prints in the elevator don't mean much," Lori Graham ventured. "She works in that building."

"Yeah, but I'm prepared to testify that she was the last person to touch that lobby button. Based on the pathologist's estimate of time of death, that's strong evidence that she was at the bottom of those stairs a few minutes before the security company's patrol came by. Add that to the hair, found *on* Pomeroy's body, and…"

Farrell interrupted.

"What about that hair? Has the lab looked at it yet?"

"Nope. But I examined it under a microscope. It looks to me like a good match to the ones I took out of her hairbrush at the house. Hair and Fibre will do the full workup on it in the morning."

Lori Graham turned to Farrell. "The daughter – have we located her yet?"

"Not yet. The father has custody. I'd like to get him to consent to a tap on his phone, but so far no one's been home. Bailey and Ashdown will try again tomorrow."

"How long has the father had custody?" a cop asked.

"Little over a month," Lori Graham replied. "It's an interim order. Date for the full hearing hasn't been set."

Mitch sucked his teeth. "So she just lost custody." He looked at Farrell. "Something else to set her off?"

There was a moment's silence. Finally, Hank looked around the table. "Questions, anyone?"

A row of haggard faces stared back at him. Farrell wrapped up the meeting.

Grace's friends were confounded by the latest disaster, but they stood fast. On Sunday morning, everyone crowded into the tiny sitting room to watch the television news. The early edition was dominated by reports of American airborne attacks on Afghanistan. Late in the half hour, there was a brief

152

mention of Cameron Pomeroy's death, with a promise of more details to follow in a later report. Pomeroy was identified only as 'a prominent Victoria lawyer'. There was no mention of the other killings, or any hint at a connection.

By noon, that had all changed. Despite world-shaking events in south Asia, Channel Six devoted a full ten minutes to the Pomeroy story. It was a sensationalised report that recapped the previous broadcasts, identified both Andre Devereaux and Cameron Pomeroy by name, and went on to name Grace Palliser as the police department's prime suspect in their murders and in the fatal shooting of one of their own. Two more photographs of Grace were added to the one from the day before. She recognised them. They had been taken from photo albums in her home. For the first time she was described as both dangerous and mentally unstable.

Debbie Paulson, the young reporter from the first report, did the wrap-up. She seemed almost elated as she speculated for the audience: "These killings may be the work of the first female serial killer in the history of Vancouver Island!"

Grace and her friends were shocked into silence.

For months, Grace had avoided phoning Myles Rothwell. She still hadn't made that call.

Now there was another call she dreaded making. Since yesterday, when she'd learned of Andre's murder, Grace had understood that she would have to call Annette. On Saturday's newscast, the overweight Inspector had mentioned that the police had not yet notified next of kin. Grace knew that Annette Devereaux was the only candidate for notification. Annette was the survivor of twins; her sister had died while the girls were still in their teens. Andre's heartbroken wife had followed her to the grave a few years later. Annette and Andre had been all that was left — the tattered remnants of a once close-knit family.

Annette lived on the mainland, in Langley Township, in the Fraser Valley. Once a farming community, Langley was now virtually a suburb of Vancouver. It sprawled over 120 square

153

miles of flood plain, between the silt-laden Fraser River and the U.S. border. The international boundary – the 49th parallel of latitude – marked the township's southern edge.

Grace and Annette had never been really close, although each had always felt that, given the right circumstances, they might have formed a bond. Geography and infrequent contact had intervened.

As well, if they were entirely honest with themselves, other less benign matters had handicapped their relationship. There were Annette's occasional percolations of resentment against Grace for spending more time with her father than she was able to. And there was Grace's deep fear of offending. Or of being thought too ingratiating. Or of being disliked by yet another woman for her physical attributes.

For the past several years, the two women had been united in one respect: their love for Andre. But, despite Andre's occasional efforts, they had never really connected. Grace didn't know much about Annette's personal life, other than the fact that she worked for a small telecommunications firm in the Fraser Valley and had never married.

Grace had good reason to dread making this call.

At three o'clock on Sunday afternoon, Grace stood under dripping eaves at a pay phone outside a gas station on Wilkinson Road. A few yards away, Raymond sat behind the wheel of his truck, which he kept running. Today, he had insisted on driving and Grace, weak from constant fear, had agreed and hugged him for his loyalty.

She had a handful of quarters. Enough for a three-minute call to Langley. Enough for an experiment.

She dialled 411 and got Annette's telephone number. She dialled the number and dropped the quarters into the slot. The line was busy. She collected her quarters from the change slot and got back in the truck. They waited five minutes. She got out and tried again. Fifty miles away, a telephone rang.

The police must have told her that I'm her father's killer, Grace was thinking. Why the hell am I doing this?

154

Annette answered. Even her simple 'hello' was enough for Grace to detect in her voice everything that she too was feeling.

Utter desolation.

"Annette?"

"Speaking. Who is calling, please?" The voice was hollow, defeated.

Grace's heart pounded in her throat.

"Annette, it's Grace.

Silence.

"I didn't do this, Annette," Grace said, as calmly as she could. "I didn't do any of it."

"Papa is murdered, and *you* call me…! You fucking-!" The voice seemed to twist in on itself; in her mind's eye, Grace could imagine the face doing the same. She could hear a moan starting in the woman's throat. Raw anguish poured through the phone line. Grace needed to strike quickly, before Annette slammed down her receiver. She started talking, very fast.

"Annette, your father uncovered something at the office – something serious! Something criminal! I tried to help him. I tried to persuade him to go to the police. He wouldn't. I know who's behind his murder, and the other killings. A man named Pendergast. And a lawyer at the firm, a bastard named Eric Nader. Pendergast tried to kill me as well! I got away! I'm not on the run because I killed your father, or that policeman, or Cameron Pomeroy! I ran to save my own life. But now I'm the suspect."

Annette sniffed. It sounded like she was wiping her nose. At least she was listening.

"If this is true, why don't you go straight to the police?"

"I tried to. Last night, I arranged with Cameron to meet me at the office so we could get Nader's file, the one your father was investigating. Then we were going to go to the police together. When I got to the parking lot under our building, I found Cameron's body! Someone showed up a few minutes later. I panicked and ran. I'm trying to stay out of custody until I can get my hands on that file. But after all this time, Nader and Pendergast have probably shredded it." Grace took a breath. "Annette, how can I get you to believe me? I didn't kill your father! I loved him! You know that. I know you know that."

"Yes. And I loved him! He was all I had left!" Annette erupted into sobs.

A recorded voice interrupted, telling Grace she had thirty seconds left on the call. Annette's crying subsided.

"Annette, I-"

Annette cut her off. "There's something here."

"What?"

"From Papa. An envelope. It came by courier."

Grace felt cold sweat on the back of her neck.

"What's in it?"

"Another envelope... and a note."

"What does the note say?" she whispered.

"It's in another room. I can get it."

"No! Annette! This call is going to be cut off! I don't have any more coins. Take down this number, then get the envelope and phone me back. I'll wait here for two minutes. Two minutes only, Annette!"

"Yes, all right."

Grace read off the number of the pay phone and hung up the receiver. She leaned against the building next to the phone. From the truck, Raymond watched her in puzzlement. A minute passed. Then another. The phone rang. Grace grabbed it.

"Annette?"

"I opened it." Her voice was dead, but not quite as dead as before.

"Read me the note!"

"It's in French. It just says: 'My dear daughter, please put this in a safe place. I will need it when I come'." Annette's voice shuddered. "He was supposed to come for a visit next week."

"What's in the envelope?"

156

"A letter. Something about a company called Arbas Investments. In the Cayman Islands. And a fiche."

"A fiche?"

"A microfiche. There's just one sheet."

A Microfiche.

Something tugged in Grace's memory. Pendergast, her house, that black gun in her face... He was looking for a 'film'.

Annette was still speaking. "I can't see what's on the fiche, but I have a reader here."

"A what?"

"A microfiche reader. It's like a projector, so you can read the film on a screen. They have them in libraries."

"Why would you have one?"

"It isn't mine. It's Papa's. He left it here."

Grace swallowed. "Annette, I need to see that letter, and I need to see what's on that film. And I need to see them before I turn myself in."

Annette was quiet. Grace could hear her breathing. Finally she spoke.

"A policeman named Farrell called from Victoria. He was trying to be kind and nice, I guess because of my father..." Her voice trailed off, as if her conscious mind was disengaging. "He sounded hard. In his voice. He sounded like my old commander."

Annette had done a tour in the Canadian Army. She was intelligent, well educated, and fluently bilingual in English and French. Andre had said she should have advanced rapidly. She hadn't. She'd resigned after five years.

Grace straightened and looked apprehensively up and down Wilkinson Road. Raymond saw her change of posture and followed her gaze.

"Annette, did you call Farrell before you phoned me back?" Grace asked quietly.

Silence.

"No. I almost did, but this envelope stopped me. Papa must have been planning to use the reader." She sighed. "He always trusted you. I suppose I should too."

157

"I need to come there. I know something about your father's investigation. That envelope could help prove I didn't kill him. It could help point the police toward the men who did."

"Where are you now? How can you get here? Your face is all over the news."

"Leave that to me. I'll call you back." She waited for protests. Annette didn't say anything. "Is that okay?"

Silence.

"Annette?"

"Yes. It's okay."

Grace hung up the phone and climbed back in the truck.

"What happened?" Raymond asked.

"Annette has some evidence. Something from Andre. I'll explain on the drive back." She hesitated. Something clicked. "Raymond, do you remember at the end of that newscast yesterday, there was a story about a man's body being pulled out of the harbour? Just at the end, when you shut off the TV?"

Raymond knitted his brows.

"Yeah. Something about a seaplane pilot running over it."

"I need to see yesterday's newspaper. I want to know if they ran a story about that body."

"Be right back." Raymond got out of the truck and went into the Mini Mart next to the gas station. A minute later, he returned with the weekend paper. Grace flipped through it, skipping past the headlines about her, the various tributes to the dead policeman, and the usual overheated treatments of neighbours' shocked reactions.

She found a short piece on the third page of the Metro section. The drowned man was reported to be a known alcoholic, with no fixed address, who had lived on social assistance. A police spokesman said that he'd had a very high blood alcohol reading and the pathologist had ruled his death accidental. His name was Edward Pozner.

"Pozner," Grace said. "This guy's name was Pozner." She threw the paper behind the seat. "I thought it might be Getz."

She turned to her friend. "Let's go back to the cabin. I need to figure out a way to get over to the mainland."

Raymond's eyes widened. He looked at her.

"I have to get over to Langley," Grace continued. "And, anyway, it's time you and the girls got clear of me. I would hate it if any of you got arrested!"

"Heard anyone complaining?"

"No, but... Well, you've done enough. More than enough."

Raymond pulled the truck onto Wilkinson and they headed south.

"There is one small thing I need to do first," Grace ventured after a few minutes.

"What's that?"

"Steal your truck again."

At eleven that night, Grace parked Raymond's truck against the curb on Courtney Street, opposite the side entrance to the courthouse. There were a few streetlights, but otherwise the block was dark. There was no nightlife here.

A southeaster was blowing, but no rain had fallen. Dead leaves swirled along the pavement and rattled across the hood of the truck.

When she'd joined the firm a decade ago, Grace had learned that each lawyer had a key to the side door of the courthouse. If any of them needed to visit the Law Library or the Lawyers' Lounge after hours, or on a weekend, they would phone a private security company, give a personal identification code, and arrange a time to enter. The system had worked for a few years, but the security company's services were expensive, so last year the Court Manager had changed the system. Users still entered by key, but then they had thirty seconds to punch in a five-digit personal code on an alarm system keypad inside the door. The same process applied when they were leaving.

Any failure to follow the procedure would trigger a remote alarm at Victoria Police headquarters.

Grace got out of the truck and zipped up her jacket. She

walked across to the small street level door. She had
Pomeroy's keys in her hand. She found the one with the
familiar stamped markings, and inserted it into the lock. The
door opened.

She slipped inside and went directly to the keypad. The
module was beeping rapidly and a small red light was flashing.

Don't screw this up!

She held her breath and punched in Andre's numbers. She
prayed that his code hadn't been cancelled. If it had, she'd
have to scramble out of there and hope to get clear of the
building before the police showed up.

The green bulb lit and the beeping stopped.

Grace mounted the stairs to the third floor. Her feet were
in agony, but she had to move quickly. Pomeroy's key opened
two interior doors, and then she was in.

In the still of night, the air in the Lawyers' Lounge smelled
stale, redolent with a hundred lawyers' sweaty pre-trial fears.
Grace's heart was pounding in her chest as she moved swiftly
through the lounge area to the robing room. She went directly
to Andre's locker and dialled in the combination.

When she raised the catch and opened the locker door, she
suddenly smelled her friend. His special human smell, all his
own, every day for all those years. She nearly collapsed.

Slowly, hanging on to the door of the locker, she lowered
herself to the carpet. She leaned her head against the cold
metal, fighting against tears. Fighting against defeat.

She set her jaw and started rummaging through the debris at
the bottom of the locker.

Umbrella. Magazines. Makeup. Her law library card. She
glanced at it, then slid it into her pocket. She went back to her
search.

Where is it?

There!

She felt the envelope. There was a card inside. She stood
up, closed the locker, and walked to the telephone desk in the
main lounge. A sign on the wall above the phone warned:
'Local Calls Only'. Grace knew it was blocked for long

distance, but not for 800 numbers. Weeks ago, she had applied for a credit card from one of the Internet's so-called virtual banks. "Introductory offer, low interest rate, we'll pay off your balance on high interest cards... blah, blah, blah." The envelope had arrived in the mail during Horace's trial and she'd dumped it in the bottom of Andre's locker on Monday, along with other accumulated briefcase junk, to make room for the CD player.

Grace tore open the envelope. The card had warning stickers on both sides: *This card may not be used until activated. See instructions.* She found the number and dialled it. A woman with a southern accent took the call.

Grace silently prayed.

"I'm calling to activate a new card."

"Which bank, ma'am?"

Grace told her.

"Thank you. I'll transfer you now." There were a few moments of tinny country music, and then a different female voice came on the line. The same accent. Before she started answering questions, Grace asked one.

"I just love your accent," she gushed, trying to sound like some witless prattler. "Where are you folks located?"

"Louisville, Kentucky, ma'am. But we're just customer service contractors. Your bank's office is in New York State."

"Oh, how interesting!" Grace breathed a quiet sigh. The crime rate in the U.S. was pretty high. And the F.B.I. was obsessed with Arab terrorists. It was unlikely that the woman at the other end of the phone line had heard of Grace Palliser, wanted for questioning in a few random killings on the west coast of Canada.

Grace completed the formalities and was told she could now use her card. Her credit limit was $10,000 dollars.

"That's U.S. dollars, ma'am," the woman added proudly, as if she was bestowing a great and signal favour.

Grace exited the building and drove back to Raymond's cabin. By the time she arrived, the rain was starting.

*

161

The small village of Brentwood Bay lay nestled against the shore of a green, picturesque cove on the western shore of the Saanich Peninsula. The town and its cove faced onto the Saanich Inlet, whose deep cold waters, in turn, joined those of Satellite Channel, some five or six miles to the north. Running east, Satellite Channel separated like an estuary into a series of short passages that threaded between the southern Gulf Islands. Finally, the eastern reaches of Active Pass — a final twisting channel between Galiano and Mayne Islands — converged with the Strait of Georgia. From there, some twelve miles to the northeast, lay the British Columbia Ferry Corporation's gigantic Tsawwassen terminal.

On the mainland.

A competent mariner, with good local knowledge, would have no difficulty navigating these waters at night. Or so Raymond had said.

Grace guessed the police would be watching the airport and the ferry terminals. Channel Six had even shown the snarl of traffic caused by a police roadblock at Goldstream Park, north of the city. From the police point of view, that was a perfect choke point. There was no other land route to the Upper Island, where manpower would be spread thin trying to keep tabs on every possible crossing point to the mainland.

Once again, Grace was forced to accept Raymond's help. She said goodbye to Millie and Verna in the cabin where she had spent much of the last forty-eight hours. Horace was in Verna's cabin, watching TV, amiably oblivious to the momentous events that had been swirling around him since Friday night. Fortunately, he never watched the news.

At times like this, no words can fill up the spaces, and good people don't need them. Grace's eyes filled with tears as she hugged her two guardian angels, they smiled gently and squeezed her hands, and then she and Raymond were in the truck and gone.

In the dark cab, Raymond reached over and took Grace's hand. "You're a fine woman, Grace. Should be easy to see that you couldn't have done these things."

They rode in silence, northbound on Highway 17, toward the Brentwood Bay exit.

The village sat right next door to South Saanich Indian Reserve No. 1. One of Raymond's cousins lived on the Reserve. Orville Chickite, who for some unaccountable reason preferred to be called 'Ned', was a fisherman. He kept his ageing gill-netter on a mooring in Brentwood Bay. For the cost of fuel, Ned had agreed to make a night run to Tsawwassen.

No questions asked.

Raymond gave Ned a pair of fifty-dollar bills that Grace, with a pang of guilt, had provided to him earlier from Cameron Pomeroy's wallet.

At two in the morning, Grace followed her two guides down the stepped gangway to the wharf. The rain had stopped. The tide was low; dark pilings thrust up thirty feet from the water on both sides of the floats. Water lapped and dripped. A few low wattage dock lights cast pale pools of illumination at irregular intervals along the wet planking. Across the inlet, a cloud ceiling stretched across the slopes of six thousand foot Mount Jeffrey, obscuring its higher elevations. The cloud's margins ran east and north, low and dense, darkening the night and deadening the sounds of their footsteps on the plank decking.

In the darkest part of a dead zone between two lights, a small skiff was secured to cleats. Ned took the centre seat. Raymond helped Grace into the bow, and then lowered himself onto the stern seat. Ned unshipped the oars. He rowed them in silence out into the cove. He was lean and short, with a gaunt face, a wispy moustache, and ragged black hair sticking out from under a woollen watch cap. He looked to be in his twenties. His sure hands gave the impression of a man who had been around boats since he was a child.

The gill-netter lay on a buoyed mooring a hundred yards out. They clambered aboard and then Ned and Raymond pulled the skiff out of the water and dumped it upside down on the deck.

Raymond guided Grace through the wheelhouse and down a short companionway into a dank forward sleeping cabin.

"Once we're running and away from shore, you can come back up on deck." The engine starter cranked, and the powerful diesel rumbled, coughed, seemed to die, and then caught. Ned revved it for a few seconds, then settled it back on a fast idle. "Ned says the tide might be against us for part of the Active Pass leg, but we should still reach the other side by six."

"Annette said she'd be there at seven."

"Will she wait for us if we're late?"

"Yes."

"Should be fine, then. I'll go ashore and meet her. You stay on board, out of sight. Till we're sure." He looked at her. She was perched on the edge of a bunk, shivering. "The engine will heat up the cabin. I'll get the stove going and make some coffee."

"Coffee would be good," Grace replied gratefully.

Raymond turned to leave.

"Raymond?"

He turned back. "Mmmh?"

"Thank you."

The night passage was uneventful. For the first time since she had fled into the gravel laneway behind her house, Grace felt a semblance of peace. She knew she had no right to have this feeling. Her best friend had been murdered, along with two other luckless men. She was wanted for those crimes. The true criminals were, so far, impervious to discovery. And what her little daughter was hearing... well, that didn't bear thinking about.

Forces, as they say, were arrayed against her.

By rights, she should be crouched in the cabin below, tormented with fear and despair.

But from the wooden bench on the afterdeck of this old fishing boat, bundled in a thick Mustang jacket, drinking hot coffee and watching the vessel's churning, phosphorescent

164

wake – from that seat, at that moment, Grace simply existed, calmly, in a private pod of serenity. It wasn't anything like the crude facsimile of calm that her pills had provided.

Grace's gaze reached out across dark ocean swells.

She felt like she'd crossed an invisible line.

They made landfall at six thirty. The huge ferry terminal occupied several hundred acres at the seaward end of a two-mile-long man-made breakwater. Four lanes of paved highway ran down its spine. At the mainland end, in a corner formed by the original shoreline and the base of the jetty, a handful of pleasure craft tugged at their moorings. The anchorage was exposed to the southwest, but on this morning the swells were manageable.

Raymond rowed ashore alone while Grace waited below. Ned sat on a stern locker and smoked a cigarette. He hadn't spoken to Grace on the passage across. He hadn't even asked her name. Clearly, he preferred not to know. He had remained in the wheelhouse, concentrating on the navigation and mumbling the occasional laconic answer to his cousin's questions.

Raymond rowed back for Grace shortly after seven.

Grace held out her hand to Ned, and he took it, nodding uncomfortably, but meeting her eyes. "Good luck, lady," he said quietly.

She climbed over the weathered gunwale and settled onto the stern seat of the skiff. Raymond rowed them to shore. He watched Grace's face as he worked the oars.

On the rocky beach, Grace hugged Raymond and kissed his broad cheek. There were no tears.

"I can never repay you," she whispered.

"No need," he said gently. "Millie and I are driving back to Port Hardy tonight. Call us there if you need us."

Raymond Vallee gave Grace a last squeeze on the shoulder with his thick hand, then pushed the skiff back in the water and climbed in. There were a few muffled thumps as he set the oars in their locks. Then he set off.

Grace turned and began to pick her way carefully up the steep slope of granite riprap to the roadbed fifty feet above.

Annette Devereaux stood waiting.

FOURTEEN

Annette Devereaux's twenty-year-old ranch style home sat on an acre of land, one of a dozen homes that were strung along the north side of a half-mile long rural roadway. The house was the last one in the row. It straddled the dead end of the street, nestled against dense woodlands.

An expanse of well-tended lawn sloped gently down to a paved cul-de-sac turnaround in front of the property. Standing in Annette's simply furnished living room, Grace had a clear view for several hundred yards along the roadway to the west.

She had to stay alert. Trusting Annette was still a calculated risk.

"Black, no sugar," said a toneless voice from behind her. She turned as Andre's daughter set two mugs of coffee on the heavy oak dining table. Annette opened a drawer in the sideboard and extracted a heavy manila envelope. She set it next to Grace's mug.

Grace moved her coffee and the envelope to the other side of the table, where she could keep a watch on the street. Annette raised an eyebrow, but said nothing.

They both sat down. They hadn't spoken much during the forty-minute drive from Tsawwassen to Langley. After an awkward hug, Annette had climbed into the driver's seat of her Buick and driven them away from the rendezvous point, both hands on the wheel, knuckles white, eyes fixed on the road ahead. After a few miles of silence, Grace had leaned back against the headrest and gazed, unseeing, out the passenger window.

Independently, the two women had struggled to find some kind of psychological mooring point to hold them against the current of unprecedented horror that had drifted into their otherwise ordinary lives. Independently, they had decided to delay all discussion until they were safely within sanctuary's walls.

167

Annette sipped at her coffee. Her hands were trembling and her normally handsome face, durable and Gallic, was hollow-eyed and gaunt over the rim of the mug. Her thick, dark hair, which Grace had always admired for its shiny good health, was dull and stringy, barely restrained from unruliness by a few cheap barrettes. It was obvious that she hadn't slept for the last few nights.

Grace hadn't slept either, but she felt oddly calm and rested. She was about to tell the truth. Here, now, sitting with her dear friend's daughter, the only thing that was important was the simple truth.

Will she recognise the truth when she hears it?

There was a note clipped to the envelope. Grace studied it. It was in French. It was in Andre's handwriting. She ran her fingers over it, feeling the indentations in the paper. There was a lump in her throat. She tried to cough it away.

"Annette, I want to tell you everything. Before we look at this."

The other woman stared into her coffee cup, her jaw set. "I need to hear it."

Grace recounted every detail. She had already decided that Annette deserved to hear it all. She knew it was her responsibility to take the first step toward creating trust. So she started before the beginning – before the killings, before the Assu trial – and related things she would never have revealed to Annette during their earlier days of distant and cautious regard.

She talked about her marriage to Brent and its steady disintegration, about the drugs and the alcohol, about losing Myles Rothwell, about the custody battle, and the unending soap opera since. Tears rolled down her face – and Annette's – when she told her about Andre's uncomplaining friendship and patience, about his many trips in the dead of night from his home to hers, just to sit by her side and listen. She told her about the abrupt and dramatic ending of the Assu case, and about the evening when she'd overheard Nader and Pendergast at the office, and about Andre's warnings and suspicions about

168

the Getz file, and about her plunge into booze and drugs the night the detective was shot. She described her escape and her barefoot flight into the night, the selfless assistance of Horace's family, and her discovery of Pomeroy's body in the stairwell. She left nothing out.

For the last thirty minutes of the story, Annette didn't move a muscle. As Grace rubbed the drying vestiges of a tear from her cheek, Annette watched, her face stone, her eyes unblinking.

"It always upset me, you know," she said.

Grace waited.

"The way my Papa loved you. All the time he spent with you. All that time he didn't give to me."

Grace groped for words, unsure how to answer. "He loved you very much. He spoke of you often – almost every day. His relationship with me was different. Not father-daughter. Uncle-niece, maybe. Fondness. Concern. We became close because we worked so well together. Then he got drawn into my personal problems. It was unfair of me to let that happen. I know that. But I had no one to turn to. Your father is incurably kind..." Her voice trailed off as she realised she'd used the present tense.

"Was there more than that between you?"

Grace should have been shocked, but she wasn't. *If Andre had been younger... if I had been older...*

Her eyes locked on Annette's. "If you'd asked the same question a few months ago, I would probably have been very upset. But he's gone now, and there is an empty space in my life that will never be filled. You have the right to ask the question, but you must accept my answer. The answer is no." Grace looked away, gazing into space, her eyes filling with tears once again. "You should also know that I loved your father very much. As far as I'm concerned, the only thing that prevented what you have just suggested was his forty-year head start on me. And, probably, his very good sense.

"And, Annette-" she turned back to her and reached for her hand "-I would have taken my own life before I'd ever harm your father."

Annette didn't draw her hand away. She looked long and hard into Grace's eyes, and then surrendered. She squeezed Grace's hand with both of hers, and let her own tears flow.

Then she lowered her head onto her outstretched arms and began to wail.

Grace got up and went to her.

She had crossed another invisible line.

"There's still Leddi Dixon. Can she be trusted?" Annette spoke between sips from a glass of water that Grace had brought her from the kitchen.

"Yes. Your father was trying to protect her appointment to the Supreme Court. Leddi must be completely shattered by all this. I tried to call her before I called Cameron. No answer. And there was no answering machine, which is strange, because she and her husband have had one for years." Grace picked up the envelope, opened the unsealed flap, and began to extract the contents. "Leddi and I have been pretty close for a lot of years. I'll try her again today."

"I'll do it."

Grace looked up, surprised.

Annette put up a hand. "I mean... you shouldn't make the call. Two lawyers from her firm have been murdered. All she knows is what the police and the press are saying. What reason does she have to trust you? If you call her, she might talk to you for a few minutes and then hang up and call the police."

"She won't know where I'm calling from."

"Most people have call display."

"We can block it."

"Grace, I work in communications. The telephone company's computer logs every call whether it's blocked or not." She shook her head. "Leddi Dixon will take a call from Andre Devereaux's daughter. Let me do this."

Grace nodded, biting her lower lip.

She carefully unfolded the pages she'd removed from Andre's envelope. A single sheet of microfiche dropped onto the table. She fingered it briefly, then set it aside and examined the documents.

The top page was a photocopy of a standard lawyer's covering letter, under the letterhead of a Cayman Islands law firm, Bellis & Matthews, addressed to the attention of 'Eric Nader, Esquire'. Something immediately caught Grace's eye.

"Interesting..."

"What?" Annette moved to the chair beside her.

"The address. This letter wasn't delivered to our office. This must be Eric Nader's personal post box. The writer addressed it to the firm – see, 'Pomeroy & Associates' – but that's not the firm's address. Nader must have specifically asked the writer to ignore the address on the letterhead and use this post box number."

Grace read through the text.

The writer, an attorney named Ward Bellis, confirmed that he had finalised the incorporation of Arbas Investments L.D.C., a Cayman Islands "limited duration exempt company" and was enclosing a copy of the Certificate of Incorporation and Memorandum and Articles of Association. He continued: "In accordance with your instructions, I have completed banking arrangements for the company with Carnarvon Bank and Trust Company (Cayman) Limited. I enclose copies of duly executed signature forms and mandates for your perusal. Due to the current structure of the Board of Directors, our indemnity insurers require that we control this account. I confirm that you have instructed us to proceed on that basis."

Grace flipped to the second page. It was a copy of a Certificate of Incorporation, dated August 17, 2001, and stamped with a seal that read *"REGISTRAR OF COMPANIES CAYMAN ISLANDS EXEMPTED"*. She returned to the letter and read through the next paragraph: "The originals of all mentioned documents lie on our file, the contents of which are not only protected by solicitor-client privilege (a principle with which you will be familiar), but also by the very strict confidentiality laws of this jurisdiction."

A short final paragraph, which had the ring of a standard recital, explained that under the laws of the Cayman Islands an exempt company was prohibited from conducting business – other than its reasonable and necessary banking affairs – within the Islands.

Grace turned to Annette. "Have you read this?"

"Yes. It didn't mean much to me. Does it have something to do with the file Papa was worried about?"

"When I told your father that I had read through the Getz file after Nader and Pendergast left the office that night, he asked me if I had come across any reference to a Cayman Islands incorporation." She thought for a moment, then gripped Annette's arm. "We had that conversation on Thursday morning. Courier companies usually date stamp their waybills to show when shipments are first received. Did you keep the outer envelope?"

Annette retrieved the waybill from the drawer in the sideboard. The date stamp read: *October 4 01 4:46 p.m.*

"The same night Papa died," Annette said quietly. "I wonder if he knew…"

"I can't imagine him taking a deliberate risk," Grace replied. "Can you?"

Annette stared out the window for a few seconds before answering.

"Yes," she said, simply. "He was like that."

Grace picked up the microfiche and held it to the light. Squinting, she could see minute reproductions of document pages.

"You mentioned a reader."

"It's in the cellar."

"That's an odd thing to have in your cellar."

"Papa bought it years ago… back in the seventies, when we lived in Ontario. He was often hired by police officers who were in trouble. He represented some of them during those federal hearings into the RCMP Security Service. A lot of the

172

files he subpoenaed were on microfiche, so he needed a reader. There was a printer with it, but I don't know what became of it."

"Why did he leave it with you?"

"He needed it for that big case against the telephone company. The trial was in New Westminster, so he stayed here on weekends. He never got around to taking it home." She paused, puzzled. "Why didn't you work on that case?"

"I had a few marital problems around that time."

Annette pushed the switch on the side of the machine. An internal light came on and the screen colour transformed from black to royal blue. She sat down and Grace pulled up a chair beside her. Annette slid the fiche between the two small sections of thin glass and pushed them under the projector lens, like a slide under a microscope. A cluster of pages appeared on the screen. She adjusted the focus until they could read the text. Columns of entries emerged. Where the tops of pages were visible, pre-printed headings appeared in German and, in one case, French.

To Grace, the documents looked very familiar. "Swiss banking records," she said. "Just like the ones I saw in the Getz file."

"Are they the same ones?"

Grace squinted at the screen.

"No." She pointed with the tip of her index finger to a spot on the screen. "See here: that's the identity number of the bank's customer. You've heard of 'numbered accounts'? I don't remember the complete number on the Getz records, but I do recall that it ended with double sixes. This one ends with five three. And look at this-" she moved her fingertip to the top of a column on a page to the far left of the screen "- that's French, right?"

"Yes."

"So these are records for other bank accounts, and I'm betting they belong to other depositors who died in the concentration camps. Let's start in one corner and see if there's any pattern to the way they're arranged on the film."

Annette slid the handle on the glass slide to the right and pages blurred across the screen in the opposite direction until they were looking at the upper left corner of the fiche. Grace leaned forward.

"That's the Getz statement! Those are some of the pages I saw printed out in the file. It looks like the dates track downwards. Let's look!"

In a few moments, they detected the pattern. In each column of documents, the pages were arranged in date order from top to bottom, continuing on to the top of the next column and so on, column after column, from left to right.

"Annette, do you have a calculator?" Grace asked.

Annette left the room. While she was gone, Grace studied the totals showing on the screen. They covered three different account numbers. Her rough calculation, just based on what was visible, added up to four million Swiss francs. She wondered what that amount would be worth in modern terms.

When Annette returned, they began working their way methodically through the account statements. Grace recorded the final totals for each bank customer. When they were finished, Grace's notes showed that there were eleven different customers who had maintained accounts at eight different financial institutions in Zurich and Geneva.

The deposits totalled over two hundred million Swiss francs.

"What would that be worth today?" Annette wondered aloud. "You know, with exchange rates and fifty years of interest?"

"I don't know. There must be some computer program that could figure it out." Grace tapped her page of notations with the end of her pencil. "You know what I think? I think Nader and Pendergast and this Koop guy aren't just running a fraud in the Getz case. I think they're running eleven different frauds. Maybe more." She looked at Annette. "And I think your father knew it."

FIFTEEN

Monday was Canadian Thanksgiving, a national holiday in the same tradition and spirit as its American counterpart. The significance of the day didn't touch Grace or Annette – there was too much grief and fear pulsing through their lives – but late afternoon brought extra traffic to the street. The activity made Grace nervous. She watched the street constantly.

Annette dialled Leddi Dixon's home number in Victoria while Grace listened on the extension.

Graydon Dixon answered with a brisk hello. Annette introduced herself. There was a short silence.

"Miss Devereaux…" His tone instantly changed. "Miss Devereaux – Annette – please let me say how shocked we are about your father. How are you coping?"

"I'm surviving. Thank you." Annette's weary voice was not an act. "People are being very kind. I've been given time off work and I have my friends to support me."

Grace had seen no sign of these supporters. She wondered. Annette continued. "Is Mrs. Dixon there?"

"I'm sorry. You've missed her. She just left to catch the plane to Vancouver. She has a meeting scheduled with the Chief Justice tomorrow morning. They're scrambling a bit with the arrangements."

"Arrangements?"

"Yes, for the swearing-in. Guest lists, protocols, a fitting session for her robes, that sort of thing."

Grace knew what this meant, and her heart sank. But Annette was confused.

"I'm sorry, I don't understand."

"Of course! You wouldn't know. I apologise. You see, Leddi is going to be a judge. She's been appointed to the Supreme Court. She'll be taking the oath at the courthouse in Vancouver on Tuesday. The Chief Justice fast-tracked the whole process. He doesn't want these terrible murders by that

Palliser woman to affect a deserving judicial candidate. His exact words, by the way."

Grace felt like a serrated blade had been plunged into her stomach.

Annette pressed him. "Would I be able to reach her in Vancouver?"

"Ah, well, I don't know..." Dixon sounded doubtful, even protective, but also slightly embarrassed.

So much for sympathy, Grace thought. He's basking in all this new prestige, and here's this inconvenient little victim, spoiling his day.

"I really need to speak to her," Annette broke in. "I need some advice about my father's affairs. I'm alone now. I have no family to help me." Annette sniffed and her voice quavered – again no act. "Would you call her and ask her to phone me?"

"I see. Yes, of course." Her palpable pain seemed to have brought him down from his plateau of smugness. "I'll be speaking to her this evening. Where can she reach you?"

Annette recited her number. "Please ask her to call me," she pleaded.

"I will. I promise."

Grace leaned against the kitchen counter while Annette made sandwiches. Thanksgiving dinner. Annette seemed to need to stay busy, and Grace sensed this, so she didn't offer to help. She watched as her new friend deftly constructed their meal.

"Who's Ruth?" Grace asked, breaking the silence.

"Wh-What?" Annette's head came up. She looked slightly unnerved. Grace pointed to a fridge magnet, one of a cluster on the refrigerator door. *Ruth's Kitchen*, it said.

Annette followed her finger. "Oh." She looked Grace in the eye. "She was my partner. We were in the Army together."

Grace returned her gaze. For a moment, she said nothing while her mind made connections. Andre had complained that Annette hadn't received the promotions she deserved.

Had he known?

"Did you and Ruth resign at the same time?" Grace asked.

"Yes, but she left me a year ago." Annette compressed her lips. This was not a subject she intended to discuss. She reached some plates down from the cupboard.

Grace tried to stop her racing mind. It insisted on running off down a side canyon fraught with unfamiliar terrain. Annette must have sensed this. She arranged the sandwiches on the plates and garnished each with a slab of dill pickle. Then she turned into Grace's silence.

"It's not catching," she said quietly, holding out a plate.

Grace took it from her hand and set in on the counter. She put her arms around Annette.

"I know. Thank you."

The phone rang while they were eating. It was Leddi Dixon. Grace wanted to listen, but Annette had already answered, so she decided not to risk being heard picking up the extension.

But as it turned out, Annette's side of the conversation, and her facial expressions, told most of the story. She nodded and made the appropriate grateful sounds as Leddi apparently offered her condolences. They discussed Andre's affairs. Annette's responses implied that Leddi was no longer in a position to help her. After a few seconds, Annette said, "Yes, go ahead," and started writing.

When she finished writing, she handed the notepad to Grace. It bore the names and telephone numbers of three of the firm's lawyers.

One of them was Eric Nader.

Annette finally came to her real reason for making contact. As she opened the subject, her tone conveyed bafflement.

"Mrs. Dixon, I'm sure you know that my father and Grace Palliser were very close friends. Grace had tremendous respect for him. I find it difficult to believe these things I'm reading and seeing on television. What possible reason would Grace have had to kill Papa? Is there something that isn't coming out in the news reports?"

As she listened to the reply, Annette's face went pale. Her eyes locked on Grace's and she slowly shook her head. At one point, she tried to interject, but was apparently cut off. Finally, after what seemed to Grace like a very long minute of one-sided conversation, Annette found an opportunity to speak.

"Well, I suppose you would know, since you worked with her all those years, but I still find it…" Her voice trailed off and her shoulders slumped and it was clear that Leddi Dixon was talking again.

"Yes, I'll call Mr. Farrell," Annette said eventually. "But I need a little time to deal with all this before I talk to him."

Annette ended the call. She collapsed onto a kitchen chair. "She won't be any help. She talked about the custody thing with Brent and your daughter. And drug abuse – she went on and on about it. And something about your father's suicide when you were a little girl-" Grace opened her mouth to speak, but Annette waved her hand to stop her. "It's all right, Grace. I don't need to hear about it. It's pretty obvious to me that you're not insane."

"My father did kill himself," Grace said quietly.

"How old were you?"

"Four."

Annette thought about that. "Did your mother remarry?"

The old nightmare stirred like a troll under a bridge. Grace sank onto a chair. "My father killed my mother before he killed himself," she said tonelessly.

Annette sat motionless, staring at Grace.

After long seconds, she drew a deep breath.

"That Swiss bankers' fund. I remember reading somewhere that it was supposed to be a world-wide settlement. They were dealing with thousands of dormant accounts."

"I think that's right. Why?"

"So… wouldn't there be a website?"

Welcome to the Dormant Assets Website of the Swiss Bankers Association…

178

On February 5, 2001, a new claims process was established to provide Nazi victims or their heirs with an opportunity to make claims...

The claims process was triggered by the publication of 21,000 names of account owners...

They were in Annette's bedroom, sitting at her computer desk. Annette leaned forward.

"Twenty-one thousand accounts!"

"Look at the links at the bottom." Grace pointed. "Maybe you can bring up the whole list." Annette followed the prompts. There were two different lists of account names, arranged alphabetically. One was for individuals. Its introductory notes stipulated that 20,825 names were recorded on that list. To shorten search time, there was a direct link for each letter of the alphabet.

The other was for corporations. There were a hundred and sixty-two of them.

Annette scrolled at random through the list of individuals. It was a stupefying catalogue – names: last, first, middle, and address, if known. All that remained of thousands of discarded lives. Innocent human beings, murdered for no better reason than to satisfy a barbaric and twisted mythology. There it was, laid out before them.

The Holocaust. Rolling up the screen. And rolling. And rolling...

After a moment of shocked silence, Grace whispered a suggestion. "Let's check the account names against this list. See if we can find Israel Getz. I'll fetch our notes."

Grace was gone for thirty seconds. When she returned, Annette said, "On the screen, Grace! 'Israel L. Getz'." Grace kneeled beside her. She checked the notepaper in her hand. "Try Oskar Tobias." Annette clicked on the 'T's'.

"Yes!" Annette tapped the monitor. "Here!"

"Yvette Alexandre?"

"Yes!"

"Adolph Wagenmann?"

"Yes!"

"Erich Harbeck?"

"Yes!"

"Okay, what about this company? I'm not sure how to pronounce it. I think it's Romanian." Grace spelled the first part of the name as Annette clicked on the corporation name link. "B-U-Z-E-S-C-U Romana Industrij, ends with an I-J." After a second, Annette sighed.

"There it is."

They checked the last five names from the fiche. They were all on the list. Grace sat on the end of Annette's bed.

"In order to target dormant accounts with big balances, Nader would need someone with access to the actual account documents. That was probably Gunther Koop. I remember him coming to Victoria last spring. There was some talk about him interviewing Getz in our boardroom – like he was some kind of investigator. I'd like to know who he really is. And, who he works for."

"Let's search his name." It only took a couple of seconds. The search engine cycled them back to the website they had just left.

Gunter E. Koop, Judge and Arbitrator, Claims Resolution Tribunal for Dormant Accounts in Switzerland. Herr Koop is one of seventeen distinguished arbitrators, lawyers and judges who make up the Tribunal's panel of claims adjudicators. These adjudicators are charged with responsibility for...

Annette's hands dropped into her lap. *"Merde!"*

After an hour of muddled discussion, both women succumbed to exhaustion. By then, Grace had reluctantly decided to surrender to the police in the morning. Annette would drive her to the local RCMP office. She had a story to tell, she had the microfiche and the letter, and she had Annette, the daughter of one of the victims. After that, well... she'd need a good lawyer.

Grace slept in the guestroom. She stripped off her clothes and crawled between cool sheets, imagining that Andre had used the same bed when he'd visited his daughter. She lay there, remembering him.

She buried her face in the pillow and wept.

*

Grace didn't hear the bedroom door open. Her first awareness came when she felt someone sitting on the edge of the bed. A hand touched her shoulder. She opened her eyes. Faint daylight was leaking past the curtains.

Annette was wearing a faded housecoat. Her eyes were wide with fear. Grace sat up quickly. She looked past Annette at the open bedroom door.

They've found me!

"What?" she asked urgently. Annette laid a folded section of newspaper on the bedcovers in front of Grace.

"This morning's *Province*," she said quietly.

Grace rubbed away the sleep and scanned the headline. She looked at the picture directly below it. Pain rippled through her chest. It was a photograph of a smiling little girl.

Her little girl.

FUGITIVE WOMAN SUSPECTED IN ABDUCTION

In a case marked by one bizarre twist after another, the latest development in the Grace Palliser serial murder investigation has the Victoria Police baffled and worried. On Monday afternoon, five-year-old Sherry Marie Taylor vanished from a community playground in Victoria's famous Beacon Hill Park. The child is the daughter of Grace Palliser and Brent Taylor, of Victoria. Mr. Taylor is Palliser's former husband. He recently won temporary custody of their daughter after a legal battle.

In a statement to the press, Victoria Police Sergeant Hank Farrell told reporters that shortly after three p.m. on Monday, the child's playmates saw Sherry Taylor get into a blue car, which then drove away.

"There were no adult observers," Sergeant Farrell said, "but the children's accounts and other circumstances of the case lead us to believe that Sherry was abducted by her mother, the fugitive Grace Palliser. We are looking for a late model four-door sedan, possibly a Toyota or a Mazda. It is dark blue in colour. We would greatly appreciate the public's assistance in

181

locating this car. We are very concerned for young Sherry's safety since, as the community knows by now, her mother is believed to be mentally unstable. Sherry is five years old. She goes by the nickname 'Shy'."

Sergeant Farrell warned that anyone who sees Grace Palliser, whether or not the woman is with her daughter, should not approach her but should immediately call 911.

Brent Taylor, the abducted child's father, declined to speak to the press. Mr. Taylor's girlfriend, Hilary Holt, advised reporters that Mr. Taylor is afraid to make any public statement, for fear that his comments might inflame his ex-wife to harm their daughter. "Grace Palliser is very unpredictable," Miss Holt said, "and she has exposed this poor little girl to physical danger in the past. After the events of the past week, who knows what she is capable of?"

Grace Arlene Palliser is the prime suspect in a series of murders that have rocked the capital in recent days. She is implicated in the death of veteran Victoria police detective Paul DaSilva, who was shot and killed in Palliser's West Victoria area home, and she is also suspected in the deaths of Andre Devereaux and Cameron Pomeroy, both lawyers who worked at the firm where Palliser was employed as a secretary. Police are currently seeking Palliser on a Canada-wide warrant. Detectives are so determined to find her that they have arranged for her case to be featured on an upcoming segment of "At Large", the well-known American television show.

Grace threw the newspaper aside and slumped back against the headboard of the bed. Annette moved closer, watching her new friend's face, ready for a deluge of horror and tears.

Nothing.

No helpless panic.

No tears.

Just tourmaline eyes, hard and cold.

"Nader," Grace said quietly.

Annette gaped at her. "How can you-?"

182

"-know that? I don't. But, who else? And the car..." Grace ran fingers through her hair. "Maybe it's nothing, but..."

"But?"

"Nader's secretary. She drives a dark blue Mazda." Grace's lip curled. "Nader's been sleeping with her. In fact, Shy walked in on them. Last Sunday, at the office."

Annette was thoughtful.

"How do we find out if you're right?"

"Shouldn't take much effort. I'll phone him."

"What?"

"Those bastards did this to flush me out. It's a signal." Grace bit down on her lower lip. "They're saying, 'Call us or we'll kill your daughter'."

SIXTEEN

On the northern side of Vancouver's deep and well-protected harbour, the District of North Vancouver lay like a draped tapestry across the lower reaches of Grouse Mountain. Over the decades since the Second World War, swank subdivisions had crawled higher and higher up the slopes in search of more stunning views of the harbour and the city below. High above the cedar-and-glass eyries of the new middle class, on clear winter nights, pristine ski runs formed a necklace of lights suspended in the heavens.

Nestled against Grouse Mountain's western skirts, a thousand feet below the Swiss-style gondola that carried yuppie snow-boarders to chalets in the sky, Cleveland Dam created a vast freshwater reservoir that wound for a dozen miles into the narrow valleys of British Columbia's Coast Range.

Directly below the dam lay Capilano Canyon Park, a wild tumble of granite cliffs and coniferous forests that somehow contrived to guide the runoff from the dam's spillway past the fish ladders of a salmon hatchery, under the Cable Pool bridge, and along the bouldered ancient beds of the Capilano River to its mouth on the ocean, five miles to the south.

It was still dark when Annette's Buick sped north through the darkness, across the Second Narrows Bridge, and turned west. It followed Highway 1 as it arrowed across the slopes of the North Shore toward the ferry terminals at Horseshoe Bay and the glitzy ski resorts of Whistler fifty miles beyond. Grace sat in the passenger seat, her eyes glued to the stretch of pavement unrolling in the pool of brightness cast by the car's headlights. As they broke over the crest of the Lynn Valley Cut, a long, straight three-lane climb that was locally notorious for unsanctioned drag races, she glanced over at her friend. She was still surprised at the transformation the past twenty-four hours had wrought in Annette. Even now, in the dampened glow of the instrument lights, she could detect the sense of grim purpose that now seemed permanently etched into her friend's expression.

We give each other strength, Grace thought.

A sign warned that they were approaching Capilano Road.

"This exit?" Annette asked.

"Yes. And then take a right at the bottom of the ramp. It's a few more miles." Grace felt her stomach knot up. She moved her gloved hand to feel the heavy object in her right coat pocket. Its presence reassured her. She hadn't wanted to carry a gun, but Annette had been adamant.

"Anything could happen. You could end up facing those two alone," she'd insisted. "You were there when Pendergast shot that policeman. What we're doing is risky enough. For you to go unarmed is crazy." She'd held out the small black pistol, butt first. "It's a Beretta nine. It's not loaded, but I have a full clip for it. Take it. It was Papa's. It's never been registered."

"Isn't that illegal?" Grace asked. Her hand closed on the grip and, despite herself, the gun's reassuring heft began to erode her natural resistance to the idea of a firearm.

Annette looked at her calmly. "It is. But Papa took a different view on certain things," she said with a half-smile. "He knew that in his line of work things could go very wrong, very quickly. In the old days, back in Quebec, he was defending hard men. He sometimes represented waterfront union members who bragged that they were-" she searched for the right word "-I think the American expression is 'connected'. To the Montreal gangs, or perhaps to the Mafia. There were times when some psycho client came looking for trouble. My father knew he couldn't always count on the police for sympathy, much less assistance, so he dealt with these situations himself, on what he called 'a case-by-case basis'."

Grace held up the Beretta and studied it. "I haven't used a gun since I was a teenager. And I've never fired an automatic," she said doubtfully.

"No time to teach you now. Just remember: if you have to fire, use both hands." She took the pistol back from Grace and demonstrated, aiming away from them. "Inexperienced people try to shoot a handgun with one hand. If they're right-handed, like you, they almost always pull to the right and fire wide."

As they neared the park turnoff, Grace was glad to have the gun. But could she use it?

Could I actually pull the trigger?

Annette glanced over at her. "Nervous?"

"Yes."

"Me too."

A small carved sign came into view on the right shoulder of the road.

"Take the next left," Grace instructed. "It's that narrow entrance that angles into the trees. I need to show you something before we go up to the dam."

Annette slowed and made the turn. They drove along a narrow paved roadway that curved gently left and then straightened. The few private residences close to the main road quickly gave way to deep forest on both sides of the car. After a half mile, the road divided into a Y intersection, with the paved main road bearing steeply down and away to the left, and a gravel track, just wide enough to accommodate a vehicle, climbing upslope into the woods to the right.

Steel gates barred both roadways. Annette stopped the car. Grace pointed to the gate on the left. "That gate opens at six. The road leads to a parking lot next to a salmon hatchery. There's a trail that leads from the southwest corner of the car park directly to the barbecue pit. It's about a two minute walk." Grace put her hand on the dash, pointing to the gravel road on the right. "This is a fire road. It leads up to the parking lot at the eastern end of the dam, where you'll drop me. That gate stays locked all the time, but the road is easy to follow on foot, even in the dark. It's about a two mile hike."

"Okay. So where's the church camp?"

Grace pointed left again. "Down this hill about a quarter mile, the road takes a loop to the right. The camp's entrance drive is on the left, at the mid-point of the curve. The camp will be boarded up at this time of year, so there won't be anyone around to bother you. If you park behind the main building, your car can't be seen from the road."

Annette sat in the half glow of the dash lights, her lips a thin line. Finally, she spoke.

"A lot of things could go wrong, Grace," she said gently.

Grace felt for her friend's hand. "I know. And, thinking about that, maybe you should be the one carrying this gun."

"No!" Annette was firm. "If this goes bad, your only chance to get Shy back will be to go face to face with them. Anyway," she added, "the Army taught me a thing or two. Don't worry about me." Annette reversed the Buick into a two-point turn. "Back to the main road?"

"Yeah. Then take a left."

The public parking lot at the eastern end of the dam bordered rolling lawns that stretched away toward the waters of Cleveland Lake. A hundred yards short of the shoreline, a chain link fence barred access. Metal "No Trespassing" signs were wired to the fence at regular intervals. The local authorities jealously guarded their freshwater resource; the entire watershed was out of bounds to all members of the thoughtless and ever careless public.

But the causeway across the top of the dam was open to foot traffic.

Grace got out of the car, zippered her borrowed ski jacket, and retrieved a knapsack from the backseat. Annette came around the car and stood in front of her. "When you're in place, try the phone," she said.

Grace nodded. "What time is it now?"

"Ten after five."

"All right. I'll need twenty minutes. Park where you can see the turnoff. The fish hatchery people unlock the gate every morning, so watch for a pickup with the hatchery logo on the

187

door. They'll just swing the gate back and keep going, so you can follow a few minutes later."

Annette stared at her through the gloom. "Can you do this?"

Grace's jaw tightened. "I have to." They hugged, then Annette got back in her car and, with a wave that didn't quite match the tense expression behind it, she drove out of the parking lot and turned south.

Grace slung her pack over her shoulder and set off toward the causeway. She stepped around a steel vehicle barrier and began the long hike to the other end of the dam. The rush of water over the spillway was a white noise that grew louder as she approached the midpoint of the dam. Vortices of mist roiled up from the canyon below, creating halos around the handful of low wattage lamps that illuminated the causeway. Behind the dam, Cleveland Lake was a black presence, felt rather than seen.

The moist darkness slid its clammy fingers under her collar, clutching at her spine and at her spirits. The metallic fears of old nightmares closed in, lurking on the edge of her consciousness.

She zipped her jacket collar higher and focused her thoughts on Shy. She kept walking.

At the western end of the dam, the pavement of the causeway terminated at another steel barrier. A gravelled service road lay beyond. Grace climbed over the rail and walked on for another hundred yards. The roadway curved into groves of thick conifers and the night deepened. She reached into her jacket pocket for the penlight Annette had given her and clicked it on. Shining the narrow beam of light on the shallow ditch and forest verge to her left, she made her way forward in careful steps.

After twenty more yards, she found it.

The trail opening.

She held the beam of light just ahead of her feet and threaded her way along the familiar pathway down the canyon's wooded upper slopes, through fern and huckleberry underbrush, to a small clearing which opened to the south through a gap in the trees.

Twenty years and nothing's changed.

As a young girl, Grace had often visited this spot to sit on the cool forest floor and eat lunches of thin sandwiches. This had been one place that her grim and remote grandparents never knew about. One secret that her boisterous and attention-disordered younger brother had never discovered and ridiculed.

Grace unslung her knapsack, opened it and removed a folded gardener's groundsheet. She spread it carefully on a flat area next to a huge cedar stump, then settled onto it. The stump was a dozen feet through, left there by the nineteenth century lumberjacks who had once clambered through cathedrals of ancient forest giants, felling them with long whipsaws and hauling them away to waiting ships and sawmills.

To Grace, this ancient stump had once been a comfortable friend and a patient confidante. She dug into her backpack and pulled out a cell phone. Last night, Annette had driven to her office at the communications company where she worked and retrieved two of the firm's demos.

She turned it on. Its illuminated display showed the time. 5:43 a.m. She punched a number on the keypad. It was answered on the first ring.

"I was getting worried," Annette said.

"I'm okay. I'm in place. You?"

"On the corner above the turnoff. I'm in a row of parked cars, but I have a good view. I'll call you when I move."

"Okay."

Grace switched off her flashlight and leaned back to wait for dawn.

The constant sound of water rushing over the spillway waxed and waned through the trees like the warning winds before a violent storm.

*

189

During their conversation, Leddi Dixon had given Annette a telephone number for Eric Nader. Grace had recognised it as his home number. He lived in a sprawling waterfront home at Moses Point. Early in her passage to the mainland, Ned Chickite's fishing boat had skirted past the cliff where Nader's house, isolated from its neighbours on either side by hundreds of feet of wooded shoreline, brooded over the dark waters of Saanich Inlet.

Grace had dialled the number on one of Annette's cell phones. There was no answer. Just a voice mail service, with a generic female inviting the caller to leave a message or dial zero for more options. Grace left no message. She'd dialled the number once every thirty minutes until seven in the evening. Finally, the receiver was picked up.

Eric Nader. He'd been expecting her call.

"The redoubtable Miss Palliser! I thought I might hear from you." His voice was oily with self-satisfaction. Grace's skin crawled. She struggled to maintain an even tone.

"I believe you have my daughter."

"Bright girl. Too bright, it would seem. But there it is. See where all that intelligence has got you? Such a calamity, my dear. And worsening every day, I believe."

"Let me speak to her."

"Not possible at the moment, I'm afraid. She's asleep."

"Asleep! I doubt it. She must be terrified!" Grace's voice crept higher as her throat constricted. "Let me speak to her!"

"Midazolam."

"What?"

"Midazolam. Also known as Versed. Injected in her cute little bottom. It's a very powerful sedative. Poor child, she just sleeps and sleeps."

Grace gasped as her vision clouded with tears of rage.

"My God, you fucking monster!"

"Not at all, my dear. Now Harvey, on the other hand... there's a man who does need to be watched." His voice hardened. "He's quite unpredictable." He let that sink in, then softened his tone. "Your daughter is alive. Alive and well

190

cared for. The sedative is harmless when it's properly used. And you'll be relieved to know that it has a most fortunate side effect. The child will remember nothing. Nothing important, that is. Of course-" his voice hardened again "-we can't keep her in dreamland forever. She'll need to eat. We wouldn't want her to starve, now would we?" He paused, and the silence seemed to fill with an inky malevolence. "I believe you have something of mine."

"And that would be...?"

"Don't play games, Miss Palliser. You have a microfiche film and, I would guess, various photocopies that the late lamented Andre Devereaux left in your custody. I require their immediate return."

Grace played for time as she mentally mapped out her moves.

"Let me get this straight. You snatched my daughter out of a playground on the chance – no, on the *remote* chance – that I would figure out that you were behind it and call you. Have I got this right?'

"An accurate prediction, as it turns out. You've called, haven't you? Now, we end the talk, Miss Palliser. A simple trade is called for – your slumbering child for my property." He paused. "You don't really need time to think about this, do you?"

"No." Grace made sure he heard her voice shake.

"Excellent. Very wise. Now, where are you?"

"You don't really expect me to tell you that?"

"You'll need to come to Moses Point. Tonight. Unless you want Harvey to get careless with the child's doses. Now, where are you?"

"For God's sake, Nader, I'm on the mainland! I can't possibly get there tonight! Even if I could catch the last ferry, I'd be spotted for sure." Grace allowed her voice to become harsh, with a tinge of rising hysteria. "Maybe that's what I should do – turn myself in with this microfiche and tell the police everything I know!"

"Do that, Miss Palliser, and your daughter will never be found." Nader spoke in cold and measured tones. He waited for his threat to sink in, and then added, "And thank you for confirming that you have the film."

"I'm taping this conversation."

"No, Miss Palliser, you are not."

Damn! Why the hell didn't I think of it?

A long silence.

"Miss Palliser. Start talking."

"I... I couldn't guarantee that I'd make it if I had to cross the Straits again. You'd risk losing the fiche." Behind the tone of defeat in her voice, Grace's mind was racing. She plunged on. "You'll have to bring Shy over here."

Grace knew that any meeting with Nader or Pendergast would probably mean her certain death. And Shy's. But she couldn't let Nader know that she was alert to the danger. She needed him to believe that he held all the cards.

Grace could hear him breathing. Thinking. Then he said, "Just a minute," and the line went dead. She waited.

After thirty seconds, Nader's voice came back on the line. It seemed clearer, louder.

"Tomorrow morning. At the Tsawwassen terminal."

"No! Please!" Grace tried to sound panicked. "All the terminals are being watched by the police. There's nowhere secluded on that jetty. Everything's out in the open. They're putting my face on that TV show, for God's sake! Look..." She took a breath. "Okay. I'm in North Vancouver. And I'm taking a big chance every time I go outside. We need to meet somewhere near here, outside, but private."

"I see." Nader sounded thoughtful, even conciliatory.

He's playing me. They are planning to kill me. Simple. Clean and effective. Kill me. Kill Shy. Make us disappear. After a few years, I'm just another cold case file.

"Where then?" Nader asked.

"Let me think."

"Remember, your daughter's face is in the news as well."

"Your Lincoln has tinted windows."

"Yes"

"Take the 7:00 a.m. ferry from Nanaimo. That way, you'll land at Horseshoe Bay. Stay in the car during the crossing. When you come off the boat, take Highway 1 as far as the Capilano Road exit, then take Capilano north, toward the Grouse Mountain gondola, but don't go that far. Take the turnoff to Capilano Canyon Park. It's deserted this time of year – especially on a weekday. Drive to the parking lot near the salmon hatchery. I'll meet you at the Cable Pool Bridge. Follow the signs."

"Your daughter won't be in any condition to walk down a trail."

"Carry her. It's only a hundred yards."

"Why the bridge?" Nader asked suspiciously. "Why not the parking lot?"

"The salmon hatchery operates all year. I don't want to be recognised by some nosy fisheries officer. We won't be seen at the bridge. I can come on foot through the woods and avoid the parking lot."

"And what time are you suggesting?" Nader asked, with a touch of sarcasm.

"You won't be off the boat until nearly nine o'clock. It will take you at least thirty minutes to get to the park. Ten o'clock."

"All right. Ten o'clock." Nader's tone was deadly. "Be there."

"Just a minute! Make sure you're carrying a cell phone. Give me a number." He recited a number to her. Then he hung up.

Grace had sketched out the details to Annette.

"Grace!" she exclaimed. "This is your break!" Grace rubbed at her temples wearily.

"What do you mean?"

"Turn yourself in, tell the whole story, and get them to fill the park with police. How are those men going to explain why they have Shy? It will prove you're telling the truth!"

"No."

"Why? I would think-"

"I don't trust the police. I watched them try to destroy a young boy's life. Now they're trying to destroy mine. Besides, there's not enough time! If I turn myself in, I'll have to do it right now! Your local Mounties will just lock me up and leave the whole thing to Farrell. I'm the crazy woman who shot a Victoria policeman, remember? Think about it, Annette! Police departments are bureaucracies. Farrell isn't going to requisition a helicopter and a SWAT team on my say-so!"

Annette's eyes bored into Grace's. "That's not it, is it? Not any of it." Her words hung like smoke in the air.

Grace took a deep breath. She answered calmly. "No. Nader is smart. If he spots a trap, Shy dies. I'm not leaving this to the police. This is my child. I need a plan I can control." She pushed her chair back and stood up. "That's why I had to convince Nader to meet me on my turf."

"Your turf?"

"I grew up near that park. I know those woods." She was thoughtful. "Listen, in their position, would you even bring Shy?"

"Maybe, maybe not. But if you don't believe they will, why go?"

"Because I have to. On the chance."

Annette leaned on the kitchen sink, looking out the window. She turned back. Her eyes found Grace's.

"A plan you can control?"

"Yes."

"Any idea what that is?"

SEVENTEEN

Grace's hips and knees were stiffening from the cold. As she got up to stretch, her cell phone rang. She checked the time on the display.

6:50 a.m.

"The hatchery truck just turned in," Annette reported. "I'm moving now."

"Call when you're at the camp."

To the east, the sky was beginning to lighten. Peering through a gap in the forest, Grace still couldn't make out any landscape details further down the canyon. But she wouldn't have long to wait. She groped in her knapsack and found Annette's binoculars. She set them on her lap.

She leaned back against the stump, tightening and loosening her leg muscles against the chill air. After a while, enough of the dawn's murk had lifted for her to make out the Cable Pool Bridge, five hundred yards down river. Her view took in its entire length. It was a wooden footbridge, solidly constructed out of hewn logs, with a thick plank deck.

After a few minutes of watching, movement at the eastern end of the span attracted her attention. A large black dog, straining on its leash, led a bundled figure into view. The person bent down and a second later the dog, now released, bounded happily across the bridge and into the forest on the western side of the river. The bundled figure followed at a slower pace.

Grace picked up her phone. She pressed a button to light the display.

7:36 a.m.

Where the hell is Annette?

She punched in the number of Annette's cell phone.

"The customer you are calling is presently unavailable or out of the service area. Please try again later."

A prickly sensation migrated down Grace's spine. The church camp buildings were on bench land near the river, between high granite cliffs. Annette must be in a dead zone where her phone wouldn't work.

She forced herself to stay calm. Annette would realise the situation and deal with it.

As if in answer to her silent prayer, the phone in her hand suddenly vibrated. She put it to her ear and immediately heard the thick hiss of static.

"I'm on-" Annette's voice faded away. The signal died, then came back clearly "-to the park road."

"I didn't get that," Grace said quickly. "Say it again, slowly."

There was more static, then: "How's this?"

"That's better."

"I said I'm on foot. The phone doesn't work down at the camp, so I left my car there and walked back up to the park road."

"Okay, is there somewhere nearby where you can stay out of sight?"

"Yes. But I'm not sure it matters. When I was walking up the last hill, re-dialling your number, a white Lincoln went by on the paved road, heading into the park."

"Could you see the driver?"

"No." A pause. "Could be a coincidence."

"I don't believe in them. Not any more. Did you have any trouble with the fiche?"

"No. That's done."

"Okay. I'm watching the bridge. Keep talking until you've found a place where you can't be seen from the road and we can still hear each other."

"I'm there now."

"Okay. I'll call you back." Grace trained her binoculars on the bridge. After fifteen minutes, her arms were beginning to ache. She was about to lower the glasses when a heavyset man wearing a baseball cap, light-coloured jacket and dark slacks appeared at the east end of the bridge and started to amble across. His gait was familiar. Grace's stomach muscles tightened. She fine-tuned the focus on the glasses. The man stopped near the middle of the bridge and leaned on the railing, studying the deep pool twenty feet below. Then he straightened and looked up toward the dam. His full face appeared in Grace's field of view. It was Harvey Pendergast.

The big man turned and continued walking across the bridge. He vanished into the woods on the western side of the gorge. Grace's pulse rate began to climb.

She kept her binoculars trained on the spot where she'd last seen Pendergast. The forest on the western bank was a labyrinth of hiking trails. As a child, Grace had explored most of them. She recalled that one trail climbed toward her general location in switchback loops through dense stands of fir and hemlock. It eventually intersected the service road that passed a few hundred yards behind her.

She stayed alert. After several minutes, Pendergast reappeared. He stopped again near the middle of the bridge and gazed up toward the dam. He seemed to be looking directly at Grace. Involuntarily, she pulled the binoculars from her eyes. She had a sudden irrational feeling that Harvey Pendergast knew exactly where she was.

After a second, Pendergast walked slowly back to the eastern end of the span. Without the aid of the binoculars, he appeared as a tiny figure on a distant bridge. Grace saw him descending the steps that led to the parking lot trail.

She called Annette. "Pendergast was checking out the bridge. Two hours early! They must have caught a ferry last night, after my call to Nader." Grace was heartsick. "You know what that means."

"What?"

"It means those bastards didn't bring Shy. Where could they keep her overnight so no one would see her?"

"How about a motel!" Annette replied rapidly. "One of those old ones, all on one level with an office out by the street and a string of drive-up rooms. They probably have her in the

197

car. We planned for that, Grace! Pendergast was just being careful. Looking over the area ahead of time."

"I know," Grace said tensely. "I just have a bad feeling." She felt light-headed, queasy. She took a deep breath. "Don't do anything yet. The meeting time is still a couple of hours away. Can you stay where you are for now?"

"Yeah. It's not exactly the Hilton, but I'll survive."

"Okay. Let's check in every thirty minutes, or sooner if something happens."

"I'll be here."

Grace resumed her watch, but within minutes Annette called back.

"They just drove by, heading out."

"Could you see how many people were in the car?"

"No. They were really moving. Caught me by surprise."

"I guess we wait."

"Yes. We wait."

At twenty minutes to ten, Grace's phone vibrated again.

"The car just went back down the hill toward the parking lot."

"Good. Wait for my call."

A short time later, a thin male figure appeared on the bridge. Grace studied him through the binoculars.

Eric Nader. He was bareheaded. Even at this distance, Grace could make out his pale face and creepy, slicked-back hair. He was alone. Grace's heart sank.

Where's Shy?

She waited, but no one joined Nader on the bridge. Either Pendergast was babysitting Shy in the car or they hadn't brought her. She ground her teeth. She was desperately afraid for Shy, but she had to force herself to stay calm and clear-headed. She and Annette had planned for three different scenarios. The first one – Nader bringing Shy with him to the bridge – looked like a non-starter. On to plan B, which assumed that Shy was being held in the car. From here on in, everything depended on communications and timing. And cool heads.

As she watched, Nader leaned on the railing and studied the moving currents below. Every few seconds, he lifted his head to check each end of the bridge.

They're setting a trap for me. But how?

It was time to find out. Grace picked up her phone and called Annette.

"Nader is on the bridge. Alone."

"Plan B. I'm moving now."

"Be careful. I don't know where Pendergast is. And these phones may not work when we need them."

"You know where I'm going to be. If you don't hear from me, improvise." Annette ended the call.

Improvise? I hope so. Or we could all end up dead. Would they kill a child?

A wave of rage coursed through her. She grabbed the binoculars and checked on Nader. He was looking restive. As she watched, he turned and looked up toward the dam, then reached into a jacket pocket and took out a small black object. He seemed to be studying it.

A gun. No. A phone.

Waiting for my call, Eric? Getting a bit nervous, you bastard?

Grace dropped the glasses. She had written Nader's cell number on the palm of her hand. She punched the sequence into the keypad on her phone, and then she held her thumb on the Send button, without pressing, and picked up the binoculars. She trained them on Nader.

She pressed the button. Before she heard her call ring through, Nader put his phone to his ear. She listened. There was a click, a short pause, then a busy signal.

Busy signal? Who's he talking to?

As the busy signal beeped in her ear, the background rush from the dam spillway carried another faint sound to her through the forest.

The sound of a ringing cell phone.

Nearby!

She jerked her phone away from her ear. The ringing quickly cut off, as if someone had answered. The sound had come from the woods to her left, further down the slope. Grace closed her eyes, straining to hear. A new sound drifted up to her. A voice, low and muffled. A male voice.

Grace dropped her phone on her knapsack and steadied her binoculars with both hands. Nader was standing sideways to her and she could only see the profile of his face, but she could see when he was listening and when he was talking.

When he was listening, the voice in the woods was talking. When he was talking, the voice was silent.

The voice could only belong to one person.

Pendergast.

Where are they keeping Shy?

Grace set down the binoculars and stood up. She yanked the Beretta out of her jacket pocket. She eased back the slide, as Annette had shown her, and checked that there was a live round in the chamber. She clicked off the safety. She stood there for a few seconds, thinking. Annette would be calling. Grace needed to warn her, tell her there might have to be a new plan.

She punched Annette's number on her phone, but all she got was the telephone company recording. She pocketed the phone. Annette would have to improvise.

Grace could still hear the voice in the woods. She moved higher up the trail she had used earlier to reach her observation post, and then began working her way cautiously through the undergrowth, following the contour of the slope. She stayed above the voice. She hadn't gone very far when the talking stopped. They must have ended the call, she thought. Nader would be waiting for a call from her.

She was wearing the sneakers that Millie had bought for her in Victoria. They were soundless on the soft needle bed of the forest floor, but the stiff branches of the huckleberry bushes scraped noisily against the sleeves of her ski jacket. She dropped to her hands and knees. Closer to ground level, the way ahead was clearer. She crept forward carefully.

After a few yards, a dense patch of ferns blocked her way. She was preparing to detour by climbing higher up the slope when she heard a scuffling sound below her, down the hill. She raised herself to a half-crouch and peered over the ferns.

Harvey Pendergast was in the middle of a small level clearing, thirty or forty feet down toward the canyon rim. He was lying prone on the uphill side of a deadfall.

Even though she had expected to see him, Grace froze in momentary shock. As she recovered, her eyes strayed to an object leaning against the log a few feet to Pendergast's right.

It was a rifle.

It looked too long to be designed for legitimate hunting. It had a military green stock and an oversized scope. Much of its extra length was derived from a black, evil-looking silencer. It looked just like something from a movie. Something a police sniper would use.

Or an assassin.

As Grace watched, Pendergast carefully folded a dark-coloured rag. He placed it on the log in front of him, then picked up the rifle and set it across the pad, tucking the stock against his shoulder. He put an eye to the scope.

Beyond him, down the canyon, Grace could see Nader on the bridge. He was a distant stick figure, intermittently appearing and disappearing behind the swaying upper boughs of the evergreens that clung to the cliff rim below Pendergast's nest. From his location, lower down, Pendergast would have a clear shot at the bridge through a gap in the trees.

He laid there, patient as a python. Waiting to kill the woman who was sitting thirty feet above him, watching. Adrenaline poured through Grace's veins like some bizarre nightclub drug. Her legs started to vibrate. Carefully, she drew her gun from her pocket.

Shoot him! a voice in her head urged. *Empty the fucking clip into him!*

Her rational brain clanged an alarm, reminding her why she'd come here. She had to get Shy back. Nader might hear the shots. And she doubted that she could actually do it. Kill Pendergast - *even him* - in cold blood.

But if he's here waiting to shoot me, and Nader's on the bridge, where the hell is Shy? Either she's their backup plan – drugged insensible in the trunk of their car. Or she's dead.

Grace's heart filled with dread. She looked around carefully. There was a Douglas fir just above her, ten feet up the slope. It was wide enough at its base to provide cover. She eased her way uphill, crawling backward, until she reached shelter behind the tree.

She settled against it. She pulled out her phone and dialled Annette. She got the recording. She set the Beretta on the ground next to her and drew up her knees.

Think, dammit!

The black dog nearly got Grace killed. She'd decided to circle back and retrieve her things, then move to a different vantage point. There were a few places on the west rim of the canyon, farther downstream, where she would be able to see the hatchery parking lot. Now that she knew where Pendergast was, if she could reach Annette on the phone, and if they timed this right...

I've got one slim advantage, she thought. I call Nader. Tell him I know where Pendergast is and what he's planning. That I'm sitting in the bush twenty feet behind him. That he can't hear me talking on this phone because of the noise from the dam. Tell him I have a gun of my own, a nice little nine-millimetre, and it's aimed at the back of Pendergast's head. Tell him that if tries to warn Pendergast, the bastard will die the second his phone rings. Tell him to release Shy in the parking lot and then drive away, out of the park. Tell him...

But then there was the black dog. At first, it didn't register. Grace was checking on Pendergast, who hadn't moved, and the jingling of a dog's collar was such a familiar sound that it didn't immediately intrude on her concentration.

Then it did.

She turned to find herself looking into a happy doggie face. In a panic, she grabbed the Labrador's collar to stop its tags from jingling. She tried to pull the dog tight against her, out of sight behind the tree, but the quick manoeuvre frightened the animal. The Lab yelped and snapped at her forearm. Its teeth sank into the sleeve of her jacket, just missing her flesh. A high-pitched whistling sound filtered through the trees from higher up the hill. Grace realised that the dog's owner must be on the service road. The dog pulled back violently just as Grace was releasing her grip on its collar, but its teeth caught in the fabric of her sleeve and she was almost pulled onto her face before the dog tore free. Her cell phone flew from her hand. The dog fled noisily through the underbrush, back toward the road, its collar making more noise than before.

Grace scrambled back to her hiding place and pushed herself tight against the tree. After a few frightened breaths, she cautiously eased her head sideways to peer around the trunk.

Pendergast had vanished.

The next thirty seconds unfolded in slow motion. Grace turned her head to check in the other direction. She didn't complete the move. A powerful force slammed against her throat, grinding the side of her head into the rough bark of the Douglas fir. On reflex, she kicked out with her right leg. Her foot found empty air. She heard a harsh laugh and the grip on her throat tightened, choking off her breath.

She was looking into muddy, bloodshot eyes.

Pendergast's voice croaked in her ear. "How fucking convenient!"

The claustrophobic panic that came from being strangled saved Grace's life. Pendergast was using his right hand to choke her. Out of the corner of her eye, Grace saw that he was holding the rifle in his left. Her clouded wits ordered her to react. Her fingers found her pistol. She swung the muzzle upward and jammed it into her assailant's crotch.

Pendergast grunted in surprise. He dropped his rifle, tightened his grip on her throat, trying to throttle her, and used his free hand to clutch at her gun. He tried to use his superior strength to force one of his fingers behind the trigger and push the Beretta down and away from his groin. The muzzle of the pistol jerked past the crotch seam in Pendergast's jeans and began sliding off target.

Choking and desperate, Grace fired.

Pendergast let out a yell and spun away, releasing his grip on Grace's throat and grabbing for his crotch. She twisted away and crawled, crab-like, down the embankment into the stand of tall ferns. Coughing and nauseous, fuelled by fear, she plunged through the tangle of ferns. Miraculously, the Beretta was still in her hand. She had no idea if her bullet had disabled Pendergast. Taking no chances, she ran for her life.

From behind, she heard a sharp noise, like an animal's cough. At the same instant, she felt a blast of superheated air on her cheek as a high velocity bullet whipcracked past her head. She dove headfirst over a rotting cedar log just as another round tore through her coat and burned a track across her rib cage. As she rolled back to her feet and scrambled away through the dense thicket, she felt warm wetness soaking down her side toward her belt line. Fear was coppery in her throat. Unaccountably, her mind remained clear.

I guess the nervous breakdown comes later, she thought insanely. *If I live.*

The firing had stopped. Maybe Pendergast wasn't in any condition to follow her. She gritted her teeth, praying that he wasn't. Praying she'd blown his balls off.

She plunged on, heading away from the river.

Pendergast didn't know these woods.

Grace did.

The top end of the switchback trail wasn't marked. Even if Pendergast had reconnoitred, he probably hadn't discovered it. Grace ran quickly, angling across and down the slope. After a few minutes, she burst out of the brush at the top of a low embankment. A loop of the trail was a few feet below her. She leaped down and started moving rapidly downhill.

Pendergast would call Nader to warn him that their diabolical little plan had failed. She cursed herself for losing her phone. There was no way to warn Annette.

Grace only had one course left. She had to get to the place where she and Annette had agreed to meet when it was over.

She had to get to the church camp.

She couldn't use the Cable Pool Bridge. And she'd be foolish to try the dam causeway. But there was another way to get across the river, if she could get to it.

Her side was burning. She was sure the bullet hadn't penetrated her abdomen, but it had torn open skin and flesh, and maybe cracked a rib. She worried about the bleeding.

She sped down the path. In a few places, she managed to save time by going straight down the pitch of the slope from one switchback grade to the next. But her headlong downhill flight was jarring her joints and aggravating her wound. She was terrified that her strength would give out before she could reach safety.

She wondered what Nader was doing. Combing the woods below for her? She had to make it to about the fourth or fifth loop above the Cable Pool Bridge. From there an old trail, which had been partly overgrown even when she was a child, looped around to another service road. It was a Water District road that ran next to a pipeline, one of the huge penstocks that carried water from Cleveland Lake to the city. The pipeline ran southeast until it intersected the canyon rim several hundred yards downstream from the Cable Pool Bridge. There the service road ended, but the pipeline continued – across the canyon. The pipe itself formed a bridge seventy-five feet above the river.

Grace and her childhood playmates had called it the 'Pipe Bridge' and had often talked breathlessly about crossing it. It had been the scariest attraction on their expeditions into the canyon park.

She almost missed the cut-off trail. She overshot and had to pull up – gasping, her breath ragged, her side throbbing – and climb back up to the spot where the faint track led west through the salal bushes. She stood there for a moment, chest heaving. She noticed that she still had her gun in her hand. She pocketed it, and set off again, jogging, trying to maintain a steady but slower pace – one that wouldn't prematurely exhaust her.

Thankfully, the traverse to the service road was shorter than she remembered. Distances always seemed longer when you were a kid.

The Water District road hadn't been very well maintained in the past twenty years. Its rutted surface looked no better than a streambed. Rainstorms had scored it with deep runnels and it was littered with tree boughs, boulders and rough gravel. It ran along beside a raised berm that hid the buried penstock. Grace felt vulnerable on the open roadway, so she climbed to the top of the berm and half-scrambled, half-slid down the other side. There was a rough pathway between the bottom of the berm and the bordering forest. Her progress was slower, but the earthwork provided her with cover.

After ten minutes, she reached the canyon rim. Ahead and just outside the tree line, a huge steel pipe, eight feet in diameter, emerged from the termination of the berm and launched itself into space. It formed a span, a hundred feet long, to the rim of the opposite canyon wall. A gantry-style walkway was welded to the top of the pipe, and a flight of metal grid steps led up to it.

Grace eased closer, still staying within the cover of the forest. Breathing hard, she leaned against a tree and studied the gantry.

One section of railing was missing at the far end on the downriver side, but otherwise the walkway seemed intact. Grace breathed a sigh. She crept forward to the edge of the woods. She wasn't able to see very well on her own side of the river, upstream or down, but she spent long seconds studying the opposite cliff tops. There was no one in sight.

She took a deep breath and stepped into the open. Quickly, she mounted the steps to the gantry. She started across.

It has been said that a soldier should never worry about the gunshot he hears. It's the one he doesn't hear that kills him.

If it weren't for a length of inch-thick steel pipe, Grace wouldn't have heard the shot that erupted from the trees on the west rim of the canyon. As it was, she didn't actually hear the silenced gunshot – only the sound of the heavy slug as it whined off the handrail next to her, missing her by millimetres.

Grace dropped to the catwalk. Her side screamed with pain, but fear suppressed it. She pressed her face into the welded grid of the decking. The shot had come when she was nearly across. She estimated that she was about a dozen long paces from the eastern end of the gantry. There was another set of metal stairs there, on the upstream side of the pipeline. The side exposed to the gunman.

Grace edged her body toward the edge of the grid, desperately trying to find cover. Maybe she could take advantage of the curve of the pipe. The shooter would be lining up another shot.

The thought conjured the reality.

The bullet passed directly under her body, between the underside of the catwalk and the top of the giant pipe below. It slammed into the base of a stanchion, next to Grace's right hip, and exploded in a shower of hot metal. The force of the impact jarred down the length of Grace's right leg and it immediately went numb.

That's not Pendergast shooting, she thought. With a scoped rifle, he wouldn't miss.

That's Nader, using a handgun.

Grace felt a surge of hope. Nader would realise he was shooting from a bad angle. He'd have to stop firing while he worked his way along the top of the canyon wall to get closer. There was no trail there. She waited, dreading another shot.

Nothing.

Sensation was returning to her right leg, but now it was pulsing painfully, in tempo with the wound in her side. She wondered if she had taken some shrapnel from the last shot.

She heard the sound of something heavy moving through the bush on the west rim. Behind her, to the left. She'd guessed correctly. It was time to run. Praying that her leg wouldn't give out, Grace lurched to her feet and sprinted for the end of the catwalk. A bullet whined off the big pipe a few yards ahead. Then another, close to her feet. She was abreast of the area with the missing railing and, in a blur, she glimpsed a flat table of dry stone. Unlike the upstream side, where the steps led down from the gantry, the cliff top on the downstream side jutted out over the river.

The drop from the catwalk was at least ten feet. As another bullet ignited the air behind her head, she leaped.

In flight, she recalled the words of a sky diving instructor, years earlier, when she'd made her one and only jump.

Tuck and roll.

But this was solid granite.

The lower boughs of an old growth cedar overhung the rock table. Grace grabbed at the branches. They broke her fall, but they slashed the side of her neck and scraped the skin off her palms as she swung to the ground. Now oblivious to pain, she lunged into the cover of the woods. A bullet ripped through the branches inches above her head.

It wouldn't be long before Nader crossed behind her. Grace wrenched the Beretta from her coat and took cover in a needle-carpeted hollow behind a tangle of roots. Steadying the gun with both hands, she aimed carefully at the far end of the gantry. The foresight on her gun's barrel oscillated with her pounding heart. She tried to steady it by holding her breath. It didn't seem to help.

She waited.

After thirty seconds, Eric Nader strode out of the forest. He looked like a man on a morning outing. Without a second's hesitation, he mounted the steps to the catwalk. He was holding a long-barrelled handgun down at his side, next to his right thigh. He started across the bridge.

His arrogance was breathtaking.

He must know that she was armed. Pendergast would have told him. He seemed perfectly confident that – gun or no gun – Grace would just keep running.

After all, hadn't she been running from the start?

Grace debated waiting until the man was in the middle of the span and then pinning him down, as he had done to her. But she needed to buy time, to find Annette. She would only be able to keep Nader on the bridge as long as she had bullets.

No. She had to drive this bastard back into the woods and make him think it was just too dangerous to cross.

She waited for Nader to take a few more steps. Then she opened up. The boom of Grace's unsilenced automatic echoed down the canyon.

Nader's confident stride disintegrated as bullets flew around him. One shot, striking the deck of the catwalk, showered him with sparks. He dropped onto his stomach and scrambled backward. Then he leaped from the top of the metal steps into the brush below. He crawled on his hands and knees into the woods as Grace put a few more slugs into the thicket next to him.

As soon as Nader disappeared from view, Grace retreated into the dark safety of the forest. She stumbled to the service road that led from the bridge and raced away inland. After the first bend, a trail led off to the right. She took it, ghosting through the trees toward the church camp.

As she ran, tears of grief and despair flooded down her cheeks. She had survived, but she had failed Shy.

My beautiful little girl...

The breakdown began.

She didn't know how she would go on.

EIGHTEEN

The church camp compound sat among ancient trees on a broad shelf above the river. The trail led Grace to the rear of a row of bunkhouses. Rain had started and fat drops fell from the branches of overhanging trees, landing noisily on the shake roofs above her. She made her way cautiously forward. Through the narrow gap between two buildings, she could see a section of the gravel parking area in front. Beyond the open space was part of a wall of another structure – the main meeting hall, she remembered.

She rounded the corner of the last bunkhouse and almost collided with Annette's Buick. There was no one in the car.

Where's Annette?

In dread, Grace moved to the passenger side of the car and looked in. The keys were in the ignition. There was a long black flashlight on the seat. The passenger door was unlocked. Grace was about to open it when she heard the wrenching sound of wood against wood. It came from the front of the bunkhouse. She dropped into a crouch, yanking the Beretta from her pocket. A second later, a figure appeared at the corner of the building.

Grace nearly shot her friend.

"Grace!" Annette's eyes were wide, her voice fearful. Grace lowered the gun, straightened, and leaned shakily against the car. Annette came quickly to her side and eased the gun from her hand. Grace collapsed against her.

"I heard shots!" Annette said. "I was worried!"

"Those were mine. They had silencers." She made her hands into fists to stop them from shaking. "It was a trap! Pendergast was on the hillside not far from me. He had a rifle, ready to pick me off when I showed up on the bridge – maybe after they got the fiche, or maybe they don't really care about it. He spotted me, but I got away from him. You heard me shooting at Nader. He's not far behind - maybe five minutes. We've got to go!"

Annette was staring at the slash on Grace's neck. "Grace, you're hurt!"

"It's okay. We better go!" Grace's face contorted with anguish. "Oh, Annette! My baby! My baby girl!"

Annette was silent. Grace wiped at her eyes to clear her blurred vision. She saw her friend's face. It wore a faint smile.

"Oh God! You found her!" She grabbed Annette's shoulders, then released her and looked in the back seat of the car. "Where is she?"

"In the bunkhouse. She's drugged, but she seems all right. Go to her. I'll bring the car around." Grace clutched Annette into an awkward hug and then ran to the corner of the building. A heavy wooden door stood open. Splinters of doorframe and a padlock, still locked to its hardware, lay on the ground in front. Grace stepped nervously through the doorway.

Shy was lying on the first bunk, wrapped in a blanket. She appeared to be asleep. Even in the semi-darkness of the unlit bunkhouse, Grace could see that her daughter's once-angelic face was now pasty and hollow-eyed. She knelt beside the bunk and kissed her, then, weeping, kissed her again and again. The child slept on, her breathing slow and even.

Joy mixed with visceral rage as Grace stroked her little girl's cheek. She was ready to take the Beretta and go looking for Nader.

The Buick crunched to a stop next to the doorway.

"Grace!" Annette's voice was urgent. "Bring her! Quickly, Grace!" Grace scooped up her little girl, blanket and all. Pain knifed through the wound in her side. She staggered to the door, almost falling. Annette steadied her and helped her arrange Shy on the back seat. Then Grace crawled in next to her, sitting on the floor next to the child's head.

Annette drove them out of the camp. The access road curved up the slope, barely more than two wheel ruts through the forest.

211

"Where was she?" Grace asked. "How did you - ?"

"She was in the Lincoln. When I went down the hill to hide the microfilm in the fire pit, like we planned, I noticed there was an upper parking lot. You didn't mention it."

"It must be new. I haven't been here in years."

"After you told me Nader was on the bridge, I got in my car and drove down to the first lot. I parked against the mountain, out of sight, and then walked to the edge. The Lincoln was the only car in the lower lot. It was parked next to the entrance to the bridge trail. The engine was running – I could see the exhaust. I figured Pendergast must be in the car, which made me think they might have brought Shy. I was just going to call you when the driver's door opened and a man got out. Not Pendergast. A young guy. Dark hair. Expensive clothes."

Grace sucked in her breath. *Preppy Boy?*

"I pushed the redial on my phone, to warn you that Pendergast might be somewhere in the park. The guy leaned on the car, smoking a cigarette."

Preppy Boy doesn't smoke. Or does he?

"I couldn't get through to you, so I said to hell with it and I went and got Shy."

"Went and got her! How?"

"The guy went into the bush to take a leak." Annette held up the heavy black flashlight that Grace had noticed earlier. "He never heard me coming – with a little luck, I gave him a nice concussion. Shy was on the back seat, under that blanket."

Annette slowed the car at a narrow section of the driveway. Encroaching boughs squeaked along the door panels.

Shy began to stir. Grace stroked her face. Annette's simple courage filled her with admiration. And gratitude. She couldn't speak. She reached over the back of the seat and squeezed her friend's shoulder. A warm strong hand covered hers briefly, then returned to the steering wheel.

When they reached the park road, Annette slowed the car to a crawl and checked for other vehicles. The road was clear.

She drove the Buick out of the bush and swung onto the pavement. They sped out of the park.

By the time they reached the outskirts of Langley, Shy was awake and mewling. She sounded like a surgical patient coming off anaesthetic, querulous and confused. The little girl clung to her mother, her damp cold fingers pinching flesh, opening the slash on Grace's neck, mixing blood and tears.

"Mommy, that man...!" She rolled forward and buried her face in Grace's breast. Sobs wracked her little body.

"Sshh, my love. Don't talk now. I know. I know about the man."

"There was a bad man in my dream, Mommy! He stucked a doctor needle in me."

Grace almost passed out from the mental picture. She struggled to think of a gentle response, something soothing. Her mind wouldn't cooperate. It went blank.

Shy saved Grace from an inadequate silence. As if to brush the cobwebs of nightmarish memory from her mind, she released her grip around Grace's neck, slid back, and abruptly changed the subject.

"I'm thirsty, Mommy. I'm really thirsty."

"We'll be home in a minute. You can have a drink then."

"Are we going to your house?"

"No, sweetie. We're going to Annette's house. She's my friend."

"Is that the lady who's driving?"

"Yes, love."

"Is she a nice lady, Mommy?"

"Yes, she is. A very nice lady. And very brave."

"Does she have juice in her fridge?"

"I'm sure she does." Shy seemed reassured. She laid her cheek on the seat and, after a second, closed her eyes. Drying tears and mucous streaked her small face. The skin under her eyes was puffy and dark. Her shallow breaths smelled foul. Not the usual sweet breath of her child. It was the breath of a child whose small body was struggling to metabolise a strong drug.

Rage, blue and cold, spread through Grace's being.

When they reached the house, Annette backed into the double garage and pressed a remote to close the door. A vintage Volkswagen Beetle occupied the other parking slot. There wasn't much room between the vehicles to manoeuvre Shy out of the back seat. Grace got out first, and then reached back to gather up her daughter. Pain ripped through her side. She went to her knees on the concrete, nausea crawling in her throat.

"Grace!" Annette wound an arm around her torso and Grace involuntarily cried out as her friend's grip closed next to her wound. Annette snatched her arm back and then pulled Grace's ski jacket away from her shoulders. Grace's sweatshirt was soaked with blood.

"*Mon Dieu!* Why didn't you say something?"

Grace forced a grimacing smile. "What do they say in the Westerns? It's just a scratch."

"Can you walk?"

Grace nodded.

"Then go in the house and lie down. I'll bring Shy."

But Grace wasn't ready to lose sight of her daughter, even here. "No. You carry her. I'll follow."

Annette deposited Shy – limply awake, but not fully alert – on the bed in the spare room. Grace brought her daughter a glass of juice and held the glass for her while she sipped, then slumped into the soft chair next to the bed. Annette brought scissors. They turned Grace's chair, so that Shy couldn't watch, and Annette cut through Grace's bloody sweatshirt and the tee shirt underneath. She laid back the fabric.

"*Merde!*" she breathed. An oozing four-inch long trough had been excavated into Grace's rib cage, just below her bra. White bone glinted through the red carnage.

Annette ran to the hallway and returned with a clean towel.

"Grace, you need a doctor," she whispered as she gently pressed the towel against the wound.

Grace raised her arm and pulled the towel away. She craned to examine the bullet wound. For a moment, she contemplated how close she had come to annihilation. She was amazed at her own feeling of detachment. Annette replaced the towel and held it tight.

"No doctors," Grace said quietly. She glanced over at Shy, who was off in some twilight zone, an after-effect of the sedative. "I'll have to settle for a strong antiseptic, big bandages, and the strongest painkillers you can find." She looked directly into Annette's eyes. "And then we need to talk."

Annette left in her car. She soon returned with bandages and tape, antiseptic, and a bottle of over-the-counter painkillers that contained a small amount of codeine. She dropped a newspaper on Grace's lap.

"Another story?" Grace's face, already tense from the pain, tightened even more.

"No. It's all about Afghanistan and airport security and the cleanup in New York. But nothing about you. Not a word." She paused. "A bit strange, don't you think?"

The towel finally stopped the worst of the bleeding, but the antiseptic – which burned so much that Grace nearly bit through her lip – started the blood flowing again. It took Annette nearly an hour to finally staunch the wound and get a pressure bandage in place. But she was paranoid, so she checked the dressing every fifteen minutes to see if blood was soaking through. Finally, she relaxed.

Together, the two women got Shy undressed and Annette put Shy's clothes in the washing machine. Before wrapping the child in one of Annette's old flannel nightgowns, Grace examined her for injuries.

There were three distinct bruises on her hips – two on one side and one on the other. There was another bruise on the fleshy part of her upper arm.

215

"This must have been the first injection," Grace said.

"How do you know?"

"This bruise has a tiny mark in the centre, like the ones on her hips, but it looks older than the other ones – see, it's starting to turn yellow around the edges. Shy says she dreamed about a bad man who put a 'doctor needle' in her. My guess is that one of those bastards, probably Pendergast, gave her the first injection right at the playground. It would take a few minutes for the drug to work, so she would have seen the man before she went to sleep. She probably wouldn't remember the later shots. So now Pendergast seems like some kind of nightmare." She closed her eyes, fighting against the feeling of helpless horror that was rising within her. "Which he is!"

"Grace, it's time to go to the police! Shy's story will support yours. She can confirm that it wasn't you who picked her up in that playground, but some bad man. She can probably identify the man. Add that to my evidence – remember, I rescued her from Nader's car – and they'll have to believe you!" Annette was animated, full of hope.

Grace was silent. If Annette's father had taught her anything in their years of work together, it was scepticism. Police officers were human, and police forces were riddled with the same foibles as the wider community.

Grace would face huge hurdles of disbelief if she turned herself in. She would be held in custody for weeks, or months, while her lawyer prodded and cajoled the prosecution into investigating her allegations.

It might take a trial to clear her.

Or not.

Nader and his cohorts would anticipate a visit from the police. They would probably disappear. Evidence would evaporate. Even if Grace were half-believed, she might be suspected of complicity in Nader's scheme. In her imagination, she could hear Farrell telling the press that Grace had been an accomplice in some complex international fraud and had fallen out with the other conspirators.

There was no Andre Devereaux to defend her.

Still… Annette had a point.

Grace turned away from Annette and looked at her daughter. Two large eyes were watching her from the pillow.

"Who's that lady, Mommy?"

"I told you, love. This is my friend, Annette."

"Do the police want to catch her too?"

"No, Shy. Of course not."

"Daddy says the police are trying to catch you cause you killed people. He says you killed Uncle Andre. You didn't killed Uncle Andre, did you Mommy?" Her little voice was full of panic. Grace sat on the edge of the bed and stroked Shy's hair.

"No, love, I didn't kill Andre. I didn't kill anybody. The police made a mistake. Annette is Andre's daughter. She knows I didn't kill her Daddy. She's been trying to help me catch the people who did. And she helped me get you back from those people who took you."

Shy seemed to think about that for a few seconds. Then she sighed deeply and said, "I'm hungry."

"How about soup and crackers to start? Just to make sure your tummy doesn't get upset. You could have something else later if you feel like it. 'Kay?"

"'Kay." Shy actually smiled. Grace blinked back tears.

Annette volunteered to make the soup. Grace thanked her, and then got out of her chair and lay down on the bed. She held Shy close against her uninjured side, feeling her daughter's heartbeat, and tried to empty her mind. After a while, she floated into a light doze.

Twenty minutes later, Annette stepped into the bedroom, carrying a tray. Seeing Grace sleeping, she beckoned Shy to follow her. She settled the little girl on the living room couch in front of the TV. When she was sure that the child was comfortable, she returned to the bedroom. Grace was awake.

"Thank you. It's important that she trusts you."

"She's a sweet angel."

217

Grace smiled. She looked away for a moment, her mind outside the room. She turned back. "Annette, there's something I have to do."

"I was afraid you would say something like that. God, woman, you've done enough! And now you have Shy!"

"I know."

"Grace, I'm a witness! I'll tell them they had Shy!"

Grace closed her eyes.

"There's something you're not telling to me!" Annette said.

Grace opened her eyes.

"I'll be denied bail."

"You don't *know* that."

"I do. I've been to a lot of bail hearings with your Dad. The prosecution can easily prove I'm a flight risk. Even if they couldn't, the charges are so serious that I'll be denied bail. I can be detained 'for the protection or safety of the public'. It's in the Criminal Code. And while I'm sitting in a cell waiting for my trial, Brent will get full custody of Shy. By the time he and Hilary are through with her, she'll hate me. Even if I'm acquitted, it will take years to regain her trust."

Silence settled like snow.

"And, if I'm stuck in a cell," Grace finally added, "I'll be relying on others to do what I should be doing myself." She took a long, careful breath. "When are you going back to work?"

"I don't know. A few weeks. A month." Annette gave Grace a quizzical look. "Or... maybe when Shy's mother comes back for her?"

"Do you think you could retrieve the microfiche for me?" Grace asked.

"Yes. Tomorrow."

"Good. Thank you. Do you have a camera? With a flash?"

"Yes."

"We'll need that newspaper you brought me. I want photos of Shy's injection sites, with today's front page in the picture." Annette stared at her. Grace held out a hand for Annette to help her sit up.

218

"I'm sick of being a victim," Grace said quietly.
Annette hesitated. "What are you going to do?"
Grace's jaw tightened.
"I'm going to change the game."

NINETEEN

Friday afternoon.

As the light from the lowering sun turned watery and pale, Grace pushed herself to her feet. Wincing from her wound, she carefully positioned a straight-backed chair near the eastern end of the long window.

For an hour she sat very still, watching the street. Traffic was light. As each new vehicle turned in from the distant intersection, she stiffened. When she was sure it posed no threat, she settled back into watchful surveillance.

Just before darkness fell, she abandoned her observation post and walked through the house to the garage. Annette's old Volkswagen Beetle was parked facing the overhead door. Grace eased her body behind the wheel and turned the key. The old car's air-cooled engine caught immediately.

She drove south through Langley Township. The main route was 200th street, but it came to a dead-end a mile north of the American border. She swung east onto a side avenue and worked her way through a series of doglegs until she reached another dead-end.

Straight ahead lay dense bush. A sign marked a paved roadway that passed in front of her.

O Avenue

Zero Avenue was a narrow two-lane road that ran east-west along the U.S. border. In her headlights, Grace could see a barbed wire fence on the southern edge of the avenue's road allowance. The fence was overgrown by blackberry vines, with thick second-growth forest behind.

Grace knew this place. As a child, during summer visits with a great aunt in nearby Aldergrove, she had picked blackberries here. Beyond the trees, a thousand yards away, there was another paved road that ran parallel to this fence. That road was located a thousand yards inside the United States.

She turned and accelerated, driving east along Zero Avenue, measuring off kilometres on the odometer. At first, unbroken forest encroached on the roadway from the U.S. side. After a few kilometres, the trees and foliage began to thin out. She passed a vast bog, looking pre-Cambrian under an early evening mist, then dairy pastures, interspersed between sections of woodland.

For several kilometres, the roadway ran next to a shallow ditch. Beyond it, fields of hops stretched away into the purpling dusk.

The farmers on the American side had extended their cultivation right up to the border. There was no fence here – only an occasional cement obelisk, three feet high, marking the forty-ninth parallel of latitude – the longest undefended border in the world.

But farmers have dogs, Grace warned herself.

After a dozen kilometres, she arrived at the Aldergrove border crossing. Canadian and American border checkpoints had been constructed on the south side of Zero Avenue. A line of produce trucks was backed up on the Canadian side, waiting to pass through U.S. Customs.

Since the attacks in September, America's earlier relaxed attitude to northern border security had changed dramatically. Now, every vehicle passing into the United States was being searched, and its occupants carefully questioned.

To Grace, sitting in the nondescript Beetle, it seemed an odd contradiction that for the entire distance she had driven the most forbidding barrier between Canada and United States had been a few rusty strands of barbed wire.

Odd, but convenient.

Satisfied by her tour, she reversed direction and drove back to the house. She backed the Volkswagen into the garage and made her preparations.

She returned to her place by the window, willing the time to pass quickly.

Two a.m. Outside, nothing moved.

Grace retraced her earlier steps. The Beetle sat waiting. A ski suit and a heavy winter coat lay draped across a bench next to the car, where she'd left them. Felt-lined boots sat on the floor nearby. She put on the ski suit, then lowered herself onto the bench and tried to push her feet into the boots.

Too tight. She bent over to pull them on. Pain knifed through her. Perspiration beaded on her brow and upper lip. She sat up and remained motionless for a moment, waiting for the worst of the pain to subside. Finally, she stood up, opened the passenger door of the Beetle, and dumped the heavy coat on the seat. She walked around the car and slowly eased herself behind the steering wheel.

She waited for her knees to stop shaking, then she started the car and activated a remote control that was clipped to the sun visor. The overhead door rose. She drove out of the garage and pressed the button again. The door came down behind her.

It would take her at least twenty minutes to reach her destination. She drove at the speed limit; she couldn't risk attracting the attention of a curious cop. The bars had closed an hour ago. She prayed silently that the night shift at the local RCMP detachment was sitting in a warm office, yawning over coffee and paperwork.

She concentrated on her driving, watching her mirrors and her speedometer, as she retraced her earlier route to Zero Avenue.

Frigid air buffeted her cheeks. She'd left her side windows down so the vehicle interior would stay cold.

There was a heavy ground mist. She strained to read the street signs as they emerged from the bright halos created by her headlights.

After one missed turn, she reached Zero Avenue. She turned and drove east for two kilometres, then slowed, craning her neck. On the north side of the roadway, she spotted the entrance to a playground parking lot. She wheeled in and cut the engine. The car rolled to a stop against a makeshift cedar curb.

Swing sets, teeter-totters, and a monstrous Jungle Gym stood silently in the mist. Grace shut off the headlights, then sat very still while her eyes adjusted to the darkness. After a few moments, she got out of the car, pulling the winter coat behind her.

She stood in the darkness, studying her surroundings. Houses were widely spaced in this rural area, but she had to be certain she wasn't attracting attention. A slight breeze rustled through the upper branches of the nearby evergreens. Otherwise, all was quiet. She quietly clicked the car door shut.

Slowly and deliberately, she pulled on a pair of diver's gloves. Then she struggled into the heavy coat. As she walked across Zero Avenue and turned west along the southern shoulder of the road allowance, she was very frightened. If her plan didn't work, she'd be sitting in an American jail within an hour.

She reached the spot she had mentally marked. For a few yards, the barbed wire fence was lying on its side. She pulled up the hood of her coat and then yanked the wooden toggles to tighten it around her head. She extracted a second pair of gloves from her coat pockets. Welder's gloves. They barely fit over the first pair. In a crazy thought, she was reminded of a televised courtroom scene – O.J. Simpson famously playing to the jury, hands aloft, black gloves half-on, half-off, a sleight-of-hand metaphor for a sleight-of-hand defence.

She didn't need to wear all this extra protection for climbing across the tangle of barbed wire looping up from the damaged fence. It wasn't the wire, or even the dense blackberry brambles, that worried her.

It was her body heat.

She'd piled on all the insulation she could find. Only her face was exposed. She hadn't been able to devise anything sensible to cover it.

I'm probably a damned idiot!

She shrugged and accepted her fate. She clambered through the break in the fence and disappeared into the woods.

3:25 a.m. The road on the U.S. side was about twenty feet ahead. Grace calculated that she was about ten miles northwest of Lynden, Washington, the nearest U.S. community. She would have to cover that distance before dawn, and she would have to be careful. This was farm country. The local residents would know each other. A strange woman walking alone on a rural highway, so close to the border, at this hour, might attract curious attention. And if some kindly country motorist offered her a ride, she'd be even worse off. She knew nothing about the area and didn't know a soul who lived there. She would be hard-pressed to offer a quick and believable answer to even the most innocent question.

She knew she had to complete the journey before first light. But now, facing the prospect of hiking along the roadway for three hours or more, in the dead of night, she was unnerved. Any patrolling Sheriff's Deputy or Border Patrol officer would be certain to stop her and ask questions.

Whatever she did, she had to get away from her present location. The Border Patrol might already be heading this way. She had no idea whether the Americans had actually installed remote infrared sensors along this stretch of the border, as they'd claimed in news reports. Those stories could have been true, or they could have been propaganda to deter terrorists or Asian 'snakeheads' whose wholesale smuggling of illegal Chinese immigrants had become such a problem in recent years. She didn't know.

She crouched among the trees, only yards from the graded shoulder of the deserted rural highway, pulled off the gloves and boots, shrugged off the heavy coat, and struggled out of the ski clothes. She retrieved a baseball cap and a pair of Nikes from the deep pockets of the coat and put them on. She hid the discarded clothing under some brush. She was ready.

She set out toward the east, inside the tree line, staying parallel to the road.

After several hundred yards, the ground cover thickened, then became impassable. She edged to the right. A mesh-wire fence separated her from the road allowance. She searched for a break in the wire, but couldn't find one. She'd have to climb over. She got a toehold next to a wooden post and then, clenching her teeth, began to climb. As she lowered herself down the other side, one of her feet slipped. She clutched at the post.

Pain seared through her side.

Gasping, she resumed her journey eastward.

There was no hint of dawn on the horizon ahead. Puffs of light breeze occasionally disturbed the deep stillness of the night. The farmhouses she passed were set deep in their properties, well back from the road. In the rising mist, halogen yard lights cast cones of incandescence onto the dew-laden ground below.

Only two cars passed. She detected the first one in time to duck into the woods before it got too close. But the next vehicle scared her badly. It came from behind, moving slowly. In those moments, the breeze was rattling dying leaves in a grove of vine maples next to the road, covering the sound of approaching tires.

Just in time, Grace sensed her danger. She stumbled for cover.

The car idled past. There was a light bar on its roof, and six-inch-high printing on the driver's door.

Whatcom County Sheriff

Nauseous with fear, Grace waited fifteen minutes before setting out again.

At last she reached a T-intersection with a flashing amber light. The name of the north-south intersecting street was inscribed on a sign hanging high above the roadway.

Guide Meridian Road   Lynden 2.

An arrow pointed south. She turned right and followed the signs.

At six thirty in the morning, Grace passed a large cemetery and then found herself in the parking lot of an L-shaped strip mall.

Her side was on fire, and she was exhausted. But she was clear of the border. She stopped in a bus stop shelter to rest and think. She needed some US cash. But someone might be tracking her credit card.

Do they know about my new card?

She huddled on the bench, assailed by indecision.

The shopping centre had been quiet when she arrived. Soon there were signs of activity. A few men, unshaven and clad in thick flannel shirts, parked mud-spattered pickups in front of a 24-hour convenience store. They pushed through the doors and came out carrying paper bags and cups of coffee.

She knew there was a good chance she'd find an ATM inside that store. She started walking.

When she was halfway across the parking lot, she spotted a Savings-and-Loan sign at the far end of the mall, past the convenience store. She changed direction.

Approaching, she saw a cash machine built into the wall of the front lobby. She stopped, uncertain.

The store or the bank?

At that moment, diagonally across from her on the next leg of the complex, an older woman in a waitress's uniform emerged from the front door of a small café. She was carrying a large chalked blackboard. She propped it against the front of the building.

BREAKFAST SPECIALS

Grace made an instant decision. She pulled the credit card from the pocket of her jeans, and pushed it into the slot next to the bank's front door. The lock clicked open and she entered the small lobby.

There were two hurdles. First, the machine. Then, if she was unlucky, the police. There was no protest from the ATM. Grace followed the prompts on the small screen. The slot opened and five hundred dollars in twenties rolled out. She shoved the money into her pocket, followed by the printed transaction slip, and then, forcing herself to breathe slowly, she exited the bank and strolled across to the cafe for the next stage of the experiment.

Grace took the booth closest to the entrance to the kitchen. She still had a clear view of the bank, and a handy rear exit from the restaurant. The waitress brought coffee and a menu. While she waited for her breakfast, she hunched in a corner of the booth, giddy with fear, clutching her coffee mug in both hands.

Her eyes were glued to the front of the bank.

She fully expected to see two or three police cruisers screeching to a halt out front, and officers fanning out in a search pattern.

Nothing happened. Relieved, Grace ate her breakfast in peace.

After paying for her meal, she left the café and found a phone booth. She checked the yellow pages. A County bus service to Bellingham, fifteen miles further south, connected to the Seattle-Tacoma Airport shuttle. Grace dialled the number.

PART II
FLORIDA
OCTOBER 13 – NOVEMBER 5

TWENTY

Grace sat in the huge main terminal hall at SeaTac Airport, trying to collect her thoughts. She was still vulnerable. Canadian and U.S. police had always cooperated, but since September eleventh, according to accounts she had read, the two countries' law enforcement agencies had agreed to link their computer databases more closely than ever before. Canadian police had already arrested several suspects who were wanted for questioning by the FBI. The Americans would be only too ready to return the favour. The only identification Grace had was in her own name. She'd be at risk as soon as she stepped up to a counter.

She ran through a checklist in her mind: air ticket to Atlanta (they'll want to see photo identification, even for a domestic flight – sorry, ma'am, Federal regulations); luggage (she had none); clothes and toiletries (putting an empty carry-on bag through the checkpoint x-ray machine would obviously attract suspicion).

She shifted in her seat, trying to find a more comfortable position. The pain in her side had eased a bit since she'd swallowed several of the codeine pills, but it still nagged and the pills had upset her stomach.

If this wound gets infected, I'm in real trouble.

Hospital emergency staff might treat her, but somewhere out of earshot one of them would be calling the police.

She mapped out her moves, then got up and strolled toward a currency exchange booth. In addition to the U.S. cash from the ATM in Lynden, she still had over three hundred dollars in Canadian currency that she'd lifted from Cameron Pomeroy's wallet. She felt a pang of guilt about that.

The exchange counter was a glassed-in booth in the middle of the terminal. She pushed the Canadian currency through the slot and requested U.S. dollars. When a printed transaction form was presented to her, she scribbled a made-up signature.

230

The bored attendant passed her the proceeds, then leaned into his microphone, offered a robotic thank you, and called for the next customer.

She wandered down a row of gift shops. She bought a wheeled carry-on bag. In an overpriced boutique next door, she picked out a couple of tee shirts, a sweatshirt, and two pairs of stretch pants. After supplementing her purchases with a hairbrush and a few toiletries, she slipped into a ladies room to clean up, change clothes, and pack her bag.

In a cubicle, she checked the dressing on her ribs. It was oozing through a little, but it looked as if it would last for a few more hours.

It would have to. She only had one clean bandage left.

A few minutes later, freshly decked out and pulling the carry-on behind her, she headed for the American Airlines ticket counter.

This was the worst moment. Grace had already used a pay phone to check on flight availability, so she knew that American's 2:15 to Dallas, where she could connect to flights going further east, had lots of space. The main problem was that even though she was paying cash, she would be asked for identification. It had been airline policy before September eleventh; since then, it had become an obsession.

Worse, her name would be entered into the airline computer system.

Grace's stomach tightened at the thought of an unwanted welcoming party at the arrival gate in Dallas. She waited her turn in front of the sales counter. Finally, a short, middle-aged woman with big hair and lacquered nails beckoned her over.

"I'd like a seat on your 2:15 flight to Dallas. When I phoned earlier I was told there were still seats available, and that I could connect to Atlanta."

"You made reservations?" The agent's long nails began tapping on her computer keyboard.

"No, actually I didn't. When I phoned, I wasn't sure that I'd be travelling. I'm hoping that you still have space available."

"Okay. Let's have a look." Tap, tap, tap. Pause. More

tapping. The woman squinted at the screen.

"Yes, ma'am. I can put you on that flight. It departs at 2:15, arriving in Dallas at 7:59. You'll have just enough time to connect to-" she knitted her brows, peering "-flight 1954, departing Dallas at 8:48. That would put you into Atlanta at 11:53 local time." She looked up. "When would you want to return?"

Grace only needed a one-way ticket, but she hesitated for a second.

Will that sound odd, a one-way to Atlanta?

"I should have mentioned – I only need a one-way ticket. I'm picking up a car and driving back."

"Certainly, ma'am." She smiled, revealing capped incisors. "Long drive." There was another short pause while she scrolled down her screen. "With our business down quite a bit lately-" she grimaced and looked at Grace with sad eyes "-we've been authorised to offer some pretty good deals. But with a last minute booking, and this being a one-way ticket, I don't have a lot of leeway. I suggest you buy a round-trip ticket. Even though you're not using the return portion, it will work out cheaper. I can give you that for five twenty-four. Actually, that's the economy fare for bookings seven days ahead, but both these flights are less than half full, so I can overlook that."

"That would be fine. Thank you."

"I'll just make the return date for seven days from now. Name please?"

"Arlene Palliser." Grace spelled out her surname.

Grace, you're a fool if you think your middle name is going to fool anyone.

She waited while the ticket agent completed the transaction. Her nerve endings were vibrating. She felt conspicuous. She looked up at the clock on the wall.

"I see it's twenty to two. Is it very far to the gate?"

"No, ma'am. You'll be fine."

A minute later, as her boarding passes were coming out of the clacking printer, a voice erupted from a loudspeaker overhead.

The opening words momentarily quelled the background din of the huge hall.

"Attention please! Attention please! A security breach occurred just before ten o'clock this morning at the North Satellite Checkpoint. The FAA has directed the Airport to re-screen all passengers for flights from the airport. As a result of this process, there may be increased congestion. Please check with your airlines for the status of outbound flights, or check the overhead monitors. Thank you for your patience."

"Any bags to check?" the agent asked.

Grace leaned on the counter. "What was that about?"

"No worries. They've been playing that recording since this morning. We had some delays with earlier flights, but you should be fine. Luggage?"

"No, just my carry-on here." The agent leaned sideways and looked through the gap created by the baggage weigh scale. "I checked it in one of those measuring frames," Grace volunteered. "It fits."

The woman nodded as she tore off extra copies of the ticket and slid them into a waste slot in the counter below her keyboard.

"Make sure you get rid of any scissors or sharp objects so you don't get held up at security. I hear they're even confiscating nail clippers."

"I suppose they're pretty paranoid these days," Grace said, as she counted out the fare in cash.

"Yes. And that reminds me. I'll need to see some photo ID, ma'am. I should have asked you earlier."

The dreaded question.

Grace made a show of looking at the clock. She squatted down, ignoring a stab of pain, and pretended to fumble with the zipper of her carry-on. She stood up and produced her Victoria Courthouse law library card from her back pocket.

"My purse is buried inside my bag. Will this do?" The card bore Grace's full name, a head-and-shoulders photograph and the name and address of Pomeroy & Associates, but place and date of birth were absent. Grace's pulse was racing; it was an unusual card to produce. She knew the agent was expecting to see a driver's license, or maybe a passport.

What do people do who don't have either?

"As long as it's government-issued…"

"Oh, it is."

The woman took the card and studied it, then looked up at Grace, comparing her with the picture. Then she focused back on the card.

Here it comes…

The agent's face lit up.

"You're a lawyer from Victoria!"

Grace was momentarily startled. Then she saw her chance.

"Yes, I am."

"My husband's an attorney. We spent a wonderful week in Victoria last year. He was attending a conference at the Empress." She handed back the card. "What a fantastic hotel! And your city! The harbour! And those Butchart Gardens! I've never seen so many beautiful flowers in one place!"

As the ticket agent prattled on about horse-drawn carriages and double-decker buses, Grace mustered her happiest smile and chatted along. After a polite interlude of nodding and agreeing, she made a point of glancing again at the clock.

"Thank you so much for all your help. I guess I'd better get moving so I don't miss the plane."

"Right. Here you go." She handed her the ticket and boarding pass. "Gate C16." She smiled cheerily, showing more capped teeth. "Enjoy your flight!"

There was a queue at the security checkpoint. A Hispanic-looking man in a security company uniform was comparing identification documents with boarding passes. Against the wall behind him, two uniformed police officers and a huge man wearing a U.S. Marshall sweater watched on with gimlet eyes. When Grace's turn came, she was sick with fear.

The security man made a perfunctory comparison of her boarding pass and her library card. He looked at the photo and then looked at her. Grace held his eyes. He thanked her and waved her on. She moved forward a few paces and lifted her bag onto the x-ray conveyor, trying not to wince from the pain in her side.

A minute later, she was walking briskly along the departure concourse. Her luck was holding.

But the ticket agent would remember her.

One day, some FBI agent would show the woman a photograph. "Yes," she'd say, "that's that lady lawyer from Victoria. Now that you mention it, she used a library card for ID."

Grace had to get to a safe place before *At Large* broadcasted her face to millions of TV screens.

She found her gate. A few dozen people were scattered through the seats, most of them reading. There was a row of pay phones against the wall on the opposite side of the concourse. None were in use. Grace rolled her bag to the last one in the row and sat on the hard plastic seat. She pulled the telephone book out of its slot and leafed through the advertising in the front until she found the map page that showed area codes. Then she dialled 4-1-1 and waded through a computer voice menu until she was speaking to a live operator.

"Directory assistance for toll free numbers, please." She finally obtained a number and dialled it. After a short conversation, she hung up.

That was done. Now for the difficult call.

She didn't have coins and she didn't want to risk using the credit card. She picked up the receiver again, gritted her teeth, and followed the instructions for a collect call. She punched in the numbers from memory.

"Operator."

"Person-to-person collect, please. To Mr. Myles Rothwell. My name is Grace."

"Yes, ma'am. Thank you." There were a few clicks, the rapid sound of automatic dialling, and then she heard a phone ringing, far away. She visualised the phone. She visualised a familiar kitchen. The phone kept ringing. Grace had a sudden thought.

He's in the Reserves. Maybe he's been called up...

Then she heard an easy southern voice. His voice.

"Hello?"

"This is the A T and T operator. This is a call for Myles Rothwell."

"Speaking."

"I have a collect call from Grace in Washington State. Will you accept the charge?" Silence. Grace could hear crackling on the line. The operator repeated her question. "Will you accept the charge, sir?" A sigh. The scraping of a chair.

"Yes, all right, operator."

"Thank you. Go ahead please."

"Hi. It's me."

"I know."

"I'm sorry I had to call collect. I can explain."

"It's okay. Washington State?"

"It's a long story."

"Oh. Okay." He obviously wasn't too interested in hearing it.

"When it kept ringing, and the answering machine didn't cut in, I wondered for a second. You know, the nine-eleven thing... and you in the National Guard..." Her voice failed. She trailed off.

"It's a young man's war. Anyway, I'm retired. I'm on the reserve list." He clipped his words. He had the upper hand and he knew it. More silence. More background static.

"Will you talk to me?"

"I'll listen."

"I owe you an apology."

"Yes, you do."

"More than an apology. More than that."

"Yes."

"It's long overdue."

"Yes, it is."

"I'm sorry, Myles. I'm so very sorry." He didn't say anything. He wasn't making it easy.

"Is it too late?" she asked weakly.

"This is a tough thing to fix," he said quietly.

"Myles, I love you. And right now, I really need you. Could you-?"

"Grace, it's been months."

She felt like she'd been knifed.

Stupid! Stupid! Grace, how could you be so stupid?

She had to get off the phone.

"All right. I'm sorry. I was an idiot to call." She tried to hang up but, agitated and fumbling, she dropped the handset. It bounced off the metal tray below the telephone and banged against the Plexiglas side panel of the booth. She grabbed at it. She was an inch from hanging it up when she heard his voice, small and tinny.

"Grace! Grace! Just a minute! Hang on!" She put the phone back to her ear.

"I'm here."

He was quiet for a moment. When he spoke, she heard the pain in his voice.

"I still feel the same way about you, Grace. I try to hang on to the good memories… the way you made me feel. But no matter what my feelings are for you, I can't have that kind of trouble in my life. Not now. Not ever. I've made too many mistakes in the past. I made those mistakes knowing they were mistakes. I won't let myself do that again. It isn't just me – I have to think about Lisa. And you have to think about Shy. Neither of these kids deserves to have constant turmoil in their lives. And I just think-"

"I lost her, Myles! At least, almost. Brent got interim custody. I've just got her back, temporarily, but unless I am very smart and very careful, he'll have her permanently."

"Grace!" He sounded stricken. "How could that happen?"

"It would take a long time to explain and I can't do it on a long distance call. Believe it or not, that's not the worst thing that's happened." She looked down at her free hand. It was shaking. She sat on it. She tried to delay the inevitable question by changing the subject slightly. "How is she? Lisa?"

237

"Fine. Healthy and happy." His tone filled with affection. "She's visiting with her cousins in Fort Myers right now, but usually she's here on weekends. We do a lot of riding. She asked about you a few times. I told her we were taking a break."

"Long break."

"She knows you live far away. I'm sure her instincts tell her there's more to the story, but she hasn't said anything." He continued before she could reply. "What did you mean when you said 'that's not the worst thing that's happened'?"

I have to tell him. Oh God!

She had to hold herself together.

"Myles, I... I-" Her lips quivered. She couldn't do it. Her voice broke and she let out a sob.

"Grace! What is it?" She didn't answer. She stifled a cry in her throat. Her eyes blurred. Panicking, she wiped them and looked frantically around to see if anyone was watching.

Passengers strolled past, oblivious to her distress.

"Grace, if this is another episode with the drugs, I'm sorry, but I'll have to hang up!" His tone had sharpened; he was preparing himself for disappointment.

"No! No!" she choked out. "I got rid of it, Myles. After Gainesville. It's out of my life."

It's only a little lie. I promise I'll tell him the truth if...

She paused, and took a deep breath. As she let the air out, her voice shook. "I'm in trouble, Myles. A lot of trouble! I have nowhere else to turn."

"What kind of trouble?" There was a loud beep from the loudspeaker above Grace's head. A female voice started rambling through a pre-boarding announcement.

"The worst kind. The kind that can't be explained on a telephone, especially since I'm sitting out in the open here."

"Are you in an airport?"

"I am. Sea-Tac. And that was my flight, so I've only got a few more minutes. Listen..."

Do it!

238

"Listen, Myles. I'm not asking you to trust me. I'm going to trust you instead. I'm going to tell you where I'm going and where I'll be staying. Then I want you to hang up and get on your computer. Log on to the Internet and find the website for the Victoria *Times Colonist*. It's a newspaper. Do an archive search. My name, Myles! Search my name! Then call me tomorrow night and tell me if you'll help me."

"The *Colonist*?"

"Yes." Grace told him where she was going.

"You're kidding."

"No, Myles, I'm not. And... Myles?

"Yes?"

"You'll read some things that will shock you. I mean, really bad things! You're going to realise how much trust I'm putting in you. You know where I'll be tomorrow night, so one word from you could end my life. I'm only asking one thing: before you do anything that we'll both regret, just spend some time thinking about what you know about me, about the person I am. Because I'm swearing to you, right now – I didn't do those things!"

Myles didn't respond immediately. She waited. She could hear him breathing. Thinking.

"Okay, Grace," he said finally, "I'll call you at the Marguerite."

Grace hung up the phone. She was calm now. By some miracle of psychiatric survival, her mind had emerged from emotional chaos into a kind of numinous clarity, like early morning after a rain.

She walked across the concourse and joined the line of passengers waiting to board the plane.

Grace took a deep breath and lifted her bag into the overhead bin. She thanked God that it wasn't too heavy. As she gingerly lowered herself into the narrow seat next to the window, her entire body was shaking. She hadn't slept in over thirty hours. She was dangerously exhausted, and she knew this long day was far from over. She needed to rest while she could, and then be alert and ready for trouble when the plane touched down in Dallas.

After what seemed an interminable wait, the plane pushed back from the airbridge. Grace had been dozing; the lurch of the aircraft startled her back to wakefulness. She was relieved to find that the seat next to her was still empty.

As soon as they were airborne, Grace reclined her seat, closed her eyes, and prayed for sleep.

And for a few hours, she found it.

The landing announcement woke her up. A headache pounded behind her eyes. She straightened her seatback and pressed her forehead against the coolness of the small window next to her.

As the 757 banked onto its final approach, memories lurked in the blackness beyond the aircraft's pulsating navigation lights.

Last spring, she and Myles had met in New Orleans for the start of a three-week vacation together. They'd driven the back roads of the lower Mississippi, paddled meandering tree-shaded watercourses in the bayous, spent evenings hand-in-hand on the sidewalks of the French Quarter, and made love for hours in the huge four-poster in their room at the Hotel de Marguerite. Then he had taken her home to Florida to meet his daughter Lisa.

Replayed in her mind, the disastrous finale to their Deep South idyll seemed like a home video of someone else's sordid and dysfunctional life.

TWENTY-ONE

Myles Rothwell was ex-Navy, ex-ATF, ex-assistant district attorney, and ex-husband. That was the past. These days, he was full-time defence attorney, running a small firm in Live Oak, Florida, and part-time Dad to a nine-year-old daughter who spent most weekends with him, riding horses in the backcountry of Suwannee County.

A year ago, in Victoria, Canada, Andre Devereaux had defended a man named William Pollard, one of four gunmen charged with the robbery of an armoured car. The evidence was strong, and Andre's best efforts had not been enough to save Pollard from conviction. At the sentencing hearing, the prosecutors revealed for the first time their belief that William Pollard, supposedly a Canadian citizen with no prior criminal history, was in fact Orville Pryce, a convicted American felon who had escaped from U.S. federal custody several years earlier. They said he had been convicted in the early 80's for planting a bomb outside a police station in Salem, Oregon. In that incident, although no one had died, three police officers had been maimed for life. It was alleged that Pryce had been living in Canada for years, using near-perfect forgeries of Canadian identification papers in the name of William Pollard.

Because of all this, Myles Rothwell had received an all-expense-paid trip from Florida to the Burdett Street courthouse in Victoria. At the time of the Salem bombing, he had been Agent-in-Charge at the Bureau of Alcohol, Tobacco, and Firearms offices in Portland, Oregon. His agents had arrested Pryce.

Myles had dealt with the man personally on several occasions before he escaped from a prison van and disappeared over the northern border. One such occasion had been just after the arrest, when Myles had rolled Pryce's fingerprints. This routine procedure had led to the oddly ironic spectacle of an American defence attorney appearing as

241

a prosecution witness at a Canadian sentencing hearing.

Myles had taken the stand in what was expected to be a brief court appearance. The courtroom was unnaturally quiet; its regular denizens – usually given to a level of informality that comes from long familiarity – seemed to be on their best behaviour as this foreign ex-lawman appeared in their midst. Just over six feet tall, with wavy salt and pepper hair, grey eyes and a healthy-looking tan, Myles Rothwell had the can-do bearing of a military man. But Grace, hunched over a notepad in her usual spot behind Andre, noticed something else about the handsome American. As she listened to him testify she couldn't quite put her finger on it. A twinkle of humour, a certain welcoming warmth in the margins, a touch of the rebel, maybe – she wasn't sure, but the qualities she detected seemed very much against-type. She'd straightened up in her seat.

After working his way through the background preliminaries, Myles had made a positive identification of the prisoner. Then he'd proceeded to link Pollard directly to the original ATF fingerprint form lying on the witness box railing in front of him. The form bore a complete set of finger and palm prints, as well as Myles Rothwell's signature and that of the suspect – the latter a scrawl, barely legible as 'O. Pryce'. The document was then marked as an exhibit.

Andre Devereaux rose to cross-examine. Although he knew that the next scheduled witness was a fingerprint expert who would testify that the prints of 'William Pollard' exactly matched the prints Myles had taken from the American felon Orville Pryce, Andre had been somewhat bemused by this southern lawyer with the easy drawl. Motivated more by mischief and curiosity than by forensic insight, he had launched into a robust cross-examination that extensively questioned Myles' memory and, more obliquely, questioned the authenticity of the exhibit document. After a moment of visible surprise at being challenged over this simple administrative matter, Myles had handled himself with quiet, and occasionally devastating, intelligence.

Within a short time, everyone in the courtroom was

laughing. Not at Myles... At Andre.

Everyone, that is, except Orville Pryce.

Smiling, Andre had saluted his adversary and returned to his seat, a gentleman accepting defeat.

Establishing Pryce's true identity had tied up a loose end and sealed the man's fate. Although sentenced to serve twelve years for the robbery in Canada, he was soon transferred to the United States under a prisoner repatriation agreement. The Canadian Justice Department knew Pryce wouldn't make parole as easily in the United States as he would in Canada.

Sitting in the first row of the gallery while Myles testified about Andre's client, Grace had felt herself strongly attracted to this fascinating Southerner with the seductive drawl. After court, she had done something she'd never done before. Eavesdropping, she'd discovered he was staying at the Empress. (*Of course!* she'd thought. *Americans were suckers for the Victorian-era charm of that old monstrosity.*) That evening, she'd managed to accidentally bump into Myles in the Library Bar, a cosy meeting place for businessmen that was tucked away in a far corner of the cavernous main lobby, away from the constant traffic past the front desk. Conveniently, Myles had been sitting alone, nursing a glass of bourbon and thumbing through a newspaper.

Grace may have been flustered at her own boldness, but Myles Rothwell had seemed amused by it. He'd ordered her a drink. His words and gestures gave no hint that he thought she was physically attractive, but his eyes told a different story. For the first time in a very long time, a man's company had given Grace butterflies in her stomach.

After an hour of comfortable conversation next to the fireplace, Myles had borrowed Grace's cell phone to cancel a dinner engagement with the chief prosecutor, put on his coat, and offered Grace his arm. They had strolled down Wharf Street until they found a seafood bistro. Over a two-hour dinner, she'd learned he was a fifth generation Floridian who had inherited his surname from Lancashire forefathers. He said he was divorced, with shared custody of his daughter, and lived on fifty acres near the Florida Panhandle. He was intelligent and considerate. He looked right at her when she spoke, his expression open and unaccountably magnetic. He had a wealth of eye-popping stories from his years in law enforcement (all true, he swore), and he'd had Grace laughing until there were tears in her eyes. Laughing more than she had in years. Grace wasn't sure if he was telling the truth about the important things – divorced, unattached – but she wasn't sure she cared. After the meal, he had borrowed her phone again, this time to change his airline flights.

Golden nights and silver mornings had followed.

Grace had expected the affair to end when she dropped him at the airport five days later. But it hadn't. Eventually, she'd learned that Myles Rothwell was a man of his word. Everything he had told her was true.

Including the part about calling her soon.

They had been together four times since then. Though separated by citizenship, geography, career paths, and family ties (five year old Shy in British Columbia; nine year old Lisa in Florida), their bond had grown very strong, very quickly.

In the end, overtaken by events, Shy never got the chance to meet Myles or Lisa. The natural progress of the relationship had foundered when Myles discovered that Grace had another love.

Prescription drugs.

Apart from Andre, no one in Victoria had known about Myles. No one at the office, none of her few friends, and certainly not Shy. At the beginning, Grace had decided to keep it that way so that Brent wouldn't try to use her affair with the American to make trouble. He would have found a way; his self-righteousness was all consuming.

Later, she'd kept silent out of shame.

After a long ride along the river, Myles Rothwell removed Dr. Pepper's saddle and bridle and sent him trotting happily off to join his pals in the north pasture. He mounted the steps to the house and went inside for a shower. For fifteen minutes, he stood motionless under the jets of water. After he'd towelled off, he pulled on his favourite jeans and an old tee shirt, poured a glass of orange juice, and padded barefoot down to the back bedroom. He sat at the computer and clicked onto the newspaper's website. For the third time in as many hours, he retraced his steps through the archive search.

He reread every article and every police news release.

He closed the program and sat back, staring at the ceiling.

After a while, he got up and went to his bedroom. He pulled a duffel bag off the shelf in the closet, packed a few clothes and his shaving kit, and then locked the house and climbed into his car. He drove north on Route 129. When he reached the junction with Interstate 10, he swung into the westbound entrance and put his foot down. The silver Audi sailed up the ramp and slid easily into the line of traffic.

As soon as he was settled in a safe slot on the inside lane, Myles locked in the cruise control and used his car phone to track down Pete Wetherall. Pete was sitting by his pool, drinking beer with his girlfriend and her sister.

Myles asked him to cover for him in court on Monday.

"Maybe Tuesday as well, Petey. I'll have to call you."

"What's up, buddy? You all right?"

"Yeah, fine. I've got a little problem to deal with. Ask Janice for the files. She'll explain where we are on them. Hell, she knows more about my cases than I do! Call you tomorrow night, pal. Okay?"

"Sure. *No problemo.* Be safe!"

Pete didn't ask questions. He was a good friend. Good thing too, Myles thought, as he disconnected. I have no idea what I would say.

Just before five o'clock on Sunday afternoon, an air-conditioned Trailways coach pulled into Union Passenger Terminal on Loyola Avenue in New Orleans. Grace stepped down into the soft Gulf Coast humidity. She took a cab to Jackson Square, in the French Quarter, paid the fare, bought some hydrogen peroxide in a drug store, and then walked two blocks to the Hotel de Marguerite. The desk clerk flipped through a card index and found her reservation. When she'd called from the departure lounge at Sea-Tac, she'd requested a specific room. It had been held for her. Grace paid cash for a two-night stay.

Room 104 was small and dark, but it opened onto a tiled courtyard and gardens. Birds chirped and darted among the flowering vines that trailed from the balconies above.

The familiar sounds and scents would have enthralled most tourists, but they filled Grace with pain.

She closed the door to her room, unpacked her meagre belongings from her bag and stripped off her clothes. Sitting on the toilet in the bathroom, she carefully removed each strip of tape from her rib cage and eased the large wad of gauze away from her skin. She stood sideways in front of the mirror and pulled her breast aside so that the light fell directly on her wound. It was seeping blood.

It looked angry but, she concluded, it wasn't infected. Yet.

It took her a half hour with hydrogen peroxide, wads of tissue from the counter dispenser, and her last pressure bandage to re-dress the wound.

She desperately wanted to take a shower, but without more bandages, that would have to wait. She didn't want to leave the room in case she missed a call from Myles.

Dusk settled on the courtyard outside. Grace's nervousness increased with each passing hour. She needed Myles' arms around her – if only to help her regain some emotional strength. Desperation was a creeping menace and, with the phone silent, it took Grace by the throat. She felt herself retreating into a bleak inner landscape. She recognised the feeling. It was a familiar visitor from the past.

There was a vinyl-covered binder sitting on the small writing desk next to the window. Grace knew there was a liquor menu under the Room Service tab. After staring at the book for hours, with the phone still silent, she flipped it open and dialled the room service number. A man with a Spanish accent answered. She ordered a bottle of scotch and a bucket of ice.

"Deed jo say 'a bottle', Mees?"

"Yes! *Si!* A bottle!"

"Hokay... Comin' soon!" The man sounded amused.

She put down the phone and sat back on the bed. She told herself that the scotch would help dull the throbbing pain from her wound, but it was an afterthought excuse and it did no good. Self-loathing seeped through her. She found extra pillows in the closet and piled them up at the top of the bed. Pushing her back against them, she drew up her knees and waited for room service to deliver the poison.

At twelve-thirty, the telephone at the bedside rang. Grace was startled from a fitful, half-drunken doze. The TV was on, filling the small room with canned laughter from some recycled 80's sitcom. She couldn't remember where she was. The telephone kept ringing. Six times, seven times... The caller was persistent. Finally, cautiously, Grace picked up the receiver. She held it to her ear, saying nothing, teetering on the edge of the bed.

"Grace?" In the distance, a familiar voice.

"Who is it?" Her tongue was thick, her head swimming.

"Grace, it's Myles. Are you all right? What's the matter?"

It took a few seconds to register.

"Myles?" She had to concentrate to make her lips form words. The skin on one side of her face burned with pins and needles. Her eyes blurred. She was going to start crying. "Just a minute, just a minute! Don't go away!"

Grace dropped the receiver on the bed and stumbled to the bathroom. She twisted the antique tap. It squeaked in protest but finally surrendered. She cupped her hands and dashed cold water in her face. She stayed over the sink, deciding whether to retch. No, the nausea was controllable. For now. She made her way back to the bed and picked up the phone.

"Where are you?"

"Near Biloxi. Is everything all right? What's your room number?"

247

"Yes. Uh, Room 104. The same room. Our room." She tried to speak carefully in case he noticed a slur. As if he wouldn't know soon enough. "You're coming here?"

"I'll be there by two. I want the whole story. Order me something from room service. I'm starving. And Grace-"

"Yes?"

"I haven't called anyone."

She listened to his breathing.

"Thank you," she said simply. She hung up the phone and fell back onto the pillows. She lay there motionless for a very long time.

Finally, she pulled herself together enough to call her Spanish friend at room service. She ordered a pot of coffee, to be delivered right away, and a clubhouse sandwich and a Corona, to be delivered at two o'clock.

Grace returned to the bathroom and knelt in front of the toilet. She shoved two fingers down her throat. Her stomach heaved and heaved again. She retched until the room was swimming and her head was pounding. Pain screamed through her side. If there had been sutures in her wound, the convulsions would have torn them out.

She retched and swore and retched and wept.

Finally, she struggled to her feet, rinsed her mouth and threw more cold water on her face. She looked at herself in the mirror and wished she hadn't. She carefully removed her tee shirt and then filled the ice bucket with warm water. She knelt over the tub and poured the water over her head.

She towel-dried her hair and brushed it as best she could and then went back to the bed and curled up against the pillows.

She knew she had no right to ask this good man for help. And she knew she didn't deserve the loyalty he had just demonstrated by driving through the night to see her. But then, Grace Palliser was quite experienced at feeling unworthy.

When Myles arrived at Room 104, Grace was dozing. Fortunately, the television volume was turned low, so his tapping roused her. She lurched off the bed, checked through the peephole, and then pulled the door open. Myles filled the doorway, a small duffel bag slung on one shoulder. He stepped in without a word. Grace stood there uncertainly, studying his face. What she saw was enough. She leaned into his chest. She felt his heart pounding, heavy and fast.

They stood frozen in the doorway.

Finally Myles lowered his bag to the floor, pushed the door shut, and slowly enfolded Grace in his arms. He pressed his face into her hair, still damp from her rejuvenation efforts.

The male scent from Myles' shirt opened a floodgate. For a few seconds, memories washed against the impervious reality of Grace's life in the present. Then they ebbed away. Defeated by exhaustion and the stress on her injury, Grace's knees buckled. Myles caught her. He lifted her effortlessly from the floor and carried her to the bed. Her side hurt, but she hid the pain. He lay her down against the pillows and sat on the edge of the bed at her side. Grace drew a rasping breath and lay silent. She felt a tear rolling down her cheek.

Myles watched her with sad eyes, then picked up the drinking glass from the nightstand and held it to his nose. He glanced around the room. Grace followed his gaze to the writing desk, where an unopened beer sat next to a room service tray covered with a linen napkin. He leaned forward and peered into the wastebasket next to the bed. Then he turned back to Grace, one eyebrow raised in a gentle question.

"I poured it out. The bottle's in the bathroom." He turned his body on the bed so he could face her squarely. "And what about-?"

Grace pressed two fingertips to his lips. "No, Myles. Not that. You can see that, can't you? Look at me. You can see that I'm clean." She felt her eyes begin to fill.

It was Myles' turn. He touched her lips with a finger and gave her a forlorn smile. It wasn't the easy, quirky smile that used to lift Grace's heart – at least, not completely – but the familiar outlines were there.

He leaned toward her. Grace put her good arm around his

neck. Holding on, her lips pressed to his ear, she whispered urgently. "I need you to know something, Myles. I was trying to say it. There was... there... was once. One time."

Myles drew back, but kept his head close to hers, watching her eyes. His expression was still open. And hopeful. Grace bit her lip.

"It was two weeks ago. When this nightmare started-" she struggled to sit up, to meet his eyes at the same level. Reacting to help her, Myles put his hands on each side of her torso and lifted.

Grace let out a scream. For an instant, her vision went black.

"Grace! What...?"

Grace was still gasping as her vision cleared. Myles was looking at his right hand. It was smeared with blood.

TWENTY-TWO

Friday.

Grace was sitting on the porch swing in the screened-in veranda. A sea of impossible green stretched away from the ranch house and disappeared into deep shadows under the moss-hung live oak and cypress trees lining the riverbank a half-mile to the west. The air was warm and soft and, apart from a few cumulus billows drifting overhead, the sky was clear.

After the events of the past two weeks, there was an eerie quality to the tranquillity of her present surroundings. Two weeks ago, wallowing in self-pity, anaesthetised by drugs and whiskey, she'd been oblivious to a tightening seine of events.

Two weeks ago, she'd begun her descent into chaos.

Has it only been two weeks?

Myles would be home soon. Grace had a batch of margaritas mixed and ready for him in the fridge. She wasn't drinking, but because in some visceral way she needed the companionship of the end-of-the-day reward ritual, she'd mixed herself a Virgin Mary.

She swirled the thick red liquid, listening to the clink of the ice against the glass. There were a few bottles of hard stuff in the dining room cupboard – no scotch, but she'd spotted a fifth of bourbon. She hadn't touched it.

She hadn't even been tempted. Not since New Orleans.

Myles had amazed her. He seemed to be handling this disaster better than she was. Not once had he spoken those words she'd expected – the almost ingrained reaction of the law enforcement veteran – the words that would have thrown her back into the world, alone and on the run: "I think you should turn yourself in. You have to trust the system. You know as well as I do that evidence of flight is evidence of guilt."

251

Not one word like that since he'd walked into the hotel room in New Orleans. Even though, by helping her, he risked his reputation, his livelihood, and probably his freedom.

On Tuesday night, as the tires of Myles' car had crunched to a stop in the gravel in front of his house, they'd both known that Grace's very existence would have to be a secret from his friends. Myles had been living alone since his divorce a few years ago. There would be awkward questions. For the most part, since their arrival back at his home, Grace had remained indoors. Myles had been careful to resume his normal workday routine: morning coffee with Pete Wetherall; lunch with his courthouse cronies; evening phone call to his daughter Lisa.

Because he didn't want Grace to have to answer his home telephone, Myles had made a stop yesterday on his way home from work. He'd bought her a cell phone and a handful of pre-paid airtime cards. They'd agreed that if she had to speak to him, she'd call his cell number. If he was in court, with his phone turned off, he'd see the missed call later.

The procedure wouldn't be much use to them in an emergency, but it would serve for the short term. Today, for the first time, Grace had actually managed to relax. She'd taped a plastic bag over her wound dressing and taken a shower. Then she'd watched an hour of scripted banter on some daytime talk show, and even skimmed through an issue of National Geographic. But mainly, she'd spent the day on Myles' computer. Looking at ads for weekly rentals.

The cell phone rang. Its penetrating warble shattered the quiet of the porch. Grace jumped involuntarily and her drink nearly capsized. She snatched up the phone from the seat next to her. Logic said that the caller could only be Myles, but the habit of fear, developed over the last two weeks, made her nervous and hesitant.

"Yes?" she answered carefully.

"It's me. I'll be home in five minutes." She closed her eyes in thanks.

Just after six, the silver Audi slid into view on the long

driveway. It disappeared behind a grove of trees, then reappeared, the late afternoon sun glinting on its windshield.

Grace rose and went inside to pour a margarita.

Sunset.

A red-tailed hawk circled above the tree line, watching for an evening meal. Myles and Grace were on the veranda swing. Grace had her good side nestled against Myles' arm and shoulder. Her long legs, bare and enticing, were tucked up beside her.

The hawk folded its wings and dropped. A moment later, it reappeared, a spectre flapping against the dark backdrop of trees. It climbed and flew south. A snake was writhing in its talons. Myles watched it until it disappeared.

He broke the silence, choosing his words carefully.

"We have a security problem."

"Security problem?" He felt her cheek press against his shoulder. "You make it sound like you're protecting an embassy."

"I have a lot of friends. Owning a few saddle horses adds to the attraction. I live a long way from town, but my friends sometimes drive out here unannounced. Pete especially. Sometimes he just comes out to try his luck in the river. Somebody's unscheduled visit could take us by surprise. And when I'm at work, just about anybody could catch you off guard – the power company guy reading the meter, somebody like that. You're going to need a bit of forewarning so you can duck into Lisa's bedroom." He got up. Grace swung her feet back to the porch deck. "I've got something to show you. Be right back."

Myles went to his car and returned with a plastic bag. It bore the logo of a national electronics chain. He dropped it on the seat next to her. "I picked this up today."

Grace opened the bag and extracted the contents. She scanned the printing on the packaging.

"An alarm system?"

"Motion detector. It has a remote sensor with a built-in transmitter. That box-" he pointed to the one in her hand "-is the receiver. We keep that here in the house. I'll mount the sensor on the gate down by the main road. The whole thing is battery-powered, both ends. Anybody who walks or drives through the gate sets off a warning up here at the house. A red light starts flashing and there's an audible warning. You just shut it off and then get out of sight."

"Myles..." She looked up at him, her eyes wide.

Myles' stomach tightened. *Those eyes!* Those damned eyes of hers had bewitched him from the beginning, when they'd sparkled like gemstones in the firelight in the little bar in the Empress Hotel. Then, her eyes had been filled with sensuality and nervous daring, exciting him. Now, on the opposite side of the continent, on his veranda, in the thickening dusk, they were a disconcerting blend of love, gratitude and alarm.

"Myles. This is so dangerous for you!"

"Yeah. Maybe. But you see, little lady," he said, deliberately adding more drawl to his drawl as he settled back onto the seat and put his arm around her, "I reckon we need to buy some time while we work out a few details. I've been reading a lot about suicide missions in the news lately." He smiled and gently squeezed her shoulder. "This one you're planning needs a bit of work."

"All I need is ID."

He looked at her. "Oh. Is that all?"

In the small hours of the previous Monday, after she'd shown him her bloodied side, Myles hadn't pressed her to talk. Of course, as he'd expected, she'd asked him the obvious questions. Had he read the news reports? Yes, he had. Did he believe she'd actually committed three murders? No, he didn't. He'd known, even as he scanned the reporter's accounts for the first time – shocked, disbelieving, almost physically sick – that this wasn't the Grace Palliser he knew. That conclusion was reinforced by the fact that Andre Devereaux was one of the victims. Myles hadn't missed the deep affection in Grace's voice when she'd talked about the courtly old lawyer.

No, he hadn't believed it. That's why he'd decided to drive to New Orleans. And after seeing the bloody bullet track gouged across her ribs, he was less inclined than ever to believe the reports. There'd been no mention in the news of Grace being shot at by the police.

Myles had repeated his reasoning to Grace. She'd wanted to start telling her story right away. To explain everything. To set his mind at ease. And her own. Tired as he was, he would have listened. But it was soon apparent that Grace's mental acuity, steeped in emotion and whiskey, and stressed by constant pain, might not be up to the challenge.

And the wound had needed attention. Myles had left to find some medical supplies. Grace had clung to his neck and made him swear to her that he'd come back. He'd located a twenty-four hour pharmacy. When he returned, he'd removed her old blood soaked dressing and smeared its replacement with Polysporin because that's all he could think of doing to stall an infection. The wound was going to leave a terrible scar.

He'd held her, stroking her hair, while she sobbed out a brief and mostly disjointed story about bank fraud, and custody battles, and whiskey and valium, and a police detective shot dead in her house, and murdered lawyers, and a midnight trip on a fishing boat, and gunfire in a wilderness park, and…

After ten minutes of rambling confusion, he wiped the tears from her soft cheeks, kissed her nose and told her it could wait until morning. She'd searched his face with her eyes, frantic for reassurance, and then, apparently satisfied, subsided into relieved silence.

Somehow, she'd seemed content just to hear in his voice the promise that he'd still be there in the morning.

So Myles sat on the edge of the bed, with Grace's legs across his lap, eating his sandwich and drinking warm beer with one hand, and holding Grace's hands with the other. In an earlier life, he and Grace had stayed together in this same hotel, in this same room, in this same bed. They'd made love. They had lain together, their bodies entwined, and talked for hours. They had made plans – rough outlines, it was true, but with the promise of permanence.

But that had been before he had found himself having to choose between the welfare of the woman he loved and the welfare of his daughter.

And so the heart had gone out of their relationship and one miserable day last spring, it had ended.

After finishing his meal, Myles stretched out on the bed beside her. She crawled awkwardly into his protection, her head on his chest. Within minutes, as he'd hoped, she was fast asleep. For a while, Myles had stared with unseeing eyes at the flickering television, where some giant reptile was terrorising a Japanese city. He'd tried to imagine the truth behind the horrific press reports he had read. Finally, he too had surrendered to exhaustion.

They passed the night in each other's arms. They awoke after nine to overcast skies. Tired and gritty from too much mental distress and too little sleep, Myles was sure that Grace would be hung over and in no condition to clear up the mystery of the murder charges and her gunshot injury. But, after a tentative kiss on his neck, she pushed herself to her feet before he could react and headed for the bathroom. He expected to hear her retching into the toilet, but she surprised him again by running water into the tub.

He got up and stumbled to the bathroom door. "You're not going to try showering with that bandage on, are you?" he called.

"No. I'm going to put an inch of water in the bath and then do a sponge-off with a face cloth. How about some breakfast?" He shook his head in admiration and went to the phone. An hour later, after devouring a plate of toast and scrambled eggs, Grace made herself comfortable on the bed and started to talk. At first, Myles interrupted with questions, which Grace patiently answered. After a while, listening to the despair in her voice, watching her otherwise pleasing features contort with replayed horror, he fell silent. Fear, anger, and confusion – all crossed the face he had once loved so much, and loved still – as the enormity of what had happened was laid out before him.

Before last spring's drug-addled incident, when Grace had disintegrated before his eyes, she had seemed to Myles a rare, if faintly troubled, creature. He had found himself inexplicably drawn to her, this talented and beautiful woman, this woman who couldn't seem to accept her own worth or her own stirring beauty. Because of this past relationship, and because of the sheer implausibility of the murder charges against her, he had been predisposed to believe any story she might tell. But the habits of law enforcement had never left him, and he had warned himself to watch for signs of deception. He had detected none.

She showed him the letter and the microfiche; he glanced at them while she talked.

When she finished, she looked at him with a resigned, helpless expression, almost as if she knew what was coming next: an explosion of anger at being lured back into her miserable, fucked up, and now dangerously criminal life. Or, perhaps, an embarrassed fumbling for jacket and duffel bag as he backed out of her hotel room and out of her life forever.

He picked up the letter from the Grand Cayman lawyer. As Grace watched nervously, he carefully read it. Then he stood up and held the microfiche against the window. Thin light from the courtyard provided indifferent definition, but he saw immediately that the fiche was covered with microscopic lines of text.

He picked up the photographs Grace had taken of Shy's injection sites. Annette Devereaux appeared in each of them, holding the newspaper. He studied them again.

"You left Shy with Andre's daughter?" he asked quietly.

Grace looked up at him. "Yes. Annette took her to St. Felicien. It's a small village in southern Manitoba, just over the border from Minnesota. They drove."

"Why take her there?"

"It's small, it's French-speaking, and it's fifteen hundred

miles from those sick bastards."

"Shy will stand out like a sore thumb. She'll arouse someone's curiosity – a social worker, a cop, a schoolteacher. Her picture has been all over the news. It's only a matter of-"

"That's what I said. But Annette said no. She says it's a very close-knit community. Less than a hundred people. Everyone is related. Annette's mother was born there. She and Annette's twin sister, who died in her teens, are buried there. The place is surrounded by English-speaking communities. Annette says no one in the village will say a word to an outsider."

"Do you know if they've arrived there yet?"

"Annette phoned me before I left her house to cross into the States. They were in eastern Saskatchewan. I talked to Shy for a few minutes. She was very excited. Annette had promised to teach her to speak French."

"How will you contact her? Do you have a phone number?"

"Yes. I told her I'd call when I was in a safe place."

For a long moment, Myles was quiet. He held the fiche up to the light, studying it.

"You can call her from my place," he said.

At 10:00 a.m. on Tuesday, in Harrah's New Orleans Hotel and Casino, near the Riverwalk market, while Myles plunked quarters into a nearby slot machine, Grace had stepped up to a casino cashier's wicket. They had agreed that if the cashier disappeared from view, picked up a phone, or seemed to be delaying, Grace would walk away. They'd meet in the parking lot.

But it had gone smoothly. Generally, casinos were only too ready to accommodate the cash advance needs of the gaming public (the word 'gambler', with its unfortunate connotations, had long ago been banished from Casinoland's corporate vocabulary). Grace's request for a nine thousand dollar advance on her credit card hadn't raised an eyebrow. Myles watched the cashier swipe the card through the transaction

258

modem. Grace stood at the wicket counter, opening and closing her fists at her side. Myles willed her to stop – he thought she looked too nervous. She glanced over to him, saw his warning look, and stopped. She leaned her elbows on the counter and relaxed her shoulders. A few minutes later, she gathered up the pile of currency the cashier had counted out for her and then walked off in the direction of the hotel lobby.

Acutely aware of the surveillance cameras, Myles had steadfastly continued his play at the slot machines for another half-hour. He suspected that Grace's card transaction would one day come to the attention of the investigators and some cop would fly down from Canada to study the casino's tapes. If that cop caught Grace's exchange of glances with Myles... He pushed the thought away.

They had put New Orleans behind them. They sped north across the Lake Pontchartrain causeway. Traffic was surprisingly light on Interstate 10. As they sifted east through Mississippi, along the Gulf coast, Myles kept the cruise control locked just below the speed limit. With a fugitive in his car, he didn't relish the idea of attracting the attention of a patrolling state trooper.

After an hour or so, Grace reclined the passenger seat and closed her eyes. Myles glanced over at her. Midday sunshine, depleted by the Audi's tinted windows, played across her cheeks. In the sepia-toned light, Grace's skin looked papery, almost translucent. Somehow, her underlying beauty survived and shone through, but it was obvious that the ordeal of the past few weeks had taken a terrible toll.

Myles hadn't let her see that he was in turmoil of his own. Questions had tortured him since the previous day. As his Audi ate up miles on the concrete ribbon of highway, he tried to approach the problem with care and logic. Conservatively, he told himself.

As a hypothetical.

He replayed part of their conversation on Monday afternoon.

"A plan?" Grace had been in the bathroom, struggling to

259

do something with her hair. Her voice sounded hesitant. "Is it so obvious that I have one?" She turned and leaned in the doorway, hairbrush in her hand. He was watching her with levelled eyes. Her cheeks coloured slightly. "Yes, I suppose it is." She turned back to the mirror and started working her hair back into a ponytail, in obvious difficulty because of the limited use of her left arm. Myles rose from the end of the bed and walked toward the bathroom, intending to help her. All of a sudden, Grace slammed the brush on the counter. "Shit! What am I doing? I don't have any damned elastics! Do you have any elastics? No, of course you don't!" she continued, answering for him. She let her hair fall and shook it out, then turned to face him again, leaning the small of her back against the sink counter. "I don't know if it will work," she said. "I'm going to need help. It's a lot to ask of anyone, especially-" she searched briefly for the right words "-someone who has a lot to lose. Like, his job, his profession." A pause. Then she added, "Maybe his life."

Myles had watched her silently for a moment, standing there against the sink, her unruly hair tumbling in a gorgeous tangle to her shoulders, framing the face that had seduced him, in his dreams, for months.

"I'm listening," he said.

After she'd told him, he hadn't known how to react, or what to say. He'd struggled within himself for a few moments, his feelings a jumble of amazement, admiration, and fear.

"You can't be serious!"

"Security is always better on paper than it is in real life. Unless there's money inside, it's usually pretty slack. You've seen it yourself."

"Grace, that's a long shot. A real long shot." He looked into her eyes. "You know that?"

She nodded. She looked dejected, but at the same time... determined. He watched her, his mind racing.

The sun was gone, leaving a riot of red sky in its wake.

"Like another drink?" Grace's voice was smoky with invitation. He remembered what that had usually meant. He turned to her. Her eyes were iridescent in fading light of dusk. He felt something inside of him let go. He took a deep breath.

"Sure. You doing the honours?"

"Yup." She got up. "And I suppose we should be thinking about something to eat." Myles had a curious feeling that she wasn't talking about food.

His eyes followed Grace's retreating back as she slipped back into the house to refresh his drink. They hadn't made love. Not once. Not in New Orleans, and not since they'd arrived in Live Oak.

Rich memories assailed him, filling his head. He could smell the sweet scent of her skin against his. Desire stirred in him. He tried to push it back. He'd been pushing it back all week long. It was a bit more difficult to do after a margarita. He needed to be careful. He needed to keep his mind clear. Sex with the most captivating woman he had ever known would only cloud his thinking.

If Grace insisted on going ahead with her plan, she would need a false identity. Myles was already harbouring a fugitive. If he took the next step, he'd be opening himself to serious criminal liability. No one knew this better than him. Worst case: Grace had been lying to him, she'd eventually be caught and convicted, and his involvement would come to light. He, Myles Rothwell, respected attorney and father, would find himself facing charges of accessory after the fact, or harbouring, or several other choice selections from a rich smorgasbord of federal and state offences. Best case: Grace had been set up and she was able to prove it. In that event, he might only be charged for obtaining the fake identity papers she'd used to clear herself.

Myles had spent the last few nights listening to Grace sleep and sweating over his dilemma. He knew he was taking a huge risk.

It was ironic. When he'd realised that Grace had a drug problem, he hadn't hesitated to choose Lisa's welfare over his love of this woman and his natural desire to help her straighten out. He'd long ago admitted to himself that his reaction to the crisis had probably been too severe. But Lisa had to come first, and, although regretful, he'd never felt guilty.

Now here was the same woman, dramatically back in his life. Addiction to tranquillisers and freaky, chaotic outbursts were nothing compared to a murder indictment. But this time he couldn't turn his back, even though that decision could ultimately visit grief and devastation into both his life and Lisa's. Why was he reacting differently this time?

Maybe because, in the final analysis, only Grace herself could have faced down her addiction. For him to attempt to help, from three thousand miles away, would have been futile. The alternative – Grace's tentative plan to move to Florida, and to obtain a court order so she could bring Shy – could have risked exposing Lisa to unforgivable dysfunction. It would have jeopardised Myles' relationship with her. It might have destroyed it.

But this problem was different. Logic told him that Grace couldn't possibly deal with this alone. Even so, she seemed determined to try. If Myles had left her in that hotel room, she would have gone ahead without him, one way or another. He knew this. He had seen it in her eyes. He still loved the woman behind those eyes. So he would help her.

But that decision had created a new dilemma. One that he hadn't discussed with Grace. They would need Pete. That was the problem. Pete Wetherall was his best friend. How could he put him in that position? How could he ask him to put his ass on the line for a woman he didn't even know?

That night, they made love. Grace sensed it was time. Myles was sitting on the edge of the bed, naked and distracted. Grace left the bathroom and came to him. In the half-light, she straddled his legs and pulled his face to her. Slowly, languorously, careful of her wound, he kissed her neck and kissed her breasts.

She feasted on the scent of his hair and the sound of him and the feel of his hands on her back. She lifted his face and feasted on his lips. He lay back. She climbed onto the bed and kissed him everywhere. Then she slid him home.

Myles lay there for a long time afterwards, stroking her hair. Finally, he drifted off.

TWENTY-THREE

After breakfast, Myles went out to mow the lawn. Grace watched him from the dining room window as he tracked back and forth on an old green ride-on mower. He seemed to be following a cutting pattern borne of long habit. His mind was obviously somewhere else.

He needs to think. I've screwed up his life. Again.

She drew a despairing breath and wandered down the hallway to the back bedroom. Lisa used this room when she came for weekends. There was an old-fashioned double-sized brass bed in one corner. The rest of the furniture looked vaguely antique, though it had a certain flea market standard about it. The top of the dresser was strewn with a few stuffed animals, a collection of hand-beaded bracelets and various fripperies favoured by North American girls on the verge of puberty. A sleek compact disc player sat on a small writing desk near the door. On the wall above it was a huge poster of a quartet of the latest teen heartthrobs, a singing group of boymen. The photograph showed them strung across the front of a vast stage, narrow chests bare and glistening with sweat, as female hands reached and pleaded from the audience.

There was one other piece of furniture in the room – a large desk with a computer.

Grace sat down and logged on to the Net. She quickly located a website. She'd looked at it a half-dozen times before. A home page materialised.

Bellis, Matthews & Associates
Attorneys-at-Law
George Town, Grand Cayman
"Island Roots – Global Reach"

Under the logo was a photograph of a pastel-coloured two-storey building, bordered by photographs of a dozen grinning men and women. The top photo was of a pleasant-looking man in his forties. The caption under his picture read, "Ward

A. Bellis, Senior Partner".

Grace leaned closer and studied the photograph of the building. There was a caption under its picture as well.

The Easton Building

The first time Grace had looked at this site, shortly after their arrival, Myles had come into the room. He'd peered at the screen and then looked at Grace. His raised eyebrow had told her what he was thinking.

But, since then, his views seemed to be, well... evolving.

Grace wondered how much longer it would take Myles to finish cutting the lawn.

Whether she should make some lunch...

Whether he'd be interested in some afternoon sex...

She felt a lump in her throat. Last night had been a blessing – a kind of oasis on a dangerous road leading to an unknowable future. For the brief time that it had lasted, and afterwards in Myles' arms, she had felt safe. And for the first time in weeks, her sleep had been undisturbed by dreams. Or by nightmares.

Myles had disappeared.

Grace was still at the computer, browsing Cayman Islands tourist sites, when she realised the mower had stopped running. She looked out the dining room window. The lawn was nicely groomed. The mower was nowhere to be seen. She went outside and looked around the house. The garage was locked. She peered through the dirty pane of glass in the side door. The mower had been put away. Myles' car was still there. There was no sign of him. Grace returned to the house, puzzled and vaguely worried. She went to the en suite bathroom off Myles' bedroom, stripped off, and stepped into the shower. Using the detachable showerhead, she was able to avoid wetting the dressing on her wound. After she'd towelled off, she went to the kitchen and poured a cup of coffee.

Still no sign of Myles.

Grace sat in the living room. She was getting nervous. Myles has been meticulous about letting her know where he was. Even on workdays. Every weekday morning he'd left her a note explaining his plans for the day – depositions, appointments at the office, court. Whatever. So she would feel connected. So she would feel safe.

She sat on the couch for twenty minutes, distractedly thumbing through a magazine. Then, just as she decided to get dressed and go looking for him, she heard sounds outside.

Crunching gravel. Heavy steps. The gate alarm hadn't sounded!

Grace bolted for the back bedroom. Before she reached the hallway, the front door of the house banged open. In her fright, the empty coffee cup slipped from her fingers and fell to the carpet.

It was Myles. He was wearing a huge grin, which momentarily faded when he saw Grace leaning against the wall, wearing nothing but panties and a bandage, her chest heaving.

She heaved a sigh of relief. "You scared the hell out of me! I thought-!"

He came to her quickly and kissed her.

"I'm sorry. I wasn't thinking." He paused for a moment, savouring the sight of her bare breasts. He kissed her again and then took her hand. "Come outside."

She looked down. "What? Like this?"

"There's no one out there. Well, no humans anyway. Come on!" He pushed her ahead of him out onto the veranda. At the bottom of the steps, two saddled horses raised their heads from the grass next to the walkway. They eyed her solemnly.

"I thought you'd like some exercise. That is, if you think your ribs can handle the bouncing around. There's lots of empty country behind the house. No one will see you."

She gave him a mischievous look. "Then I guess I can go like this, huh? Work on my tan!"

Myles' arms wrapped around her from behind. His hands cupped her breasts. "I've just thought of a way to check," he whispered.

"Check what?"

"Whether you can handle the bouncing."

266

"Would you take advantage of the walking wounded?" Grace asked, her voice husky.

"Only if she insists."

They spent an hour in the bedroom before heading out for their ride.

For Grace, the afternoon was the most carefree and exhilarating that she had experienced in a very long time. For his part, Myles was disappointed and he said so. He'd been hoping Grace would ride topless.

That evening, the outside world came calling. Grace was featured on *At Large*. Over breakfast, Myles had spotted a brief digest of the show's line-up in the television guide. Half an hour before the show was due to start, he broke the news.

Grace was pale and tense when they sat down to watch. Myles put a blank tape in his VCR and set it to record the broadcast.

"Good evening, folks. Welcome to *At Large*." The camera panned across a bustling, high-tech network set and swooped in toward a group of technicians in headsets. The crime show's famous host, a grey-haired man with an angular face, stepped out of the staged activity, talking as he moved. "I'm Wendell Forbes. Once again, we're looking for your help in apprehending America's worst criminals." The angle changed; Forbes choreographed a quarter-turn of his body to face the new camera. "We'll be telling you about a dramatic arrest in West Virginia, thanks to calls from some of you. And we'll be asking for your help in tracking down a serial rapist in the Midwest, and an escaped murderer in the Oregon. But first, we bring you a horrifying story from north of the border. The City of Victoria is the capital of the Province of British Columbia, on the Pacific coast of Canada. A few weeks ago, that city's usually genteel tranquillity was shattered by a series of killings that almost defy belief. Victoria police say that this woman-"

Even though she was expecting it, Grace gasped as her face – carefree, complete with her trademark smile – filled the

267

screen.

"-is responsible for the violent murders of three men, one of them a police detective..." It was all there: Andre, who (it was now said) had been burned alive; Detective DaSilva, shot in her house; and Cameron Pomeroy, bludgeoned in the stairwell at the firm's offices.

"...serial killer. Her motives have not been determined. Police warn that Grace Palliser is highly intelligent, an accomplished liar, and extremely dangerous. Members of the public who encounter her are advised to use extreme caution and immediately notify their nearest police agency.

"Detective Sergeant Hank Farrell, of the Victoria City Police, is the primary contact. He recorded these comments to assist us with this broadcast..."

Farrell appeared on screen, sitting at a squad room desk. Grace knew what to expect. She put her hand on Myles' shoulder and got up from the couch. "Watch the rest," she said. "I can't."

She fled down the hall and threw herself on Myles' bed. Even though she'd known this was coming, she felt as if she'd been watching her own funeral. A few minutes later, Myles came into the room. Grace lay in anguished silence, staring vacantly. He sat on the edge of the bed.

"Where did they get the photos?" he asked gently.

"They must have gotten the first one from my house", she said vaguely, not looking at him.

"There's a beautiful photograph of you sitting in a field of wildflowers. It's not the picture of a killer, Grace."

Grace shuddered. "They've cropped it", she replied woodenly. "Shy was sitting beside me. She always brings out my best smile." She turned to Myles. Her eyes were wet. "I can't believe this!"

Myles squeezed her leg reassuringly, but she didn't respond. She lay frozen, staring at her feet. Myles took a deep breath and then broke the silence, talking quickly.

"Listen to me, Grace. We're going to need Pete's help. If you want a new identity, it has to be airtight. I used to have pretty good contacts, but they're from way back. Pete's contacts are current. He's the only person I know who can do this. And we've got to change your appearance. I mean radically. You can't look anything like those photos on television."

Grace didn't say anything. She didn't have to – her face was a frozen mask of fear. What Myles was suggesting involved a huge gamble. If he misjudged Pete Wetherall's loyalty, or if Pete wasn't prepared to risk his career, or if he had second thoughts later, Grace would be arrested. Arrested and extradited. Then her only chance would be Annette.

Could Annette's testimony save me?

And what about Myles? Even if he were never convicted of any crime, he would be disbarred. Grace drew a breath, and took the plunge.

"Just how do you propose to get a fellow attorney to obtain false papers for a serial killer?"

"By appealing to his dark side."

"His dark side?"

"Yeah. The side of him that just loves to prove the cops are stupid. The Victoria police aren't *our* cops, but they're cops. Pete was a hippie, a child of the sixties, retired from it now, maybe, but definitely unrepentant. I'm an ex-cop and ex-prosecutor, but he's forgiven me my trespasses because, as he says, I've seen the light."

Grace thought about this for a while. It was a warm evening, but she began to shiver.

Over Sunday morning coffee, they discussed what Grace might do to change her appearance. Then Myles picked up the phone and hit a speed dial button.

"Hi Pete. You alone?"

"It's Sunday morning, Myles! Whaddaya think?"

Pete sounded like he was still in bed... and definitely not alone.

"Okay... Just answer yes or no. Is Madeline still working at the library?"

"Yeah. Part time. It's just a volunteer thing." Pete sounded confused.

"You know those microfiche readers? The ones folks use to search the library's collections?"

"Yeah."

"I need to borrow one."

"Why?"

"Come for steaks tonight and I'll show you."

"Mmm… Library closes at six on Sundays. Maybe I could-"

"Great! See you at six-thirty."

"Okay. What's this about, Myles?"

"I'll tell you tonight. Bring the reader. And, Pete…"

"Yeah?"

"Don't bring Madeline."

TWENTY-FOUR

The gate alarm went off at ten after five. Myles reset it while Grace put her drinking glass in the dishwasher and then disappeared into the bedroom. She pushed the door almost closed, leaving it open a few inches so she could hear what was going on, then took a pillow off the bed and dropped it on the floor. She sat on it, her back against the wall, her ear next to the gap between the door and the frame.

The last time she'd eavesdropped like this, she'd been sitting in Leddi Dixon's office, listening to Nader and Pendergast.

A pickup skidded to a stop in front of the porch. It was a late model vehicle but it wore a few signs of negligent contact with immovable objects. "Wine dents", Peter Wetherall had once described them to Myles, looking sheepish. The driver's door swung open and two muscular, sun-tanned legs, clad in shorts, swung out and planted a pair of worn sandals on the gravel. The rest of Pete Wetherall's tidy frame followed. Pete was well into his fifties, but his face was still ruggedly handsome. There wasn't an ounce of extra weight on his compact body. Although middle age had streaked his hair with grey, he still wore it pulled back into a short ponytail, as he had for over thirty years.

Many women of a certain age, as he liked to say, and the occasional younger model, found something irresistible in Pete's throwback looks. He had never lacked for companionship, but his companions seemed to come and go with an almost predictable regularity. Pete was the first to admit that he preferred it that way. He had been married once, in his early twenties, but because fidelity had never been one of Pete's strong suits, the union had ended in divorce. Fortunately, there had been no children.

"Hey, man!" Pete called, as Myles came down the steps. "Hang on – be right there." He hustled around to the other side of the truck's cab, his quick movements barely containing

271

the irrepressible energy that had earned him the nickname 'Eveready' in some quarters of the legal community. He wrenched open the passenger door and started wrestling a large object off the seat.

"Got that fiche machine here. Told Madeline I needed it to look at some discovery material. Hated lying, but I couldn't think what else to say."

"Good thinking," Myles said, coming around the truck. "Good guess, too." They lugged the reader into the house and they set it on the dining room table. Myles could see that his friend was burning with curiosity. He'd let him stew for a bit; maybe get a couple of drinks into him before playing his hand.

"How about a cold one?" Pete stared at him, then nodded, apparently deciding it was too soon to start a cross-examination. They went to the kitchen. They drank beer while Myles finished making the salad Grace had started. He checked on the Hoppin' John in the oven – it was a Caribbean recipe that Pete always raved about. Then Myles produced two New York strips from the fridge, sprinkled them with a homemade blend of spices and started rubbing it into the meat, preparing it for the grill.

Pete leaned against the counter, watching Myles work and rambling on about the Cordero case, a burglary trial that was scheduled to start the next day. Pete was relishing the prospect. His client had the distinction of being charged with breaking *into* the sheriff's office – bypassing a pitifully inadequate alarm system – and prying off the door to the property room. A number of drug exhibits and firearms had gone missing. None of the stolen items had been recovered. As a result, the police had been unable to produce evidence in several prosecutions of other offenders and their cases had been dismissed. Understandably, the whole fiasco had resulted in some very red faces, so Pete's upcoming trial was attracting media attention.

After a while, Myles handed Pete a second beer and played his first card.

"Thanks again for covering for me last week," he said, as Pete twisted the cap off the bottle. "Word is you did a great job on Slaney. He's a prickly little bastard."

"Yeah, thanks." Pete took a pull from the bottle. Then, expanding on a running joke between them, he added, "You know, maybe that's the trouble with you ex-cops who switch sides. Maybe you think it's still your job to persuade criminals to plead guilty. Maybe you think an attorney-client interview is just another form of interrogation." He waved the amber bottle at Myles. "Maybe that's why up-and-coming recidivists like Slaney tend to get 'prickly' when their lawyer tells them to plead out to their second felony indictment! I'm thinking, maybe that's why-!"

Myles interrupted. "You copped a plea, didn't you?"

"Yeah," Pete replied, grinning. He swung himself up on the counter. "That scumbag had no defence at all!"

Myles laughed. "That's what I told him, but he wouldn't believe me. When I told him 'I practise law, buddy, not magic', he just stared at me and then offered some observations about my brainpower and my parentage."

"Yeah, well I made him a believer." He reached out and clapped Myles on the shoulder. "You see, my son, it's all a matter of style."

"And bullshit."

"That too."

A long second passed.

"You've never asked me where I went last week."

"Guess that's your business. I suppose you'll tell me when you're ready."

Despite Pete's pretension of only mild interest, Myles could see that his friend was dying to know the story behind his mysterious three-day trip.

"Well, Peter, old friend," Myles said, trying to sound nonchalant even though his pulse was quickening, "I may need your help on this one. And you'd have to trust me. And I mean, trust me more than I have any right to ask."

"Myles, my man, you've known me a long time. If you think

273

I can deal with it, I guess I can deal with it." He grinned, half-joking. "It ain't illegal, is it?"

"Yes, Pete. It is."

His friend's eyebrows went up. "Shit, Myles! You, of all people!"

"Petey, this little enterprise could put us in jail. I have good reasons for getting into it. The best reasons. You don't. In fact, there's no damned reason on earth for you to help with this."

"It's nothing to do with all this terrorist shit, I hope?"

"Of course not. Listen-" he dropped his voice, trying to let his tone demonstrate that, no matter what Pete decided, he would never hold it against him "-if your guts are already churning, tell me. It's all right. We're friends and we'll always be friends. We can just forget we had this conversation."

Pete eyeballed his friend. His reply was tinged with heat. "Myles Rothwell, you're probably the only lawyer in this damned town who stood by me when that dickless judge and those State Bar assholes tried to ruin my life. If it weren't for you, I'd be back working on a shrimp boat. I already owe you my ticket! Tell me what's going on! Whatever it is, it's gotta be a lot more sensible than me fucking that judge's wife!"

"It was his daughter."

"Oh...? Yeah. That's right."

"Suppressed memory syndrome?"

"Maybe. Or, old age..."

Myles tried not to smile. "Don't commit yet." He stepped to the sink. He rinsed and dried his hands. "Come with me."

He led Pete into the living room, opened a drawer in the wall unit and took out a videocassette. He slid it into the player and turned on the television. Then he picked up the remote, pushed the play button and motioned for his friend to sit down.

"Watch this. No questions. I'll explain when its over." A familiar musical theme filled the room. The *At Large* segment about Grace Palliser played across the screen. At first, Pete's expression was puzzled, then, after a few minutes, intensely interested. Myles sat on the arm of the couch, watching his friend's face. When the taped section ended and the screen flickered into snowy static, Myles stopped the tape. For several seconds, Pete continued staring at the darkened television. He turned slowly to face Myles. He looked like he'd been watching an autopsy. Myles could almost hear Pete's imagination spinning: *Holy shit, what's this got to do with Myles? Beautiful woman... all those killings...! Gotta be some kind of psycho...*

Myles broke into his friend's turmoil.

"What would you say if I told you she's innocent – that she's been set up?"

Pete stared at him. He answered slowly.

"I guess that would be a matter for the cops up in Canada." He trailed off, and his look sharpened as he asked the obvious question. "What's this got to do with you?"

"Well, see, I'm kind of hoping to marry her." Myles let that sink in. Pete's eyes bugged. "But before I can do that, I'll need your help to get her out of this mess."

Pete's jaw was working, but no sound came out of his mouth. Then his eyes shifted past Myles and an expression of utter shock materialised on his face. He scrambled to his feet just as Myles detected a soft footstep behind him and Grace's hand settled gently on his shoulder.

Peter Wetherall stood gaping at Myles Rothwell and Grace Palliser, his eyes darting uncertainly back and forth between them.

"Holy shit!" he stammered.

Grace hadn't intended to come out of the bedroom unless Myles came to fetch her. In truth, she hadn't really expected him to come for her at all, except maybe to explain that his recruitment plan had backfired and that they'd have to find somewhere else to hide her. But, listening from the bedroom, she'd heard the theme music from *At Large*. Fifteen minutes later, she'd heard Myles tell Pete that he'd been hoping to marry her. She'd been stunned, grateful, confused. And she'd made an instant decision.

Screw it! He's risking everything for me. Now he's risking his friend's career. I'm getting this over with. If Pete goes south on us, I'll just give up and turn myself in.

As Grace stepped into the living room, she was thinking that turning herself in was exactly what she should be doing anyway.

The next few hours changed her mind. Myles dug a third steak out of the fridge, prepped it, and went outside alone to fire up the grill. He took the meat platter with him.

"Listen to her," he said to Pete quietly as he left. "That's all I ask." Only Grace could bring Pete around, and all three of them knew it.

Grace sat on the couch with Pete while he stared at her, apparently at a loss for words. Finally, he spoke.

"You're better looking in person."

"Thank you... I think. Let me show you something." She started pulling up her tee shirt. Pete's eyes widened slightly. "It's okay, Pete, only Myles gets to see everything. But I need you to see this." She exposed the dressing on her ribcage. "Under this bandage is a wound from a rifle bullet. It only grazed me; I was lucky. Myles has tried to treat it. We don't think it will get infected now, but it's taking a long time to heal." She dropped her shirt. "On that broadcast, you didn't hear anything about the police shooting at me, did you?"

"Sounded like they never laid eyes on you. Except maybe that detective who died in your house. But they said his gun hadn't been fired. What's this got to do with-?"

"I'll explain. I'll explain everything. But there's a lot of ground to cover, and I wanted you to know about this injury right now. There are also some photographs of my daughter – I'll show them to you later."

"Okay, but first I have a question. How is it that I don't know about you? Myles and I are good friends. Myles just said he wants to marry you. Knowing Myles, that means you two-"

"We knew each other before all this happened. We met last year, when he testified in Victoria on that old ATF arrest. You know about that?" Pete nodded. "We kept our relationship to ourselves. We both have daughters. We were living in different countries. We were just seeing how it went. And it went beautifully, until… until I did something stupid and I broke it. We stopped seeing each other last May." She drew a breath. "I'll let Myles tell you if he wants to tell you. It's not my place. He's a very private man. I'm sure you know that."

Pete nodded his head. He suddenly remembered the beer in his hand. He took a long drink. "Seeing you sitting here, four feet away, I guess I can understand Myles wanting to keep you all to himself." He tried to smile, but couldn't quite pull it off.

"Excuse the language, ma'am, but this whole thing sounds like a fucking movie." Grace, Myles, and Pete were sitting around one end of the dining room table. The microfiche reader Pete had brought still squatted, as yet unused, at the other end of the table. They hadn't bothered to clear away the supper dishes, and the remaining scraps of their meal had long ago congealed on the plates.

"I wish it was a movie," Grace replied. "I could just wait for the credits and then make for the exit and go back to my humdrum, chaotic little life."

Pete picked up a sheet of paper from the table in front of him. It was a printout of the Bellis, Matthews law firm's home page. "Grand Cayman, huh? You're gonna need a passport."

"The Panamanians, Pete," Myles said quietly. "That case you did in Tampa. You said some of those guys had fake identities, but the passports were genuine articles. I remember you saying that when your client walked on all those charges, his gratitude was almost embarrassing. You were saying that if you ever needed to disappear, like to get away from a woman-" Myles deadpanned "-you knew where to go for a new identity."

"Just bullshitting over bourbon, Myles."

Myles looked into his friend's eyes.

"Was it, Pete?"

Pete held Myles' gaze for a few seconds before looking away.

277

"No."

"Can you do this?" Grace asked. He looked at her, then back to Myles. The skin along his hairline had gone white. Grace might have made him a believer, but he was a frightened one.

"I could make a few calls," he said quietly.

Pete had promised to deliver the microfiche reader back to Madeline tonight, so she could return it to the library in the morning. Myles plugged it in and he and Pete studied the microfiche Grace had brought with her from Canada. Grace didn't join them. She'd already combed through those entries at Annette's house. Maybe fresh minds would see something she'd missed. She decided it would be better if she didn't hover over them, so she stretched out on the couch while they talked.

When Myles called her, she rejoined them.

"Grace, there's not really anything in here, standing by itself. I think you know that."

"I know. That's what I've been saying. I'm sure Nader has made the Getz file disappear. I've never heard of the other ten names on that fiche. If those accounts have been emptied, they've done it some other way. I suspect they used ghost files. If so, I don't know how they slipped up on this one. But we can be pretty sure that, by now, the paper trails have been erased. So how do I clear myself? I've got a gouge across my ribs that I say is from a bullet. Others might doubt that, especially now that it's partly healed. I have Annette's testimony to back me up, and there'll be shell casings in the woods in the park – unless Pendergast collected them up. I've got the photos of the needle marks on Shy's body and I've got evidence of the Cayman incorporation." She pointed at Bellis's letter.

"Not a bad case," Pete ventured. "I'd be happy to defend it. If the cops wouldn't listen, a good PI could connect the dots. You'd have a strong chance of walking on this."

"A 'strong chance' isn't a guarantee," Grace replied. She

was standing near the table, leaning on the back of one of the chairs. "I'm not a lawyer, but I know enough to tell you that I wouldn't get bail. So while I'm locked up in Victoria, waiting for that Farrell guy to follow up on my story – or a private investigator I can't afford, hired by a lawyer I can't afford – any evidence that might be sitting in the Cayman Islands will evaporate. Nader would make sure of that. The huge balances on that microfiche tell me he's running a fraud worth millions." Her voice rose. "The lengths they went to just to see me dead tell me that if they think there's even the remotest chance of exposure he and Pendergast will vanish. And whatever money they've got hidden, or whatever records there are, will vanish with them! The way I see it, the only way I can get out of this is to stay out of jail and finish it myself!"

Both men were staring at her. She realised that she'd allowed her rage at what happened to Shy seep into her voice.

"Anyway," she added, pulling the chair back and sitting down, "Pendergast used to be a cop. There's a good chance that if I was in custody in Victoria, he'd make arrangements for me to commit suicide."

"You know any cops you can trust?" Pete asked gently. Myles looked at him. The question sounded a bit odd, coming from Pete.

"Not for sure. But I know one that I *think* I could trust." She told them about the Horace Assu trial, and her brief encounter with the RCMP officer named Tom Naaykens. "He gave me a good feeling. He said all the right things about those two bent investigators."

"You could call him," Pete suggested. "Maybe arrange a meeting."

"I wasn't ready to take that chance while I was still in Canada. I'm not saying I wouldn't, if I had more evidence to show him." The two men were silent for a moment, mulling over Grace's words.

"Anything else we should know?" Myles finally asked.

"Yes." Grace replied. She spoke softly, but her tone was adamantine. "Those bastards made a very big mistake."

"What was that?"

"They killed my best friend and abducted my five-year-old daughter and injected her with drugs. I'm going to make them pay for that."

Pete stayed late. His pending burglary trial didn't seem as important to him as it had before he met Grace. Around midnight, Myles got up from the table and went to the sideboard. He returned with three short glasses and a bottle of Jack Daniels. He set the glasses down and poured a finger of whiskey into each of them.

While Grace and Pete talked, he unobtrusively placed a glass next to Pete's elbow. Then he slid one in front of Grace.

He's testing me.

Grace picked up the glass. She gave Myles a level look and took a sip. Soon she felt the bourbon coursing in her veins. She relaxed. The liquor potentiated her sense of unreality. She, a fugitive, charged with three murders. They, a pair of country lawyers risking their futures to help her.

Grace had only one drink.

During the night's discussions they agreed that, because of Grace's accent, her new identity would have to be Canadian. It would be too difficult to fake a background from some other jurisdiction.

Pete left at two. The two men loaded the fiche reader into the cab of his pickup while Grace watched from the steps. Before he drove away, Pete walked over.

"You look the same right now as you did on that videotape. That TV show pulls big ratings all over North America. And I'm betting they get the Miami channels down in the Caymans. You're damned good looking. That means you'll get noticed. Wearing a hat and sunglasses isn't going to cut it. How tall are you?"

"Five eight."

He looked her up and down. "And a half, right?"

"Yeah. And a half."

"Hmmh," he grunted, visibly worried. "Can't do much

about that, but you'd better stay off heels. Wear flats. Cut your hair short and change the colour. Start wearing glasses — whatever. And do it soon. I can't get started on your new identity until you decide what you're going to look like."

TWENTY-FIVE

The phone rang at six thirty on Monday morning. Myles was getting ready for work. Grace was in the kitchen, grinding coffee. She checked the call display, memorised the number, and recited it to Myles as he came out of the shower.

"That's Lisa," he told her, padding dripping wet into the bedroom, quickly rubbing his head with a towel. "I wonder why she's calling so early." He picked up the extension.

Grace also wondered, so she hung in the doorway for a moment, admiring Myles' naked buttocks, until she was sure there was no brewing crisis. Then she returned to the kitchen.

Lisa lived with her mother in Gainesville, sixty miles to the south. Grace hadn't wanted her own inconvenient presence to interfere with the father-daughter routine, so Myles had talked with Lisa regularly since he and Grace had arrived back from New Orleans. Lisa's time in Fort Myers had been great fun, apart from breaking her little toe on the leg of a coffee table, but the girl really missed her Dad. Months ago, before her 'fall from Grace', as Grace had labelled her personal train wreck in her mind, Myles had mentioned that Lisa would rather live with him than with her mother. But, because his job often required him to travel, such an arrangement wouldn't be practical. Lisa would have been forced to spend two hours a day on a school bus, and at times she'd be left alone overnight.

In any event, Myles' ex-wife, Josie, had violently objected to the idea. Myles knew that if he got into a court fight with her, he didn't have the ammunition to win.

That hadn't stopped Lisa from adoring her father. Human nature being what it is, their enjoyable weekend visits, horseback riding along the river, probably encouraged the girl's desire to be with her Dad. Grace had no doubt that when Lisa was older, she'd become a permanent resident of the little bedroom at the back of the house. Listening to one end of their phone calls – Myles joking, talking to her about school and music, giving her advice about boys, gently warning her about some friend's apparent disloyalty – she had come to almost envy the man's easy and loving relationship with his girl. Not because she didn't have the same relationship with her own little Miss Bossy Boots, but because Myles could visit with Lisa whenever he wanted. It would probably be a long time before Grace could visit Shy again.

But at least they'd been able to speak on the phone a few times.

Grace had made her first call on Saturday afternoon, after she and Myles returned from their ride. A woman had answered the call. She'd answered in French. She sounded very old. Grace recalled enough from her high school French to stammer out a request to speak to Annette. The old lady grunted, there was some animated discussion in the background, the sound of clattering dishes, and then Annette came to the phone.

"*Allo?*"

"Annette, it's me."

"Thank God! Where are you? No, don't say. Are you safe?"

"Yes, I am. I'll tell you more in a second. How is you-know-who? Is she there?"

"Here, speak with her for a moment, and then you and I will talk. How long can you stay on this call?"

"Long enough. Don't worry."

"*Bien.* Here she is." Grace heard Annette's voice, speaking in French, directed to somewhere away from the telephone. There was a child's squeal, a rustling sound, and Shy came on the line.

"Mommy? Mommy?" Grace's resolve melted, and she started to cry.

"Yes, my darling," she managed to say. "It's me. I'm here."

"Where are you, Mommy? Are you coming to get me now?"

"Oh, baby, I can't just yet. But I will soon. I will. I promise." Grace knew she might be lying. She was dying

283

inside. Myles, sitting next to her on the porch swing, put an arm around her shoulders and held her tight. Seeing Grace weep, his own eyes filled with tears.

Grace could not now remember the rest of the conversation. A terrible emotion, a raw, indescribable yearning for her little girl, had detonated like a grenade in her mind. She could recall Shy talking excitedly about learning French, and of course she had to try it out on her mother, who had laughed, amazed through her tears to hear the little girl's almost perfect inflection. There was much talk about making special decorations for Christmas, even though it was two months away, and about doing school work at the kitchen table, but the lessons were all in French, so some of it was hard, and... other stuff that Grace just couldn't remember.

Finally, Annette had come back on the line, and after Grace had assured her that she was safe and that her injury was healing, she asked her if there was any news.

"Nothing here. We are a little bit isolated, and *Tante* only watches the French channels. I've been picking up the Winnipeg papers, but they seem to be filled with the war in Afghanistan and all the new anti-terrorist laws. Nothing about... you know. Not even in the back pages."

"I guess that's good. How long can you hold out there? I mean, Annette, you have a job back in-"

"I'm on indefinite compassionate leave. Besides, I have a new job."

"A new job?"

"*Mais oui.* Looking after a little girl who I love very much."

"God bless you, Annette. I don't know how I..." Grace trailed off, tears running freely. Myles gently took the phone out of her hands.

"*Mademoiselle*, your friend is having difficulty speaking right now. She is safe here. Let me say that we are both extremely grateful to you. We will try to finish this business quickly. I've been sitting here listening. I hear that a certain little girl is already making Christmas decorations. I have been thinking about my own daughter. She has never experienced a white

284

Christmas. It occurs to me that Christmas celebrations in a certain francophone village would be just the thing for her. For all of us, *n'est-ce pas*? Yes, thank you. You are very kind." Pause. "A real sleigh? I don't believe it! I thought that was only in beer ads!"

Grace's eyes widened as she listened. Myles nodded and smiled as Annette was replying. Then, to Grace's complete astonishment, Myles switched to French. He and Annette continued speaking for a few minutes. When he handed the phone back to Grace, she was gaping at him, her tears forgotten.

Grace and Annette agreed that Grace would call again before moving on. Grace ended the call, and then turned to Myles with an expression of wonder on her face. He grinned.

"What? Ya think jes 'cause us south'n corndawgs talk like this we's all stoopid?" The exaggerated hee-haw drawl actually got a laugh out of Grace. She hugged him until her bandages came loose from their moorings.

Myles appeared in the kitchen wearing a robe. He had just put down the phone.

"She wanted to catch me before I left for work."

"She needs to see you, Myles. It won't sound right if you start putting her off."

"That's just what I was going to say."

"I know. What did you tell her?"

"She wanted to come for the weekend. I've been expecting this, so I had my counter-offer ready."

"Counter-offer?"

"Yeah. I told her the ranch was getting a bit boring – hell, Grace, if she only knew-" he laughed and leaned close, kissing her temple "-so I suggested she and I spend the weekend at the beach. Go over to the Atlantic side, Jacksonville, or maybe Daytona, hang out on a boardwalk, catch a few movies. She jumped at it. I'm picking her up in Gainesville on Friday night. I'll be back Sunday."

Grace didn't respond immediately. She was thinking about

being alone for two days. She quickly reproached herself for being selfish. "Good idea. With luck, I'll be gone before her next visit. Better warn Pete."

"Warn him?"

"Yeah. I've seen that shotgun in your closet. Warn Pete that I'll be alone and I'll be nervous, so if he's coming to visit – especially after dark – he shouldn't just rely on the gate alarm. He'd better call me on the cell and sound his horn when he's coming up the driveway. Otherwise, he's liable to get a load of double-ought buck through his windshield."

"Double-ought is what the cops use in their pump actions. It's basically for killing people. How do you know about it?"

"I read it on your ammunition box."

On Monday afternoon, Myles left his office early and drove to Jacksonville. He prowled a couple of shopping malls and arrived home with hairdresser's scissors, hair colour, tinted non-prescription contacts, and a couple of fashion magazines. He and Grace spent the evening transforming her into a blue-eyed blonde with a low maintenance haircut. Grace was surprised to discover another of Myles' hidden talents: he was quite handy with scissors and a comb. The job on her hair looked almost professional. Myles stood back and surveyed the result.

"We have a problem."

Grace looked in the mirror. "What problem?"

"Any way you look at it, you're still too damned good looking. We should've done your hair some mousy shade of brown. Maybe we should get you at pair of glasses for wearing indoors. Something with big dorky frames, as Lisa would say."

Grace gave him a mock pout.

"Sorry, my love. What I'm saying is that we need to take away some of the lustre so you aren't so easy to remember. When you're outdoors, a hat and sunglasses can still help some. Maybe you should try to lie out in the sun every day – get a really dark tan." He looked closely at her face. "I like the freckles, though."

286

Grace leaned close to the mirror. A sprinkle of light-coloured freckles had appeared high on her cheeks and across her nose. "Yeah. Sunshine brings them out. Must be from when we went riding."

"They're not a bad thing. Anything that makes you look different from the photos on television is good. I seriously think you should work on a tan. You should be safe lying on a blanket behind the house. Take the gate alarm receiver with you. Just make sure you leave the back door unlocked so you don't have to run around to the front porch to get in the house." He stood close behind her at the mirror. The top of Grace's head came to just below his eyes. "There's not much we can do about your height."

Reflected in the mirror, Grace's expression was forlorn. Myles wrapped his arms around her and kissed her neck. After a moment, she broke free, and turned to face him. Her new look couldn't alter the seductive curve of her lips. He found himself inches from a bewitching blonde with china blue eyes. Grace took his hand and led him toward the bedroom.

"Come with me," she said. "I'm betting the idea of making love to a strange blonde gets you pretty excited."

The next day, Myles cancelled his morning appointments and drove Grace to a shopping centre on the western outskirts of Jacksonville. She went on a quick tour of a department store, wearing sunglasses and a ball cap just in case, and picked up some sale-item summer wear. Then Myles led her down the mall to a camera store. A sign in the window said "Instant Passport Photos".

Myles handed the pictures to Pete Wetherall that same afternoon.

The two men met in the parking lot behind their office. Pete had made some calls. He had a contact in Tampa, and a meeting set up for Wednesday night. He was obviously nervous, but he claimed to enjoy the adrenaline rush.

"It's a four hour drive each way, so I'll be pretty late getting home. If you want, I'll call you when I get in. Let you know how it went."

"No, Pete. Thanks, but let's keep this thing off the phone. Tell me tomorrow morning. Then again, maybe I should ride down with you. You can drop me off in the neighbourhood and I'll watch your back. This is where my discreditable background comes in. I have some experience running surveillance. Old hippies like you usually don't."

"*No necessario*, my son," Pete replied quickly. "Roberto will be with me. He still hasn't forgotten that he was the only *hombre* out of the five defendants who left the courthouse through the front door." Pete gripped Myles' shoulder. "You're the one who needs to watch his back, buddy. You get caught hiding that girl and you can kiss your ass goodbye."

On Saturday night, Grace lay on Myles' bed, wearing one of his tee shirts, trying to read. She couldn't concentrate. Myles had left the night before to spend the weekend with Lisa. He'd hugged her and held her and earnestly instructed her not to worry. "Lay low," he'd said. "If you go outside, take the gate alarm. But don't go wandering around in the pastures, because the alarm has a limited range. Oh, and keep your cell phone with you. I'll call you if I get a chance, but I can't promise. Lisa sticks pretty close to me. She's a bit of a teen wannabe, but mostly she's just a kid."

Grace had smiled and told him to go spoil his daughter.

So far, he hadn't phoned. Maybe he'd be able to manage a quick call tomorrow morning, while Lisa was showering or something. Grace hoped so. She was feeling lonely and adrift. And, after more than a week spent mostly indoors, she was definitely feeling confined.

It gave her a mild taste of how prison would feel.

She turned out the light and lay on her back in the darkness. Her mind was a tumble of emotions. Myles and Pete were sticking their necks out to help her. So far, she was safe. She was three thousand miles from two manhunts – womanhunts? – one by the police, another by Pendergast and Nader. And Shy was safe in Manitoba...

288

Count your blessings, Palliser! By rights, you should be dead.

Grace was just drifting off when she heard it. Movement outside, near the front of the house.

Whoever it was didn't seem to be hiding their presence.

Footsteps on the porch.

The front door rattled.

Grace sat up, instantly alert.

More footsteps.

Then silence.

Her heart rate soared.

Could it be Pete?

The gate alarm hadn't sounded. She glanced at the bedside clock. 12:40. Pete wouldn't come here this late without calling first.

Pete wouldn't come at all without calling first.

Earlier in the day, Myles' friend had spent two hours with Grace, drinking beer on the porch, telling her about the ID problems. A Canadian passport was possible, he'd said, but not certain. His source had assured him that the best people for Canadian passports were the Jamaicans, and that he had a few contacts with them. With some luck, they'd know by tomorrow night. What will it cost? Grace had asked. Three grand, he'd replied. He waved his hand. "Don't worry about it right now. It's taken care of." Grace had marched into the house and come back out and handed him the full amount in crisp new hundreds. Pete's face had gone bright red.

"No, no, Gracie girl," he said, handing the money back. "Not necessary. Let's just pray your little plan works and you don't find yourself locked up in some third world toilet."

"Pete, I have the money! I expected to pay!"

"It's all right," Pete had said, looking embarrassed. "Myles took care of it."

No, there was no reason for Pete to come back tonight.

Grace got off the bed slowly and crept toward the closet. As she reached its doorway, there was a thump under the bedroom window. A scraping of shrubbery branches against the siding. Then, hard scuffling. Grace was gripped by a sudden, insane fear.

Pendergast!

She ducked into the closet and grabbed the shotgun from the corner. She knew it was loaded because she'd insisted that Myles fill the magazine with shells before he left. Grace's hands were suddenly sweaty. One at a time, she wiped them on her shirt.

She positioned herself just inside the closet doorway and fixed her eyes on the bedroom window. In the dim light, she noticed the window starting to slide up.

Shit! Why didn't I lock it?

Hands appeared and a large male figure boosted itself partway through the window opening; shoes scraped against the siding.

Grace was sick and tired of being afraid. Grimly, she stepped out of the closet. She worked the pump action of the shotgun, forgetting there was a round in the chamber. It ejected and landed on the carpet as another live round was racked into place.

The sound was unmistakable.

The intruder froze.

"You move one more inch and I'll blow your fucking head off!" Grace's voice was clear; her intention unmistakable.

"Okay, lady! Okay! Don't shoot! Please don't shoot me!" It was the voice of a teenager. Another little punk break-in artist like dozens she'd seen in juvenile court up in Victoria.

Grace stood there, momentarily uncertain.

"Uh, what do you want me to do?" the kid bleated, hanging on the windowsill.

"Just don't move!" Grace walked slowly past the bed and over to the window. She shoved the muzzle of the shotgun hard against the boy's forehead. He squealed with fright.

"Pleeeease, lady!"

"You just slide back down that wall, sonny, and get the hell off this property!" Grace shouted. "You run and you keep running. The police are on their way. You hear me? You come near this house again and you'll be leaving in a body bag!"

The kid released his grip on the sill and fell into the shrubbery. He scrambled backwards, pushing with his feet. Grace watched his figure disappear into the woods between the house and the road. After a few minutes, she heard a car start and then accelerate away, spraying gravel.

She sat on the bed until she stopped shaking.

Then she pulled on some clothes and walked around the house, turning on the lights in every room. She switched on the stereo and found a country station. She played the music loud.

After a few hours, she fell asleep on the couch.

TWENTY-SIX

The sound started as a background disturbance, distant and nagging. It rapidly grew more insistent. Like a fingernail on a blackboard, it intruded into the red swirl of her dream. Her dream about her mother.

Her mother wasn't lying on the cold concrete. She was lying in the hot sun.

But Mommy wouldn't wake up. Grace twitched in her sleep. The terrible noise went on and on. Groggily, Grace stirred. Her arms thrashed involuntarily.

She woke up.

She was lying on a blanket on the lawn behind the house. Perspiration ran in rivulets off her body. Judging by the position of the sun, it must be late afternoon. Myles would be home soon. He'd phoned her at nine, from Daytona Beach. Lisa was in a clothing store, trying on outfits. Myles was out on the sidewalk, promising Grace he'd be home by eight.

She hadn't told him about her little adventure last night. It would have worried him, and Lisa might have noticed a change in his mood.

Grace had burdened the man's life with enough stress already.

What the hell is that noise?

Grace turned her head. Her heart thudded.

The gate alarm!

She jumped to her feet, grabbed her cell phone and Myles' shirt, and raced through the back door into the house.

What's the matter with me? Myles warned me about this!

She sprinted down the hallway to the kitchen and switched off the alarm. There was a knock on the front door. She walked softly to the dining room window, pulling the tee shirt over her head. Cautiously, she peered out.

There was a police car parked in front of the house. Grace backed away from the window. Her face went hot.

There are no vehicles here, she thought. No reason for them to think anyone's home. Hide in the bedroom! As she was processing the thought, a uniformed deputy stepped to the window and peered in. He looked right at her. Now she had to answer the door. Her knees turned to rubber.

As she swung the front door open, she found herself facing an imposing figure. The officer was young, late twenties or early thirties, several inches over six feet tall, and fairly good looking in spite of some permanent scarring from teenaged acne. He was so broad in the shoulders that his uniform shirt gaped slightly at the chest buttons, as if he was still wearing shirts issued to him before he'd started a weight-training program.

"Deputy Johnson, ma'am. Suwannee County Sheriff's Department. May I speak to you for a minute?" Forcing herself to stay calm, Grace stepped back and allowed him to enter. He ducked as he entered and carefully shut the door behind him. He removed his Stetson.

"Ma'am, I'm sorry to disturb you. I'm investigating a burglary at a residence just along the road. The owners are pretty sure their place was entered either yesterday or the day before. They've been away since Friday morning; came back early today. I'm checking with the neighbours to see if anyone saw or heard anything. Have you been home over the last few days?"

"I have been, yes. But I don't actually live here. I'm only visiting."

"Uh huh", he nodded. "So, have you seen anything suspicious, anyone hanging around, maybe a car that didn't seem to belong, anything like that?"

"Not really. Of course I wouldn't know who belongs here and who doesn't. And I haven't been outside much, except to sit out in the sun, or walk down to the river."

The deputy regarded her curiously for a moment.

"Can't help but notice your accent, ma'am. You from up north?" Grace was too shocked and nervous to dream up a lie.

"Yes, uh, actually from Canada. I'm on vacation."

The officer didn't respond. He continued to watch her closely. The silence was nerve-wracking.

"Ma'am?" Something in his tone made Grace feel nauseous.

"Yes?"

"I think we'd better sit down for a minute. There's something you and I need to talk about." He walked to the dining room table and pulled out a chair for her. He stood there until Grace followed him and sat down.

The officer pulled out the chair opposite, placed his hat on the table, sat down, and took a notebook out of his shirt pocket. He flipped it open, found the page he was looking for, and placed the small booklet carefully on the table, framing it with thick hands. He referred to the open page in front of him.

"About two o'clock this morning, Jimmy Barnes, one of our deputies, pulled over a 1991 Honda Civic. Speeding. Pretty routine. The driver was one of our local badass teenagers. Name's Ephraim Polk. 'Polk the Punk', we call him." He looked up. "Please don't repeat that, ma'am." He went back to his notes. "No one else was in the car, but the officer observed that the back seat was piled with stereo and video equipment. There was even a thirty-two inch TV jammed in there. Naturally, Deputy Barnes was suspicious, so he took the kid in. Checked the serial numbers and so on. Nothing reported stolen. But there was an open bottle of whiskey in the car – turns out it's the same brand as one that went missing from the house up the road here. Polk had booze on his breath and, since he's under age, Barnes locked him up. Mainly so he'd have a little more time to check on the stuff in the back seat of his car.

"This morning, the folks from up the road here came in to our office to report the break-in. They identified all the electronic equipment found in Polk's car. They're careful people – kept all their receipts. The serial numbers check out."

"So why are you calling on the neighbours if you've already caught the guy?" Grace asked. But even as she spoke, she'd guessed the answer.

"Because, ma'am, I just spent an hour grilling that kid, and he told me a story that I'm obliged to check out." He flipped over a few more pages in his notebook, and started reading. "Kid says he decided to hit another residence right after he finished the first one." The policeman looked up, his expression deadpan. "Guess he wanted to fill up the passenger seat as well, ma'am." He returned to his notes. "Says he spotted a driveway just along the road from the first one. He parked out on the road, climbed the fence and walked into the property through the bush. The description he gave of the house matches this one. There were no lights on and no cars around, so he tried to break in through a bedroom window. Says he never made it. Says some woman caught him when he was half though the window and stuck a shotgun in his face. Says she jammed the barrel between his eyes and threatened to blow his brains out. Scared him so bad he soiled his pants." Johnson looked straight at Grace, with a hint of amusement on his face. "Deputy Barnes confirms that."

Grace responded with a faint smile, but she wasn't sure what to say. If she denied that she was the scary shotgun-wielding woman, the deputy might ask her to accompany him to the office for further discussions. She was pretty sure she hadn't broken any laws – Americans were pretty firm on the right to defend home and property – but the police would certainly wonder why she wouldn't just admit to it. That might lead them to think that she had something to hide. It was time for some damage control.

Deputy Johnson interrupted her thoughts.

"So, ma'am. You got anything to tell me?"

"Yes, okay. That was me." Grace took a deep breath. "He made so much noise climbing in, he woke me up. I remembered seeing a shotgun in the closet, so I grabbed it. I don't even know if it was loaded," she lied, trying to sound naive. "I was pretty damned scared."

"Maybe. But you sure got your point across. Polk's got this nice red circle on his forehead where you nailed him with the muzzle. Should make an interesting bruise." He paused and gave her a stern look. "Why didn't you call it in, ma'am? And why were you playing dumb with me?" Grace had been working on her answer.

"Three reasons." She counted them off on her fingers. "One: he was just a kid. I didn't see his face – it was too dark – but I could tell by his voice. Two: there was no harm done and the boy got a good scare. He was squealing like a two-year-old. And three: I'm just a visitor here. I really like Florida, but I don't want to come all the way back from Canada just to testify about a teenaged burglar."

The deputy was about to reply when Grace's cell phone rang. She'd left it on the kitchen counter. She got up to answer.

"I'd like to see that shotgun."

"In the master bedroom closet." Grace pointed toward the hallway. "Second door on the right."

The officer headed toward the back of the house. Grace crossed into the kitchen to answer her phone. It could only be Myles or Pete. No one else had the number. Her stomach was still churning, but her mind was racing.

How am I going to handle this call with a cop in the house?

"Hello"

"Grace! It's Pete. I should be there in about ten minutes. I'm bringing something with me that I think you'll like. And I figure you must be getting sick of your own company, so I bought some swordfish steaks and a few other goodies. We can light the barbecue and wait for-" Pete was ready to ramble on, so Grace cut him off.

"Hi, honey," she said sweetly. That shut him up. She didn't know if the deputy was eavesdropping, but she hurtled on. "Glad you called! There's a policeman here, a Sheriff's deputy. He's investigating a burglary at one of the neighbour's places. Sounds like it was that same kid who tried to get in here last night when you were out at that meeting. The officer is wondering why we didn't report it. I told him about what we'd decided – about the kid being scared enough just by having me shove a shotgun in his face, and me not being able to identify him anyway..." She paused, to let that sink in. "Maybe you can talk to him when you get here."

There were a few seconds of dead air.

Come on, Peter! Think fast!

When Pete finally spoke, he caught Grace off guard.

"Your name! Did you tell him your name?"

"Uh, no, I-"

Oh shit! Of course!

"Sydney Cates."

"What?"

"Your name! Your name is Sydney, ah - just a minute! Sydney Ellen Cates. Sydney is spelled S-y-d-n-e-y, Ellen is... you know, the usual, and Cates, C-a-t-e-s." He seemed to be reading to her and trying to speak clearly, but he sounded a bit panicked. "Birth date is September second, nineteen seventy-two. Got that? Born Toronto, Ontario. Tell him you're a legal secretary at – Christ! Make something up! Anyway, did you get that? Want me to repeat it?"

"No." Grace had been concentrating. She knew her life depended on a good memory.

"Okay. I'll be there as fast as I can! Now listen! If he asks to see some ID, you left your knapsack in my car. With your ID in it. Okay? So if he asks, tell him your passport will be arriving in a few minutes. You and I – we're... friends. Be coy. Make it sound illicit, you know? Friends, in quotation marks! We met in Tampa earlier this week. At... at the Doubletree on Old Tampa Bay. We met by the pool. And we've borrowed Myles' house because he's away and it's out of the way and I have a girlfriend in town. Okay? Got all that?"

Grace was impressed. "Okay, lover," she breathed. She hoped the deputy was listening. "See you in a few minutes."

She disconnected. Then she remembered the gate alarm. She grabbed it, switched it to standby, and shoved it in a drawer.

A moment later, Deputy Johnson reappeared. He had his notebook in his hand.

"Okay, ma'am. I just made a note of the serial number of

the shotgun. Whose place is this?"

"His name is, uh… Myles-something. It belongs to a friend of my friend. He's away right now. He's letting us use it for a few days."

"So who is *your* friend?"

"Pete… uh, Peter Wetherall. He's a lawyer. That was him on the phone. He'll be here in a few minutes."

"Pete Wetherall, huh?" The deputy's expression changed slightly. His eyes took Grace in, their earlier professional detachment displaced by male appraisal. Grace thought he lingered a bit too long over her legs, visible below the hem of the tee shirt.

"You know Pete?" she asked cautiously.

"Pete? Oh, yeah. He's a defence attorney, I'm a cop. We run across each other once in a while." A pause, still looking at her. "Quite the boy, old Pete."

"Oh?"

"Yes, ma'am. Long story. Quite a few long stories." The deputy moved back to the dining room table and sat down. Grace followed, but, pointedly, she remained standing. Johnson took out his pen. "Now then, ma'am. May I have your full name please?"

"Sydney Cates." She spelled both names for him.

"Middle name?"

"Ellen."

"And your date of birth please, ma'am?"

"September second, nineteen seventy-two." Grace rattled it off, trying to make it sound like second nature. "You're really not going to need me on this case are you, sir? I mean, you did catch the boy with all that stolen property."

"Well, it's like this, ma'am. Our DA might be inclined to file an extra charge of attempted burglary, even if it's only for leverage, you understand? Might help persuade Polk and his attorney to plead guilty to the other break-in without filing a string of motions. So I'll just go ahead and record your statement and we'll see what comes of it. I'll need your address and phone numbers in Canada, so we'll know where to find you, just in case."

Grace didn't know her address. She was wondering what to say next. Whatever she might make up would be a stab in the dark.

Pete said I was born in Toronto...

Grace had spent a couple of days there, years ago, but she couldn't remember the names of any streets.

What's the area code for Toronto?

The officer stood up.

"I'll just get my clipboard out of the cruiser. I'll be right back."

Deputy Johnson went out the front door, leaving it ajar. Grace watched him through the window. He opened the passenger side of his patrol car and leaned inside.

Pete, where the hell are you?

The sound of Johnson's boots coming back up to the porch sounded to Grace like a death march. But just as the deputy reached the top step, she spotted a momentary reflection over the officer's shoulder, in the trees near the driveway. Pete's pickup came into view.

Hearing the moving vehicle behind him, Johnson turned, watched for a second, then went back down the steps and stood by his patrol car. Pete pulled to a stop ten feet from him. Grace could see her friend's face through the windshield; it wore an expression of cheerful recognition.

Johnson's back was to her, but she half-imagined the deputy might be smirking.

Pete Wetherall emerged from his truck, carrying a bag of groceries and a black packsack. He and Deputy Johnson met at the rear of the police car. They stood there talking. Grace felt it was best for her to stay out of the way. She went to the fridge and got a cold soda, not because she was thirsty but because she wanted to appear unconcerned. She grabbed the phone book and quickly checked the area code map.

Toronto: 416

Then she sat near a window and pretended deep interest in a magazine.

Looking up warily after a few minutes, she saw that Pete and the deputy were now in a huddle behind the police car. Pete was talking a mile a minute. After a while, both men straightened up. Pete held out his hand; Johnson took it and they shook. Then they walked together toward the house.

Pete entered first. Grace rose from her chair. He walked quickly to her, gave her a hug, put a hand on her ass, kissed her, and whispered, "It's okay."

Deputy Johnson hung in the doorway, watching. Pete turned toward the officer, but spoke to Grace.

'It's okay, honey. Carlyle and I had a talk and he's agreed to sit on this until tomorrow. Then he and I will meet with Charlie Hudson. He's the DA. I know Charlie pretty well. I doubt he'll want to spend all that money to bring you back from Canada to testify in some penny ante case like this. As I mentioned to Carlyle, if the kid's confessed to both cases, they've got him cold. And if for some reason his confession is ruled inadmissible, well... you can't identify him anyway, so your testimony wouldn't be much use."

"Well, I don't know about that, Pete," the deputy interjected for the doorway, grinning. "Your lady did put her brand on the kid's forehead.

"Yeah. Well, anyway, I'll talk to Charlie tomorrow."

Grace was relieved. Very relieved. She turned to the Deputy, who was still standing in the doorway, grinning. Grinning a little too broadly, she thought.

"Thank you, Mr. Johnson." She stepped toward him, extending her hand.

The deputy took it gently. "Pleasure meeting you." He smiled down at her. "I do mean that, ma'am. You made young Polk mess in his pants. Don't know of any cops ever scared him that bad."

Johnson retrieved his Stetson from the dining room table, and then turned to leave. Before Grace closed the door, he turned back.

"One more thing. That gun was loaded. Three in the magazine and one in the breech. I ejected the shells. They're on the bed."

Grace watched the police car pull out of the driveway and turned to Pete.

"How did you do it?" Grace asked.

"Like they say, it's a guy thing. Live Oak's a small town, Grace, and he knows I'm seeing Madeline. And now he thinks I'm getting laid by some gorgeous Canadian girl who's here on vacation. Cops love to know things about lawyers. Anyway, he agreed with me when I said I can't see the DA dipping into his piddling budget to fly you back from Canada to testify." He paused, thinking. "But this kid is one of the Polk clan. They're like a plague around here. No saying what Charlie Hudson might say. You better get ready to move on your plan... like, tomorrow."

Grace went cold inside at the thought. She took a deep breath.

"I owe you, Peter."

"No problem. It was kind of a rush!"

"A rush? Rattling off my vital statistics over the phone and praying I'd remember them?"

"No, girl. Grabbing your ass. *That* was a rush!"

Pete had certainly come through. After the deputy left, he laid Grace's ID on the coffee table in front of her: an Ontario birth certificate and a Canadian passport. To Grace's untrained eye, they looked genuine. Pete beamed.

"Roberto is magic. I told him I needed clean documents that would get a Canadian through Immigration in one of the Caribbean islands, and-" He saw Grace's alarmed expression. "Don't worry! I didn't tell him your real name and I didn't tell him where you were going."

Grace had already examined the passport. She picked it up again and flipped it open to the page with her photograph. "This says it was issued at Kingston, Jamaica in 1999."

"It had to be issued in Kingston."

"Why? Why wouldn't it be issued in Canada?"

"Look at the inscription under your photograph, across the

bottom of the page."

She looked, and then read out loud. "'This Canadian Passport is not machine readable'."

"Roberto says the ones issued in Canada *are* machine-readable. The Immigration guys can swipe them through a reader, just like a credit card. Those ones are really hard to forge. But most overseas embassies have to be able to issue passports to their citizens, and a lot of those embassies don't have the proper encoders. Anyone asks, your passport was stolen in '99 while you were on a trip to Jamaica and the replacement was issued by the embassy."

Myles drove in at eight fifteen. Grace and Pete were waiting on the porch. The barbecue was warmed up and the meal was ready to go. Grace ran to the car and threw her arms around Myles' neck. She hung on, not saying anything. After a few seconds, he eased her away from him and held her at arm's length. Grace's eyes were damp.

"Well now, little lady, seems you're glad to see me. Boring weekend, huh?"

Grace looked at Pete and they started to laugh. That only complicated matters. It took a marathon of explanations to wipe the suspicious look off Myles' face. A delicious supper of salad, rice and grilled fish helped. Myles was impressed with Pete's illicit acquisitions. But after he'd inspected the passport and birth certificate, and after Pete had answered the same questions Grace had asked, Myles went quiet. Grace knew why. The time had come, and their idyll was about to end.

After Pete hugged them both and drove away, Grace and Myles crawled, exhausted, into bed. Myles was scheduled for a deposition at ten the next morning, but in light of what was about to happen, Pete had agreed to take the file.

Lying in bed, with his strong arms around her, he whispered to Grace how much he loved her. He had said the words before, but never like this. Grace cried, and Myles tried not to. She held on to him. Eventually he fell asleep. Grace didn't. She lay there for hours, blinking at the ceiling.

302

PART III
GRAND CAYMAN
NOVEMBER 6 – NOVEMBER 15

TWENTY-SEVEN

Pirate's Lookout Guesthouse, on West Bay Road, was neither a lookout nor a guesthouse, but it offered cottage rentals by the week. At the going rates, Grace's one bedroom cottage was expensive, but it was adequate for her purposes. She didn't plan to be there very long.

Unit eight sat at the rear of the establishment's lush acreage. Mature lime, mango and Poinciana trees partially shaded the cottage's weather-beaten front door from the worst rays of the hot Caribbean sun. The back door, its frame and jamb swollen from the humidity, was difficult to budge, but when Grace finally wrenched it open she discovered a small patio with a pair of moulded plastic chairs. Beyond was a border of grass that ended, twenty feet further away, in a jungle-like tangle of tropical shrubbery.

She unpacked her single suitcase and put away her clothes. Then she tried calling Myles on her cell phone. As she'd feared, it wouldn't work. A recording instructed her to take her phone to the nearest Cable and Wireless office to register a new account. That wasn't going to happen.

She tossed the phone back in her bag, pulled on her ball cap and left the cottage. She walked back to the guesthouse office and bought a pre-paid phone card. Then she hiked out to West Bay Road, the busy thoroughfare that ran the length of Seven Mile Beach, and found a pay phone.

Myles had taken Monday off and they'd spent the day together, mostly in bed. That night, they'd loaded her bag in his car and driven to Tampa. They'd stayed in a hotel near the airport.

The next morning, he'd wanted to come into the terminal to see her off, but Grace objected. She reminded him that there was a war going on.

"While you've been at work, I've been watching the news," she'd said. "Airport security is really tight – surveillance cameras everywhere, and lots of federal agents watching monitors. As it is, I'm taking a pretty big risk. Even though the security people are probably concentrating on Middle-Eastern-looking men, it wouldn't be smart for you to show up on some surveillance tape walking arm-in-arm with me."

So he'd driven her right past the departure level drop-off zone and pulled his car to the curb a hundred yards beyond. He'd turned the engine off and looked her in the eye.

"Please don't try any soft option angles. Do you know what I mean?"

Grace shook her head.

"I mean, using your female wiles. You have an effect on men. Just remember what happened to Mata Hari."

"Remind me."

"She was shot as a spy."

"Don't worry. I'll stick to Plan A."

"Okay. Go do it."

Then he'd hugged her until she couldn't breathe and driven away. Grace felt sick to her stomach as she stood and watched his car disappear around the last corner.

"Thank God!" he said, as soon as he heard her voice on the phone. "Any trouble?"

"None. I sailed through."

"How's your place?"

"It'll do. Take down the directions? In case I-"

"Yeah. I know. Shoot." Grace explained carefully how to find her cottage. Myles had insisted before she left that if anything went wrong, she was to call him immediately. "I'll be there on the next flight," he'd said. "If the cell's turned off, use my office voice mail."

Grace told him about her cell phone. "It won't work here unless I open an account with the phone company. I'm not going to do that. The calls could connect you to me. I bought one of those pre-paid long distance cards instead, and I'll just have to use pay phones."

They kept the conversation short. Before Grace disconnected, Myles added a warning. "Get this done. Get it done as soon as you possibly can and get back here. You're exposed. Do you hear what I'm saying?" Myles wasn't talking about the police.

"I know. Thank you, Mister. I love you."

"And I love you, Missus. I want you back."

Grace hadn't bought groceries yet, so she went in search of a restaurant. She stayed on the eastern side of West Bay Road, away from the beach hotels. She had decided to stay out of the large resorts. Despite the travel industry's much-lamented business downturn since September eleventh, Cayman's beachfront hotels were likely to be crowded with tourists, mostly Americans. In other words, crowded with people who might have seen her on TV. It would only take one observant busybody to end Grace's career as a fugitive.

She found a small café. It was filled with customers who spoke with Caribbean and Spanish accents. A few heads swivelled, giving her the once over, then went back to their conversations.

She sat at a small table near the back and ordered a vegetable roti. It was delicious.

By the time she left the restaurant, the day was ending. She crossed the road and followed a paved walkway between two large condominium complexes. It led to the beach. The soft evening breeze was just strong enough to stir palm fronds above her head. They rattled gently, making a sound like rain on a tin roof.

She stood at the water's edge. The sinking sun transformed the sea into molten glass. She turned south and walked along the shoreline. Gleaming white sand curved away toward George Town harbour, three miles distant. There, a quarter mile or so out from shore, three white cruise ships lay at anchor on the turquoise water. Motorised tenders, painted rescue orange, bobbed toward them with loads of tourists returning from their day ashore.

Grace took off her sandals and walked on the tide line. Warm Caribbean waters lapped against her ankles and hissed on the sand. The experience seemed surreal. A mile further along, a beach bar called The Royal Palms was noisy with drinkers. The atmosphere was informal; most of the patrons were clad in shorts, brief tops and sandals. At one corner of the four-sided bar, five or six admiring males crowded around a pair of nubile young women. The girls were squealing with laughter. There was a dance area, but it was almost deserted. One couple clumsily stumbled through unfamiliar steps as a small steel band pounded away.

Grace bought a fruit punch and sat at the end of a low wall that separated the bar area from the beach. She sipped her drink and marvelled at her situation – a counterfeit stranger in a strange land. As she sat listening to the sea wash the sand, a wiry male, barely out of his teens, shuffled along the beach and passed by. He wore a Dick Whittington hat and carried a can of beer. After a dozen steps he stopped, as if he'd just realised something, and then reversed course. He lurched up the sandy slope to where Grace was sitting. Her heart sank at his approach. The young man stood, swaying, looking her up and down with unabashed interest.

He swept off his hat in a Gilbert and Sullivan bow.

"M'lady, I would be truly honoured if I could have this dance." He managed the offer with only a slight slurring of the words.

Grace tried to be polite. "Thank you, but no. I'd just like to be alone this evening." She tensed herself for trouble. The young man's bloodshot eyes marked a serious hangover in the making. In the meantime, the alcohol might fuel a streak of troublesome persistence. The last thing she needed was a drunken would-be stud, several years her junior, getting the wrong idea and trying to follow her home. It wasn't as if she could call the police.

Her fears were misplaced. The young man accepted her rebuff in good humour, plopped his silly hat back on his head and stumbled off up the beach in search of a more compliant female.

The next morning, Grace found a motorcycle dealership that catered to tourists and rented a 100cc scooter. She welcomed the helmet that came with it. It made her even less identifiable.

Although it was only mid-morning, the day was already humid and very warm. Grace spent fifteen minutes doing a practice ride along the streets and lanes near the dealership. She soon had the hang of it. There were no gears to change, the scooter was easy to ride, and the warm breeze felt good on her skin.

She joined the traffic on West Bay Road and headed south toward George Town. She knew when she was close. As she followed the waterfront into the small city core, she spotted a fresh flotilla of cruise ships lying offshore. The road on either side was lined with tee-shirt shops, fast food outlets, duty free shops and fancy jewellery emporia. The sidewalks were crowded with sunburned tourists.

She came to a traffic light. She turned left, heading inland. She had no interest in the waterfront carnival. She was looking for the Easton Building.

She found it tucked into a corner of George Town, several blocks back from the water, on a cross street connecting two main avenues. There was a parking lot extending along the front and down one side of the building and, across the road from the building, a small, triangular public park.

Grace parked her scooter and went for a stroll in the park. Apart from a foursome of tourists sprawled on the grass in a one corner, it was empty of people. What caught Grace's eye was a huge rubber tree. Its boughs, branches and leaves formed a tight, impenetrable tangle of dark green that almost touched the ground on all sides. But at one point in the massive tree's circumference, maintenance staff had sliced a hollow into the verdant matrix and positioned a small park bench in the space.

Grace tried the bench. From her position, she could see a slice of the park... a stretch of roadway... and the Easton

Building's front entrance.

She returned to her scooter. As she strapped on her helmet, a late-model Bentley Azure convertible turned into the street. Grace looked at the driver as the car glided past her.

Bingo.

Grace watched the Bentley swing into the Easton parking lot and reverse into a stall next to the front steps. The convertible's top rose out of the tonneau cover and slipped silently into place.

A fit-looking man in his forties stepped out of the car. He was wearing an open-necked shirt and dress slacks.

Ward Bellis.

He disappeared into the building.

Grace checked her watch. Nine fifty.

Banker's hours. I wonder when he takes lunch...

Grace started up her scooter and rode away.

Two hours later, she was back. She parked her scooter behind the rubber tree, plucked a grocery bag from the carrying basket on the back, locked her helmet to the bike, and settled onto the little bench under the rubber tree boughs. She removed a wrapped sandwich, a bottle of water and a book from the bag.

She watched people come and go from the Easton building while she pretended to read.

At twelve thirty, she ate her sandwich and sipped some water.

At five minutes after one, Bellis emerged from the building, accompanied by another man. They walked off down the street, engrossed in an animated discussion.

Grace pocketed her book. She collected up her trash and dropped it in a bin.

She followed the two men.

As she walked, she heard Myles' voice in her head. "Stick to Plan A!"

No harm. I'm just curious.

Bacchanalia Restaurant and Wine Bar was packed with a

luncheon crowd. There was a handful of tourists, mostly occupying the sidewalk tables outside, but the majority of the patrons were clearly local office professionals.

Grace found an empty table near Bellis and his companion. She ordered a glass of cranberry juice and a salad. She watched and listened as she pretended to read her book.

Ward Bellis had a permanent tan and a wide smile. His teeth were so alarmingly white that Grace's first thought was that they'd been chemically treated. Seen from this distance, he had the slightly embalmed look of an over-the-hill Hollywood actor. Unexpectedly, he had a Brit Midlands accent. The down-class accent didn't quite fit the look.

His companion was a short, wiry man with a crooked nose and thinning blond hair. When Grace heard him speak, she realised he was either an American from one of the northern tier States, or an eastern Canadian.

By the time Grace's salad arrived, a few nearby tables had emptied, lowering the din of lunchtime chatter. She picked at her meal slowly, stared at her open book, and strained to listen.

"Ed Scully over at Monetary said he circulated the blacklist to all the firms," Bellis's companion said.

"What list is this?" Bellis asked.

The other man's face flushed. "The FBI list! All the front organisations suspected of providing financing for terrorists. A raft of individuals too. Coupla hundred names, he said! I felt like an idiot!"

"Why?"

"Because I've never heard of it! He says they've issued three versions since September!"

"Kathleen probably received it and gave it to Corporate. We have over four thousand registered companies, Pat! Thousands of beneficial owners! It's going to take weeks to screen every file. That's a lot of staff downtime that we have to pay for!"

"Ward, that job should've started weeks ago! What happened to the earlier versions?"

"Never saw them."

"You expect me to believe that?"

Bellis's eyes went cold. "If you plan to accuse me of something, Pat, there are two things to remember: one, don't do it in public and, two, make sure your CV is up to date."

The other man paled. "Ward, I-I didn't mean…!"

"Good." Bellis smiled. He picked up the dessert menu. "How about something sweet?"

The two men finished their meal. Bellis paid the waitress and the other man left the tip. As they rose from their table, Bellis caught a gorgeous young blonde woman looking at him. Their eyes locked briefly. She deflected with a quick smile and returned to her book and her coffee.

Bellis hadn't seen her come in. His gaze flickered appreciatively over her body, then returned to her face. She was a knockout. Involuntarily, his imagination formed an image.

She'd be sensational…

As Bellis suppressed the thought, something else replaced it. He watched the woman sip her coffee. She was aware of his gaze and she was studiously ignoring him. Something nagged at his mind.

He and his associate exited the restaurant. They passed in front of its large front window. Bellis glanced in. At that second, the young woman lifted her head from her book. She turned and looked out.

Then he knew.

TWENTY-EIGHT

Shortly after six that evening, Grace returned to her post under the rubber tree. The Bentley was gone, but she wasn't there to watch Bellis. There were a few cars left in the parking lot, but by six thirty they were gone.

Sunset would be at six thirty-nine. Grace had checked.

She waited.

Darkness fell.

She waited.

A van appeared and turned into the parking lot. The sign on its side panel read 'Bushell's Janitorial'. Grace checked her watch. Seven thirty.

The vehicle parked near the front doors and five uniformed cleaning staff spilled out. They were a mixed group of black and Hispanic-looking women. One of them swiped a security card to gain entry through the front door. They all trooped inside.

After a few minutes, the top floor lights came on.

Grace waited.

After what seemed an interminable time, the main floor lights came on. A short while later, the last light on the top floor was extinguished.

Grace checked her watch. Nine thirty.

She waited.

Eventually, the front door opened. A cleaner propped it open and started carrying swollen trash bags out of the building. She disappeared around a corner with her first load.

Grace checked her watch. Ten forty-five.

She kept watching. The cleaner returned for two more loads.

Fifteen minutes later, the lights on the lower floor went out and the cleaners left the building.

Grace waited until their van drove away. Then she rolled her scooter out from behind the rubber tree and headed back to her cottage. She stopped at a pay phone on the way and called Myles.

"How did it go?"

"As predicted." They had agreed to be careful about what they said on the phone.

"From when to when?"

"Seven-thirty till eleven."

"And... the other thing?"

"It's workable." Based on experience, Grace knew that cleaning staff could be pretty lax about security while they were working on premises. She'd known there would be some weakness to exploit, but she hadn't quite counted on waltzing in through the front door in plain view of the street.

"You need to know their pattern."

"I've got tomorrow and Friday. Monday's a holiday here. Remembrance Day. Better set the appointment for Wednesday."

Myles knew what this meant. Grace recalled their conversation before she left Florida...

"You have a problem," Myles said. "You have to find a particular file in a building that holds thousands of files, most of them locked away in filing cabinets or vaults. Right?"

"Right."

"So if you can't get to the file, you have to get it to come to you."

Grace didn't answer immediately. Her mind was processing.

"How?"

"Say an existing client makes an appointment. Would a true professional wait until that person is sitting in his office, and then call for the file?"

Grace nodded. "He'll want to review the file. Show the client he's on top of things... switched on."

"And if the client happened to book the first appointment of the day?"

A second passed.

"Now you're going to tell me a certain client might call from

313

overseas to book an appointment."

"That's what I'm saying."

"You don't exactly sound like Eric Nader."

"I'll use a slightly French accent. The receptionist won't know the difference. I'll be in a hurry. Tell her it's just a quick visit. I'll ask her to put me in his diary for Wednesday morning."

Grace thought about that. "You keep getting in deeper."

Myles had shrugged. And smiled.

"Wednesday it is," Myles said.

"Will you do me a favour?

"You have to ask?"

Grace took a breath. "No. Guess I don't. Would you call A? Tell her we're getting close. I don't want to call her myself. I'd only want to talk to S, and then I'd probably break down."

"I spoke to her this morning. Everything's fine. A certain little munchkin is learning to speak a foreign language. Very fluently, I'm told." His tone changed. "Listen, I know this sounds cruel, but I want you to push her out of your mind. You need to concentrate. Okay?"

A mental picture of Shy flashed across Grace's consciousness. She wanted to linger over it, feel the love, remember the sweet smell of her baby girl...

She pushed the image away.

"You're right," she said.

Grace resumed her vigil on Thursday evening. There were still several vehicles in the parking lot when she arrived. One of them was the Bentley. As dusk settled, she checked the front corner office windows at each end of the building. The lights were on in one. It stood to reason that the senior partner would occupy a corner office.

Is that his office?

Just before seven, the office's lights went out. Two minutes later, Bellis emerged from the building.

It is. Thank you, Mr Bellis.

314

Grace retreated against the foliage behind the park bench as Bellis drove away. Then she waited for the cleaners. They arrived an hour late, and they didn't leave until nearly midnight. Grace was so tired she rode straight home and fell into bed. It was nearly noon on Friday before she called Myles.

"Grace! Where were you?"

"Sorry. I slept in."

"You have to get out of there!"

"What? Why?"

"I called the receptionist. I tried to book the appointment..."

Grace's heart sank. "Tried?"

"Yeah. She said I couldn't."

"What do you mean, 'couldn't'?"

"Because I already have one, on Tuesday! She read it to me: 'You-know-who, Tuesday, November thirteenth, eleven thirty a.m.'. I had to do a bit of fast talking... sound confused... blame my secretary... thank her for straightening me out."

Grace was silent.

"Get out of there, Grace! Today!"

She was thinking.

"Grace?"

"Why?"

"What?"

"Why should I leave? This is perfect!"

"Are you kidding? This just got a whole lot more dangerous!"

"They're meeting to cover their tracks. They're not expecting me! Monday night-"

"You said Monday's a holiday! The cleaning crew won't be working!"

"I talked to the manager where I'm staying. Friday night is party night. Most cleaning firms skip the Friday night shift and do the work on Sunday night. On long weekends, they do it on Monday night." She paused. "It's worth a look."

"You asked the manager? You shouldn't be asking those kinds of questions."

"We were just talking about the Caribbean lifestyle. Friday night's a big deal here."

"He's bound to remember the conversation."

"I doubt it. He loves to talk. He talks to everyone."

"Grace, I'm serious! Don't do it!"

"I'm serious too, Myles. I'm not giving up."

Grace had an early supper on Friday and then stayed inside, watching television. She surfed the Miami channels, looking for anything that would take her mind off her worries. It was late when she finally fell asleep.

On Saturday, she returned her rented scooter to the dealership and bought a bicycle. Bicycles made less noise.

Then she stayed close to home and waited for Monday night.

Hank Farrell's stomach was bothering him. Too much coffee and too little sleep for too many weeks were combining to destroy his insides. His squad kept telling him he'd end up in the emergency ward if he didn't ease up. Returning from the men's room for the third time this morning, he was beginning to think his detectives were right. Lori Graham was waiting at his desk. She was grinning.

Farrell lowered himself gingerly into his chair. He eyed her suspiciously.

"I just talked to an FBI agent in Seattle", she said. "His name is-" she squinted at her note pad "-Rob Harwood. I think we just caught a break."

Farrell straightened in his seat. He pointed at the chair next to his desk. Lori pulled it closer, still talking as she sat down. "Because of all this terrorist shit, the FBI's been running computer checks on airline passenger manifests, looking for matches with their intelligence databases. At first they concentrated on international flights, but recently they've been looking at the domestic ones too."

"And?"

"And... do you remember Grace Palliser's middle name?"

"Like I'd forget it. Arlene."

"Harwood told me that a woman using the name 'Arlene Palliser' booked a ticket from Seattle to Atlanta on the thirteenth of last month. She had a connection through Dallas, but she failed to board the onward flight. He says when that happens it usually sets off alarms, but only if the passenger has checked luggage. This passenger didn't."

Lori's words took Farrell's mind off his grumbling innards. He tapped the desk with his pen. "She left from Sea-Tac?"

"Yes."

"Sea-Tac is a major airport. There's gotta be surveillance cameras. Did you-?"

Lori nodded. "There are cameras, but the tapes are recycled after thirty days. Harwood checked with airport security before he called us. No go. The cassettes for that day have been taped over."

Farrell glanced at his calendar.

"Thirty days isn't up yet!"

"They ran short and started using the oldest ones last week."

Farrell threw down his pen. "For Christ's sake!" he barked. "They have four hijackings in one day, and it doesn't occur to somebody to start hanging on to those fucking tapes! What about Dallas?"

"He's checking. He'll call me back."

"Good." He stared at her, thinking. "I suppose it'd be stupid to ask if she gave the airline a contact number."

"They don't ask for one when you buy your ticket at the airport and fly the same day."

"Is that what she did? It fits."

"That's what I thought."

"She'd have to produce ID. At least tell me she did that!"

"She did, but it was just entered in the computer as 'photo ID seen'. No description."

"What ID? We have her purse!"

"Don't know yet. Harwood agreed to track down the ticket agent and interview her. See if she can remember anything."

"Send him the eight-photo lay-down. No, wait..." He

317

paused, thinking. "One of us should be at that interview." He leaned forward. "Feel like a trip to Seattle?"

"Fine with me."

"Okay. I'll fix it with the pencil necks upstairs. You call this FeeBee guy back and make the arrangements." He shuffled through a pile of papers on his desk and extracted a memo pad. "Pack a few extra clothes. If this is a hit, you might need to keep going."

"Keep going?"

"To Dallas. Better talk that over with Agent Harwood as well."

"Right, boss." Lori stood up. "Shit, I almost forgot..." Farrell looked up. "There's a Mountie waiting downstairs. Wants to see you. An Inspector from Courtenay. Has sort of a Dutch-sounding name... Naaykens, I think he said."

"Tom Naaykens? No kidding? Now there's a name."

"What do you mean?"

"I ran across him on a firearms course at the Argyll Street compound. He used to work out of that RCMP building in South Vancouver – the one the Mounties call the Puzzle Palace. He was one of those NCIS spooks."

"Why's he 'a name'?"

"He was on the team that took down that snakehead freighter a few years back. The one with the ninety Asian illegals in the hold."

"I remember. Some bad guys got killed, and one cop took a bullet." The penny dropped. "Him?"

"Yeah. And it was two bullets. Nearly died."

"They kept it kind of quiet."

"That's because the Operation Commander screwed up and Naaykens got left on his own. He killed three of the bad guys before he passed out. He spent a month in a hospital and then he disappeared."

Lori Graham shook her head.

"You look at a guy... you never think..."

"Courtenay, huh?" Farrell looked up at the map of Vancouver Island on the wall beside him, frowning. "What's he doing in a dink hole place like that?" He stood up. "Better go see what he wants."

TWENTY-NINE

At nine o'clock on Monday evening, Grace rode her bike out of Pirate's Lookout and turned south on West Bay Road. Traffic was light. The air was thick with humidity and she was soon perspiring through her tee shirt. When she reached the outskirts of George Town, a set of headlights fell in behind her. They maintained their distance. Just to be safe, she wheeled into a gas station. It was closed, but the pump islands were well lit. She pretended to check the air in her tires.

The vehicle swung into a side street. Grace glanced over her shoulder. It was a police cruiser.

In the town centre, she passed a few pedestrians, but most businesses were closed and most of the small downtown area was empty of people.

She turned into the Easton Building's street. As she peered into the parking lot, she felt a surge of adrenaline.

The Bushells van was there.

She rolled past the building. Nearly every window on the top floor was alight. The main floor was still in darkness. She rode slowly on, through the next intersection, made a wide turn and headed back. She wheeled silently into the park and into the shadows behind the rubber tree. She laid her bike on its side and slid it under the foliage, out of sight. She took a seat in her usual spot on the little bench. She waited. Only crickets disturbed the stillness of the night.

At eleven fifteen, a cleaner propped the front door open. Grace stood up. She eased out of the space under the tree and checked the street in each direction. The cleaner disappeared around the corner of the building.

Grace ran across the street.

When she reached the steps, she dropped to the ground beside the porch, out of sight to anyone using the front door. She waited.

The cleaner returned.

Silence.

Hell! What if that was her only load of trash?

The cleaner came out with a second load. As soon as she disappeared from view, Grace jumped up and, in a few bounds, ducked through door.

She almost tripped over two full trash bags that were positioned just inside the door. She dodged them just in time. She found herself in a large ornate lobby. She darted across it and into a darkened passageway to the rear.

She came to a door with a small window in it. Beyond was a lighted stairway. She ducked through it and moved swiftly up the stairs. The door shut behind her with a loud click.

As she passed the first landing, she heard the door below open. She froze. She could hear breathing, but no footsteps. Her throat closed, shutting off her breath. She risked a peek over the railing. A large woman in a Bushell's uniform stood in the doorway on the bottom landing. Listening.

The woman muttered to herself. She disappeared. The door clicked shut. Grace allowed herself to breathe.

Carefully, she mounted the last flight. She cracked the door. The second floor lay in darkness.

She slipped through the doorway and eased the door shut behind her. She set out toward Bellis's office, threading her way past the dim shapes of desks and partitions.

There was a gold-embossed sign next to the door to the corner office: "Ward Bellis, Managing Partner".

Thank you, God, for egotists.

The thick door was closed.

What if it's locked?

She drew a breath and tried the handle. It opened. As she stepped in, a large figure loomed from behind the desk. She nearly fainted.

It was Bellis's chair, backlit by light from outside. She closed the door quietly behind her.

Faint light leaked into the office from a streetlamp across the parking lot. In the semi-darkness, an enormous hardwood desk dominated the room. Save for a small reading lamp, a computer monitor and a tacky-looking penholder, the vast desktop was devoid of clutter.

Letting out a shaky breath, Grace moved quickly around the desk and pulled the chain on the small lamp. A pool of light appeared on the work area in front of the chair. There were no files. Grace tried every desk drawer. The bottom one on the right was locked. She scanned the room. There was no filing cabinet. She shifted her attention back to the locked drawer, studying it uncertainly. She rummaged in the other drawers until she found a letter opener. She groped under the desk for the lock, found it, and squatted down.

She was about to shove the tip of the letter opener into the keyway when she spotted something on the credenza across the room. She stood up and walked over. There were four or five folders sitting in a plastic tray. Grace thumbed down through the tabs. The third one bore a neatly typed label.

ARBAS INVESTMENTS LDC
File WB23857.001

The folder was an inch thick. She extracted it from the pile, returned to the desk, and sat in Bellis's chair. She opened the cover. A thin binder sat on top.

Memorandum and Articles of Association for Arbas Investments LDC.

She quickly flipped through the tabbed contents. They were the usual corporate documents. The incorporation certificate, dated August 17, 2001. It bore the seal of the Registrar of Companies for the Cayman Islands. Stamped across the seal were the words, "Exempted Limited Duration Company". She'd seen a copy of it before, stapled to Bellis's letter to Nader. The named directors of the company were companies themselves: Carib Corporate Services Limited and Carib Nominees Limited. Ten ordinary shares in Arbas had been issued and the sole subscriber was Carib Nominees. She looked for a banking resolution. She found it a few documents down: Carnarvon Bank and Trust Company (Cayman) Limited.

Who has signing authority on the account?

A standard-form bankers' mandate answered the question.

Ward Bellis, Director, Carib Nominees Limited.

Grace remembered what she'd learned working with Andre on the Jensen case. There could be a bearer warrant, giving the beneficial owner the right to buy all the shares in Arbas for a nominal amount. Or there could be some kind of trust.

She started working her way through the folder. After a few minutes, she had the answer. There was a manila envelope mixed in with general correspondence in the file. She opened the flap and pulled out a document. It bore a red seal. It was a trust deed.

Grace scanned the contents. It was briar patch of paragraph-length sentences and arcane legalese, but the essentials were clear enough. Carib Nominees had been appointed sole trustee of the issued share capital of Arbas Investments LDC, to be held by it for the exclusive use and benefit of... *The Chatila Relief Foundation*

What the hell is the Chatila Relief Foundation?

She examined the signatures and execution date at the bottom of the page.

Given under my hand and seal this 4ᵗʰ day of October, 2001.

David Samuel Getz

The notary's signature was a scrawl, but Grace had seen it before. A red wafer seal bore a legible imprint:

Province of British Columbia

Notary Public

Eric K. Nader

Grace sat back in Bellis's chair, her mind in turmoil.

What were they doing?

Her fingers detected a slight bulge at the bottom of the manila envelope. She turned it upside down and shook it. Two savings account passbooks spilled onto the desk.

She snatched up the one on top and opened the front cover. Customer number. Account number. Currency: USD. No name. She checked the account number against the one written on the bank mandate for Arbas Investments. They matched.

I'm holding the Arbas bank account in my hand.

She leafed through the book. It was empty except for the first page, which only showed eight or nine entries. Every entry except the first one was for an interest credit. The opening balance was $15,858,294.

Grace picked up the second book and flipped back the cover. The specified currency was also US dollars, but the account and customer numbers were different. Again, no name. She thumbed over to the first page. There were three entries. A deposit of $17,620,326. Then two withdrawals, ten days later. One for $15,858,294. Another for $1,762,032. Ten percent of the opening balance. The current balance was zero.

Grace laid the open passbooks side by side. After a moment, she saw it. The ten percent was Bellis's fee. The second book belonged to David Getz. But Getz probably had no idea it existed.

On an impulse, she turned on Bellis's computer. In seconds, the desktop display materialised. She waited for the inevitable password demand.

Nothing.

Must be protected for file searches only...

She clicked the Internet icon and arrowed through to a search engine. She typed in one word.

Chatila

The results appeared instantly. The advice bar claimed over twelve thousand hits.

Grace scrolled down the first page on the screen.

Chatila festival, Budapest. Tradition goes back to...

Chatila, Dr. Eduardo. Renowned expert on indigenous...

Chatila Marine Electronics. Your headquarters for...

Chatila and...

The fourth hit looked strange. Grace opened it. It took a few seconds to load. She started reading.

"Sweet Jesus!" she muttered. She backed out and scrolled down through the search results, checking each new site as she went. Some were in foreign languages, but most referred to the same subject. As an experiment, she jumped ahead and assayed a random page. More of the same.

Chatila and Sabra. Memorial to...

The site opened into photo galleries. She wandered through them, intermittently clicking on a thumbnail photograph to enlarge it. The images made her feel ill. Her gaze settled on the row of tiny photos at the bottom of a page.

She moved the cursor, picked one and clicked the mouse.

The screen filled.

For long seconds, she stared at the image before her.

Her face went hot, and then cold.

Her hands were shaking as she backed out of the site. She popped down the History window and deleted her searches. She burrowed through the operating system until she found a folder marked 'Temporary Internet Files'. All of her Chatila searches were listed there. She deleted them, exited, and shut down the computer.

Grace had what she needed.

And more. She was still reeling from her discovery.

She spiked the loose paperwork back on its metal fastener and tucked the incorporation binder back in the folder. Then she switched off the lamp and sat in the darkness, allowing her eyes time to adjust. Her hands were still shaking.

She moved the chair closer to the window and waited for the cleaners to leave. Finally, she saw the van drive away. She left the room, shutting the door behind her. As she made her way toward the stairs, the two bank passbooks slipped out of the file and dropped to the floor. She scooped them up and shoved them in her back pocket.

In the lobby, she ducked behind the reception desk and searched through drawers until she found a plastic bag. She shoved the file into the bag and knotted the top.

She exited the building and quickly crossed the street. She rounded the rubber tree. She stopped. She stood very still. She could almost feel the hair stand up on the back of her neck.

Something was telling her to get far away – now!

She stooped to retrieve her bicycle.

An odd smell drifted past her nostrils, faint and unpleasant. She stood up quickly.

There was a rustling noise behind her. She wheeled toward the source. A man's thick arm snaked around her neck and clamped hard against her throat, cutting off her air.

"Hello, Grace," a familiar voice whispered. Harvey Pendergast's grip was like iron. For a few seconds, Grace struggled like a mad woman. Then everything went black.

She was in a moving vehicle. Lying on her side. The vehicle was pounding over a rough surface. Her cheekbone banged painfully against hard metal. Her throat hurt from the choking. She struggled to get up, but discovered she couldn't. Her ankles and wrists were bound with tape. So was her mouth. She tried to turn over. When she did, her feet kicked something hard. She craned to see what it was. Her bike. Grace was lying in the cargo area of a van.

The vehicle slowed. Grace lifted her head to peer forward. Pendergast grinned at her over the back of the driver's seat.

"Morning, bright eyes!" He laughed, delighted at his own idiotic humour. He turned back to his driving. "I've got to hand it to you.," he called out. "You're one smart bitch." He held up the Arbas file. "Smart, but short on luck! We sent your photo to Bellis. After he spotted you in that restaurant, he called Eric." He drove on for a moment, and then he banged his hands on the steering wheel and shouted back at her. "You shoulda kept running!"

He subsided into silence. After what seemed like an interminable time, Grace felt the van slowing and then turning. It crept along in low gear, and then stopped.

Pendergast got out and slammed the door. After several minutes of silence, Grace heard footsteps and the van's back doors crashed open. Rough hands seized her feet and pulled her body toward the door. Pendergast cut the tape from her ankles, then scooped her up as if she weighed nothing and dropped her on her feet. He frog-marched her through a high wooden gate.

She had a glimpse of wooded property, old trees, and a single-storey house.

He hurried her onto a patio that faced open water. Grace frantically twisted her head to see, trying to memorise her surroundings. She saw a white flagpole rising out of an expanse of lawn. It had a cross-member near the top, like a sailing mast. She had the impression of white decking near the water's edge, possibly a dock.

Water lapped gently; there was no sound of breaking waves. On just about any Cayman shore, the rush of surf was constant. She guessed that the house faced North Sound, the forty square mile lagoon that lay behind Grand Cayman's north reef.

As Pendergast dragged her across the patio, she caught a glimpse of a white geodesic dome. It looked to be a mile or two away, along the shoreline.

Pendergast forced her through open French doors into a darkened living room, and then into a dimly lit hallway. After several paces, they climbed a flight of steps and made a sharp turn through a narrow doorway. He pushed her to her knees on a tiled floor. Then he straightened up, towering over her.

Grace's breath was coming fast; she looked wildly about. She was in a tiny unfurnished room. She struggled against her bindings and tried to shout at her captor. The tape across her mouth turned the words back.

"Quiet!" Pendergast slapped her across the side of the head and then kneeled down, grabbing her by the hair. He pulled her face close to his. His breath was foul. "Listen carefully! This is what some people call a hurricane room. Strongest room in the house. Nice and small, with extra thick walls and an oak door-" he patted the thick wooden door standing open against the inner wall. "It'll pretty much withstand anything, except maybe a twenty-foot storm surge. Soundproof, too. You'll be very safe here." He grinned malevolently at her. "Enjoy your stay."

He stood up to leave, then turned back. "There's no outside lock on this door. But not to worry, because I'm going to fix that for you right away."

Pendergast slammed the door behind him, plunging the tiny chamber into blackness. Only a thin thread of light was visible where the door met the tiled floor. After several minutes, Grace heard noise outside. Seconds later, the crash of nails being hammered home almost burst her eardrums. Then everything went quiet.

Half dozing, Myles waited for Grace's call. He used the time to torment himself. More than anything, he needed to *do* something. Sitting and waiting while Grace took the risks was wearing him down. He was ashamed. He'd been trained as an investigator. He knew more about her case than the cops who were trying to arrest her. She was in danger of becoming a victim of the justice system. His own country had seen plenty of examples of it – again and again, DNA had demonstrated just how wrongheaded, even plain stupid, some investigators could be.

Innocent people had been executed.

Myles knew he owed Grace more than this. More than just sheltering her and arranging her new identity and sending her off to some glorified sandbar somewhere in the Caribbean south of Cuba. Knowing what he knew, he should be booking a flight.

Then, there was Pete's idea. It was a long shot, but maybe... Just maybe...

He looked at the clock beside the bed.

4:10 a.m.

Where the hell is she?

THIRTY

Apart from fitful dozing, Grace didn't sleep. She kept shifting her position on the hard floor, but found little comfort. Her flesh went numb wherever it pressed against the tiles. The slit of dim light under the door never changed. She had no sense of time.

Hours passed.

Then she heard a distorted sound coming through a ceiling vent.

A jet aircraft taking off.

She had no idea whether Pendergast was still in the house or if he had left her to starve.

Outside, hidden from her eyes, a bright Caribbean morning slipped into afternoon.

Grace's half-doze was disturbed by a sudden shuffling in the hallway. Shadows flickered along the slit of light. There was a harsh squeal of metal against wood. As Grace listened, nails dropped one by one to the floor. She pushed herself into a corner. The door flew open and she was blinded.

"Showtime, Gracie!" Pendergast's enormous torso loomed over her. Without another word, he yanked her roughly to her feet and hoisted her over one shoulder. His body reeked of stale sweat. In her fear and revulsion, Grace almost vomited into her duct tape gag. Her captor wheeled, almost smashing her head into the doorframe, and started down the hallway. He carried her down the stairs, through the living room, bright with afternoon sun, and into a large modern kitchen. He lowered her to her feet but, before she could catch her balance, pushed her onto a straight-backed chair. She reeled with dizziness.

Pendergast produced a roll of duct tape. He methodically bound Grace's upper body to the chair back. Wherever the tape gum might stick to the bare flesh of her arms, he carefully inserted sections of paper towel. He repeated the process with her legs.

Why is this sick bastard being so careful about my skin?

When the job was done, Pendergast rose and surveyed his work. He gave the upper binding an experimental tug, then grunted in satisfaction.

He pulled up a chair in front of her and sat down. He stared for a few seconds, his eyes as featureless as a predator's, and then, without warning, he reached out and tore off the tape that was covering her mouth.

The outrage to her skin was like an electric shock.

Pendergast inspected the sticky side of the tape. He held it in front of her.

"You should thank me," he smirked. "A lot of women pay a fortune to have those embarrassing little moustache hairs removed."

Grace's rage overcame her fear.

"Are you insane? Whatever the hell you've got planned, you'll never get away with-!" Her mouth was still open, forming the next word, when the blow landed. Bright light exploded behind her eyes. Her chair rocked sideways and nearly went over. She cried out in pain and surprise. She blinked against her tears.

"Quiet please, Miss Palliser," Pendergast whispered. "Stay very quiet." His face appeared in double vision, a foot from Grace's eyes, as he emphasised his next words. *"Unless I ask you a question!"*

Grace sat there, stunned. Her right ear shrieked with pain.

Her tormentor leaned in closer, inspecting the right side of her face. He touched her ear. She winced and pulled away.

"Mmm. Not too bad," he muttered, mostly to himself. "It'll swell a bit, maybe get a bruise. One bruise won't matter. But that cut... musta been my ring." He made a fist with his right hand. It looked like a club. He was wearing a heavy ring with a dark stone.

He went to the sink, wetted some paper towel, and then gently dabbed at Grace's ear. When she tried to pull back, he held her by the shoulder.

"Cut it out, girlfriend. Should be no problem for a tough bitch like you." He was quiet for a moment. "Might need a couple of stitches. Sorry. No time for that." He finished dabbing. There was a large spot of bright red blood on the towel. He went back to the sink, soaked more paper towel under cold water, then returned and held it against her ear.

"I suppose I could cut your hands free so you could hold this thing yourself, but you might get stupid ideas. So, I'll just sit here until the bleeding stops and in the meantime you and I can have a little talk." His voice softened just slightly. "What did Devereaux tell you before he died?"

"He didn't die, you bastard!" Grace rasped. "You murdered him! How could you do that?"

"He was a meddling old fool. You'll be pleased to know that he died quietly, not a sound. Now answer me! What did he tell you?"

"Nothing... 'Get out of the firm'. 'Find another job.' Nothing!"

Pendergast's free hand shot out and clamped onto her throat. He squeezed hard.

"Cut the crap! You think I'm a fool! Two months after I set you up with that dead cop, here you are on Grand Cayman, sneaking into an office building in the middle of the night and coming out with the Arbas file! That old bastard had a hand-held tape recorder in his car, but it was empty. There were no tapes in his pockets and there were no tapes in his car. He'd been following me – I don't know for how long. Where are the tapes? What the fuck did he tell you? How do you know about Arbas?"

Grace was choking. Pendergast released his grip. *"Answer me!"* It took Grace a few seconds to recover her breath and find her voice. She struggled to fabricate.

"I found a tape in his house, before I left Victoria," she gasped. "It's in a safe place. It explains everything he found out. About Getz. About the fraud. Anything happens to me, it goes to the police! You and that creep Nader are fucked, Harvey! It's only a matter of time." A pause. "Where is he, anyway?"

"Coming. Got delayed in Switzerland." He leaned close. "You're lying! If you had a tape like that you wouldn't be on the run. You would've turned yourself in! What did he tell you about Arbas?"

Grace switched gears to a new lie.

"He read the Getz file. He'd figured out the scam. He'd made some copies and he was going to show them to me. But you killed him before he could do that. I broke into his house after the cops left and looked for the copies. I couldn't find them. But he'd told me enough." She fixed angry eyes on him, spitting her words. "How could you ever believe you'd get away with it? I had a reason to dig into this! The best reason going – you framed me and you took my daughter!" She stopped and looked at him, trying to sound reasonable. "Why are you in this anyway, Harvey? Nader's just using you. When you've outlived your usefulness, you're a dead man!"

Pendergast removed the compress from her ear, looked at it, looked at her ear, and then nodded, apparently satisfied. He smiled that old smile. The one from another time, another place.

"My end's covered. I've got my money. Nader will need me again – he doesn't like wet work. But just in case, I've got a passport he doesn't know about and a beach house in Panama. Just a few more loose ends and I'll be lying on a hammock with a blender drink in my hand."

He grinned at her as if he actually believed he was clever and cunning. Grace stared back at him. Her response, when it came, was deliberately calm, her words measured.

"You're really a piece of work, Harvey. Since I'm one of your loose ends, I guess you're planning to kill me. Go ahead. You'll still be caught – you and that reptile you work for. Other people know what I know. It's all documented!"

Pendergast's lip curled. "What are you talking about?"

"How do you think I got to the Cayman Islands? I'm a wanted killer! The cops in Victoria even put my face on American TV! I didn't just fly in here on my own passport, you idiot! I've got a complete new identity! How would I do that, huh, Harvey? How would a dumb secretary know where to go for a fake passport?" She sneered back at him, putting everything into it. "You might kill me, Harvey, but you're still screwed! Any way you look at it, you're screwed big time!"

"Skip the bullshit threats! They won't work." His eyes narrowed. "You'll soon answer my questions." His tone was ominous. "And you can start with who's helping you?"

"What, you think I'm going to tell you? So you can kill them too? No limits, huh, Harvey? One body, ten bodies, what's the difference, as long as you get your money!" She paused, tilting her head back. "Is it really the money, Harvey? Or do you just get off on killing people? Is that how you get your rocks off? Can't get it hard unless someone's screaming for mercy?" She shouted at him. "Fuck you, Harvey! I might end up dead, but I still get the last laugh!"

Grace steeled herself for another backhand. She didn't care. She was going to die anyway. At the same time, in the back of her mind, she knew that anyone could be forced to talk. She needed a cover story that would stand up no matter how brutal things got. A story she could stick with – one Pendergast could never be sure about. But to make it real, she'd have to make him work for it. That meant pain. Probably lots of pain. If she gave it up too soon, he'd think she was lying. She needed to worry him. Scare him.

By now, Myles would be worried. She wondered if he'd tried calling Pirate's Lookout. He'd keep trying. Then he'd drive to Tampa to catch a flight. He'd never find her. He wouldn't have a clue where to look. Her heart felt like lead.

I'm on my own with this monster.

Pendergast didn't hit her.

"You think I'm going to work you over, don't you?" he breathed. "Slap you around? Rip off your clothes? Fuck you up the ass? Real psycho stuff, right?" He got up from his chair.

"Sorry girly, that's not the real me. It *is* the money, and this is business. You get to leave here with your sweet little ass intact and only one bruise on your pretty face." He tapped a finger on her sore cheek. It hurt like hell; she jerked her head away. He smiled. "It's your lucky day."

Pendergast strolled to the refrigerator.

"Thirsty? Like a drink?"

"Yes."

He opened the freezer. "Ice?"

"Doesn't matter."

He reached into the freezer and pulled out an ice tray. Then he reached into a cupboard. When he turned back to Grace, he was holding a bottle of liquor.

"Water's fine, thanks."

"Really? Thought you drank this stuff straight."

"I don't drink anymore. Water's fine."

"Now, now, Grace. No fibbing to your friends. As I recall, last time we met, you were knocking back the expensive stuff. Your place, remember?" He held up the bottle. "Sorry. Not your brand, but it ain't bad stuff. It's Eric's, but he won't mind me sharing it with a special guest like you."

"Very generous, but I'm not drinking." His smile told her he wasn't listening. "That's just the point, Gracie darling. That's just the point."

Suddenly, she knew what he was planning. Fear clawed through her guts. Pendergast set the ice tray and a large tumbler on the table next to them. He twisted the cap off the bottle. Grace stared at the label.

Oban. Single Malt Whiskey.

Pendergast sat down. He dropped a few ice cubes in the glass and poured whiskey over them until it was almost full. Grace clenched her jaws shut.

"There! Just the way you like it. Drink nicely. I'll hold the glass for you."

Her jaws remained clamped. She radiated hatred.

334

"Right," he said resignedly. He set down the glass and picked up the bottle. "Just so you know, that was the easy way. This is the hard way!" His free hand shot out and locked on her jaw like a talon. After a few seconds of pressure, despite her determination, her mouth opened involuntarily.

Pendergast poured the liquor straight from the bottle into the back of her throat, then clamped her mouth shut. She had to swallow or drown. She swallowed most of it, but some streamed back out her nostrils and onto his arm. He grinned triumphantly and repeated the procedure. Then he released her for a moment so she could gasp for air.

She coughed violently, spraying whiskey and mucous.

"Care to reconsider?"

Grace nodded, tears streaming down her face. He held the glass for her. She took a sip. He held the bottom of the glass higher. She took another swallow.

"Good girl! You know, this is really great!" He chortled like a kid at the circus. "Pretty soon you're going to tell me everything I need to know. Then maybe you'll drink yourself to death. Too bad. They'll say you just couldn't take the strain – being an international fugitive and all. Couldn't live with what you've done. Finally cracked. Maybe they'll make a movie-of-the-week about your life. Deprived childhood, revenge on society... the whole formula. Think of it!"

Grace hadn't eaten for twenty-four hours. Already she could feel the alcohol. She knew it wouldn't be long before she was drunk, and then, if Pendergast kept pushing scotch into her, comatose.

As the heat from the alcohol began to spread toward her limbs, Grace forced herself to visualise some benchmarks. If she went through the exercise now, early, maybe the last things on her mind when she was still rational would become her obsession when she was drunk. She eyed the level of scotch in the bottle, silently calculating. Then she muttered bitterly, for Pendergast's benefit.

"God damn you, Harvey! If you're going to force me to drink, at least give me something to eat! I haven't eaten since yesterday!"

"Never mess with a good thing." He topped up the glass and held it to her mouth. Grace glanced at the bottle. Nearly a third of it was gone.

Half of that bottle will put me out.

Grace focused on trying to appear drunker by the second, praying Pendergast wouldn't get suspicious. She exaggerated her symptoms, first making them slight, then more pronounced. Timing was crucial. She had to stay ahead of the real level of absorption, far enough ahead that she'd still have a shred of mental function left when Pendergast believed she didn't.

It was a delicate balance. If he got too much booze past her lips, she'd never wake up. She concentrated on her story. The one she'd have to tell. The one that might make Pendergast think twice about killing her.

Pendergast kept pouring whiskey into her. She swallowed some and dribbled as much of it as she could down her chin. She let him see her eyes wandering crazily. She let her head loll forward

Without warning, he put the glass aside and stood up. "Work on that for a minute," he muttered at her. He left the kitchen.

Christ! Don't leave me here, you bastard! Ask your fucking questions while I can still think!

Waves of dizziness assaulted her brain.

Forty minutes. That's what the experts always said in those impaired driving cases. When a drunk driver killed someone, the prosecutors always called the crime lab witnesses to the stand. Their testimony had great impact on a jury. "Forty minutes for full absorption, assuming an empty stomach."

My stomach was empty! How long since he forced the first drink into me?

Grace twisted her head around, casting about for a clock on the wall, or built into some appliance. There was a digital glow

336

from the microwave, but she couldn't read it, her eyes wouldn't focus. She gave up.

Where the hell did he go?

Heavy steps reached her buzzing ears, and then Pendergast reappeared. He set a small white bottle on the table.

RUBBING ALCOHOL   WARNING! POISON!

He's going to poison me.

Myles, I'm sorry...

I love you.

Pendergast opened a drawer next to the sink.   Grace pretended to be semi-conscious. She watched him from under hooded lids. He turned around. He was holding a huge knife. Grace knew she only had seconds to live. She tried desperately to move, to get away, but her legs didn't feel connected to her body. They were immobilised, taped together and taped to the legs of her chair. Her feet jerked uselessly back and forth. If Pendergast noticed, he didn't react. He stepped behind her.

He's going to cut my throat.

Grace's mind separated from her body.

She waited for the end.

THIRTY-ONE

Pendergast squatted and pushed the knife blade through the dowels of the chair back. He sawed through the tape that bound Grace's wrists, then stepped around her and eased her numb forearms forward, placing her hands on her lap. He plucked the scraps of tape from her wrists. Then he pulled a rag out of his pocket and soaked it with rubbing alcohol.

He rubbed her wrists, one at a time, dissolving and wiping away all traces of adhesive on her skin. He was very gentle. He talked to her while he worked.

"Grace! Are you with me?"

She mumbled, pretending to be roused from a stupor. Her hands began to tingle, restored to full circulation for the first time in hours. The rubbing aggravated the pins and needles, but she endured in silence.

"Grace, how did you get a passport? Who helped you?"

"Can't tell n'body. Not 'lowed to tell."

The alcohol effect was still rising. Her slurred speech was no act.

"Gracie, girl-" He dabbed at the inside of a wrist. "Just tell me and maybe no one else will get hurt. Maybe I can just leave you somewhere to sleep it off and I'll drop out of sight and we can both get on with our new lives."

"You woan ged away. They know yer... know yer here."

"Who, Grace? Who knows I'm here?"

Even through the alcohol haze, Grace detected a faint note of worry. She remained silent, playing on it.

"Who knows I'm here, Grace? Tell me!"

Silence.

"Tell you what, Grace. Let's have some more to drink, shall we?" Pendergast stood up. A part of Grace's brain was still working - ponderously, but working. It told her she'd have to risk one more drink, if only to make the coming revelation more believable.

She stayed quiet. She drooled.

Pendergast resumed his seat. He dribbled more whiskey past her lips. She pretended to choke so she could spill most of it on her shirt.

The bottle was half empty. Pendergast held on to the glass, watching her.

"Grace?" She didn't answer him. For some reason, her own name didn't register in her brain.

I'm Sydney, not Grace. Doan-know-no-Gresh. Sydney.

He slapped her. Hard, on the left cheek.

Not like last time. Didn't hurt as much.

But it got her attention.

"Grace!"

"Whah?" She pretended to cry – no, she was crying.

Goin' under soon... Do it now, drunk girl! Now! Then you can rest...

"Who knows I'm here? Who, Grace?"

Grace stayed silent until she heard Pendergast shift in his chair.

Gonna hit me. Now or never.

"F-F-Farrl."

"What was that? Say it again, Grace." He put his head close to her mouth.

"Fah-rrell. Cop."

"Farrell? The cop? The Victoria cop, Grace?"

"Yeah. Sen-me-here. Asked him... t' sen me. Knows 'bout you." Grace slumped forward in her tape bindings. She wasn't faking anymore. The room was dipping and spinning like a fairway ride. Her field of vision was a half-lit tunnel crawling with vague shapes.

Pendergast sat back in his chair, staring at her. Through cracked lids, Grace made out his face. It was pale under a two-day stubble. A thought registered in her liquor-sodden brain.

He believes me.

An hour ago, he may not have believed Grace was working with the police. But now he'd be thinking: she's paralytic... on the verge of passing out.

Could she be lying now?

For Grace, the end of conscious thought came in a red rush.

In one instant, she was trying to work out whose mind she was thinking with – Pendergast's or her own.

In the next instant, thinking stopped.

The sky had been clear most of the day. Now it began to produce weather. Thunderheads were forming in the northeast. They towered into the stratosphere. The trade winds nudged them toward Grand Cayman's northern shore.

Pendergast stood at the window. North Sound stretched away in three directions, a giant lagoon behind the north reef. He checked the time. It would be dark soon. One of the advantages of the Island's latitude – or disadvantages, depending on your point of view – was that day and night were almost equal in length. For him, today, it was an advantage.

He returned to Grace Palliser. She was out cold. He squatted and methodically cut away the tape that bound her ankles. He wiped away every stray shred of adhesive material from her skin. After a final inspection, he tilted her head back.

She was definitely out of it.

She was a sexy woman. He'd had lots of fantasies about her. *Shoulda screwed her before I got her drunk.*

He released her chin. Her head slumped forward. He left her there, grabbed a set of keys from the counter, and walked through the house and out onto the patio. A hundred feet away, a Campion cruiser rocked and tugged on its moorings. The Yank landlord had included the boat in Nader's lease agreement.

Pendergast strode across the grass and out onto the dock. A passenger jet thundered overhead. He looked up in annoyance. Grand Cayman's main airport was the one drawback to this location. The upwind end of the runway was only a mile along the shore to the west.

He boarded the boat, checked the fuel levels, ran the bilge exhaust fan for thirty seconds, and then started the twins. They caught immediately. He ran them up for a few seconds, then pulled back on the throttles. They purred, tuned to run in harmony. He left them to warm up and proceeded forward, down the companionway to the small forward cabin. He checked the hatch over the v-berth. It was padlocked on the inside, a modification designed to deter thieves.

He glanced around the cabin.

This would hold her.

A forty-five minute ride and she'd be shark food.

He returned to the controls and shut down the engines. Then he sat on a stern locker, watching schools of minnows in the shallow water next to the boat.

He wondered about what she'd said.

Any way you cut it, the bitch is a witness.

If Farrell was letting her run – maybe had some kind of deal with her - then she's a prosecution witness.

Fuck Farrell!

No evidence, no case.

He checked the horizon. The sky was still bright in the west, but it was dark overhead. He moved. He switched off all the lights on the ocean side of the house. Then he returned to the kitchen. Grace hadn't moved. He cut away the last bindings that held her to the chair. She started to topple. He caught her and hoisted her over his shoulder. He carried her into the living room and dumped her on the couch. Then he went back outside and checked the neighbours' properties. There was no one in sight.

He carried Grace to the boat, over the gunwale, and down the steps into the forward cabin. He unloaded her in a sprawl onto the v-berth, then left and closed the door behind him. After re-starting the motors, he dropped the mooring lines and settled into the pilot seat behind the wheel. The big twins rumbled as he backed away from the dock. He swung the bow and headed north.

Although it was a slow process, the pitch and roll of the cruiser underway brought Grace around. The urgency of impending seasickness finally forced her hibernating consciousness back

341

through woollen layers until she returned to some semblance of awareness.

She strained to remember where she was.

A kitchen. A hard chair.

This isn't a kitchen.

She was lying on some kind of mattress. And it was moving.

Waves of horrifying nausea washed over her. She groped tentatively in each direction. When she found the edge of the mattress, she pulled herself over and vomited violently into the space beyond. Heaving again and again, she rid herself of Pendergast's most recent contributions to her wretched state. A pungent smell of booze and bile assaulted her nostrils, making her retch some more.

Tearful and exhausted, she crawled back. The vomiting brought some slight relief, but she knew more misery lay ahead.

What *was* ahead? Why was she in a boat? Her mind was a jumble – she didn't remember Pendergast saying anything about a boat. But there was something she did remember: he'd said she was going to drink herself to death.

He's going to dump me in the ocean.

She looked around. Faint light was coming in through two oval portholes, one on either side of the hull. She was lying on a v-berth. She recognised the configuration. Her grandfather had owned an old Chris Craft cabin cruiser.

On her hands and knees, she crawled to a porthole and looked out. The light of the boat's running lights glowed off wave crests; beyond that lay darkness. She couldn't see the horizon. She crawled to the other side. There was a low shoreline in the distance, lit here and there by pinpoints of light.

Peering through the portholes made her head swim. Her stomach threatened to rebel. The dark confined cabin filled her with a primitive sweaty apprehension. She crawled back to the edge of the berth and stuck two fingers down her throat, forcing herself to retch again onto the cabin sole. She needed to get any unabsorbed whiskey out of her system.

Hardly anything came up. It was probably too late. Grace knew she was very drunk. Her coordination was off and she had to concentrate to move her limbs. The signals from her brain to her muscles were unaccountably delayed. She knew she had to concentrate if she was going to survive.

There had to be some kind of light in the cabin.

Where's the switch?

Rising terror began to clear her mental processes.

On her hands and knees again, she groped along the underside of the storage lockers that overhung the berth on each side. Forward, under the bow peak, her fingers found a small locker door.

Find a light. Check the locker later.

Groping aft along the port side, she finally located an object mounted on the bulkhead near the foot of the berth. It felt like a dome light in a vehicle. There was a switch. She pressed it.

Light.

It was a small reading lamp, one of a pair. There was another switch at the foot of the starboard berth. She turned it on. She examined her prison. It was a typical forward cabin, cramped but functional. There was a hanging locker built into the aft bulkhead, on the port side, and a number of smaller storage lockers to starboard. There was a small area where a person could stand upright, a few square feet of finished hardwood sole, most of which was now splattered with malodorous vomit. The rest of the space was filled by the v-berth, overhanging storage spaces, and a small locker forward, under the peak of the bow. A deck hatchway was located directly above the v-berth. She reached up. It was padlocked.

Grace turned her attention to the cabin's teak door, set in the aft bulkhead. She lowered herself to the floor, avoiding the pool of vomit, and lurched across to the door. She was wobbly on her legs. She hadn't put weight on them for hours, and now she was standing in a moving boat with a mega-dose of alcohol in her bloodstream.

She turned the knob carefully and – as gently as she could in her condition – she tried to pull it open. It was locked from the outside.

Of course it's locked, you idiot!

There was a light switch on the wall inside the door. Looking up, she saw a recessed light in the main ceiling. She didn't need the extra light, but seeing it made her suddenly wonder if the light from the reading lamps could be detected through the crack under the door.

She pulled off her booze-soaked tee shirt and stuffed it in the crack along the bottom of the door.

Weariness overcame her.

Maybe I should lie down for a minute...

No!

As methodically as she could, with shaking hands and a spinning head, Grace searched every locker. Most were empty, but one of the portside lockers contained a beat up tackle box. She opened it, praying for a fish cleaning knife. The top tray held a few scraps of tackle. She couldn't think of a way to use fishhooks as weapons. She lifted the tray to search underneath.

Spoons and spinners, a few spools of clear line.

Pendergast was very strong. She needed a knife, or something heavy to hit him. She dug through the bottom of the tackle box. An incongruous shape caught her eye. A shotgun cartridge. Another one.

Must be flares. Flares look like shotgun shells.

She held one close to a light. The alcohol blurred her vision. She squinted to focus. There was etching in the brass ends of both cartridges.

00 Buck

They were the real thing.

Where's the shotgun?

The v-berth mattress was split down the centreline of the berth, forming two sections. She pulled up one half. Underneath, she saw a lift-out hatch giving access to the space below. She shoved the mattress over onto its mate and frantically yanked up the hatch. Light from the reading lamp dimly illuminated the void within.

An inch of filthy water sloshed in the bottom. Otherwise, it was empty. She repeated the process on the other side of the berth. Nothing.

The cruiser ploughed on through the night. The wind was picking up. Waves banged against the hull and the cruiser's pitching became more pronounced. And there was a new sound. Grace could hear rain drumming on the deck above.

The only space she hadn't searched was the forward locker, but it was too small to conceal a shotgun.

She was defenceless. The realisation made her sick with terror.

She vaguely remembered that bow lockers were normally used to store anchor chain. A length of chain might do some damage. She crawled forward and pulled the small door open. With the light coming from behind, her shadow interfered with the view inside. She crawled as far as she could to one side and pressed her head against the frame of the doorway. She peered in.

Rope. Lots of it.

She reached in, feeling for chain. If she could find a short length, maybe with a turnbuckle on the end, she might take Pendergast by surprise. She prodded around the edges of the rope, feeling for metal. Her fingers closed on something. A box. It was wedged between the rope pile and the side of the locker. She tugged at it until it came free.

The box was made of hard black plastic, about ten inches square and four or five inches thick. Its lid was secured with plastic catches. She could read some words stamped into the lid, next to a familiar corporate logo.

Crossen Small Arms
Marine Flare Pistol

There was some smaller print under that. She squinted to read it.

12 Gauge Conversion

Grace closed her eyes in silent thanks, then opened them quickly as her dizziness intensified. With trembling fingers, she released the snaps and lifted the lid.

The flare pistol lay in its pre-formed plastic bed, along with six flare cartridges. The flares didn't interest her. She picked up the gun and, fumbling, released the catch so that the full length of the barrel hinged away from the frame. Like most flare pistols, it was designed to break for loading like an old fashioned double-barrelled shotgun.

The adapter! Where's the adapter?

It was in the barrel.

She slid the tempered metal sleeve out of the breech and examined it. It was in good shape. The adapter acted as a barrel within a barrel, with a flange at one end for seating. It was a simple conversion, with only one interchangeable component. All that was needed to convert the marine flare gun into a twelve-gauge handgun.

Grace had never had much use for her grandfather. The life he'd provided for her and her brother after they'd been orphaned had been joyless and inflexible. But on this mouldy bunk, on the dark Caribbean Sea, sick with liquor and fear, Grace Palliser thanked the Lord for the old man.

Her Grandpa had owned one of these guns. They were illegal in Canada. They were probably illegal in the Caymans as well, which could be why this one was hidden away in a rope locker. But Grandpa had never permitted such niggling details to get in his way. He'd bought his gun second-hand from a commercial fisherman at Friday Harbour, in the American San Juan Islands, and carried it on his boat for years.

And, bless the old bastard's heart, one summer evening he had shown a teen-aged Grace how to use it.

She slid the adapter back in the barrel. She loaded it with one of the shotgun shells. She snapped the barrel closed, locking it in place. She fingered the extra cartridge; she knew if she missed with her first shot, she'd never have time to reload.

She'd only have one chance to save her life.

*

346

The soft darkness of early evening had rapidly transformed into the Blackness of the Pit. As vast thunderheads bore down on North Sound, convection caused the wind to intensify and shift direction. A following sea developed, then whitecaps. The cruiser was urged forward into the path of the advancing maelstrom. Lightning arced from cloud to cloud, thunder ripped through the violated air and, to the east, the lights of Rum Point disappeared behind sheets of rain.

Pendergast eyed the clouds through the cruiser's windshield, his apprehension growing. He had planned to dump Grace Palliser outside the reef. He'd heard the tourist boat operators talking about people stupid enough to go snorkelling out there. "Next stop - Cuba!" they'd joked.

The idea had suited him. With luck, Grace Palliser would disappear without a trace.

But Pendergast was inexperienced on the water, and this weather was scuttling his plans. It had already started to rain, and he knew thunderheads could produce gale force winds over a local area. With the decreasing visibility, he doubted he could even find the channel through the reef.

Plan A – drunk chick goes skinny-dipping in six thousand feet of water, disappears forever.

He peered through the windscreen. It was starting to rain.

Plan A was out.

He checked the reading on the depth sounder.

Twenty-eight feet.

The whole of North Sound had an average depth of about fifteen feet. If he dumped the woman here, eventually her body would be found. He turned that over in his mind. It could work. Plan B – drunk chick goes for a night swim at Rum Point and drowns. Turns out she's a fugitive. Working with the police? Maybe she'd fooled the cops. Maybe she was guilty after all and couldn't live with herself. Or, maybe it was just an accident.

Shit happens.

He'd strip off her clothes before he tipped her over the side. As soon as he got back, he'd drive around to Rum Point, lean her bike against a tree and dump her clothes on the sand.

Pendergast eased off on the throttles and swung the boat through a hundred and eighty degrees. Now the bow faced into the rising sea. He locked in the autopilot. That should hold it for the one or two minutes it would take. The nearest land was a couple of miles away. Even if the dunking brought her around, the booze and the waves would finish her off.

He'd prefer to cave in her skull first, for insurance, but that might make the locals suspicious. He switched off the running lights and all the inboard lighting. The cabin and the rear deck were now completely dark. He stood on the rear deck and scanned the horizon. There were no other boats around.

He moved forward, down the companionway to the forward cabin door. The sliding lock was designed to take a padlock, but for this trip he'd just hooked a fishing gaff through the mechanism. He removed it, slid back the bolt and opened the door. The cabin was pitch black and it stunk of vomit. The thud of the heavy seas pounding against the hull was louder down here. Pendergast smiled to himself.

"Gracie, time for your swim!" he called. He switched on the overhead light and took a step forward. He stopped. The berth was empty. He stepped forward and peered up at the deck hatch. The padlock was in place. As he turned to check behind the door, his eye caught a flash of red. He dodged left. A hard metal object glanced off his skull above his right ear and smashed onto the point of his shoulder. He grunted, more from sheer surprise than from pain. He was still holding the fish gaff; he lashed out downwards and backwards and felt the hook strike something soft. There was a shriek of pain. He tightened his grip on the gaff handle and pulled forward violently, trying to pull the woman off her feet. He was rewarded by a scream of agony, but instantly a tremendous weight struck his right wrist. Bone cracked. His hand went numb and, as he dropped the gaff, a fire extinguisher clattered to the floor in front of him. At that instant the boat pitched forward and, aided by gravity, the woman shoved him headlong onto the berth.

Pendergast pushed himself upright and spun around. Grace was stumbling up the steps to the pilot deck, the gaff hook embedded in her right calf. Blood streamed down from the wound. He lunged for the trailing handle of the gaff, but his feet slipped on something wet just as the cruiser climbed another wave. He was thrown against the edge of the swinging cabin door and then he crashed, half-stunned, onto the hard cabin sole. His head and shoulders lay in a pool of evil-smelling vomit.

After a few seconds, he climbed unsteadily to his feet. He picked up the fire extinguisher with his good hand and started up the steps. This bitch was going in the water.

But first I'm going to crush her fucking skull!

Grace had known the risks. In close quarters, she was no match for Pendergast.

At first, she'd switched off the light and crawled up to the far end of the berth. She'd waited there in the darkness, knees drawn up, with the loaded Crossen ready in her hand. But her alcohol-soaked brain had continued to ponderously analyse her chances. In this position she was, quite literally, cornered. If he went for her, she'd have to shoot. If she killed him, fine. But if she missed, or only wounded him, he'd have her by the ankles before she could reload.

You need more options, her brain had told her. *More room.*

She'd seen the fire extinguisher earlier, mounted on the portside bulkhead. Its potential had finally registered in her sodden imagination. She'd crammed herself against the hanging locker behind the door. When she heard him coming, she'd raised the fire extinguisher over her head.

Grace staggered through the covered pilothouse and onto the open rear deck. The wind was howling through the boat fittings and she was instantly drenched in rain and spray. The effect was sobering. She had hoped to lock Pendergast in the cabin on her way out. That would have given her a chance to work out her next move, maybe even beach the cruiser before he could break out. That chance was gone.

The boat had fallen off the seas and was wallowing beam-to. The autopilot was attempting to correct, but that only seemed to make things worse. It was impossible to remain standing on the rolling deck. Grace collapsed onto a cushioned locker seat next to the transom and examined her injured leg. It was throbbing with pain. The gaff hook had penetrated nearly two inches of muscle. If she pulled it out, she'd bleed more. She unscrewed the handle and laid it on the seat next to her, leaving the hook in her flesh. Blood was leaking from the wound onto the deck. She would have to deal with it soon.

But first things first. Pendergast wasn't out of this fight. Even if she'd broken his wrist, he could probably overpower her with one arm.

All she had was the Crossen. Even out here, she'd only have time for one shot. After that, her only escape route was over the side. Blinding rain slashed at her as her mind worked furiously. A life jacket! She moved off her seat, kneeled and lifted the cushion she'd been sitting on. There was a locker underneath. She groped inside. No life jacket.

The corner of her eye caught movement. She turned.

Pendergast was lurching up the steps. He had the fire extinguisher in his left hand. His right arm dangled at his side. He glanced at her, then worked his way to the wheel, fighting the roll of the boat. He dropped the extinguisher on the seat and released the locked wheel. He increased power, swung the bow into the wind, and locked the autopilot again. Then he opened a small locker in the fibreglass dashboard and groped inside.

Grace reached behind her. Her fingers tightened on the grip of the flare gun tucked in her waistband. Pendergast removed a rag from the compartment, held it out the vent window to get it wet, and then wedged himself between the pilot seat and the dash while he methodically wiped Grace's puke from his face.

"You lied, Palliser!" he yelled. "Said you don't drink. If you can handle that much booze and still be makin' trouble, you just gotta have a drinking problem!" He dropped the rag on the deck and flipped a switch on the dash. A rear deck floodlight came on, turning the rain and spray into a dazzling curtain. Grace was momentarily blinded.

Pendergast grabbed the fire extinguisher and stumbled toward her. Grace raised the gun and pointed it at his chest. He saw the muzzle. He stopped ten feet from her, just under the pilot deck cover. He swayed back and forth, trying to keep his feet under him on the pitching deck.

"A flare gun?" He started to laugh. "Good plan, girlfriend! You shoot me with a flare, it scorches my shirt, then I take that gun away from you and-" He didn't finish. He seemed to notice that her eyes weren't afraid. And her hands were steady.

He spotted the brass end of the second shotgun shell sticking out of her bra.

"Extra shells? Is that so after you kill me with the first one you can signal for help?" He mocked her with fake laughter. Lightning flashed overhead. Grace saw insane rage burning in his eyes. "I'll tell you what, bitch. You go ahead and shoot that popgun! Then I'm going to take it away from you and shove it up your ass! *Then* you're going over the side!"

"You try that, Harvey." Grace's voice was calm. She held the gun steady, using both hands, as if she'd been trained for it. The muzzle was pointed at the middle of Pendergast's chest. The bow of the cruiser climbed a wave. Grace tried to compensate. Her aim wavered.

"Fuckin' bitch!" Pendergast rushed at her, raising the extinguisher high, ready to smash it down on her head.

When Pendergast was five steps away, the cruiser crested the wave. When he was four steps away, the deck rolled forward, slowing his momentum. When he was three steps away, Grace squeezed the trigger.

The Crossen roared.

The fire extinguisher flew from Pendergast's hand as he pitched violently backwards. He landed like a sack on the deck. He lay there, heaving and quivering. Grace quickly broke open the pistol and extracted the spent casing. She pulled the extra shell out of her bra. She reloaded.

She crawled toward her tormentor's writhing form. The blast had torn out his throat. Rivers of blood poured from the ruined tissues. There was a hideous sucking sound as his lungs made futile attempts to breathe. Grace positioned herself where he could see her. She sat on the deck and calmly pointed the pistol at his face. His face wore an expression of utter disbelief.

She saw he was dying. She lowered her weapon. Pendergast's eyes followed the gun down, then tracked back up and locked on hers. They pleaded her to shoot again, to end the agony.

Grace shook her head.

"Andre Devereaux was my friend."

Grace Palliser sat unblinking on the rolling deck, in the rain and the blood, watching Harvey Pendergast die.

THIRTY-TWO

Fifteen minutes after Pendergast died, another squall struck.

By then, Grace had managed to extract the gaff hook from her leg. She screamed at the heavens as she pulled the metal from her bleeding flesh. Almost fainting from the pain, she staggered to the forward cabin to retrieve her tee shirt. She bound it around her calf and knotted it tightly. Her search for a first aid kit was cut short by a rogue wave that threw the Campion on her beam's end. Grace was flung against the pilot seat pedestal, striking her head and nearly losing consciousness. The twin props shrieked as they came out of the water. She struggled to her feet and hauled herself onto the pilot seat.

For awful seconds, she puzzled over the autopilot, then realised that she'd already disengaged it by moving the wheel. She spun the helm frantically, swinging the bow into the oncoming seas, and then ran up the throttles until she felt the hull making way.

She located the toggle for the afterdeck spotlight and switched it off. Her own distracting reflection on the inside of the windshield vanished and she could see ahead more clearly.

She gripped the wheel and tried to navigate each new wave as it loomed. She prayed.

After several minutes, the roar of agitated water reached her ears through the general din of wind and rain. The sound came from astern. It grew louder. She kept looking over her shoulder, but only saw blackness. She groped on the dash until she found the spot light switch and flipped it on.

The light's glare reflected off an area of boiling water and flying foam, fifty feet behind the transom.

A reef!

Grace boosted the throttles to maximum power. The boat wallowed in a trough, its engines shrieking. She kept peering over her shoulder, willing the boat forward. For long seconds, she couldn't gauge whether she was making progress, but gradually, over the deafening whine of the twin power plants, the roar of breaking water started to recede astern. She heaved a grim sigh, her breath ragged with fear.

The encounter with the reef made her realise that she needed a compass reference. If Pendergast had run them outside the reef, she was now heading away from Grand Cayman, out into the open Caribbean. In that case, a compass would show a northerly heading. If she were still inside the reef, somewhere in North Sound, the bow should be pointing generally south. A compass heading was critical.

The dash lights were dark. She ran her hand down a row of switches, trying them: anchor light, cabin lights, running lights... There! The panel lights blinked on with the running lights.

She scanned the dials: fuel tanks, batteries, engine temperature, oil pressure...

Depth sounder.

26 feet.

Compass!

South-southeast.

I'm still in North Sound.

On this heading, she'd eventually reach shore.

The boat ploughed on through the wild night. Her head still felt the whiskey, but, strangely, the nausea was easing. An hour passed. An hour spent peering nervously at the compass. An hour spent fighting the helm, her strength fading.

Then the rain stopped and the wind eased. The huge thunderhead clouds moved off to the west, giant Chinese lanterns lit from within by brilliant displays of lightning. The sky cleared astern, and then overhead. A few stars appeared. The waves diminished into disordered slop. In the distance, over the bow, she could make out a few scattered lights.

Now I've got another body to answer for.

I have to get back to Florida.

But I need a head start...

She glanced back at Pendergast's corpse. In the chaotic seas, it had rolled from its original position. Now it was wedged tight against the rear bulkhead of the pilot cabin.

He was going to dump me over the side.

Grace locked the helm. She limped back to the body. She leaned down and grabbed it by the ankles. She began dragging it across the deck.

It was well after midnight when she found her way back to the house. She hadn't even planned to search for it.

It had taken several minutes to tip Pendergast's corpse into the Sound. Then, using a cut-down plastic bleach container from one of the deck lockers, she'd sluiced the blood off the deck and out through the scuppers.

When she'd returned to the helm, she'd spotted navigation lights. It wasn't another boat. It was an aircraft. The plane had just taken off. It was climbing out toward the east. Grace adjusted course a few degrees to where she'd first seen the plane and held the bow on that heading.

As she neared the southern shoreline of the Sound, she saw the white dome. She'd seen it before. She knew it had something to do with the airport. Radar, maybe. Using it as a point of reference, she began idling her way east, a few hundred feet out from the shoreline. She studied the outline of the houses. Finally, she saw a flagpole that looked like a ship's mast.

She manoeuvred the cruiser toward the unlit dock. The house beyond was completely dark, almost indiscernible from the surrounding foliage. She was too tired and in too much pain to moor up properly, so she ran the Campion shoreward, parallel to the dock, until it went aground. She shut down the engines, clambered painfully onto the dock and limped toward the house.

It was the right house. She knew it the moment she stepped onto the patio. But now she was here, she wasn't ready to go in. After all the torments she had endured within its walls, and on the waters behind her, she was no better off. Her future looked even more hopeless than before.

She lowered herself onto a lawn chair and looked at the sky. Every muscle in her body ached with tension; her injured leg throbbed. She sat motionless for a long time.

Another jet climbed overhead, turbines whining.

Relentless pain from the wound in her leg finally drove her into the house. That, and roiling nausea.

The door was unlocked. She switched on a light. The living room was nicely furnished, an eggshell-toned tribute to fine tropical living. The elegance was incongruous, given the activities of the home's most recent resident. Grace sat on a plush chair and examined her leg. Her tee shirt bandage was still in place. It was soaked in blood.

She got up and limped desperately through the house. She found two bathrooms, but there was nothing in them that she could use to clean or dress her torn calf muscle. She worked her way to the kitchen. The chair where Pendergast had tormented her still sat in its place, trailing scraps of duct tape. Spilled whiskey glistened on the table and floor. The scene revolted her.

She lurched to the table and grabbed the rubbing alcohol. On her way to a bathroom, she found a clean pillowcase in a closet. She tore it into strips. In the bathroom, she propped herself on the edge of the tub and removed the makeshift tee shirt bandage. There was a ragged wound in her calf. Blood began to flow.

Gritting her teeth, she ran warm water directly onto the wound. The heat increased the bleeding. She let it drip for a few minutes, hoping to clean out any brewing infection.

Then she poured alcohol on her leg until she heard herself wailing. Her hands shook violently as she tried to dress her ravaged leg with strips of pillowcase. She finally succeeded.

She stumbled from the bathroom. She felt light-headed. The wall decorations in the foyer doubled and then tripled as her eyes lost focus. She barely made it to the living room. She flopped on the couch and was unconscious within seconds.

*

It was raining in Atlanta. A cab sped along a broad avenue, sliding expertly through traffic, dodged around a bus and pulled abruptly to the curb. The driver jerked a thumb toward a tall building across the street.

"It's over there. U-turn's illegal."

Pete Wetherall stared out at the downpour.

"Couldn't you go around the block?"

"Got another fare waiting. A regular." The driver sat there. Pete stared in disbelief.

"Thanks! I'll remember to never use your company again." He paid the fare and jumped out. He was wearing a light shirt, jeans and sandals. He had no hat, no coat and no umbrella. He darted across the street, defying honking horns and fingering drivers. He was soaked when he reached the opposite sidewalk.

He ducked under the cover of the tall building's broad entrance. He made a vain attempt to brush off the worst of the wet. Then he stepped into the revolving door to the lobby. Above his head, under a huge logo, gold lettering spelled out *Continental Broadcast Center*.

Pete stopped inside the door, still dripping. His eyes swept the lobby. He spotted a security guard. He walked straight toward him.

When Grace awoke, it was mid-afternoon. The after-effect of tension had left her feeling drained. Her throat was parched. She found some bottled water in the refrigerator. She gulped it down.

Then she went looking for the file. She started at the back of the house. The first bedroom was empty. A few sticks of furniture, a bare mattress, empty drawers, an empty closet. She moved along the hallway to the next door. The room smelled of Pendergast. Grace's lips curled involuntarily and she almost gagged. She switched on the ceiling fan, hoping it would help clear the dead air.

The bed was unmade, its sheets sweat-stained. In an open closet, a few shirts hung lopsidedly on plastic hangers. A battered suitcase lay on the floor. She started with the bureau drawers. They were empty. She pushed the mattress off the bed. Nothing. Methodically, she checked the rest of the room. Nothing.

Now the suitcase. She lifted it onto the bed and released the catches. Breathing through her mouth, she rifled through the contents: underwear, cotton pants, shoes, a couple of belts.

No weapons.

No ID. His wallet must have been in his pants when she dumped him into North Sound.

No file.

Grace moved to the next room. It was twice the size of the first two bedrooms. It was expensively furnished, with an ensuite bathroom.

Men's clothes were neatly arranged in the closet – lightweight shirts together, then several pairs of casual slacks. On a low shelf, shoes and leather sandals were set out side-by-side in a perfect row. Grace removed a hanger and held up a shirt. It was too small for Pendergast. She pulled a pair of slacks off a hanger and held them against her hip.

Nader's?

Methodically, she took the room apart. The nightstands were empty. She moved to the dressers. There were two, and they held clothing. One by one, she pulled out the drawers and dumped the contents on the bed.

She found a thin briefcase in the bottom drawer of the second dresser. It was half full of loose papers, most of them of no interest. But, behind a clipped panel inside the lid, her fingers closed on a sheaf of documents. She pulled them out. They were credit card statements. She'd seen the logo before.

Carnarvon Bank and Trust

The addressee on each statement was Arbas Investments LDC. The front page of each bore a red ink stamp:

'Hold Mail'.

358

The statements dated back nearly a year. Grace sat on the bed and examined them one by one. Eventually she came to one dated October 25 2001.

What the hell?

She sat motionless, staring at a single expenditure entry.

She folded the page and shoved it in her pocket.

Grace parked Pendergast's van behind a small strip mall, two blocks from Pirate's Lookout. She had already searched the vehicle, but now she searched it again. This time, she checked behind each side panel in the cargo area. Then she moved her bike, which still lay where Pendergast had thrown it, and felt for storage compartments built into the floor.

No compartments.

No file.

Pendergast wouldn't have destroyed the file without Nader's permission. He would have phoned him after he'd snatched Grace from the parking lot.

Grace had no doubt that Nader had ordered Pendergast to dispose of her.

The file was probably in a courier packet, on its way to Victoria.

Or Switzerland.

But she still had the passbooks. Incredibly, Pendergast, the ex-cop, had been so confident when he retrieved the file that he hadn't bothered to search her.

Grace climbed out of the van. The gash in her calf was pulsating. She didn't think she could ride her bike, so she left it. By the time she'd limped to her cottage, she was dripping with perspiration and blood was seeping through the makeshift dressing on her leg. She moved the flowerpot where she'd hidden her key.

It was gone.

Nader!

Fear coursed through her. Then rage. She'd had enough. She limped around the side of the cottage, pulling the Crossen out of her pants as she went. She cocked the hammer. She had never locked the back door. It was swollen and stuck in its frame, so she'd never bothered. She stepped onto the patio. She leaned back, lifted her good leg and kicked the door in. She took three steps into the kitchen, the flare gun tracking with her line of sight. The dark figure of a man appeared in the bedroom doorway. Grace swung the gun toward him. He dove out of sight a millisecond before she pulled the trigger. The gun kicked in her hand and six inches of doorframe exploded in a shower of splinters right where the man had been standing.

"Grace! It's me!"

Grace dropped the gun and staggered across the kitchen. She collapsed sobbing into Myles Rothwell's arms. The front door opened. Grace stopped crying. She stared uncomprehendingly at the man in the doorway.

"Jesus Christ!" Pete Wetherall blurted. "What happened to you?"

Grace sat in a soft chair. The wound on her leg was freshly dressed. The table next to her was strewn with wads of bloody gauze and scraps of medical tape. A cloth floated in a bowl of steaming water.

Myles and Pete were talking in the kitchen. She was too tired to try to overhear. As the two men rejoined her, Pete's cell phone rang. He stepped back in the kitchen to answer.

"It's time we ended this, Grace," Myles said quietly.

From the kitchen, she heard Pete say,

"She's here now."

"Sounds like you already have," Grace replied. "Better book our flights."

"Already have, in a manner of speaking."

From the kitchen, Pete was saying, "Yes… and we'll need a doctor." There was a pause. "Okay. See you then."

"Explain 'in a manner of speaking'," Grace demanded.

Pete reappeared from the kitchen. He was grinning from ear to ear.

*

The white twin-engine Gulfstream V stood on a taxiway apron, silhouetted against the brightening eastern horizon. Except for U.S. registration numbers stencilled on the cowlings of the twin Rolls Royce power plants, there were no identifying markings. The main door was open and the steps were down. A uniformed Immigration officer stood nearby, waiting. The limousine nosed up to a chain link gate. The Immigration officer walked across the tarmac to the fence, removed a padlock and swung the gate open. The long white car rolled through the gap and drove straight over to the aircraft. Behind it, the gate clanged shut. The car stopped at the bottom of the step. Myles and Grace got out. The officer examined their passports and allowed them to board. Grace limped slowly up the steps. Myles followed with their luggage. A young cabin steward materialised in the doorway above and descended to meet them. His nametag read 'Daniel'. He offered Grace his arm. They entered the aircraft. He helped her move forward. Myles followed. She stepped through an archway into a hushed little world of pile carpet, soft divans and a small conference table. Further forward was a neat, modern galley.

Pete Wetherall and a grey-haired man were sitting on leather club chairs, talking. When Grace, her escort and Myles entered the cabin, they both rose. The man with Pete was tall and lank, dressed in slacks and an open-necked shirt. Grace recognised him instantly. The man approached Grace and extended his right hand. In that same instant, a man appeared in the galley doorway. He had a television camera on his shoulder. He focused it on Grace and her greeter.

"Good morning, Miss Palliser. I'm Wendell Forbes. Your attorney here-" he paused imperceptibly, indicating Pete "-is a very persuasive and determined man."

"My attorney…?" Despite her earlier determination to remain cool, Grace found herself gaping at the famous face in front of her.

"Very persuasive." Forbes repeated.

Grace looked at Pete.

"So I've been learning."

Pete grinned.

"It also didn't hurt to have a former federal agent in your camp." Forbes was looking at Myles. Myles found her hand and squeezed it reassuringly. Forbes smiled gently and put a hand on Grace's shoulder. "We understand you've been injured. We've brought a surgeon. Please make yourself comfortable while I fetch her." As Grace settled in a comfortable seat, the Gulfstream's engines started spooling up.

PART IV
BRITISH COLUMBIA
NOVEMBER 16 – JANUARY 4

THIRTY-THREE

The Gulfstream halted on the runway threshold while the cockpit crew ran the final checks. Then the twin turbofans powered up, the brakes released, and the aircraft leaped forward. It tore down the runway, stood on its tail and climbed out over North Sound in a steep, banking turn to the northeast. The passenger cabin was eerily quiet. Even at full power, the noise of the engines barely intruded upon the soft hiss of the ventilation system.

Grace gazed out the window as the shoreline disappeared under the wing and the emerald waters of the Sound began sliding past below. After a few seconds, the dark green of the inshore waters transformed into an artist's swirl of lime and cerulean and topaz. Then a long white thread of breaking water appeared. It ran east-west, straddling their flight path.

The North Reef.

Harvey Pendergast's body was down there.

Grace rubbed her eyes.

It all felt unreal.

Myles had told her that he'd waited until nine on the morning after her break-in at the Easton Building. Then he'd phoned Pete Wetherall.

"You heard from Grace?" Pete had asked.

"No."

There was dead air on the line.

"Shit, Myles!"

"You know your idea?"

"Which one?"

"The crazy one."

"You're kidding!"

"I'm not. I'm heading for Grand Cayman. You go to Atlanta."

Pete had had to think that over for about... one second.

"On my way!" he'd said.

And now here she was, flying back to Canada on an American television network's private jet.

She'd talked to Annette and Shy on the telephone last night. It had been a long call, filled with love and excitement and relief. Then Grace had asked the question.

"Annette?"

"Yes?"

"Could you and Shy fly back to Victoria? We can arrange to get your car later."

"Can't do that, Grace. I don't have any ID for Shy! They wouldn't let me take her on the plane!"

"You're right." Grace had looked at Myles and Pete. "I'll call you back." The long nightmare would soon be over. Or... not. What if their scheme went wrong?

The Mounties might simply decide to turn her over to the Victoria Police and let them sort it out. Myles didn't think that would happen. He'd spoken to Tom Naaykens. "The man sounds solid, Grace. Your instincts were right." But Grace couldn't get the doubts out of her mind. She kept imagining it all going wrong. A huge media circus. Farrell making sure the cameras got just the right shot of him, striding with awful purpose through the front doors of the Burdett Street Courthouse. Everyone politely overlooking the fact that his attempts to apprehend her had failed completely. The press hounds cranking out background profiles on her victims. The story of her mother's grisly death and her father's suicide unleashing endless rounds of speculative 'in-depth' reports about psychotic motives.

At least there were a few consolations. Her case was so notorious that top defence lawyers would be queuing up to represent her. Of course, many of them wouldn't give a damn whether she was actually innocent. They'd just want to trade on her notoriety in the hope of getting some of their own.

Grace lay on blankets on the conference table, with her injured calf nestled on a bed of sterile pads. Wendell Forbes stood a few feet away, chatting with Pete, while Myles held Grace's hand. A young Japanese-American doctor was carefully suturing Grace's wound. The cameraman was perched on the back of a club chair, recording every move. By agreement, his camera's audio pickup had been switched off during the procedure. Yoshi Walker cinched the final suture. She had been enticed by the network's offer to pay off her entire student loan account in return for her services on this bizarre mercy flight. "And," she'd confided to Grace when Forbes wasn't listening, "in return for my notarised undertaking to keep my mouth shut until the story hits the evening news."

With a clatter, Yoshi consigned the last of her instruments to a surgical tray. With deft hands, she dressed the wound. Then she stood up and peeled off her latex gloves. In tight jeans and a short tee, Yoshi Walker looked like an Olympic gymnast on a training break.

"That should hold you. I'm going to give you a tetanus shot in a minute. And I brought some antibiotics with me, as a precaution. I'll give you a seven-day supply, and I want you to finish the course. What about painkillers? When that local anaesthetic comes out, it's going to feel worse than before. How about some T-3's?"

Grace was silent. She felt Myles become still.

Painkillers.

Pills. Always the damned pills.

"No. Thanks anyway. I want to keep my head clear for my interview with Wendell. And for when we land in Victoria. If I could put up with a bullet wound, I suppose I can put up with this."

"Show me."

Grace pulled up her shirt and lifted her arm. Yoshi examined the scar across her ribs, still an angry crimson after two months. The cameraman zoomed in over Yoshi's shoulder. Forbes tapped him on the shoulder. The cameraman switched on the audio pickup.

"Doctor Walker," Forbes asked in his interviewer's voice, "is this scar consistent with a grazing wound from a rifle bullet?"

"Definitely. I spent three years working shifts in an inner-city emergency room. This damage is what I would expect to see if a bullet grazed or glanced off the ribcage and the wound was not promptly treated by a physician." She spoke to Grace. "It looks pretty ugly now, but a good cosmetic surgeon should be able to do a revision so it won't look so bad."

Grace smiled. "Least of my worries." She held out a hand for Myles to help her off the table.

Yoshi put a hand on her back. "No. Stay there for a minute. The tetanus shot goes in your backside." She addressed the gathering. "No cameras, please. And, for that matter, no audience. Why don't you gentlemen go to the galley and make the ladies some coffee."

An hour later, the taped interview began. Grace had got most of the way through her story when the Gulfstream landed in Winnipeg.

"We have clearance to land, folks." The co-pilot's Oklahoma accent broke the sombre quiet of the cabin. "Winnipeg Tower has just passed on instructions from the Canadian authorities. When the aircraft stops, no one will be allowed off. Two passengers will board. We will take on some fuel. We will then immediately take off."

The jet landed. Ten minutes later, Daniel escorted Annette and Shy into the main cabin.

Shy squealed and ran into her mother's arms. Annette cried. Grace cried. Shy understood nothing, but she cried because the adults were crying.

Forbes' cameraman recorded every emotional second on film. Then Grace sat down with Wendell Forbes and resumed her interview. When that was finished, he interviewed Annette. And finally, it was Shy's turn. It took a while to record her small part of the story because she kept switching into French.

After three more hours in the air, the co-pilot's voice came back on the intercom:

"Ladies and gentlemen... Victoria Tower has instructed us to proceed to Taxiway November and park in front of a row of small hangars. The captain has spoken with an RCMP supervisor on a separate frequency. He says our aircraft will be put under guard as soon as we shut down the engines. No one is to disembark until the police give permission. When we open the doors, officers will come aboard. Miss Palliser will be escorted off the plane first. Mr Rothwell and Mr Wetherall will follow. Miss Devereaux and the child deplane next. The rest of us will meet with police and immigration officials on board." A pause. "Mr. Forbes, sir. You will be asked to surrender your interview tape for copying. The original will be returned before we leave."

It was almost dark when the Gulfstream lined up with the runway on its final approach over the black waters of Patricia Bay, swooped in low and fast over a lit-up pair of moored Coast Guard cutters, and touched down on the numbers.

The pilots quickly bled off speed and the aircraft was soon bumping rhythmically over runway expansion joints. It made a left turn into a remote taxiway near the far end of the runway, continued for a few hundred yards and rocked to a stop. One by one, the engines shut down.

Let the show begin, Grace thought.

"I see I'm moving up in the world," Grace commented, looking up at the fifty-foot sliding door. RCMP Sergeant Ed Parnell didn't immediately reply. He clamped a big hand on a welded flange and pushed. The heavy door rolled a few feet. He stood aside. "There are two gentlemen here who wish to speak with you."

Grace stepped through the gap. The hangar was small, designed to accommodate a light plane. Two men were seated at a large table near the rear wall. A television set, its screen a solid blue, and a microfiche reader sat on one end of the table. The reader had a projection device mounted on top, directed at a pull-down screen on the wall.

Out of uniform, Tom Naaykens looked younger than when he and Grace had first met. She didn't recognise the other man. He was thickset, with dark, wispy hair and a sallow complexion. As Grace entered the hangar, he studied her with intense eyes.

Grace hesitated uncertainly in the doorway. The men rose to their feet. Tom Naaykens walked toward her, followed by the other man. Grace's knees went weak. Sergeant Parnell whispered to her.

"Relax, Miss. Cops don't usually stand for murderers."

"They haven't even heard my story yet."

"Tom Naaykens is a very smart man. That's all you need to know."

Larry Nixon's urgent voice echoed through the hangar.

"I'd love to get my hands on that Arbas file! There might be some names. Contacts. Telephone message slips." The FBI agent was far more expansive than he'd been when Grace had first taken her seat at the table. For the first twenty minutes of Forbes' interview tape, Nixon had sat back with crossed arms, his dark eyes occasionally cutting to Grace's face. His body language dared her to convince him. But, by the time she reached the late night visit to Bellis's office and the harrowing events that ended with Pendergast's death, the man was leaning forward, fascinated, all scepticism gone.

Now, four hours after she stepped into the hangar, Larry Nixon was addressing Grace by her first name.

Tom Naaykens clicked a ballpoint pen. "Nader isn't a fool. He would have ring-fenced his relationship with Ward Bellis so the lawyer wouldn't come into contact with anyone else in the network. And Bellis won't be a man who asks too many questions. It sounds to me like there's only one true God for him, and that's the dollar." He looked at Nixon. "Your government has an MLAT with the Cayman Islands, doesn't it?"

"Yeah."

"What's an MLAT?" Grace asked.

"A mutual legal assistance treaty," Nixon explained.

"You could probably persuade the Cayman Islands police to arrest this Bellis character," Naaykens continued, "but I doubt he'll give you much more than a small section of the paper trail. This is what the money-laundering guys call a 'walking account'. And you can bet it's walking now."

Nixon grunted. "You're right. We can only implicate Nader and Bellis and that bent banker, Koop, in the fraud on the Holocaust Fund." He leaned forward. "We need to work our way up the chain and not only find out where the money went but, more important, what these bastards are spending it on. We've got the CIA sniffing around for us, but who'd want to rely on those guys? September eleventh caught them flat-footed.

"If you guys pull Nader in and search his office and his house, you're going to get zilch in the way of documents. By now, the man's nervous. He hasn't heard from his personal thug for a few days, so I'm thinking there's no way he'll go to Cayman. He's either hunkering down in Switzerland or he's heading back here. We could use our best people to interrogate him, but they won't get Word One out of him. He's patient and he's careful and he's damned smart. Shit, Tom, this guy's been practising law in your country for years! That's what the Soviets used to do – run sleeper agents against us. Eric Nader won't talk. He'll never talk. He won't give us squat."

Nixon picked up a half-eaten Danish from a plate in front of him and took a bite. He chewed, thinking. "We need a way to get this guy talking. We don't know where this money's going, and that scares me." Nixon looked Naaykens in the eye. "It's your call, Tom. It's your show."

"I'm listening."

"We need to rattle his cage."

Grace had been sipping coffee. She put down her cup.

"Rattle his cage?" she asked.

Tom answered for Nixon. "Old expression. You tap a target's phones. Then a couple of detectives pay him a visit and ask a lot of pointed questions. Then you sit back and listen to his phone calls. Sometimes it works. Sometimes it doesn't." He looked at Nixon. "I can't see it working here.

Your people have given too many interviews on CNN about 'homeland security'. As you said, Nader's smart. I don't really see him picking up a telephone after a couple of detectives come calling. I see him dropping out of sight. Sure, I could put Special 'O' on him, keep him under surveillance, but if they lose him, we'll never get him back."

The group was silent.

Larry Nixon pushed back his chair and stood up. A section of the microfiche was projected on screen. He stood in front of the image, studying the bank balance of a long-dead Holocaust victim. Its reflection cast an umber glow over his skin.

"You know, we've got over four thousand agents working on the 9-11 investigation. We haven't told the media this, but we're sure there was a fifth crew of hijackers. They were booked on an early morning flight from Phoenix to Chicago. Our intel guys think they were planning to blast the top off the Hoover Dam. Personally, my money's on one of those obscene mega-hotels on the Vegas Strip. Anyway, when they were driving to the Phoenix airport, their car collided with a load of pipe that fell off a semi-trailer. Four of them were killed. The survivor was medi-vac'd to a Phoenix hospital. By the time our people put two-and-two together, someone had paid off his hospital bill and he'd disappeared." Nixon turned to face them, weary frustration in his eyes. "We've identified the four dead ones. They were Lebanese. And that scares the shit out of us. You know why?"

"Because", Tom answered, speaking slowly, "it could mean that Hezbollah and Al Qaeda have joined forces."

"That's right! Hezbollah were behind the suicide bombing of our Marine barracks in Beirut, back in '82. But they've never tried to harm us in our own country. Their primary target has always been Israel. They're a real dangerous bunch. Some of the CIA guys call them 'the A-team'. If they've joined up with Bin Laden's crazies, we're in real trouble."

While Nixon was speaking, Grace was watching Tom's face. He didn't look at all surprised at Nixon's revelations.

"Just a minute! Is Nader a Lebanese name?" she asked.

"Actually, it's German." Tom answered. "But yes, the Beirut phone book is full of Naders. Eric Nader came to Canada when he was in his early twenties. Supposedly, he was a refugee from the civil war in Lebanon. He had a degree from the American University of Beirut, so he was accepted into law school back in Ontario. After September eleventh, the FBI asked us to run some specialised searches on our Immigration data bank. Because of the federal privacy laws, we had to wait for the new anti-terrorist legislation to come into effect before we could do it. Nader's name came up in the first run." He looked directly at Grace, his tone apologetic. "I was suspicious about your case from the minute it hit the news. It just didn't sound right. When I saw your old law firm's name on that list, right next to the entry on Nader, I went to see Hank Farrell. I asked him a few questions. I didn't much like his answers. Or his attitude."

Grace looked at Larry Nixon. He'd returned to his chair. His face was sombre and he seemed lost in thought.

She took a deep breath. "Let me help."

"Help?" Tom looked confused. "Haven't you done enough?"

"That's what Annette said. And that's what Myles will say. But let me do it."

The two men looked at her.

"Do what?" Nixon asked.

"Rattle his cage."

Naaykens shook his head.

"The young man in the park," Grace went on. "The one Annette brained with her flashlight. Her description of him sounded like Michael Dimitri. He's a first year lawyer at Pomeroy's. Nader pushed the partners into hiring him. Some members of the firm were against it. Michael Dimitri's uncle is a long-time client of Nader's, a man named Armand Dimitri."

Tom straightened in his chair. "*The* Armand Dimitri?"

"Yes. The odd thing is, the last time I saw Armand was on the Sunday before Andre was killed. He was in the office lobby, waiting for the elevator. He said he'd just finished meeting with Nader."

"Who is *the* Armand Dimitri?" Nixon asked Tom.

"Businessman. Owns a string of upscale coffee shops. A bit like Starbucks."

"Is he Lebanese?"

Grace answered. "That's what it says in that little history blurb on the back of his company's coffee bags." She paused, pondering. "There's something else. I need to get on a computer."

Galleries of photographs. Children whose play had been interrupted for a picture to be taken and a moment captured. Old men and women with sad, haunted eyes. Some of the photographs were faded, apparently taken decades ago. The subjects' eyes seemed brighter in those. Some of them reminded her of the photos she'd seen in the Getz file, in Victoria. Only the backdrops were different. Instead of cobbled streets... broad tiled plazas. Instead of linden trees... date palms.

Young women, coltish and full of hope.

Young men, trying to look cool.

A cyberspace gallery of the dear departed.

The dead. The missed. And the missing.

Like the photos in Holocaust museums.

Like the photos on the walls and fences of lower Manhattan.

The grief of survivors poured off the screen.

There were hundreds of photographs, but Grace knew where to look. She scrolled quickly until she found the page.

"It's loading now," Grace said softly to the two men standing behind her. A photograph materialised, filling three-quarters of the screen. Beneath it, lines of text appeared in Arabic, French and English.

Grace pointed to the bottom of the screen. "There."

The two men leaned closer. The Arabic was indecipherable, but the English was perfectly clear.

"Print that," Larry Nixon said.

373

THIRTY-FOUR

Detective Sergeant Hank Farrell sat at a worktable in the Palliser incident room. He was alone. The room was fairly large, but it looked smaller because of the clutter of desks pushed together at odd angles. Telephone and data lines hung from the ceiling and lay in serpentine coils on the cheap carpet, connecting the phone, fax and computer terminals to the outside world. A photocopier hummed in one corner. There were no windows. When the whole team was in here working, the ventilation could barely keep up.

This incident room was Hank Farrell's brainchild, an improvisation that he had managed to slip through just below the budget officer's radar. It was located in the basement of the headquarters building.

Over the past two months, Farrell had spent a lot of time here. The worktable in front of him was covered with reports and statements and printouts – detritus from hundreds of investigative dead ends. The wall to his left was plastered with photographs and diagrams.

Each crime scene was represented. The burned out basement in the Radcliffe Building. There was Andre Devereaux's body, carbonised beyond recognition. The front room and hallway in Grace Palliser's West Vic rental. There was Paul DaSilva's body, face down in a pool of blood. The parking garage stairwell at the law firm's building. There was Cameron Pomeroy's body, lying in a stew of blood and brain matter.

The park playground where Palliser had abducted her daughter. So far, at least, that one hadn't yielded a body. There were more than a dozen photographs of Grace Palliser, culled from a photo album they'd found in her house. One head-and-shoulders shot looked like a professional job. It could have been a publicity photo for a Hollywood starlet. At Farrell's request, the Ident office had enlarged it and

374

reproduced it on a poster. Under the picture, four-inch-high letters shouted: "HAVE YOU SEEN THIS WOMAN?"

There were three photographs of Grace Palliser's little girl, Sherry Taylor. On the wall directly in front of Farrell's seat, someone had pinned up a glossy photograph of Farrell standing beside Wendell Forbes, the famous host of *At Large*.

Despite all this, the triple-murder investigation seemed as stale this morning as the air around him.

It was only eight a.m., but Farrell was already on his third cup of coffee. The latest reports from Lori Graham, e-mailed to him from New Orleans, were laid out on the table. He was going through them for the third time, making notes with a stubby pencil. Lori was flying back today. She was scheduled to brief the entire team tomorrow morning.

Rob Harwood, FBI agent and now – so it sounded on the phone – Lori's special new friend, had done some first class work. Farrell thumbed through Lori's latest investigative summary again, hoping for inspiration.

On October thirteenth, Grace Palliser had taken a bus from Dallas to New Orleans. This was a certainty because, since the events of September eleventh, the security director at the Dallas Trailways depot had ordered his staff to preserve all surveillance tapes for ninety days instead of the usual thirty. Lori had sent Farrell a batch of still photographs the FBI lab had developed from one of the Dallas videotapes. The images were grainy, but Grace Palliser was clearly identifiable under the peak of a baseball cap as she boarded the express coach for New Orleans.

It hadn't taken Harwood very long to track Palliser to a small hotel in the French Quarter. She'd spent two nights there. Strangely, she'd registered under her own name. The desk clerk remembered her. He'd picked her out of a photo lineup of eight pictures. He'd said she was alone. In other words, she wasn't travelling with a child.

Where was the kid?

Even more intriguing, the woman had used a credit card – also in her own name – to obtain a nine thousand dollar advance from the cashier's wicket in a casino. Lori had sent another set of prints, these made from the casino surveillance camera. There was Grace Palliser, bold as brass, collecting a stack of hundred dollar bills.

Farrell wouldn't have known about her extra credit card if he hadn't obtained a court order to intercept her mail. The card issuer's November statement showed two cash advances that had effectively maxed out the credit limit.

Obviously, she'd used the money from the bank machine in Lyndon to pay for her airline ticket.

But the airline ticket had cost more than that first cash advance.

Where did the rest of the money come from?

And what was she using for ID?

Farrell ran his fingers through his thinning hair.

Where the fuck is she now?

And where the fuck is her kid?

Despite all the publicity about heightened law enforcement vigilance, an ordinary legal secretary with no known underworld connections continued to elude the combined police forces of two countries.

Hank Farrell chewed on the end of his pencil. He was tired. He was tired and he was sick and he was frustrated. He swivelled in his chair, drawn to the poster-sized photograph of his elusive prey.

The woman was alluring. She'd be hard to forget. It was a face a man would remember. He'd always told himself that would be how they caught her.

As he swung his chair back, his eyes settled on his own photo, standing next to Wendell Forbes.

Maybe last night's show will shake out a decent lead.

He still couldn't understand why the producers hadn't contacted him about the update on the Palliser case. Farrell hadn't even known the story was scheduled. After watching the ten-minute segment, he'd phoned the network office in Atlanta. They gave him the run-around, and then told him he'd have to talk to the RCMP.

376

But the Mounties weren't talking. No one would return his calls. He took a gulp of cold coffee and swirled it in his mouth. The whole thing was pissing him off. The RCMP had stuck its nose into his case and screwed everything up and, because of that, the broadcast had been way off base:

"Even though investigators say there is strong evidence that this fugitive was in south Florida as recently as last month, they now believe that she has left the Sunshine State and is travelling north. They also say that she may now be accompanied by her daughter, Sherry Taylor, pictured here. Folks, the woman is extremely dangerous. If you see her, do not approach her. Just call the toll-free number at the bottom of your screen, or your local FBI office, or any detachment of the Royal Canadian Mounted Police.

"Now, in our next story..."

Florida? Accompanied by her daughter? Where the hell did they get that? And why the hell didn't they mention our *toll-free number? Why did they just give the Mounties' number?*

Farrell would have to report the entire fuckup to the Chief. The Old Man was a bit too smooth for Hank's liking – too much of the politician, not enough of the cop – but he was well connected. At least he'd have enough clout to get some phone calls returned.

Answering the thought, his telephone rang. Irritated, he rolled his chair over to his desk and grabbed the handset.

"Farrell," he growled.

A rich voice greeted him.

"Hank? You're sounding a bit edgy down there! Drinking too much of that paint remover you people call coffee?"

Farrell's tone changed instantly. "No, sir. I mean, yes sir. Probably. On my third cup."

"That shit'll kill you, man! It's not even eight-thirty! How long have you been holed up in that room this morning?"

"Since six, sir."

"Six, hey? Well, leave whatever you're doing. You can pretend to finish it later. Come up to my office." The Chief's voice softened. *"Now,* please, Hank."

"Right there, sir. Good timing, in fact. I was just going to call Natalie and ask for an appointment. I want to talk to you about that *At Large* show last night." Farrell faltered. "Sorry... what was that about 'pretend to finish'?"

"I'll explain later. Just get up here. Oh, and Hank..."

"Yes, sir?"

"Cancel your plans for the day."

Hank Farrell could only remember three times in his entire adult life when fear or nervousness had actually dried up the saliva in his mouth.

The first time, he'd been a two-year constable. After an adrenaline-charged high-speed chase, he'd shot and killed a robbery suspect. The man had fired first, taking a chunk out of Hank's thigh, but that hadn't eased the shock he'd felt after taking another man's life.

The second time was fourteen years ago, on the day he married his wife. That was the day he had finally admitted to himself – too late – that Janey was not the woman for him.

The third time, it turned out, was today, in the executive offices of Dennis E. Carlton, Chief of Police for the City of Victoria.

When Farrell knocked and then entered, Chief Carlton was leaning against the front edge of his desk. Hank was immediately startled by his boss's appearance. The Chief was usually in full uniform. Today, he was dressed in a golf shirt and wrinkled slacks.

Farrell had the weird impression that Chief Carlton was still wearing his clothes from last night.

The casual attire didn't detract from the man's physical presence. His fringe of white hair and the lines on his face put him in his sixties, but his body was lean and hard. He exuded an aura of refined power.

The Chief was in mid-sentence as Farrell walked into the room.

"-discuss that later with Commissioner Reichert." Chief Carlton straightened as Hank entered, then moved toward the door to greet him. "Morning, Hank! Come in!" As the Chief shook his hand, Farrell felt a prickling sensation on the back of his neck. There was something about the Old Man's manner...

A tall man in a leather jacket was standing behind the Chief's desk. He was inspecting the Chief's golf trophies. He turned slowly.

Tom Naaykens.

Naaykens? What the hell is he doing here?

"You know Inspector Naaykens, I think?" the Chief asked, following Farrell's glance. "In case you're not up to date, Tom is now deputy head of the Mounties' anti-terrorist unit. He works out of that air base up near Courtenay."

Farrell stared at Naaykens. Not long ago, the man had visited him in the incident room, asking a lot of questions. He'd seemed interested in one of the lawyers at the Pomeroy firm.

"Come and join the others, Hank." The Chief put a hand on Hank's shoulder and gestured toward a sitting area around a corner to the right of the doorway. "I have some guests you should meet."

Hank Farrell hadn't sensed others in the room. The police chief's sitting area consisted of a long couch, two matching easy chairs, and a coffee table. In the past, Farrell had occasionally been invited to join the Old Man and other senior officers there for briefings on sensitive cases.

Two men were sitting on the couch. They rose as Chief Carlton and Farrell moved toward them. The heavier-set man was dressed in a rumpled business suit; the other wore casual clothes and a light jacket. They were strangers to Farrell, but there was something about their appearance that he recognised instantly.

Cops.

"This is Special Agent Larry Nixon." As Chief Carlton began the introductions, Hank Farrell's eyes were drawn to the left, to a third person who had remained seated. "He's a senior agent in the FBI's New York office. And this gentleman is

Myles Rothwell. Myles is a practising attorney in Florida, but he's also ex-ATF, so we've agreed not to hold his current profession against him-"

Hank Farrell barely heard the introductions.

He was staring at a woman sitting in a chair facing him. She was wearing a dark sweater, faded jeans and sneakers. His eyes locked on her face as the Chief droned on. The hair was shorter. And she'd dyed it blonde. But there wasn't any doubt.

Grace Palliser.

What the fuck!

Hank Farrell's feet were rooted in place. His arms, nerveless at his sides, wouldn't respond to the offered handshakes from Larry Nixon and Myles Rothwell. He stood frozen, gaping.

Tom Naaykens moved close to Grace Palliser's chair. The move seemed almost protective. Farrell looked the woman up and down.

Her wrists. Her ankles.

He wasn't dreaming.

There were no handcuffs. No shackles.

His eyes darted crazily from face to face.

"-and, of course you know who this is."

Farrell's knees sagged. A strong arm took him around the shoulders.

"Sit down, Hank," the Chief said gently. "Here. Take this chair next to Grace-"

Grace?

"-she has a few things to tell you. And, Hank-" the rich voice hardened "-listen to me! Hank!" Farrell tore his eyes away from Grace Palliser and turned dumbly to face Chief Carlton. Darkened eyes, full of warning, met his shocked gaze. "In a little while, you're going to watch a videotaped interview of Miss Palliser that-"

Miss...?

"-will explain a lot. After that, Grace and these gentlemen will answer your questions. And then they'll have questions for you. You will give them your complete cooperation. Do you understand, Hank?"

Farrell stared at the Chief, uncomprehending, his jaw working. After a few seconds of shocked silence, he managed to nod.

"And remember this, Hank," Chief Carlton continued. "Whatever you learn in this office remains in this office. You don't talk to anyone about this! That's an order! That means you don't say a word to any member of your team. I want your detectives to keep working on Grace's case just like before. More importantly, I want them to continue believing in it. I'm sorry, but the best way to ensure that is to keep them in the dark. That's where you come in. Not only are you going to keep your team working, but you're going to re-kindle this case in the local press." He smiled. "That probably sounds insane to you right now, but by the time you leave this room, I guarantee you'll understand."

Hank Farrell was speechless.

He was three feet from the fugitive, Grace Arlene Palliser.

His fugitive. The woman who killed Paul.

She sat watching him curiously, without expression, without the slightest sign of nervousness or discomfort.

Or did she?

Did she kill Paul?

It began to dawn on Hank Farrell that he might have made a terrible mistake.

That was when his mouth went dry.

The session with Farrell had taken a lot out of Grace. But there was something else she had to do before the day was over. Tom Naaykens thought about it, and agreed. Annette and Shy were staying in a safe house. He had them transported to the RCMP headquarters in Victoria. Grace and Myles were already there, waiting.

Naaykens escorted everyone to the officers' lounge. "I'll be right back," he promised. He left a guard on the door.

Ten minutes later, they heard voices. The door opened. Brent and Hilary walked in, followed by Tom.

Shy let out a whoop and ran to her father. He scooped her up, hugging her desperately. In her inimitable way, Hilary managed to smile and frown at the same time. After a show of hugs and kisses, Hilary turned to eyeball Grace, who was standing with Myles and Annette.

Naaykens asked Brent to come with him.

"What about my daughter?"

"She can stay here with her mother and Miss Holt. We won't be long."

Brent stared at the officer as if he was insane.

Naaykens opened the door. Two plainclothes officers stepped in. "Since you seem worried, these men will keep your daughter safe. Come with me, please." Seeing Brent still hesitating, Naaykens added, "This is not a request, sir."

Brent set Shy down. The little girl immediately ran back to Grace and Annette. Brent watched, looking confused. He followed Tom Naaykens out of the room.

Hilary stared at Grace. She turned to one of the officers. "Why isn't she in handcuffs?"

"You'll have to ask Inspector Naaykens, ma'am."

Grace and Annette sat down on a sofa. Shy squeezed between them. Myles found a soft chair. Hilary took a straight-backed chair on the other side of the room.

Shy and Annette started talking. They switched back and forth from English to French. After a moment, Myles joined in. Grace smiled at Hilary and shrugged. Hilary's eyebrows shot up.

Nearly an hour passed. Then Brent and Tom returned. Brent looked completely shaken. He ignored Hilary and walked directly over to Grace. Grace stood up to meet him. Brent took her hand. "We'll work this custody thing out. I promise, we'll make it work."

Grace's eyes filled. "Yes, we will." She hugged him. He hugged her back so hard he nearly squeezed the breath out of her.

Hilary watched, blinking with chagrin.

Grace knelt and held Shy's hands. "I want you to go with your Dad and Hilary. I have a little job to do. I'll see you soon, okay?"

Naaykens had been waiting. He spoke to Brent. "These officers will escort you home. They'll stay with you until this is over."

Hilary sidled over. "Until what's over?"

"These officers will explain," Naaykens replied.

"Why isn't that woman in a cell? Somebody needs to explain that!"

"Hilary…"

Brent got her attention.

"What?"

"Shut up!"

Hilary's body jerked as if she'd been slapped. Grace stifled a smile.

Annette, Myles and Grace all hugged Shy. Then Brent took his daughter's hand and nudged Hilary toward the door. Before they left the room, Brent turned back. He looked at Grace, then looked hard at Naaykens. "Keep her safe, Inspector."

"I plan to," Naaykens said.

"Their agents are still checking with Amtrak and the bus companies and, of course, with the airlines. They're also checking used car lots in and around New Orleans. Palliser may have used some of that money to buy a car. Rob Harwood promised to call us the minute something turns up. But it's been over a month since Palliser booked out of that hotel, so the trail's getting cold. We don't even know what direction she went."

The Palliser investigation team, eleven detectives plus Hank Farrell, were spread through the incident room, sitting on desks and chairs.

"Well, it probably wasn't south," one of the detectives called out, laughing. "Unless she's a hell of a swimmer."

"Yeah, but what about Cuba?" another put in. "Cheap to live there. If she was careful, nine G's would last a few years."

"It'd be almost impossible for her to get there from the States," Lori responded. "You guys know the politics. Any flight from the States would be a charter and the State Department has to sign off on those."

There was general muttering and speculation, but Lori Graham's briefing was basically finished.

"Hey, what's with that story on *At Large*?" Art Naylor called out.

Lori Graham looked puzzled. Farrell realised she didn't know about the broadcast. "I'll deal with it, Lori," he muttered to her. She sat down and Farrell climbed to his feet. He felt his body sway. He gripped the corner of his desk and hoped no one would notice. It had been twenty-four hours since his visit to the Chief's office, but he was still trying to get his bearings in an upside down world. A world where Grace Palliser had interrogated him, instead of the other way around. A world where Grace Palliser had watched the strings of dry spittle on *his* lips. Instead of the other way around.

Impotent rage burned in his gut.

Not rage at Grace Palliser, although, for Christ's sake, he had to blame her for fleeing, for running away from the police instead of toward them.

No, to be fair, his rage shouldn't be directed at Grace Palliser. In the end, her headlong flight, and her brushes with death, had made the crucial difference in solving what was likely a far more deadly crime than Pendergast's killing spree.

And he had to give her credit. She'd managed to kill the prick. No, his rage was reserved for that other bastard. But there wasn't a thing he could do about Nader, or whatever his name was, because Chief Carlton had specifically excluded Farrell from the operation. Instead, his assignment was to wait on the sidelines and mislead his own squad.

As he began to speak, his voice echoed inside his head – dead, spiritless, almost alien. He couldn't help it. He despised what he was about to do.

"Okay, people. Cut the side talk." The room went quiet. "Thank you, Lori," he heard himself intone. "Excellent work."

Lori raised a questioning eyebrow.

She knows you, Farrell. Be careful. Make it real.

Hank picked up a folder from his desk. "The network story might be right on the money. I haven't told Lori about this-" he smiled at the young woman apologetically; she tilted her head to one side, her expression questioning "-or any of you, for that matter, because this information just came to me this morning. It comes directly from Chief Carlton. I thought I should let Lori bring all of you up to date on her work down south before I added this latest development."

Farrell took a deep breath.

Lori Graham watched him.

"Some of you may be wondering about that broadcast. For those who didn't see the show, it was billed as an 'update'. Wendell Forbes said there was evidence that Grace Palliser had recently been spotted in southern Florida, but that she was now on the move and might be accompanied by her daughter." Lori Graham's eyes widened. "I should tell you that I, personally, had nothing to do with the broadcast. No one from the show called me or Gus Fisher or anyone else in this Department. It seems the Mounties fed them this information, without bothering to give us a heads up. I say this because this NCIS report-" Farrell opened the folder in his hand "-is dated last Wednesday, and it says that Grace Palliser is in possession of a Canadian passport in the name of-" he read from the report "-Sydney Ellen Cates, DOB oh-two September seventy-two, birthplace Toronto. The passport itself is real. It was a blank, stolen from one of our embassies. The name and DOB relate to a real person, but she died when she was four. The usual trick – someone got the name off a grave marker." Farrell looked up from the paper. "It's anybody's guess where, or how, Grace Palliser got her hands on a false passport. But we know she has money, and money talks. It doesn't matter now, because here's the important thing." Farrell waved the folder. "Sydney Cates took a direct flight from Miami to

Seattle last Monday. So we've got to ask ourselves, why would Grace Palliser head back in this direction? To turn herself in? Doubtful. She could have done that in Florida. And why go to the trouble of obtaining false ID if you're going to turn yourself in? We don't know what she's up to, but if there's any chance she's heading our way, we've got to act now. You'll each be provided with a copy of this report. It includes a faxed copy of the Cates passport picture." He held the page up. "The copy's pretty dark, but it sure looks like her to me." Hank Farrell stopped talking and looked around. "We might have a shot at closing this case, people. I want fresh alerts posted at the border crossings, at the bus and ferry terminals, and at the airports. I want more of those posters-" he pointed to the wall "-spread around Vancouver Island and the mainland. Most of all, boys and girls, I want this case back on the front page."

Over the next few hours, assignments were made and team members hit the streets. Lori Graham hung back. She placed a call to her FBI friend. He was back in the FBI's Seattle office. She brought him up to date and he promised to pay another visit to the security director at Sea-Tac Airport.

Lori made a few more desultory calls and then worked on her travel expense reports.

By eleven, only she and Farrell remained in the room. She rolled her chair over to his desk and plunked herself down, making as much noise as possible. He continued thumbing idly through a batch of investigation sub-files, making notes with his stubby pencil, deliberately ignoring her.

Finally, he gave up. He set down his pencil and leaned on his elbows.

She eyed him. "Okay, boss. I'm not buying. Out with it."

Hank Farrell sighed. He put his head in his hands.

THIRTY-FIVE

"Michael Dimitri?"

"We haven't made any direct approaches. That would jeopardise this operation. But we know he has an alibi. When you and Annette Devereaux were in Capilano Park, he was in Calgary with another man from your office. A lawyer named Gordon."

"Lance Gordon. He does a lot of work for the oil and gas industry. You're sure of this?"

Tom nodded. "Yup. But the Proceeds of Crime unit is still doing background checks on the uncle."

"Hmmh. What about Joan Van Zant? The description of the car that took Shy away from-"

"She's disappeared, Grace."

"Disappeared?"

"Hasn't been seen since Shy was taken. The Victoria police received a missing person report back in mid-October."

"Who filed it?"

"Nader."

The radio crackled.

"Tom. Ticket booth."

"Go ahead."

"Back seat's clean. The windows are tinted, but these argon lights cut right through them."

"Good."

Eric Nader's Lincoln crept slowly down the loading ramp, obeyed the deckhand's signals, and rolled to the front position in Lane 4. A second deckhand kicked chocks against its wheels. A few minutes later, a retired bakery delivery van, its vintage engine coughing and smoking, boarded the car ferry and came to a stop, two car lengths behind the Lincoln. The outside temperature was just above freezing. A plume of exhaust drifted up from the Lincoln's tailpipe.

"Tom. Deck One. His engine's still running. Looks like he's staying."

"We see that."

"Shit!" Larry Nixon muttered. "The guy's been sitting in that car for three hours. When's he gonna take a leak?"

Surveillance teams had been shadowing Nader from the moment he pulled out of his driveway at Moses Point. They had expected him to leave his car before now, if only to relieve himself. So far he hadn't. When he'd disembarked at Saltspring Island earlier in the evening, he'd followed Grace's instructions and parked in the first turn-around and waited. After the six o'clock boat left, he'd rolled back down the hill to the ferry ramp so he'd be first in line for the eight o'clock sailing back to Swartz Bay. So far, he hadn't budged from the driver's seat.

Inspector Tom Naaykens, clad in jeans and a windbreaker and packing a Glock in a shoulder holster, sat on a padded bench in the darkened interior of the bakery van. Larry Nixon sat to his left, next to Sergeant Ed Parnell. The Sergeant was in the black uniform of the Emergency Response Team. Grace, dressed in a sweatshirt, jeans, and a zip-front Cowichan sweater, sat cross-legged on a bunk to Naaykens' right.

They were watching Eric Nader's car on two closed circuit TV feeds, part of a bank of terminals mounted on a bulkhead behind the passenger seat. Camera lenses in each of the van's clearance lights fed their signals to the video equipment below. The cameras could cover the entire three hundred and sixty degree perimeter around the vehicle.

The van's front cab was curtained off from the workspace behind. Two undercover RCMP officers, a male and female, occupied the forward seats. The male, Teddy, had long greasy hair, acne scars on his cheeks, and a stringy goatee. Before joining Tom's unit, he'd turned in perfect scores on the RCMP pistol team. Tonight, he slumped against the driver's door, pretending to doze. His companion, Rose, a petite brunette with a rock hard body under her soiled dress, lounged carelessly in the passenger seat, picking at her toenails.

Earlier, Tom had introduced the pair to Grace.

"Grace, meet Teddy and Rose. We call them 'The Granolas'. They're our very own alternate-lifestyle nomads."

"What he's really saying is that we're the unit's token hippies," Rose had added impishly, as she shook Grace's hand, almost crushing her knuckles. "Tom didn't believe us when we told him we never inhale."

"Hippie cops?" Grace had raised her eyebrows while she flexed her recovering hand. "Gee, I know a certain defence lawyer in Florida who'd have a stroke if he met you two." She remembered with fondness Pete Wetherall's colourful views on life and law enforcement.

Pete had flown home on the network's Gulfstream to keep his and Myles' neglected law practices from tanking completely.

The car deck filled with vehicles. After fifteen minutes, the ship's horn sounded and the loading ramp lifted. A few seconds later, the huge boat shuddered as the engine room fed power to the main shafts.

The *Skeena Queen* eased out into the black waters of Fulford Harbour.

Teddy's voice drifted back from the forward cab. "He's cut his engine."

On the video screens, remnants of the Lincoln's exhaust dissipated into the night air. The team waited, watching.

"Come on, you prick!" Larry breathed. "Take a walk." The driver's door opened and Qari Khalil Nadim, also known as Eric K. Nader, stepped onto the steel deck. Tom spoke quietly into his radio.

"Neil. Get ready."

"Yes sir."

Grace's breath stopped in her throat. She hadn't seen Nader since that day in Capilano Park. He stood next to the open door of his car, his eyes sweeping his surroundings. He was wearing a long open raincoat over a thin sweater and cargo pants. He examined every vehicle that was parked close to his. His gaze lingered on the bakery van for a few extra seconds as he apparently studied Teddy and Rose.

389

He seemed satisfied. He closed the car door and clicked the remote on his key ring. His car's lights flashed briefly.

"Neil? You get that?"

"Yes sir."

"As soon as he's out of sight, get over here."

Nader left his car and threaded his way across the car deck to a heavy green door marked STAIRWAY TO PASSENGER DECK. He pulled the door open and disappeared from sight.

"Now, Neil!"

A man appeared from the darkened area at the forward end of the car deck. He was the same deckhand who had directed Nader to his parking lane. He was carrying a portable two-way radio. He wove between the rows of cars to the passenger door of the bakery van and passed the radio to Rose. She handed it back through the curtain.

"Tom. Lounge. He just went in the can."

"Someone follow him in and see if he's carrying."

Larry Nixon opened the top on his laptop computer. The screen lit up. He plugged a lead into Neil's portable radio, and punched some keys. "This won't take long." For several seconds, an unintelligible program blurred across the screen. There was a two-tone chirp and a small window materialised on the screen. "Done!" He opened the back of the radio and removed a small black object. He handed it to Tom. It was a keyless-entry remote for unlocking vehicle doors.

"We've programmed this to work on the Lincoln's locks," Tom explained to Grace. He activated his radio. "Okay, let's make sure this guy isn't packing a stowaway." He handed the remote back to Larry. "Pass this to Teddy." Then he keyed his radio again.

"Lounge?"

"He's still in there. Wayne's with him."

"I want to know when he comes out. Neil?"

"Ready."

On the screen, Grace could see Neil standing next to the trunk of Nader's car. He had one hand under his coat.

"Tanner, where are you?"

"On my way."

A rotund man wearing a watch cap and deckhand's gear appeared on screen from the right. He took a position at the Lincoln's offside rear door. He was holding his left hand behind his back. Grace heard a window being rolled down on the other side of the curtain.

"Now, Teddy!"

Grace watched the screen. The Lincoln's trunk lid popped open and swung upward. The trunk was empty.

Neil slammed it closed and he and Tanner moved to the front doors. They opened them simultaneously and leaned into the car. Neil's voice came over the speaker on the bulkhead. "Three fifty-seven under the driver's seat!"

"Talk to me!"

"It's silenced."

Tom Naaykens' looked at Grace. Larry and the SWAT team officer were looking on. Tom spoke quietly into his mike.

"Is it loaded, Neil?"

"Yes, sir."

Everyone stopped breathing. There was a long second of frozen silence.

Grace held Tom's eyes, her face set.

"Tell him to put it back," she said.

Neil's voice came over the speaker. "Your call, boss..."

Tom keyed his mike and spoke slowly. "Put it back."

The radio went dead. Then, "Should I unload it?"

Ed Parnell leaned closer, his face a map of strain. "Sir! Tell him to unload it!"

"No!" Grace said. "Nader might check it before I get there." She paused, and then added, "I'll just have to take it away from him."

"How are you going to do that, little lady?" Larry asked quietly.

"I need a pair of pliers."

"Pliers?"

"Yeah. A little something I learned from one of Andre's clients. Trust me."

Tom stared at her. "Trust you with *your* life?"

"I made it this far."

The radio crackled.

"Sir?"

"No, Neil." Tom was still staring at Grace. "Put it back the way you found it."

There was a short pause, then, "Yes, sir." They could hear the disbelief in Neil's voice.

After a moment, the car doors slammed and the two officers moved away. There was a chirp as the doors were re-locked, and then Teddy handed the remote back through the curtain. Tom passed it to Grace.

"Put this in your pocket. If Nader locks you in, this will get you out, even if he uses the child lock." He squeezed her knee. "Can you do this?"

"Yes."

"All right. Do the transfer and then get out of the car and walk away. If the thing goes south, *bail!* Parnell and Hollis have orders to take him out if you're in any danger. They'll have him in their sights the whole time you're there. If he tries to drive away with you, dive onto the floor. Face the rear and pull your legs up to wedge yourself tight. Cover your face, because glass will be flying. And Grace-" his mouth twisted into a suspicious smile "-do *not* try to take this man yourself! He's a lot smarter than Pendergast."

"Tom. Lounge. He's on the move."

"Is he armed?"

"Didn't spot anything. Hard to tell with that coat he's wearing."

"Grace!" Larry Nixon squeezed past Tom and kneeled next to her. His eyes were a bit wider than normal. "The word from the CIA is that this Nadim creep was once pretty high up on the Mossad's hit list. People don't get on that list unless they've killed Israelis. Don't underestimate him!" He stopped and blinked, his throat working. "I know I pushed you a bit on this, but I…"

Grace closed her eyes and nodded. "It's okay, Larry. I know about your brother. I have my reasons too."

"Tom. Target's on the car deck."

Nader appeared on the left-hand screen, walking toward the Lincoln. Naaykens thumbed his mike.

"Okay, folks, we're good to go. Boat docks in ten minutes. Swartz Bay team, you hearing?"

"Yes, sir. Woods are clear."

"Hollis?"

"In position."

Tom Naaykens leaned back and whispered to Grace. "Want to call Myles?"

"Yes."

Tom had pulled a few strings. Myles was riding with the Swartz Bay secondary team. Tom took his cell phone out of an inside pocket. He pressed a pre-set code and handed the phone to Grace. Myles answered.

"Hi, beautiful," he said softly.

"Hi, love. Sounds like you were expecting my call."

"Made Tom promise. I've been listening. Sounds like a go."

"Yes. I'm going to do this, Myles."

"There's a loaded gun in that car."

"I have that covered."

"I love you."

"I know. I love you too."

"Kinda like to see you back."

"You will."

"Okay. Bye for now."

"Bye, my love."

THIRTY-SIX

Grace followed Ed Parnell along the trail in the woods. Their route had been marked by tiny chemical glow sticks, left there during daylight by the Swartz Bay team. Grace was already familiar with the forest path – she'd walked its length twice with Tom and Myles.

When they reached the edge of the forest, Nader's Lincoln was already parked on the shoulder of Land's End Road, a hundred yards further up the hill from their position. The headlights were off, but they could hear the engine idling. As Grace watched, the car's passenger side windows slid down.

They moved closer, staying inside the tree line. When Parnell was satisfied with the angle, he set up next to a large Douglas fir. Grace squatted behind him, watching the car while he positioned his rifle. From their position, Grace could just make out the right side of Nader's head.

Parnell whispered into his mike. "Tom. Parnell. I have the target. Hollis, give me a landmark." He listened on his headset, then used his night-vision binoculars to scan the tree line on the opposite side of the road. He turned and whispered to Grace. "Hollis is in the brush next to a big arbutus, roughly there." He indicated. "You could probably pick out the tree when you're walking to the car, but I'd advise you to keep your head pointed straight ahead. Nader might be watching you in his mirror." He pressed his earpiece, then held out a hand. "They want to test your wire."

Naaykens' technical support unit had stitched the intercept gear into the seams of Grace's ball cap. The apparatus, consisting of hearing aid batteries, fibre optic filaments and a microphone about the size of a grain of rice, was almost weightless and virtually undetectable.

Grace pulled off her cap and handed it to him. He handed it back with a nod, pointing at his earpiece.

"They heard me say that. It's working fine. Are you ready?"

"Let's make him stew for a minute." She knew Parnell wouldn't be fooled by the cool remark. Nor would the listening surveillance team. But she needed a minute to calm her nerves.

She replayed through her mind a conversation she'd had with Tom a few hours ago. Larry Nixon had climbed into the bakery van and Grace was about to follow. Tom had stopped her.

"Grace," he said quietly, "Larry is a driven man. For him, the Trade Center is personal. His brother was in a subbasement under one of those towers. They haven't found him yet. I know this is personal for you as well, but Shy is alive and you've got her to think about. So I'll say it again: you're not a cop and you don't have to do this. My men can move in right now and arrest this guy."

Tom's mention of the World Trade towers had made her remember some photographs she'd seen in a magazine. Disturbingly clear photographs, taken on a sunny Tuesday morning in New York City. To the thousands of people working in the World Trade Center, September eleventh must have seemed like just another day at the office.

Except that, before they'd had time to finish their morning coffee, hundreds of them had faced a horrifying choice.

Incineration or annihilation.

Burn to death...

Or plunge eighty floors to the pavement. In one photograph, two doomed, courageous souls had jumped to their deaths holding hands.

Grace's mind had flashed to Andre. Even when her life had been a train wreck, the old man had never lost faith in her. She'd given Tom Naaykens a quick hug and then followed Larry into the van.

Nader was craning his neck back and forth. He was starting to get impatient. It was time. Grace took a deep breath and tensed her legs to stand. Parnell touched her arm.

"Hollis and I will be listening to what's going on in that car. If your meeting goes sour, get out of the vehicle and onto the ground. Stay low and crawl away backward, so you can watch the car at all times. If for any reason you can't get out, hit the floor. Even if you think it's over, don't get up until one of us comes for you." Parnell patted her arm. "I don't want to have to tell your daughter that I shot you by accident."

Grace nodded grimly.

Parnell whispered into his mike. "She's moving now."

Grace straightened up slowly. She moved away from Parnell's position and then stepped into the open. She started walking toward the car, approaching on the vehicle's centreline as Tom had instructed. When she was within a dozen paces of the back of the car, Nader's head snapped up and he turned to look out the rear window. Grace quickly closed the distance to the Lincoln, then veered to the driver's side, opened the back door and got in. She slammed the door shut.

"Evening, Eric."

"Miss Palliser." He twisted his neck to look at her. "Wouldn't you be more comfortable in the front?"

"This suits me fine. Keep looking ahead and keep your hands on the steering wheel." He faced forward and grabbed the wheel.

"What now?"

"First, a bit of housekeeping." Grace's hand snaked around the driver's headrest. She clamped a pair of electrician's pliers on Nader's right ear and yanked backwards. He let out a yell of pain and surprise. She squeezed hard and pulled back until the right side of his head was halfway over the seatback.

"What are you doing, woman!" he screamed.

"Give me your gun!"

"What gun? I don't have a gun!"

"I'm guessing you still have the gun you tried to kill me with. The question is… is it under your coat or under your feet?" She jerked on the pliers. "Tell me!" she hissed at him, "or I'll tear your fucking ear off!" Nader yelped. The sound filled Grace with a crazed satisfaction. She wanted to hear it again. She gave the pliers a twist.

The man who had kidnapped her daughter yipped like a dog under a car.

"Where is it, Nader?"

"Okaaaay!" he shouted. "Under my seat!"

"Can you reach it?"

"No! Not like this!"

"I'm going to let you lean forward. Move very slowly, or you lose your ear." She shook the pliers. "Understand, Nader?"

"Yes! Yes!" he gasped.

"Okay, here we go. Use your left hand. Leave your right one where I can see it. Pick up the gun by the barrel with two fingers only. Show it to me." She eased forward. "Do it now!" Grace kept the pliers clamped on his ear and eased her body forward. Nader matched her movement. He groped between his feet and then raised his left hand. He was holding the revolver by the silencer. He eased his body back toward her, presenting the firearm over his shoulder, grip first. She took it and dropped it on the seat beside her.

When Nader was upright, Grace gave his ear another hard twist.

"Eeaah! What? What now?"

"Take off your coat!"

"I can't! Not when you've got my ear!"

"Try. We'll dance, but you'll manage."

After a several seconds of bending and tugging, Nader squirmed out of his coat.

"Throw it out the window!" Grace ordered.

Nader complied. She released the pliers, grabbed the gun and pointed it at him.

"Turn off the engine, switch on the interior lights, and then slide over to the passenger side. Do it now, Nader!"

He did as she asked, and then shifted across the console to the passenger seat. His hand went to his ear, feeling for damage. He leaned forward and drew in a few rattling breaths.

"You didn't learn that in secretarial school, woman!"

397

"I am what you've made me, Nader! Okay. Now we've got the sticking points out of the way, let's get started."

Nader was still investigating his insulted ear with a fingertip. "Why did you have me take those pointless ferry rides?"

"To be sure you were alone."

"Once again, you have arranged to dictate the terms of our meeting. It is perhaps understandable that you don't trust me. But tell me why should I trust you?"

"You set the rules, Nader. You sent Pendergast up on that hillside with a rifle."

"Yes, Miss Palliser, I did. But tell me... What were you doing up there?"

Grace ignored the question. "I believe I have you to thank for my current – a how shall I say it? – 'lifestyle'. I got another passport, but the police discovered my new identity."

"Yes, so I understand. I've been following your progress, Miss Palliser. Amazing! You have even become something of a celebrity on that ridiculous American crime show."

"Yes. I still made it to the Cayman Islands, Nader. And back."

"I won't deny that you have been very resourceful. Harvey has kept me up to date on your movements."

"You haven't heard from Pendergast lately, have you?"

Nader didn't answer.

"It's really pretty straightforward, Eric. You ordered him to kill me. He botched the job. I killed him instead."

Nader turned his head slowly and gaped at her. Then he laughed. But the laugh was hollow. She could hear his mind racing.

"Excellent, Miss Palliser. Fantastic, of course, but-really-quite-excellent." His smile was icy. "In fact, Harvey is close by, watching and listening, waiting for my orders."

"Nice try, Eric. But, you see, Harvey is dead. I watched him bleed to death." She sat back. "You haven't heard from him for nearly a week, have you?"

Silence.

398

"Ask yourself how I know that!" Grace raised her voice. Anger helped her to keep the fear at bay. "Listen, you cockroach! Pendergast took me for a little cruise. I'm sure you know the boat. A Campion. He thought the job would be a breeze. All he had to do was force whiskey into me until I was paralysed, take me ten miles out, and drop me over the side. If someone found my body, a post-mortem would show that I'd been drunk when I drowned. But things didn't work out quite the way you and Harvey planned. His body will probably wash up in Cuba in a couple of months. Parts of it, anyway." She let Nader think about that for a moment. "Let's finish our business, Nader, and it will be over between us."

"What exactly do you want, Miss Palliser?" Some of his arrogance had leaked away.

"I told you when I called. I'll give you all the evidence I've collected against you. In exchange, you will give me money. Five million dollars. You and Pendergast ruined my old life. So now I need seed money to start a new one. My daughter's coming with me. From what I've seen, five million should be nothing to you. You and Koop must've stolen ten times that from those fools in Switzerland. I might have had a conscience about that a few months ago. Not any more. Five million will keep my mouth shut for a long time."

"So would a bullet," Nader said quietly.

"Maybe. But you're not the one holding the gun."

"What makes you believe this so-called evidence is worth that much money to me? A photocopy of a letter? Photocopies are easily forged and, in any event, the file respecting that company no longer exists. The microfiche? A meaningless scrap of celluloid that cannot be connected to me."

"You thought that scrap was important enough to abduct my daughter!"

"Yes. An overreaction. I admit it. But circumstances have changed." He turned in his seat, facing her. "The truth is this, Miss Palliser, you have nothing. No leverage whatsoever."

"I have this." Grace reached inside her sweater and pulled out an envelope. She passed it to him. "I'm sure you'll recognise it."

Nader opened the envelope and pulled out a folded sheet of paper. He glanced down at it. His entire body jerked. He looked up, his expression confused, then wary.

"That's my insurance, Nader," Grace said calmly. "You know... in case anything should happen to me or my daughter. Tonight. Or anytime in the next century."

"I see." His black eyes seemed to show grudging respect.

"How do I know you won't use this after you receive the money?"

"You don't," Grace replied. "You'll just have to trust me on that one. You'll just have to hope like hell that I'm able to use your money to buy an ironclad identity."

"Do you expect me to produce this vast sum now? Tonight?"

"Not in cash. You of all people should know that. I didn't risk a trip to the Caymans to work on my tan. I know you transferred the Getz deposit somewhere. I have the passbooks. And I counted ten other dormant accounts on that fiche-"

"You have the passbooks?"

"Harvey was so intent on drowning me that he didn't bother to check my pockets. Play straight with me, Nader, and you can have them back. Did you bring the account numbers? And the passwords?"

"They are in my head, Miss Palliser."

"Good. Give me your cell phone." Nader didn't move. He took a deep breath. "Miss Palliser. Your demand is five million US dollars."

"Not a cent less, Nader."

"Yes. Well, as you have so shrewdly deduced, my colleague and I diverted a somewhat larger amount. Surely you do not expect me to reveal the current location of this money? Or the account codes? You could then help yourself to the balance after we part."

400

Nader's objection had been planned for, but Grace pretended to ponder his words. After a few seconds, she sighed.

"Fair enough. When they ask for the destination, pass me the phone." Nader took a cell phone out of his shirt pocket. He placed a long distance call. Grace listened to the tones. Three numbers... *zero one one...* three more numbers... *must be country code...* six numbers... *only six local numbers? Must be a small place...*

Grace didn't try to memorise the series. The man's precautions were useless. Tom Naaykens had obtained a court-ordered intercept for Nader's cell phone. Each time the man pressed a number on the keypad, it appeared simultaneously on three monitor screens. In the bakery van. At RCMP headquarters in Vancouver. And at the FBI Special Projects lab in Quantico, Virginia.

The bakery van was parked a quarter mile further up the hill, around a corner, behind a five-car RCMP roadblock. There was a similar roadblock below Nader's position, on the Swartz Bay ferry terminal exit lanes, preventing anyone from using the Land's End Road cut-off. Teddy was still lounging in the driver's seat of the van, keeping the engine ticking over and monitoring radio traffic between the surveillance teams. Earlier, Rose had climbed in the back with Naaykens and Nixon. Without giving a thought to the male presence, she'd stripped off her hippie garb, suited up in field gear, and strapped on a sidearm.

The audio from Grace's wire was coming through to a speaker on the CCTV console. While the officers listened, their eyes were glued to a computer screen on the bulkhead.

A series of numbers began to appear. After the sixth digit, Larry Nixon stabbed his index finger at the screen. "That's the country code for Nauru Island," he announced. "It's a tax haven in the Pacific. An FATF target." More numbers appeared, then a line of text materialised below them.

Pillar Pacific Trust

Larry gave a triumphant laugh and thumped Tom on the shoulder.

"You go, girl," Rose said softly.

When he finished dialling, Nader put the phone to his right ear. He quickly pulled it away and shifted it to the left. Grace suppressed a smirk.

"Good evening, Operator. Oh, of course. Good morning then. I need to arrange a transfer. Yes, I will wait." A few seconds passed. "Yes, I'm here. Yes. I am starting now." Nader punched a ten-number group on the keypad.

"Yes. Today it is 'tarpon'. I'm sorry? I understand. Tomorrow it is 'moray'. Yes. I am starting now." He pressed a long series of numbers. Grace counted twelve. Nader listened again. A full minute passed.

"Five M-I-L-L, operator. Yes. Mike India Lima Lima. Correct, operator, zeroes." Nader listened, then said, "One moment, please" and handed the phone over the seat. "She wants routing and account." Grace took the phone.

"Good morning, operator. I have routing and destination for this transaction. I do not wish to provide this information by voice. Are you equipped to receive any series by keypad?" She listened while the operator replied. "Yes, thank you. I am starting now." Grace punched in a series of numbers, paused and listened. "Yes, correct. Second series, SWIFT November November November." She paused again. "Yes, correct. Now, the remainder of that series." Grace held the phone pad towards her in one hand and used her thumb to press a series of numbers that Larry Nixon had spent an hour drumming into her head. "Please read that back, operator." Pause. "Correct, thank you. Third series, now." Grace entered the last set of numbers, then spoke into the phone. "Could you read that back...? Yes, that is correct." Pause. "Yes, I will hold for confirmation." Grace held the phone to her ear, waiting. Seconds passed. Nader was beginning to fidget. "Fine, operator. Thank you for your assistance."

Grace ended the call and punched some function keys until she found what she wanted. She held the key down for several seconds, then passed the phone back to Nader.

"I deleted the re-dial memory. I don't know your numbers. You don't know mine."

"I begin to understand why Andre Devereaux had such respect for you, Miss Palliser." Nader's mention of Andre's name made Grace nauseous. Her face twitched and the gun shook in her hand. She resisted an insane desire to pull the trigger.

In the NCIS van, Larry's cell phone rang softly. He snatched it off his belt.

"Nixon." He listened, said, "Thank you," and disconnected. "Quantico says it went through."

Five million dollars of the stolen money had just been transferred to a special FBI account in Washington, D.C. During the next few minutes, the entire balance in Nader's Nauru account would follow it.

Grace slid across the seat to the right side of the vehicle and tugged on the door handle, releasing the catch. She kept Nader's gun pointed at him. "Move back over to the driver's side. When I step out, drive away. Don't look back."

Nader put one leg over the console. Grace rolled her hips to the right, ready to step out of the car. She felt a lump in her back pocket. The full weight of her upper body sank onto the keyless entry remote Tom had given to her. From behind her, there was an audible click, then a thump.

The next few seconds unfolded in slow motion.

Grace didn't immediately understand what had happened. Instinctively, she looked back. She found herself staring at the top of the trunk as it finished its upward swing and stopped, bouncing against its hinges.

Then she felt the revolver being snatched from her hand.

In a panic of realisation, she turned back to face Nader. In the three tenths of a second that elapsed before his free hand

403

shot over the seat and grabbed her by the hair, Grace had a fleeting glimpse of the face of Qari Khalil Nadim, angry with sudden comprehension, filled with ruthless purpose. Then the hand yanked her forward. His other arm appeared between the front seats, holding the gun. The muzzle of the silencer was pointed at her.

The gun bucked and a blow like a jackhammer drove into Grace's chest. She felt her body being thrown backwards against the corner of the seat. Excruciating pain radiated out from her chest and down both her arms. She gasped for air, but couldn't find any. The door next to her swung open and she fell sideways through the gap. Her mind willed her dead arms to break her fall, but they wouldn't respond. The night air around her seemed to turn blue.

Then indigo.

Then grey.

Then black.

While the bank transfer was in progress, Parnell had listened to the conversation and watched the two heads in the car through his scope. Finally, he saw Grace move to the right side of the car. The rear passenger door started to open. It inched outward, then wavered and stopped. He cursed under his breath.

Grace's head and shoulders were blocking his view of Nader.

"Hollis, she's in my line of fire. You got him?"

"Dead to rights."

"Okay. Stay on him. She's getting out of the car." Because of his cross talk with Hollis, Parnell didn't hear Grace's instructions to Nader to move, but the man reappeared in his field of view as he crossed toward the driver's seat. Parnell breathed a sigh.

"Come on, girl! Get out of that car!"

Then, without warning, the trunk popped open and arced up, blocking his view of the interior of the car.

"Hollis! The trunk! I'm blocked!"

"I see it! I've still got him!"

"Stay on him. I'm moving."

Tom's voice cut in.

"What is it?" Parnell was about to answer when, in one violent motion, the back door of the car swung open and Grace fell out. Her upper body pitched onto the ground, shoulder first.

"Grace is down!" Parnell yelled into his mike.

Naayken's voice roared back into his earpiece. "We heard it! Take him out, Parnell! Everyone move in! MOVE! MOVE! MOVE!"

Parnell dropped his rifle and drew his sidearm. He broke cover and ran forward, his weapon levelled, yelling into his mike.

"Take him, Hollis! I have no shot!"

Seventy-five yards away, in the salmonberry brush under a gnarled arbutus tree, Rick Hollis already had the green dot centred behind Nader's ear.

He fired. At that very instant, Nader leaned between the front seats and tried to pull Grace's body back into the car. Hollis's bullet drilled a hole through the windshield and burned past Nader's head, missing him by two inches. The next shot hit the rear view mirror. It exploded in a shower of plastic and glass.

Nader dove over the seats, landing on Grace's legs.

Hollis was distracted by a branch in his face and missed Nader's movement. He brushed the branch away and then scoped the car, scanning for movement. Scanning for the next shot. Nothing.

"I think I missed the shot, Ed! He's out of sight! He's still in the car!" He saw Parnell's running form, crouched, holding his handgun in front of him. "Tom! Parnell's going in! GET DOWN HERE! Ed, wait for back up!"

Three hundred yards up the hill, tires were squealing. Parnell reached the rear of the car. Grace was lying half in and half out. She coughed weakly.

She's alive!

Parnell pointed his automatic directly ahead, stepped forward and wheeled left. Nader was lying on his back on the floor of the car. Waiting. He fired two quick shots.

The first slug hit the policeman in the armpit of his gun arm, destroying his shoulder joint and spinning him clockwise. The second one shattered his jaw.

Parnell went down, spraying blood. Hollis saw Parnell reel back and drop from sight.

"Parnell's been hit!"

Tom Naaykens' voice came back.

"We're coming. Take that bastard out, Hollis! Do it, man!"

Hollis was already scoping the car.

Nader crawled out onto the ground. Staying low, he seized the back of Grace's sweater and hauled her legs out of the car. She moaned.

No blood...

Nader pulled up the front of her sweatshirt.

Kevlar!

He swore in Arabic. He cocked his head. The night air was filled with the sound of car tires on pavement, approaching at high speed. He raised to a half-crouch, trying to determine where the rifleman was.

Hollis saw movement between the trunk and the body of the car. He could see part of Nader's head, but most of him was behind the upraised trunk lid.

He moved his sight to the right, to where the centre of the target's head would be. He fired. The shot made a neat hole in the window of the back door, then the rear window, and then the trunk lid – right where he'd aimed.

The bullet tore off Nader's left ear. He dropped to his knees. In a rage, he kicked Parnell's twitching body, then grabbed Grace by the back of her vest. He started dragging her. He kept the car between him and the shooter. He dragged Grace into the forest.

Car doors were slamming and men's voices were shouting. Myles found Tom Naaykens and Rick Hollis kneeling next to Parnell. As he approached, Tom snapped his cell phone shut and stood up. "Ambulance is two minutes away!" he called out to everyone. Teddy ran up, packing a first aid kit. Tom pointed at a pair of uniforms from the lower roadblock. "You two! Take care of this man until the ambulance arrives."

Myles noticed that Tom was holding Grace's baseball cap in his hand.

"Myles, Nader dragged her into the bush. Parnell took one through the jaw, so he can't talk. But he's conscious. He pointed over there." Tom indicated the line of brush and mature conifers next to the Lincoln.

"Tom, please, I... I..." Myles tried to speak, but his throat seemed to choke off the sound. Larry Nixon walked up. The stocky FBI agent threw a thick arm around Myles' neck.

"I know," Tom said gently. "We'll get her back. We *will*, Myles! There's no blood in the car, so her vest must have stopped the bullet. She's got to be alive or Nader wouldn't have bothered with her."

Myles cursed, tears in his eyes.

Tom shifted his gaze to Larry. A silent message passed between them. Tom drew his Glock. "You remember how to use one of these?"

Myles stared at the gun. He straightened and took it from the Mountie. "Damn right."

"Okay. Here's an extra clip. I've got more firepower in the van. You go with Red team, Myles. Go with Rose. She'll fix you up with a radio. Just remember your training. I'm trusting you. Teddy's going to drive Larry and Hollis and me around to that lane behind the woods." Naaykens put a strong hand on Myles' shoulder. "We'll get her back, Myles. I've got thirty officers on their way here, and the army's sending a chopper with a dozen guys from JTF Two. We'll have this end of the peninsula sealed off in less than thirty minutes."

Grace's first inkling of awareness was the deep pain in her chest.

Did I have a heart attack?

Then there was the sensation of unwelcome movement, of being dragged over rough ground. She came awake suddenly. Someone was dragging her by the straps of her Kevlar vest. The top edge of the vest was pressing on her throat, cutting off her air. She struggled to get free. The dragging stopped. She was dropped to the ground.

Nader's face appeared inches from hers. There was blood streaming down the left side of his face and neck. He shoved the muzzle of a gun against her cheek.

"Get up!" he hissed.

Grace rose shakily to her hands and knees. Nader grabbed her and pulled her roughly to her feet. He was stronger than he looked. She tottered, light-headed. She reached out and steadied herself against a tree. Her chest pounded with pain.

Nader stood in front of her. She saw his ear was missing.

"Lost an ear, after all, eh Eric?"

He seized her under the chin. Faint sounds of activity drifted through the woods behind them.

"Who are they?" Nader rasped.

"Mounted Police. FBI. *And* Special Forces," she lied. "You won't get away."

"No? Well, 'I have insurance', as you people would say. It is obvious that you are very important to them. They will be forced to let me pass." He paused. "Let... *us*... pass!"

"Don't you want to be a martyr? Or is that just for the poor fools you people brainwash?"

He swatted her on the side of her head. "Be quiet and move!"

She stumbled forward. After a hundred yards of thickening underbrush, they broke out onto a cleared path. A few feet ahead, one of the glow stick markers lay on the forest floor, a tiny cylinder of blue light. Another was visible, twenty feet further east. Nader guessed their purpose. He twisted Grace's arm, threatening to break it. She cried out in pain.

"Where do they lead?"

"To a lane! Behind some houses."

"Excellent! We'll need a car. Go!" He knuckle-punched her in the small of the back, urging her in the direction of the next marker.

After a half-dozen markers, the woods began to thin. Light from the Swartz Bay complex, reflected off the low cloud cover, bathed them in a faint yellow glow. Grace knew that her chances of survival were diminishing by the second. The path widened. Nader urged her on. The trail curved to the right. They rounded the bend.

To their right, the ground fell away into a hollow. The trail itself curved left. A dozen yards ahead there was a thick stand of pine.

Something wasn't right.

Fear had heightened Grace's senses.

Her eyes caught a faint ripple in the fabric of the darkness, like heat waves off a desert road.

At first she wasn't sure.

Nader prodded her. She stumbled forward a few more steps.

The night rippled again. For a millisecond, a tree disappeared.

Then reappeared.

Grace was sure.

She took a few more steps, and then faked a stumble. She dropped to one knee. Nader had a grip on the back of her sweatshirt. Her action caught him by surprise. He was pulled slightly off balance trying to hang on to her.

Grace twisted violently sideways, wrenched free, and dropped to the ground. She rolled down the slope, desperate for cover.

Nader fired. The slug tore into the base of a tree an inch from Grace's trailing arm, blasting splinters into her wrist and hand. She scrambled away into some undergrowth, waiting for another shot... Wondering if she'd been seeing things in that grove of trees ahead.

Where is that cop?

Glancing behind her in the dim light, she saw Nader bending and turning, tracking her progress through the undergrowth with his pistol.

"Now you die, woman!"

He can't see me. He's going by sound.

Grace froze in one spot with her back against a log. Her chest was heaving and it hurt like hell. She held a hand over her mouth, struggling to stifle the sound of her ragged breathing. The pistol swung toward her. She looked around desperately for something to throw. Something to distract him.

Suddenly, a bright beam of light pierced the darkness from the trail ahead. A flashlight. It was trained on Nader. A female voice shouted.

"Drop the weapon! Now!"

Nader dropped into a crouch.

"Who are you?" he shouted.

"Police! Drop your weapon!"

"Not much point now!" Nader croaked. He sprang left and unleashed a shot toward the source of the light.

Three things happened in quick succession. A grunt of pain. The flashlight spinning to the ground. And an answering roar from a heavy calibre handgun.

Nader stood up. The bullet had missed him. He moved like a cat toward the policewoman. He had almost reached the still burning flashlight when...

"Drop it!"

A male voice.

Nader swung and fired. Two shots replied in quick succession. The booms echoed through the woods. The bullets struck Nader full in the chest. He windmilled backward and toppled over the edge of the embankment. His body slid like a bobsled down the slope on a carpet of conifer needles. It came to rest five feet from Grace.

The male voice called out.

"Grace Palliser?"

"Here!"

"Move away from him!" Grace retreated along the slope. The man worked his way cautiously down. He spoke quickly into a portable radio while he kept his weapon trained on the prone form. He kicked away Nader's gun.

At that moment, Red team exploded out of the brush on either side of Grace. They formed a protective arc around her, their guns sighted on the lone man standing over Nader. Myles was with them. Grace slipped behind him.

The man near the body flashed a shield. "We need an ambulance. Not for him..." He nodded at the body. "For my partner." He gestured up the slope, where a young woman stood holding her arm.

Two Mounties holstered their weapons. One checked the downed man while the other ran up the slope to help Lori Graham.

Grace limped over to Hank Farrell.

"How did you know?"

"Been hanging around. Wanted to see how it went. We were listening to the radio traffic." He turned to her, frowning. "Didn't like what I was hearing."

Grace slipped her bloodied hand into his.

"Thank you, Sergeant."

"Don't mention it. I owed you one." He smiled at her. "Call me Hank."

THIRTY-SEVEN

Myles went for the phone. While Grace waited, she rubbed the stallion's cheek with her gloved hand. She threw back her head, soaking in the perfection of the heavens overhead. Pale winter sunlight angled through a cobalt blue sky, unblemished by cloud or ice crystals. St. Felicien, she had discovered, was a place of stark and unexpected beauty. In every direction, the land stretched away, flat and seamless, to the far horizon. In the southwest, the lowering sun transformed the snow-bound landscape into a sea of fire.

Shy and Lisa were oblivious to the vista that surrounded them. Within an hour of their first meeting, Lisa Rothwell had adopted Grace's daughter as her little sister. At that moment, the two of them were giggling under a rug in the back seat of the sleigh, waiting for the expedition to start.

The front door slammed and Myles' boots squeaked toward them through last night's fresh snowfall.

The girls cheered.

Grace returned to Earth.

"Who was it?"

"Tom. He sends his love. He says Chief Carlton and Hank Farrell called a press conference and announced that you had now been cleared of all charges. They promised to provide details later. The local news types didn't like that much, but a deal's a deal, and Wendell Forbes sure earned his exclusive. He's put together an edited version of the interview, and the brass have given the go-ahead." He patted the horse's neck. "Know something?

"What?"

"Tonight's show will be the first time one of these crime shows has helped prove a fugitive's innocence. Wendell's feeling pretty good about it. He says he wants to meet with you for a follow-up, but Tom convinced him to back off for now." He drew her away from the sleigh, out of earshot from

412

Lisa and Shy. "They found Pendergast's body. The Cayman Police are sending a CID officer to take a statement from you. Tom promised me he'd brief the guy first, then sit through the interview with you. I'll be there as well."

"When's Tom coming back for us?"

"Monday morning. A police car will take us to the airport. Oh... and he had some other news. Bellis waived extradition. He wants to cut a deal."

"Did he launder the other deposits?"

"Looks like it."

"What about Joan van Zant? Have they found her?"

Myles went quiet.

"Myles?"

"I wasn't planning to tell you this right now," he said quietly. "Did you know there was a boathouse at Moses Point?"

"No."

"It's at the foot of the cliff, below Nader's house. Tom says there was big inboard in there, suspended on slings. When they lowered it, they found a knapsack stuffed with cash and a couple of guns. And there was one of those big sail bags, wrapped in anchor chain. Joan was in the bag. Or what was left of her." Grace's eyes widened. "Tom figured Nader was ready to skip. He probably planned to dump her body in deep water and then transfer to a freighter out in the straits. They're checking the Vancouver shipping calendar to see if they can narrow the list of suspects." Myles kicked at the snow underfoot. "She was shot through the back of the head, Grace."

Grace stared at him for a long second, her face pale. Shy's voice brought them back to the moment.

"Mommy! Mister Myles! No more growed-up stuff, 'kay! Pleeease, can we go now! We want to go for the sleigh ride?"

"Yeah, Dad!" Lisa called out. "Cut the mushy stuff! Let's go!" She started chanting. "Sleeeeigh ride! Sleeeeigh ride! Sleeeeigh ride!" Shy joined in, punctuating her contribution with raucous shrieks of laughter.

Myles and Grace put on their best smiles and crunched back to the sleigh. Grace's accumulation of injuries made her movements a bit slow. Myles helped her up into the front seat, and then followed. He covered their legs with a heavy blanket, then sat looking at the reins.

"You know how to drive this thing?" he asked in a stage whisper.

"Nope," Grace replied.

"Wa'll, I'm not so sure myself. First time I've ever seen one of these here contraptions!"

"Maybe we shouldn't risk it, then," Grace said with mock sadness. She turned in her seat. "Sorry, girls. All these straps and hooks look pretty complicated. Maybe Myles and I should take some lessons first. You could ask Annette to take you for a ride when she and *Tante* get back from Winnipeg." Squeals of protest erupted from the back seat. Myles and Grace laughed. Myles picked up the reins.

When evening fell, they were still gliding over the Manitoba snowscape, singing *Sleigh Bells* for the umpteenth time.

THIRTY-EIGHT

The private chambers of Madam Justice Dixon were carpeted in plush red pile. The rich dark mahogany furniture and soft leather chairs might have been more impressive if Grace hadn't noticed that every judge's room they'd passed was furnished in exactly the same way. The government-issued faux opulence was a bit forced.

While her former employer changed out of her court robes, Grace lounged on a visitor's chair in front of Leddi's desk, studying the titles on the bookshelves. Some of the thick volumes were familiar; they had previously lined Leddi's shelves in the old office at Pomeroy's. Others were new, and appeared expensive. Some of the judge's personal touches – framed certificates, photographs, and keepsakes – were dispersed here and there between the rows of books.

Leddi Dixon emerged from her ensuite dressed in street clothes. Apart from shadows under her eyes, she was as arrestingly beautiful as ever.

"Now then, Grace, my dear girl. Some tea? Yes?"

"That would be nice. Thank you."

Leddi spoke briefly into an intercom. Then she came around the desk and pulled a chair closer. She sat down and put a manicured hand on Grace's arm.

"I knew you were coming, but I still couldn't believe my eyes when you showed up in the back of my courtroom. I've been following the story, of course." She shook her head. "Grace! What's been done to you is unspeakable!"

Grace took a deep breath. "That would be an understatement, Leddi."

"And Shy! Is she all right? Where is she?"

"She's in Victoria, visiting her father. On Monday, I'll be taking her back to Florida with me. Brent agreed to give up custody."

Leddi's eyebrows went up. "Give up custody! After all those months of agony he caused us?"

"He asked me to take her. I'm no longer a criminal, you see."

"You weren't a criminal before. He just treated you like one."

"Hilary left him. She moved out a month ago."

"Ah! So now he's lost interest in raising the child."

"He's a much better Dad now, but… yeah."

"And you're moving to Florida? Isn't that where the American lawyer lives? The one who helped you?"

"Yes. I need a quiet place to recover from all this. And to get to know my daughter again."

There was a knock and the door opened. Leddi's assistant entered, carrying a tray. She set it on the desk.

"Would you like me to pour, Ma'am?" she asked nervously. The question was addressed to Leddi, but the young woman's eyes were fixed on Grace. She appeared quite flustered.

"That's all right, Marie," Leddi replied gently. "We'll attend to it."

"Yes, Ma'am." Marie backed away, still watching Grace. She shut the door softly behind her.

"She's a bit star-struck," Leddi observed. "You've become something of a celebrity."

"I guess I am. Some Hollywood agent called me the other day. Something about buying my life story."

Leddi shook her head. "To Americans, everything is a commodity." She poured a cup of tea for Grace, passed it to her, and then dropped two sugar cubes into the other cup and filled it.

Grace leaned back with her tea. "I've paid a heavy price for my fifteen minutes of fame, Leddi," she said simply. She nodded at her bandaged wrist. "And I don't just mean physically."

"Your story might last longer than fifteen minutes. Book deals, movie deals…"

416

"Maybe. But that's the last thing on my mind right now. All I can think about is spending time with Shy." Grace changed the subject. "You looked very impressive up on that bench. As if you were born to it. But you're looking a bit tired. Is it the caseload?"

"Yes, but you know me. I've never been afraid of work. My hours aren't as long as they were at Pom-" she caught herself "-at the firm, but spending day after day in court can be pretty exhausting."

"How is Graydon handling the separation?"

"Quite well. I fly over to Victoria almost every weekend. Gray doesn't complain. He is a true stoic, that man." She set down her cup. "Really, Grace! Compared to your life, mine is mundane. Your story is on every network! I watched that special broadcast on that crime show last week, and the press conference you did with that policeman, Farrell. I know judges are supposed to be cool and detached, but I was quite moved when you hugged the man who had been hunting you for months."

"I was just relieved, Leddi. Relieved it's over."

"And it's all true, Grace?"

Grace nodded wearily.

"It just seems so unbelievable!" Leddi exclaimed. "Things like this happen to somebody else, not to us! Eric Nader! And Pendergast! I never liked that man. I am so sorry, my dear girl. It must have been terrifying." Leddi looked away, momentarily lost in thought. "I must confess – and I mean no offence, really! – that I feel very fortunate to have been offered this appointment. While you were running from the police, the publicity was vicious! Most of the long-time clients moved their files to other firms. New business was nonexistent. I hear the remaining partners are barely hanging on."

"You were appointed in October, weren't you?"

"Yes." Leddi looked pained. She shook her head regretfully. "My fellow Judges sometimes talk about the momentous day when they got the call. Mine was memorable for all the wrong reasons. An hour after the Chief Justice telephoned me with the news, I learned that Cameron had been murdered."

"There's something I have to ask you, Leddi."

"Yes?"

"Why did you turn your back on me?"

Leddi recoiled in her chair. "Turn my back? Grace, Grace! What do you mean? I never heard a word from you. Of course I would have helped you!"

"Do you remember when Graydon passed you a message to call Annette Devereaux?"

"Yes. I was here in Vancouver. I was having meetings with the CJ and his staff. I called her as soon as I could."

"I was standing beside her when you called."

Leddi's eyes widened. "Really?"

"Yes. Afterwards, Annette told me what you'd said. You already had me convicted."

Leddi appeared shaken. And embarrassed.

"Grace, I…" She took a deep breath and let it out slowly. "For a while there… Well, I remembered what you'd told me about your mother and father-" she shook her head apologetically "–I'm sorry to mention that, and… and I began to think you might have been carrying around some deep-seated psychosis. And, Grace, I knew about your drug problem! I want you to know I never told the police about that. I admit I thought you might be guilty." She leaned forward. "On the other hand, if you had called me yourself, I would have listened. And I would have found you a good criminal lawyer."

"You gave Annette a couple of names of lawyers who could deal with Andre's estate. One of them was Nader!"

"Cameron Pomeroy was our best probate lawyer, Grace. But Cameron was already… deceased. Personally, I couldn't do anything for Annette Devereaux! I was about to be sworn in as a Supreme Court Judge! I thought Eric or one of the other lawyers might help her, or at least refer her to someone who could. I had no idea about Eric's… background." Leddi's voice trailed off.

Grace didn't respond. She watched Leddi. The older woman shifted in her chair.

"Nader never did probate work." Grace said finally. "Peter McCormick did. Two or three of the associates, maybe. But Nader?" Grace shook her head.

Leddi Dixon pressed her lips together. "You're right, of course. It was a foolish suggestion. But think back! In the middle of all that turmoil, the Chief Justice offered me a lifeline. He said he didn't want to lose a deserving candidate. He assured me that my appointment would not be affected by the crimes of 'a renegade secretary'. I'm sorry, but that's the way he put it. I was delirious with relief. I know that must sound selfish, but put yourself in my place! Those murders could have wrecked my career. I probably wasn't thinking straight when I called Miss Devereaux."

She stood up, agitated, and gestured at Grace's teacup. "Would you like something stronger than Earl Grey?"

She didn't wait for Grace's answer. She circled behind her desk and opened a bottom drawer. When she returned to her seat, she was carrying a liquor bottle and two cut crystal glasses. She set the glasses on the desk and twisted the stopper out of the bottle.

Grace looked at the label on the bottle and then looked at Leddi. The older woman saw her expression and froze.

"Of course, my dear!" she blurted, embarrassed. "I'm sorry. After your experiences, you probably don't drink. I should have guessed. Would you like some more tea?"

"In a moment, thank you."

Leddi poured an inch of scotch into one of the glasses and settled back into her chair, swirling the pale liquid. "Grace, I do owe you an apology. I see that now. From your point of view, I must have appeared disloyal. But please believe me when I say this: if you had called and told me everything, I would have done anything I could to help you. I would have taken you to the police myself, and we would have found a first class criminal lawyer to take your case." She took a swallow of whiskey.

419

Grace watched, her face impassive.

"Oban."

"What's that?"

Grace gestured at the bottle on the desk.   "Oban. Pendergast tied me to a chair and poured half a bottle of scotch down my throat. That was the brand."

"You talked about that in that interview.   You must have been terrified!"

"Pendergast told me it was Eric's bottle. Odd coincidence, don't you think? You and Eric Nader drinking the same brand of whiskey?"

Leddi's eyes narrowed.   "Yes.   But that's all it is.   A coincidence."

"Hmmh."   Grace settled back in her chair.   She brushed some lint off her slacks.   "Do you know what I found in that house down there, Leddi?"

"What house?"

"The one where Pendergast tortured me."

"Oh.   No.   What?"

"After I killed him, I searched the whole house, looking for that Cayman lawyer's file I'd taken.   I found this little briefcase in Nader's bedroom.   Inside it were some credit card statements from a Cayman bank.   The FBI is very interested in them because they show some of Nader's movements over the past couple of years.   But one of the statements was very interesting to me personally.   It was from last October."

"Interesting to you?   Why?"

"Because it had a charge from September, from a resort in Arizona.   A place called the Maroon Mountain Inn."

Leddi licked her lips.

"What are you saying?"

"I'm saying there are two coincidences.   You and Nader drink the same brand of whiskey.   You and Nader stay in the same Arizona hotel at the same time.   I remember looking at the photos from your trip.   There wasn't a single picture of Graydon.   He wasn't there with you, was he?"

Leddi ignored the question. "You think I was sleeping with Nader."

"Were you?"

A theatrical sigh. "What if I was? That was then, Grace. Long before... all this." She sipped her drink.

Grace kept her eyes level. "I don't think you were sleeping with him."

Leddi worked up a bit of outrage. "What? You think that I had something to do with... the fraud? The idea is-!"

"The credit card statements were addressed to Arbas Investments – Nader's phoney company. The one he used to funnel the stolen Swiss deposits through the Cayman Islands."

Leddi stared at her.

"What do you mean by all this? Why did you come to see me, Grace? To reproach me? To accuse me of having some hand in this scandal?" She stood quickly and walked to the window. She stared out at the skyline of the city, her jaw working. Then she turned. "Eric was my lover! But that was *all*, Grace! Someone to have sex with. I had no idea about the rest. In fact, I broke off with him before any of this happened. I found out that he was also sleeping with his secretary." Leddi's eyes filled with tears of rage and disgust. "He was sleeping with that tramp, Joan!" She returned slowly to her chair, wiping her eyes with her fingers. She picked up her glass and took a drink. "I'm the first to admit that my behaviour was shameful, Grace, but it is all in the past. No one needs to know this. Bringing it out now would serve no purpose, and it would ruin my reputation!" Now Leddi was pleading.

Grace waited before replying. She carefully set down her cup.

"Yes. I suppose," she said slowly, "the public might be upset to learn that one of its Supreme Court judges used to sleep with a terrorist financier."

"Yes!"

"Especially since he was also her brother."

Leddi froze.

"I have to hand it to you, Leena," Grace continued. "That was a first class performance. You missed a career on Broadway."

Leddi's body jerked as if she'd been slapped. She slopped scotch on her lap, but didn't appear to notice. Her face went white.

"What did you just call me?"

"Leena. That's your real name, isn't it, Judge?"

Leddi stared at her, dumbfounded.

"Isn't it?"

Leddi licked her lips and looked away. She didn't answer.

Grace continued. "That Cayman lawyer's file was for a company called Arbas Investments. It mentioned a certain Islamic charity. I did an Internet search and found hundreds of web sites devoted to the massacres at Chatila and Sabra refugee camps. One of the links led to a memorial website devoted to the victims. I toured that site. Do you know why, Leddi? Because the photographs reminded me of the ones I'd seen in the Getz file. Different people, *same fate*! Ordinary people, Leddi, full of promise, exterminated for no good reason! That's why I looked at those pictures." Grace stood up and walked to the bookshelves behind Leddi's desk. She picked up the framed portrait of Leddi's mother. "Funny thing, though…" She set the picture down in front of Leddi. "I found a picture of this lady."

The air seemed to go out of Leddi Dixon.

Grace tapped the frame. "There was an inscription underneath the picture on the web site, like you'd see in a newspaper obituary. It appeared in three languages. The English version said something like: '…lovingly remembered and missed by her devoted son, Qari Khalil Nadim, and her loving daughter, Leena Faiza Nadim'." Grace sat down. "Pretty careless of you and your brother, Leena. Posting that. I might have made the connection earlier, but you don't sound like Eric. You don't have an accent."

Leena Nadim, a.k.a. Leddi Dixon, was still staring at Grace. Her eyes weren't focused. Her mind was somewhere else.

Somewhere in the past. After long seconds of silence, she returned to the present.

"Accent?" She shook her head. "No... No, I was the youngest. My parents sent me to the American School." She shifted her gaze to the photograph on the desk. "My mother wasn't just killed in that camp, Grace," she said. Her lower lip trembled slightly. "She was raped. Then she was disembowelled. Then she was decapitated. By Phalangist Christians! Israeli soldiers allowed those men to enter the camps. Then they just stood back and watched. What happened there is beyond forgiveness."

"I've seen the photographs."

"My mother was not Palestinian. She was Lebanese. She was a nurse and she was there in the camp for only one reason: to care for sick people. But on that day, while my brother and I were safe in another part of the city, she was raped and mutilated by those monsters. Those Christians!" She spat out the words. "The pain of being left behind can be worse than death itself, Grace. You wouldn't understand."

Grace had a flash from a nightmare. She smelled her mother's blood seeping across the concrete. She swept the image away.

"Considering that you and your brother are responsible for killing at least five people and destroying even more lives, I won't even dignify that with an answer. And what about my daughter, Leddi? Abducted and drugged! After what your family endured, how could you do that to a child?"

"Qari didn't consult me! He brought in help from outside, without telling me. When I realized what was happening, I tried to get him to stop. But by then, he was obsessed with you. He wouldn't listen." She hesitated. "You said five people are dead?"

"Don't insult my intelligence, Leddi. Andre, Detective DaSilva, Cameron, Joan... and Mr. Getz. He's disappeared, so you must have killed him as well."

"Pozner."

"What?"

423

"His name was Edward Pozner."

Grace had a sudden flash of memory. Sitting in the cab of Raymond Vallee's truck. Reading a newspaper article.

"The man they pulled out of the harbour?"

Leddi nodded wearily.

"I confronted Eric after the police came to the office looking for Andre. He told me Pendergast had drowned Pozner and then killed Andre because he'd caught him pushing the body into the inlet." Leddi's toneless reference to cold-blooded murder gave Grace a chill. Leddi took a drink of whiskey. "Pozner was our last project." She said it as if that excused everything.

"Who killed Cameron?"

"I don't know. It must have been Pendergast."

"You're lying."

"I'm not."

"When I was on Fort Street that night, I saw a black car come out of the parking garage. It looked familiar, but at the time I didn't know why. Now I do. Graydon drives a black BMW, but he was away in Switzerland. So that must have been you driving his car."

"Victoria is full of black BMW's, Grace."

"Perhaps. But no one who worked in our building owned one. And no one's spouse owned one. I checked."

Leena Nadim chewed on her lower lip. "You were always quite good with details, Gracie." She got up and walked around her desk. She opened the top drawer and reached in. Grace stiffened.

A gun?

The hand reappeared. It was holding a package of cigarettes and a lighter. Leena settled into her big chair and lit a cigarette, drawing deeply on it.

"I thought you were against smoking."

"Call it nerves. Even I have them."

Grace watched the woman's hands as she smoked. They were steady. Leddi exhaled.

"Why did you kill Cameron? He was harmless."

"After you phoned him, he came to my apartment. He was desperate to talk. Andre had already told him about his suspicions – about Eric and Harvey using the firm to commit some kind of fraud. Cameron was convinced that you'd been framed. He was quite dramatic about it. He told me about your plan to meet at the office – that the two of you were planning to retrieve the Getz file and take Joan's computer and go to the police. He wanted me to come. He wanted to show the police we were standing behind you. I left him for a minute and tried to phone Eric, but he followed me into the bedroom, begging me to hurry. I couldn't make the call, so I decided to go with him."

"Why take the BMW?"

"Pomeroy was a wreck, shaking and babbling. I told him he shouldn't be driving in that condition. He agreed with me." She took a drag on her cigarette.

"His skull was crushed, Leddi!"

"It's 'Leena', since you know." She took a drag on her cigarette. "Graydon was always afraid of being carjacked. He kept a tire iron under the seat." Leena Nadim's voice was arctic, empty.

"Where is Gray now? Have you killed him too?"

"Don't be stupid. He knows nothing. He travels a lot, which is very convenient."

"Does he know about Eric?"

"No. He believes what everyone believes. That I was born in Macedonia."

"Who does he think you were with in Arizona? Why did he pretend that he'd been there with you?"

"He thought I was having an affair. I've had a few, but they've never bothered him." Leena's lip curled slightly. "Gray prefers men. That's a handicap for an ambitious banker. He has benefited very nicely from our little charade."

"Why go on a vacation with Eric?"

"It wasn't a vacation. It was… a meeting. Others were there. Charitable causes require the same management attention as any other business."

"Charitable causes!" Grace raised her voice. "Since when is murder a 'charitable cause'!"

"What are you talking about?"

"The fifth team of hijackers," Grace replied quietly. "You paid the hospital bills for the one who survived the accident."

Leena Nadim's eyes bored into her. She replied slowly. "You're very well informed, Grace." Her face seemed to transform. Her hairline retreated, stretching the skin on her forehead. Her lips drew back, showing her teeth. She leaned forward.

"Tell me something," she hissed. "Why did you meet with Qari before he was killed?" She pronounced her brother's name with perfect Arabic inflection. "To get the bank account numbers?"

"Yes."

"Did you get them?"

"Yes."

"Why did he give them to you?"

"You know the answer."

"You used me to blackmail him."

"I didn't have to. I just handed him a copy of your mother's picture."

"And he gave you the numbers?"

"Not directly. He gave me money. Five million."

Leena's body seemed to wilt. She looked away. "But he tried to kill you anyway?"

"When he realised he was under surveillance, he shot me. He didn't know I was wearing a vest."

"And were you also wearing a microphone?"

"Yes."

Leena's eyes scanned the front of Grace's body. "You're not wearing a vest now, Grace."

"No. Should I be?"

"Are you wearing a microphone?"

"Yes, Leena. I am." Grace tensed herself.

"Can they hear me right now?"

"Every word."

Leena Nadim slumped against the back of her chair.

"After the massacres, we were taken in by a relative who lived in the Bekaa Valley. They helped us channel our grief."

"That's an interesting way to put it."

Leena ignored her.

"We joined Hezbollah. Qari went on some raids against the Israeli soldiers who were occupying southern Lebanon. We both worked on perfecting our English. Then we learned that Qari's name had been added to a target list. A list kept by Israeli intelligence." She lit another cigarette. "The Mossad's assassins are very efficient, Grace. Since Qari and I both had university degrees, our leaders decided to send us here. To fight against Israel in a different way."

"By murdering people who have no connection to all that insanity?"

"If the Americans insist on supporting Israel, then they must share the blame for Israel's crimes. And they must share the same punishment. Crime and punishment, Grace. Isn't that what you North Americans believe in?" Leena Nadim's voice rose, foaming with sudden passion. "In nineteen eighty-two, nearly three thousand people were butchered at the Chatila and Sabra camps. Most of them were women and children. The killing went on for three days. The women were raped repeatedly, and then mutilated. Babies were shot through the head. Men were lined up and machine-gunned. Some were castrated first and shot later. Hundreds of men and teenaged boys were marched away to a sports stadium in Beirut. The Israeli army controlled that stadium, Grace! Those young men were never seen again.

"Tell me how this was different from the Jews' holocaust? This *too* was a holocaust! But was there an outcry in North America? In Europe? No! You all looked the other way! A few brief news reports, and then it was forgotten. For twenty years, you ignored the slaughter of three thousand Palestinian and Lebanese people. But when an equal number of America's precious citizens died in New York, you all went mad with grief and outrage.

427

"Our people were killed under the eyes of the Israeli generals. *Israeli* generals, Grace! Jews! The last people on this planet who should ever countenance atrocities! The Israeli army sealed off those camps so that no one could escape. Their air force dropped flares all through the night so the Christians would have proper lighting to do their butchery."

Leena Nadim got to her feet. She paced.

"Your governments talk a lot about justice and democracy, but they don't *offer* it, they *impose* it! Everywhere they trample on rights in the name of rights! Everywhere they destroy cultures! Qari and I devised our own notion of justice. The concept is simple. I'm sure you and your new friends-" she gestured generally at Grace's blouse and its hidden microphone "-will appreciate the neatness and irony of it: steal the money of dead Jews, and use it to help the victims of living Jews. We diverted only a small part of the total fund. Seventy million. That is less than *six* percent of the total, Grace! We paid commissions to Koop and Bellis, and a couple of million to that mutant, Pendergast, and we still had more than fifty million for our *own* holocaust fund. Already we've paid for houses and schools and clean water for hundreds of our people." Leena Nadim smiled at Grace, grimly satisfied. "It is a good thing we have done."

Suddenly, Grace felt very tired. She stood up slowly. Leena was refilling her whiskey glass.

"I thought Muslims didn't drink alcohol."

"They don't. But I'm from Beirut. We've never known which world we belong to."

"That stuff will kill you, Leena."

"Probably."

Grace crossed the plush carpet. When she reached the door, she turned around.

"We trusted you. We made you a judge."

"Yes…" Leena dropped into her chair. "Silly, eh? It appealed to my ego."

Grace opened the door.

"Grace?"

"Yes?"

"It was never personal."

"Our friendship? Or you trying to destroy my life?"

Leena Nadim put the crystal glass to her lips.

"Both," she said.

Also from www.hirstpublishing.com

Seeker
By Andy Frankham-Allen

The Ancient nodded. "The book will explain this to you. One day the Seeker shall appear, and with my blood in your veins you will know him..."

Meet Willem Townsend: London-based entrepreneur; loving friend; loyal uncle. He seems to have everything going for him, but deep down Will is trapped by work, family and the sheer mundanity of daily routine. Stepping outside his comfort zone he begins an internet romance, and, despite the reservations of his best friend Jake, Will arranges to meet his lover for a weekend getaway. The weekend passes, and not a word is heard from Will. Jake organises a search for his friend, fearing the worst, and as the frenetic hunt progresses, he begins to realise that Will may have meant more to him than he was willing to believe. In Southend, a naked man is found in a garden, suffering from a trauma that he cannot recall. And when the memories come flooding back, they are borne by blood. He holds the key to a secret world, where the price of entry is death...

Also from www.hirstpublishing.com

Diary of a Parallel Man
By David Elham

Imagine a world where God is a proven reality. Adam and Eve have passed the test of obedience and have been granted everlasting life for themselves and their offspring. In time the borders of Eden are extended until the whole earth is a paradise populated by sinless people who enjoy perfect health and never age. What if a man born in that world suddenly found himself in ours? This is the story of Mahershalalhashbaz, told in his own words. It is the story of a massive clash of cultures, of ethics, of truths; the story of a man who deals only in absolutes having to live in a world where nothing is certain, where people struggle with conflicting beliefs, and live only to die. Surviving on Manchester's streets, he relies on the one person to have shown him kindness in this bewildering reality, a young woman named Kirsty. She is a staunch atheist – he knows that God exists for sure. But as their friendship grows, both of them begin to see life from fresh perspectives. This is a love story like no other. After reading it, you may never see things the same way again.

Also from www.hirstpublishing.com

Match Day
By Darren Floyd

A comic thriller about three people having three different days, on the same match day in Cardiff.

Cathy is a woman disappointed in life when her dream turns into a nightmare, and mires her with debt which she doesn't have a hope of paying off. Suddenly she is offered a chance of a new life in Australia, but first she must take a desperate gamble...

Martin is a bitter policeman with decades on the job, and a shameful secret in his past. He finds himself wrapped up in events that he could never have anticipated.
Leigh is a supporter; he just wants to get into see the match. Unfortunately he gets split up from his mate who has his ticket. He finds himself alone in a city full of sports fans. Now if he can only find a ticket...

Gradually these three people's paths collide, and none of their lives will be the same again...